C0-ATS-832

ALSO BY SALLY ROONEY

*Beautiful World, Where Are You*

*Normal People*

*Conversations with Friends*

# INTERMEZZO

# INTERMEZZO

A NOVEL

SALLY ROONEY

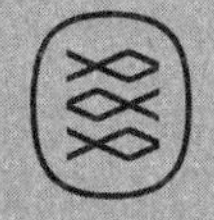

FARRAR, STRAUS AND GIROUX

NEW YORK

Farrar, Straus and Giroux
120 Broadway, New York 10271


Printed in the United States of America
Published simultaneously in the United States by Farrar, Straus and Giroux
and in Great Britain by Faber and Faber Ltd
First American edition, 2024

Grateful acknowledgment is made for permission to reprint the following material:
Lines from "Church Going," by Philip Larkin, from *The Complete Poems* © Estate of Philip Larkin and reprinted by permission of Faber and Faber Ltd.
Lines from "Those Winter Sundays," by Robert Hayden, from *The Collected Poems of Robert Hayden* © Erma Hayden, published by Liveright and reprinted by permission of W. W. Norton.
Excerpt from "Against Interpretation," from *Against Interpretation*, by Susan Sontag. Copyright © 1964, 1966, renewed 1994 by Susan Sontag. Used by permission of Farrar, Straus and Giroux. All Rights Reserved.

Library of Congress Cataloging-in-Publication Data
Names: Rooney, Sally, author.
Title: Intermezzo : a novel / Sally Rooney.
Description: First American edition. | New York : Farrar, Straus and Giroux, 2024.
Identifiers: LCCN 2024014010 | ISBN 9780374602635 (hardcover)
Subjects: LCGFT: Novels.
Classification: LCC PR6118.O59 I58 2024 | DDC 823/.92—dc23/eng/20240415
LC record available at https://lccn.loc.gov/2024014010

Signed Edition ISBN: 978-0-374-61900-8
International Paperback Edition ISBN: 978-0-374-60853-8

*Designed by Gretchen Achilles*



This edition was printed by Lakeside Book Company.

1 3 5 7 9 10 8 6 4 2

Aber fühlst du nicht *jetzt* den Kummer?
("Aber spielst du nicht *jetzt* Schach?")

But don't you feel grief *now*?
('But aren't you *now* playing chess?')

—LUDWIG WITTGENSTEIN,
*Philosophical Investigations*

# PART ONE

# 1

Didn't seem fair on the young lad. That suit at the funeral. With the braces on his teeth, the supreme discomfort of the adolescent. On such occasions, one could almost come to regret one's own social brilliance. Gives him the excuse, or gives him in any case someone at whom to look pleadingly between the mandatory handshakes. God love him. Nearly twenty-three now: Ivan the terrible. Difficult actually to believe the suit on him. Picked it up perhaps in some little damp-smelling second-hand shop for the local hospice, paid in cash, rode it home on his bicycle crumpled in a reusable plastic bag. Yes, that in fact would make sense of it, would bring into alignment the suit in its resplendent ugliness and the personality of the younger brother, ten years younger. Not without style in his own way. Certain kind of panache in his absolute disregard for the material world. Brains and beauty, an aunt said once. About them both. Or was it Ivan brains and Peter beauty. Thanks, I think. He crosses Watling Street now towards the apartment that is not an apartment, the house that is not a house, eleven or is it twelve days since the funeral, back in town. Back at work, such as it is. Or back anyway to Naomi's place. And what will she be wearing when she answers the door. Slides his phone from his pocket into the palm of his hand as he reaches the front step, cool tactility of the screen as it lights under his fingers, typing. Outside. Evenings drawing in now and she's back at her lectures, presumably. No reply but she sees the message, and then the predictable sequence, the so familiar and by now indirectly arousing sequence of sounds as behind the front door she comes up the old basement staircase and into the hall. Classical conditioning: how did it take so long to figure that out? Common sense. Not that. Everyday experience. The relationship of memory and feeling. The opening door.

Hello, Peter, she says.

A cropped cashmere tank top, thin gold necklace. And black sweatpants fitted slim at the ankle. Not elasticated, she hates that. Bare feet.

May I come in? he asks.

Down the staircase and into her room without seeing any of the others. Fairy lights glowing dim pinpricks against the wall. Takes his shoes off, leaves them by the door. Laptop lying splayed open on the unmade mattress. Fragrance of perfume, sweat and cannabis. In whose blent air all our compulsions meet. Curtains hanging closed, as always.

Where have you been? she asks.

Ah. I'm afraid something came up.

She's looking at him, and then not looking, with a scoff. Off on a late summer holiday, were you? she asks.

Naomi, sweetheart, he says in a friendly voice. My dad died.

Stunned, she turns to look, saying: Your— Then she falls silent. Jesus, she adds. Oh my God, fuck. Peter, I'm so sorry.

Do you mind if I sit down?

They sit on the mattress together.

Christ, she says. Then: Are you okay?

Yeah, I think so.

She's looking down at the soles of her feet, crossed on the mattress. Blackened with the dirt that never seems dirty exactly. You want to talk about it? she asks.

Not really.

How's your brother doing?

Ivan, he says. Do you know he's about your age?

Yeah, you told me. You said you wanted to introduce us. Is he okay?

With love, irresistibly, Peter smiles, and to avoid the spectacle of smiling with irresistible love at Naomi herself, he smiles instead, as if humorously, at the inside of his own extended wrist. Oh, he's doing— I actually have no idea how he's doing. What did I tell you about him before?

I don't know, you said he was 'a curio' or something.

Yeah, he's a complete oddball. Really not your type. I think he's kind of autistic, although I guess you can't say that now.

You can, if he actually is.

Well, not clinically or whatever. But he's a chess genius, so. Peter lies back on the bed now, looking up at the ceiling. You don't mind, do you? he adds. I have to head on somewhere else in a bit.

From outside his line of sight, Naomi's mouth answers: That's cool. A pause. He toys with the inseam of her sweatpants.

She lies down beside him, warm, her breath warm, the scent of coffee, and something else. Her breasts warm under the little cashmere top. Which he bought for her, or the same one in another colour. 'Paris grey'. Letting him touch with his fingertips her damp underarm. Chalky scent of deodorant only masking the lower savoury smell of perspiration. Hardly ever shaves anywhere except her legs, below the knee. He told her once that back in his day, the girls in college used to get bikini waxes. That made her laugh. She asked if he was trying to make her feel bad or what. Not at all, he said. Just an interesting development in the sexual culture. She's always laughing. Those Celtic Tiger years must have been wild. Anyway, you like it. And it's true, he does. Something sensual in her carelessness. Cold feet. Soles always black from walking around this kip half-dressed, smoking a joint, talking on speakerphone. She murmurs softly now: I'm so sorry. His fingers under the cashmere. Eyes closing. Everything very languid and dreamy like this. Her skin unseen beneath his hands with that soft downy quality almost velvet. He asks what she got up to while he was away. No answer. His eyes open again and find hers.

Listen, she says. I feel stupid telling you this. But some stuff came up a few weeks ago. Like for college, I had to buy some books. So I needed money. It's not a big deal.

Slowly he nods his head. Ah, he says. Okay. I could have helped you out, if I'd known.

Yeah, she says. Well, you weren't really replying to my texts. Screws her mouth up into a pained smile. Sorry, she adds. I didn't know about your dad, obviously.

Don't worry, he says. I didn't know you needed money. Obviously.

They look at one another a moment longer, embarrassed,

irritable, guilty. Then she turns onto her back. It's cool, she says. I didn't even have to do anything, the pictures were from ages ago. Feeling his body tired and heavy he closes his eyes. One of these guys who comments on all her posts, probably. The emoji of the monkey covering its eyes. Or some sad married man with a credit card his wife doesn't know about.

That's fucked up about your dad, she says. When was the funeral?

Last week. Two weeks ago.

Did your friends all go?

He pauses. Not all, he says. After another pause: Sylvia. And a few others.

I guess you didn't want me to be there.

He turns to look at her face in profile. Full lips parted, sweep of freckles on her cheekbone. Silver stud glinting in her ear. The image of youth and beauty. He wonders also how much the guy paid. No, he says. I guess not.

Without looking at him she grins. What did you think I was going to do? she says. Try to seduce the priest or something? I have been to funerals, you know.

I just thought people would probably ask me who you were, he says. And what was I going to say, we're friends?

Why not?

I don't think anyone would believe me.

Thanks a lot, she says. I don't look classy enough to be friends with you?

You don't look old enough.

Tongue between her lips now, grinning. You're sick in the head, you know, she says.

I know, but so are you.

She stretches her arms thoughtfully, and then settles the

back of her head down on her hands. Do you have a girlfriend or something? she asks.

He says nothing for a moment. Since in any case she doesn't seem to care, and why should she. Thinks of saying: I did, once. And now might be the time to tell her about that, mightn't it. About the funeral, and afterwards. Not that anything happened. Just the feeling, memory of a feeling, which was nothing in reality. In the car found himself mumbling stupidly: Don't leave me alone with Ivan, will you. That was why she stayed. Only reason. Up in the old childhood bedroom, throbbing against her like a teenager. Too dark blessedly to look her in the eyes. She slept beside him, that was all. Nothing to tell. In the morning she was up before he was. Downstairs in the kitchen with Ivan, speaking in soft tones; he heard them from the landing. What did they have to say to each other? Nice little outpost for the knight on d5, was it? She probably would too. Humour him. Forget about it.

If I did, he says, why would I be hanging around with you?

Turning her body to face him, she touches with a fingertip the thin gold chain at her neck. Because you're sick in the head, remember? she says.

He remembers, yes, and remembering touches his hand to her small face, his palm resting on her jaw. Is she laughing at him also. Yes, of course, but is it only that. At her birthday party in the summer when he brought champagne and she drank from the bottle with her painted lips. In the kitchen her friend Janine said you know I think she likes you Peter. Different from the others, he knows. Something of the challenge he liked when he met her. At the bar in her tiny silver dress, hair down nearly to her waist, stud in her nose glinting red under the lamps. Her friends showed him the website, pretending to ask if it was legal. Fuck off, she said. Don't tell him about that. Flashing him a glance then: animal intelligence. Just between the two of them, he knew. Different from the others. Men who send her deranged threats of sexual violence on the internet, stupid whore, I'll kill you, I will slit your throat. Thumbing through the inbox she laughs. The absolute cringe, imagine. Beneath her to be frightened. If it happened she would die laughing, he believes. Stupid not to reply to her texts. Some of them very nice too. His fault. He wonders how badly she needs the money, and then he feels— what? Ashamed, or whatever. As usual. She lies face down with her head in her arms. Familiar choreography, rehearsed together and with others, both. What lips my lips have. There is no one else, he could say. Someone, but not. I'm sorry. I love you. Her. Both. Don't worry. Don't say it. Christ no. Christ commands us universally to love one another.

Nine already by the time he leaves. Four minutes past. Also a little high because they smoked together afterwards. Types into the white box: Running about 20mins late, sorry. Cool darkness gathers around the lighted screen. Trees waving silent branches overhead, tram running past with faces in the windows. Locks the phone and pockets. James's Street at night. Has to walk quickly to try and make up the time now. But it is a pleasure, isn't it, on a crisp September night in Dublin to walk with long free strides along a quiet street. In the prime of his life. Incumbent on him now to enjoy such fleeting pleasures. Next minute might die. Happens every day to someone. And the man was no age, as everyone kept saying, sixty-five, that was all. Peter halfway there himself now, thirty-two and six months. Already middle-aged by that calculation. Frightening how quickly it all falls away. No, he'll say, my father's no longer with us, I'm afraid. People will be sorry, naturally, but not shocked. Different for Ivan. Almost like an orphan in his case, for all the good their mother has done him. Why they ever had children in the first place God knows. At the funeral, she muttered to Peter: The cut of him. And although Ivan did actually look absurd, and although Peter himself had only seconds before been thinking about how absurd Ivan looked, he replied: Well, his appearance may not have been foremost on his mind this week. Christine glancing back at him. Her tasteful skirt suit, navy merino. Nothing wrong with your turnout, she said. Always like that with her. He avoided her eye, watching Ivan loitering miserably alone at the table of sandwiches. Yes, he answered. Thanks. Past the old bank now towards Thomas Street and Sylvia's reply vibrates in his pocket, against his hip. Used to have a different ringtone for her messages, didn't he. In the old days. Dublin in the rare, etc. Can't remember now how it sounded. What make or model the phone was, how it weighed in his hand. Obsolete now presumably, no longer in production. Just to hear that sound once again, he thinks. To feel that his life has been preserved somewhere and not forgotten, gathered around him, packed protectively around him still. Early-morning bus journeys to the intervarsities. Prepping for the final in a back corridor while the audience waited in their seats. The record-breakers. Despised, they both were, of course. In love with one another and themselves. On the lock screen now: No problem. Have you eaten? Sensible woman. Wearing good sturdy shoes no doubt and the warm tweed coat. No. Looking out for him, that's all. Twenty minutes late and she wants to know if he's had his dinner. Twenty-five minutes.

And she is, to say the least, not stupid. He thinks sometimes the nature and extent of her suffering has lifted her free from the petty frustrations of mere inconvenience. Half an hour late, so what. When you're in and out of hospital every other week with a needle in your arm, doesn't matter much, probably. Overhearing the doctors talking about you behind the curtain. Patient female thirty-two years old. History of chronic refractory pain following traumatic injury. Road traffic accident. No, no kids, lives alone. And few could know. For himself he would rather die than go on like that. No fuss, just get it over with. She must know that other people think so. Knows even he does, maybe. But then they say one adjusts. The old life of pleasure gone and never returning: accept, or else delude yourself, all the same in the end. The will to live so much stronger than anyone imagines. Like a kind of death, what happened. A kind of death you survive out of politeness, respect for others, out of selfless love. Christ also survived his own death. And was dignified and exalted.

Past the art college now, students milling around in denim jackets, plastic boots, torn stockings. Formless teenage faces floating pale under the streetlight. At the outer door of life. He knows they're watching. Brains and beauty. Amused as he passes. One head turning to follow. Well, good for her, you only live once. He could be halfway through his days already. Allows himself to glance back with a smile. Not even pretty, but why not, and she smiles also, crookedly. Half an hour late at least. Naomi would be beside herself. God, men are disgusting. She only looked about sixteen. Oh, and it's illegal to smile now? At children. Actually he does smile at children. Also elderly people. Likes to convey to the world at large a genial disposition. Even smiles at other men sometimes. Differently. No you don't. He does if there's a reason. Mishears them speaking, or walks in front of them by accident, that kind of thing. Smiles, yes. At his rivals and enemies. You hate men more than I do, says Naomi. Obviously true, since she goes to bed with them of her own free will. Peter only goes to bed with people he likes. Most women ultimately very likeable individuals. Men, as everyone knows, disgusting. Not all: not his father, not like that. And Ivan? Different. Used to think he was one of these sexless beings you read about. Sort of amoeba blob floating in a jar. Then Peter brought a certain girlfriend home for dinner and saw him staring. Ah, your brother's a little bit awkward, no? Yes, I'm sorry. I think he liked you. Later, of course, he went to college, made friends with girls. But then, his friends are— Well, anyway. No, go on. They're what? Ugly? No, perfectly nice-looking as far as it goes. Some of them in facial symmetry terms quite attractive. Lack of taste, that's all. Naomi would be in bits. And a snob on top of everything else. But is it snobbery? Not about money, nothing to do with that. Black sweatpants tapered at the ankle, not elasticated, she hates that. And anything knee-length she hates. Discerning eye. Ivan's friends not ugly, not at all, but the dress sense. Criminal. And the turns of phrase, the gestures. Maybe it is snobbery, of a different order. Highly intelligent young women, of course. Mathematicians and chess players. None of them remotely interested in Peter and the feeling mutual. Some of them, come to think of it, probably in love with his brother. Smiles to himself at that. Feeling never appeared to be mutual there, but what does he know. Did catch him looking at the lovely Giulia that time however. Green silk blouse with the top three buttons undone. Mother of pearl. White teeth laughing, loud healthy Roman laugh. Past Christ Church now, lit up at night, stone walls bleached grey-yellow. Texts her: Almost there. No haven't eaten, what about you? And what about her. Sylvia. Beyond him entirely. Not actually very good-looking, never was. Makes the beauty of others seem excessive. Her small plain face. Of course the clothes are always right. Gets ideas sometimes for gifts he could give Naomi – high-necked sweaters, coloured silk shawls, an ankle-length raincoat. Only to realise later how wrong they would look: pretty girl dressed up as old lady. Dowdy, prudish. Sylvia never in the least. He went to one of her lectures in the spring. Slender woman at the top of the room talking about eighteenth-century prose forms. Every pair of eyes fixed on her. Voice very clear and low-toned. Contralto. Not another sound in the place. When she was finished, they all broke out in applause, what, two hundred of them, more, and she smiled and nodded, used to it, probably. Sheer charisma. Made him want to say: I know her. Ex-girlfriend of mine. So embarrassing, imagine. Think she's interesting on the subject of amatory fiction, you should try getting her into bed. Though can't now. She can't. Too much pain. Again vibrates. She has found a table in an Italian restaurant in Temple Bar, pin dropped, what does he think? Types back: See you in 5. Lord Edward Street at night, walking down towards the college gates. Scenery of old romances, drunken revelries. Four in the morning getting sick there outside the Mercantile, remember that. Scholarship night. Young then. Mixing memory and desire. Dark remembered walkways. Graveyard of youth.

Waiting for the bill, they go on talking while he eats absentmindedly the final piece of soft oily focaccia bread. Hadn't realised how hungry he was until. And then, the heavy curtains, iced water, candlelight, all so conducive to appetite. There it is again: conditioning. Across the table she's drinking her water. Faint muscular movement of the white throat while she swallows, and then, resettling her glass on the table: What are you going to do about the dog?

Oh God, says Peter. I don't know. Christine is looking after him until— I don't remember when. Next Friday, she said? Or maybe the Monday. We'll have to think of something.

The man returns with their bill and Peter takes his card from his wallet, insisting, and keys in his pin. Now, after eating, he feels better, more relaxed. Realises at last how tired he is. Effect of her presence: stills the nerves. Other feelings he notices also as they wait together in the dim warmth of the restaurant for the man to bring their coats. Had believed once that life must lead to something, all the unresolved conflicts and questions leading on towards some great culmination. Curiously underexamined beliefs like that, underpinning his life, his personality. Irrational attachment to meaning. All very well as far as it goes, the question of constitutionality arises, and so on. Couldn't go to work in the morning if he didn't think something meant something meant something else. But what is it all leading up to. An end without an ending. The man helps Sylvia into her coat as Peter looks on. Calmer now. Attuned to the quieter feelings. Under what conditions is life endurable? She ought to know. Ask her. Don't.

Outside, it has been raining and the streets are wet, reflecting in fragments the diffuse light of headlamps, traffic lights, shop windows. Empty pizza boxes discarded by the opposite wall, disintegrating. Let me walk you home. She's knotting her scarf. Thank you. She takes his arm. Her fine small hand almost weightless. Fingers in the creases of his jacket. Were you seeing Naomi earlier? How is she? Good. Yeah. Walking up towards Dame Street again. You like her. I do. Fond of her, very fond, very much so. He wants almost, and at the same time wants not, to tell Sylvia what happened, that Naomi, etc. The website, etc. For what reason? To show that it's okay: her, the others, himself, nothing to worry about. Relationships these days. Or conversely to weasel some sympathy. Sexual humiliation, little bit of a turn-on maybe. She's asking again now about Naomi's tenancy situation. Building owners secured court order before the pandemic, instructing previous group of tenants to vacate property. Which unrelatedly they already have, none of them left now. Legally can't be valid for the current crowd, Sylvia agrees, and yet. What's to stop them. Always the possibility. Gardaí take one look at the paperwork, correct address, and wave them in. Doesn't bear thinking about. But go down the route of proving the invalidity of the order, legal letters, etc., and you just give them all the more reason to get a new one: then you're really fucked. Because the tenancy is, no one suggests otherwise, in fact illegal. Better to stay quiet and hope the owners forget. How many properties do they keep lying vacant anyway, lost count probably, bloodsucking parasites. A conversation he and Sylvia have had many times, and they are this time, as ever, ad idem. Which they would be anyway, purely from the ideological perspective, both being fully paid-up members of the same tenants' union and Sylvia in fact chairing one of the working groups. The fact of Peter's ongoing sexual and also quietly financial relationship, of eight months' duration, with a participant in this particular illegal tenancy is, from the legal-philosophical, socio-political points of view, a thing of nothing. Never told his father about her, for instance, even when asked. No, no one at the moment, he said. The idea of them meeting: too awful. No. Could have told him there was someone: nothing serious, just a girl he's been seeing. What difference would that have made? Quite literally none. Why think about it then? Why these regretful feelings, and for whom? His father, himself? Pointless. Depressed even thinking about it. Depressed in general probably. Thoughts rattling and noisy almost always and then when quiet frighteningly unhappy. Mentally not right maybe. Never maybe was. Small weightless hand on his arm.

I never really got to know him, he says. Sorry. Just thinking. It's sad.

She glances. Everything communicated. Enveloped in the depth of her understanding. I know what you mean, she says. But you did know him. From her bag she takes a little rectangular sachet wrapped in plastic film. Packet of tissues. For Christ's sake, is he crying? On George's Street? Anyone could see him. And will, probably. How's life Peter, still at the bar are you, saw your name in the paper there not long ago, fair play. Quietly he accepts a white square of tissue smiling and wipes his face, saying only: Hm. She walks by his side at the same speed he walks, always. He loved you, she says. He didn't know the first thing about me, Sylvia. We were allergic to each other. Never had a real conversation in our lives. Folds the tissue up and puts it in his pocket. Oh, you take conversation too seriously, she says. Life isn't just talking, you know. He looks at her while she replaces her hand on his arm. That's a cryptic remark, what does that mean? She's laughing. Prettier then. But what does she mean: life isn't just talking? Love's austere and lonely offices perhaps. Taking their school uniforms from the tumble dryer on Wednesday nights, Ivan's little claret-coloured tracksuit and Peter's shirt and trousers, hot, crackling with static.

And in the morning, warming milk on the range. At Sylvia's side on Stephen Street now he breathes the perfume of car exhaust and dark night air. Consoling in its own way. Everything about her nearness is. And why. He knows why, doesn't, doesn't want to know whether he does or not. Comfort of long companionship then. Opens up space and quiet for him to feel at last how tired he is, how depressed. Better off perhaps staying at Naomi's, getting high and playing *Call of Duty* with her roommates, medicating himself to sleep. This way accepting consolation he must accept also that he needs it. Because his father, with whom he was never particularly close, has died in his sixties after five years of cancer treatment. An eventuality, once expected, so long delayed that he began to think it would never come, until it did. Peter somehow inexcusably unprepared for the anticipated event. Somehow suddenly head of a family which has at the same time ceased to exist.

They walk along by the Green together, gates shut, yellowing leaves. In their autumn beauty. Talking about students. Her lectures. Seminars he teaches to pay the rent. He asks after her friend Emily and smiling she gives the usual story, more administrative hassle at work, and she hasn't been able to find another sublet. Emily, little absentminded academic who always seems to have a headcold, always sneezing into a handkerchief and talking about Karl Marx. Friend of their youth, the old debating days, not that she ever had much success, hopelessly off topic and refusing every point of information. Used to spend a lot of time at their place, his and Sylvia's, even slept on the couch for a while, when he, when they. Nights they would all three sit up together drinking tea, bickering over nothing, getting into hysterics. Sylvia the cool collected friend, Emily the disaster. Says she's staying with Max for the moment, good old Max. See him sometimes at Sylvia's still. Useless he was too in competition. Too nice, not ruthless enough, always seeing both sides. Funny though. All her friends are. Lightly she has to hold the world, lovingly but lightly. Have you been talking to your brother? she asks. Ah, well, he answers. Life isn't just talking, you know. She prods him with her elbow. Nice actually to feel her so close. He's alone, she says. Aren't we all? Though Ivan admittedly appears to be more alone than most. At that, almost spiritually alone, and perhaps best left that way. What were the two of you talking about in the house the other day? he asks. Oh, she says. He was telling me— You mean at breakfast? He was telling me about some chess event he's doing in Leitrim the weekend after next. Do you know about that? No. Some kind of exhibition game, and he's giving a workshop afterwards. He was thinking about cancelling it, with everything going on. But he's decided to go ahead and do it anyway. Passing the gates of the Huguenot Cemetery. Why was he thinking about cancelling it? She's looking up at him. Because— Well, you know. Because his dad just died. Wincing now frowning, overwarm, and tired. Label under his shirt collar rubbing the back of his neck. Baggot Street lit up and busy, too busy, lights in his eyes, everything too much. Do you think he's upset? he asks. She's still looking at him, and idiotically he tries to smile. I mean, obviously, he adds. I think he is upset, she answers. I think he's lonely. Yes. Yeah. Sure. Closer and closer they draw to her apartment, the end point, and how lonely he will be then, or not. Why in God's name is everything so loud all of a sudden. Sylvia, he says. No, wait until it's quieter. Yes? Nearly there now anyway and could make it sound more casual at the door. Like just tired of walking even. Would you mind— I don't know. Can I sleep on your couch? I won't— No, no, Jesus, don't say it: I won't touch you. Don't. I'm just kind of— Her hand gentle tender on his arm not moving, still, still. All quiet and stillness gathered at the point of her merciful touch. Of course, she says. No problem. Don't say it. I'm in love with her. You, if only. Is that what you think? Under these conditions, is life endurable. He waits while she opens the door. She understands and knows everything. Be nice if you got in touch, she says. You could text him. In what language. 1. e4. Yeah, he answers. You're right. I will do that. I will.

# 2

Ivan is standing on his own in the corner, while the men from the chess club move the chairs and tables around. The men are saying things to one another like: Back a bit there, Tom. Mind yourself now. Alone Ivan is standing, wanting to sit down, but uncertain as to which of the chairs need to be rearranged still, and which of them are in their correct places already. This uncertainty arises because the way in which the men are moving the furniture corresponds to no specific method Ivan has been able to discern. A familiar arrangement is slowly beginning to emerge – a central U-shape composed of ten tables, and ten chairs along the outer rim of the shape, and a general seating area around the outside – but the process by which the men are reaching this arrangement seems haphazard. Standing on his own in the corner, Ivan thinks with no especially intense focus about the most efficient method of organising, say, a random distribution of a given number of tables and chairs into the aforementioned arrangement of a central U-shape, etc. It's something he has thought about before, while standing in other corners, watching other people move similar furniture around similar indoor spaces: the different approaches you could use, say if you were writing a computer program to maximise process efficiency. The accuracy of these particular men, in relation to the moves recommended by such a program, would be, Ivan thinks, pretty low, like actually very low.

While he's thinking, a door comes open – not the main town hall door, but a smaller kind of fire exit door at the side – and a woman enters. She's carrying a set of keys. The other men hardly seem to acknowledge her entrance: they just glance over in her direction and then away again. No one says anything to her. It's probably one of these situations that other people find instantly comprehensible, and everyone other than Ivan has already worked out at a glance exactly who this woman is and why she's here. She happens to be noticeably attractive, which makes her presence in the room at this juncture all the more curious. She has a nice figure and her face in profile looks very pretty. After a moment Ivan sees that the other men, although they have not directly acknowledged the woman, seem to be behaving differently in her presence, lifting the tables with heftier motions of their arms and shoulders, as if the tables have become heavier since she walked in. Showing off in front of her, he realises: and he even seems to see her smiling to herself, maybe because she has come to the same conclusion, or maybe just because they're all pretending to ignore her. Now, perhaps noticing Ivan watching, she suddenly looks back at him, a friendly kind of relieved look, and with her keys in her hand she approaches the corner where he's standing.

Hello there, she says. My name is Margaret, I'm a member of staff here. I'm sorry to ask, but do you know whether the little man has arrived yet? This chess prodigy. I think we're supposed to keep an eye on him.

He looks down at her. She has said all this in a smiling, funny, almost apologetic tone of voice, as if sharing a joke with him. She looks somewhat older than he is, he thinks, not a lot older: in her thirties, he would guess. Ah, he says. You mean Ivan Koubek?

She looks back up at him expectantly. That's right, she says. Is he here?

Yes. I am him.

She gives an embarrassed flutter of laughter at this, lifting her hand to her chest, jangling her set of keys. Oh my God, she says. I'm so sorry. Crossed wires, obviously. I thought— I don't know why. I thought you were about twelve.

Well, I was once, he says.

She laughs again at that, sincerely it seems, and the feeling of making her laugh is so nice that he also starts to smile. Ah, that explains it, she says. No, I am sorry, how silly of me. Did you have an okay time getting here?

He goes on looking at her a moment, and then, as if belatedly hearing her question, he replies quickly: Oh. Right, it was okay. I got the bus.

Still gently smiling she says: And I was told you might need a lift back to your accommodation after the event, is that right?

He pauses again. She goes on looking up at him, her eyes friendly and encouraging. Definitely it would be creepy of him to read too much into her friendly looks, since she's literally at work right now, being paid to stand here talking to him. Although, he remembers, he is also kind of at work, being paid to stand here talking to her, even if it's not really the same. Yeah, he says. I don't know where it is exactly, the accommodation. But I guess I could get a taxi.

She's putting her keys into the pocket of her skirt. No, no, she says. We'll look after you, don't worry.

The club captain comes over finally and introduces himself. His name is Ollie, he's the one who collected Ivan from the bus station earlier. The woman says again that her name is Margaret, and then Ollie lifts his hand in Ivan's direction, saying: And this is our guest, Ivan Koubek. She exchanges a glance with Ivan, just a very quick glance of amusement shared between the two of them, and then she answers: Yes, I know. Ollie begins talking to her about the event, what time it will begin and end, and which of the studio rooms they'll be using tomorrow morning for the workshop. In silence Ivan watches them talking together. She works here, the woman named Margaret, here at the arts centre: that explains her sort of artistic appearance. She's wearing a white blouse, and a voluminous patterned skirt in different colours, and neat flat shoes of the kind ballerinas wear. He begins to experience, while she stands there in front of him, an involuntary mental image of kissing her on the mouth: not even really an image, but an idea of an image, sort of a realisation that it will be possible to visualise this at some later point, what it would be like to kiss her, a promise of enjoyment simply to picture himself doing that, which is harmless enough, just a private thought. And yet he also feels at the same time an abrupt desire to draw her attention back to himself in real life, which he suspects he could achieve just by addressing her, just by saying something or asking a question aloud, it doesn't even matter what.

Do you play chess? he asks.

They both look up at him. Too late now, he realises he's being weird. He can see it, it's perceptible in her face and even in Ollie's. How weird, to ask her for no reason whether she plays chess, and it wasn't even related to what they were talking about. Cheerfully, however, she answers: No, I'm afraid not. I don't have a brain for that kind of thing. I suppose I know what the pieces do, and that's about it.

With grim regret at having spoken, Ivan nods his head.

Gesturing to the hall behind them, Ollie says: We don't have much to boast about in the gender equality department, unfortunately.

Oh, I wouldn't worry, she says. We had a knitting group in the other week, they were just as bad. Anyway, I won't keep you. If you need anything, I'll be upstairs in the office. You can ask for me, my name is Margaret.

Ollie thanks her. Ivan says nothing.

Glancing up at him, she adds: And good luck with your match later. I might come and watch if I get a minute.

He looks at her a moment longer before saying: Right. Thank you.

She goes back out the side door then, closing it behind her. Probably it's a special staff entrance and that's why she had those keys, to unlock it from the other side. He doesn't think she will get a minute to come and watch. She will probably get a minute, that is, but she won't use that minute to come and watch Ivan play chess. Maybe if he hadn't asked her that question she would have, because they were getting on better before. Now she probably thinks he's psychotically fixated on chess and can't talk about anything else: amazing how many people get that impression of him. Almost like there might be something to it.

Nice woman, Ollie remarks.

Ivan says: Yeah.

They go on standing by the wall together, watching the other men set up the chairs and tables. What does it mean when people say that kind of thing, like 'nice woman'? Is it a coded way of saying the person is attractive? Ivan wonders if Ollie also experienced a certain captivated feeling when this woman Margaret looked into his eyes. Why did it take him so long to come and speak to her then? But maybe, like Ivan, he gets shy around the opposite sex. Ollie is small and portly, and wears glasses, and might be fifty years of age. Also, he wears a wedding ring: married. It's difficult to imagine him experiencing feelings of captivation while talking to a beautiful woman. But a person's outward appearance does not define the boundaries of their internal feelings, Ivan knows. Plain, unappealing people are by no means exempt from the experience of strong passions. Anyway, whether the woman named Margaret was wearing a ring, Ivan didn't notice. The fact of her being so good-looking was impossible not to notice: she's probably sick of hearing about it from men. Ivan understands that it must be awkward to receive unwanted sexual comments and invitations, and there was that one occasion even in his own case, which was also a man, which probably just goes to show. He would personally go to great lengths to avoid ever encountering that guy again, not that anything bad happened, but purely from the awkwardness. Then imagine being an attractive woman and it's not just one man you have to avoid, but almost all of them. Ivan accepts that it must be dreadful. At the same time, how to reach a mutually agreeable situation without one person making an advance on the other which may turn out to be unwanted? It's like the problem with the tables and chairs. In a haphazard and inefficient way, without any fixed method, solutions can be reached, and evidently are reached all the time, considering that someone like Ollie is married. People get to know each other, things happen, that's life. The question for Ivan is how to become one of those people, how to live that kind of life.

Now, says Ollie beside him. What can we do for you before things get started? Would you like a cup of coffee? They have a nice little coffee shop out the front here.

Ivan nods his head slowly. The chairs and tables are all set up now, ten tables, evenly spaced, ten chairs. One of the men is even starting to lay out the chessboards. Sure, says Ivan. A coffee would be good, thank you.

I'll pop out for you, says Ollie. How do you take it?

Just espresso if they have it. No milk or sugar. Thanks.

Back in a tick, Ollie replies.

Ivan watches Ollie leave the hall, through the main doors, towards the lobby. Soon he will return with Ivan's coffee, and then the event will begin, and Ivan will play ten chess games at the same time. He finds in his experience it's better not to dwell on these matters in advance. To contemplate the approach of the event gives him an intense physical sensation, or rather a coordinated array of physical sensations: in his chest, his hands, his stomach, a hot feeling, tightness, nausea, shading even into light-headedness, a sense that he can't see properly, that something is wrong with his eyes, and then he starts feeling like he's going to be sick. On certain occasions he actually has been sick, after contemplating too deeply the inexorable approach of a scheduled event. At the same time, he's not at all nervous about the chess. That aspect will be easy, and, he knows, ultimately pleasant. Nothing will, or even really can, go wrong. The physical anxiety that accompanies chess events – exhibition games, tournaments – does not bear any meaningful relationship to the events themselves, except a chronological one: it arrives beforehand and goes away afterwards. His mind knows this, but his body does not. For this and other reasons, Ivan considers the body a fundamentally primitive object, a vestige of evolutionary processes superseded by the development of the brain. Just compare the two: the human mind weightless, abstract, capable of supreme rationality; the human body heavy, depressingly specific, making no sense at all. It just does things: no one knows why. It begins for some reason to attack itself or to proliferate cells where they don't belong. No explanation. Does the mind do that? No. Well, in the case of mental illness, he thinks, okay, sure, it can do similar things, but that's different. Is it different? Anyway. Ivan's own mind is far from perfect, often incapable of completing the relatively straightforward tasks with which it is presented, but at least the mind responds to reasoning. Sentience, he thinks. The body is an insentient object, animated by a sentience it does not share, like an insentient car is animated by a sentient driver. More or less everyone can accept the death of both body and mind past a certain point, like past the age of ninety, say, or at least it's acceptable in theory if you don't think about it too much. But to accept that because the body dies, at any point in time, the mind must die also, just literally whenever?

Ivan's brother Peter, who is thirty-two and has a graduate degree in philosophy, says this school of thought on the relations between body and mind has been refuted. To Ivan, this is like when people say the King's Gambit has been refuted. People are always using that word 'refuted', just because they read it on some forum somewhere, King's Gambit Destroyed in One Move or whatever, and then the move will turn out to be 3 . . . d6.

Thank you, Bobby Fischer! Not that Peter is someone who says things just because he saw them on forums. He's an adult man who has a social life and might not even know what forums are. But mutatis mutandis. He probably just heard in a lecture once that the mind and body are not considered to be separate anymore and he was like, got it. Peter is the kind of person who goes along the surface of life very smoothly. He talks on the phone a lot and eats in restaurants and says that schools of philosophy have been refuted. At one time Ivan's feelings towards him were more negative, even approaching full enmity, but he would now characterise the feelings as neutral. In any case he has to admit that Peter organised pretty much everything around the funeral and all that, Ivan himself did nothing, he can admit that freely. Probably he should have shown more gratitude on that front. As for the whole thing about Peter giving the eulogy and Ivan not, that was a mutual decision. Obviously Ivan regrets that now, he's been over that already, the regret, again and again, but it's his own fault, not Peter's, not even shared, but exclusively his own. He didn't think about it enough beforehand, clearly. But what's the point in dwelling? It's not as if there's going to be a second funeral for his father at which Ivan can make up for his mistake by saying all the things that later came into his mind to say. The human mind, for all the credit he was just giving it a minute ago, is often repetitive, often trapped in a familiar cycle of unproductive thoughts, which in Ivan's case are usually regretful in nature. Minor regrets, like asking that woman Margaret whether she played chess, horrible, and major regrets like declining or rather failing to say anything at his own father's funeral. Major regrets like devoting his life to competitive chess only to watch his rating drop steadily over several years to the point where, etc. He's been over all that before, the irretrievability of the past, what's done being done, and now is not the time in any case. Instead he's going to eat the small chocolate bar he brought with him in his suitcase and drink a cup of coffee. It's good to visualise these actions in advance, how he'll unwrap the chocolate bar, what the coffee will taste like, whether it will be served with a saucer or just in a cup by itself. These are the right kinds of things for him to think about at this moment: precise things, tangible, replete with sensory detail. And then the games will begin.

By the time Margaret finishes dinner, it's dark outside the window of the bistro, the glass blue like wet ink. Garrett behind the till asks her what they have on tonight and she says the chess club are in. Cheerfully he answers: Each to their own. Every week or two, the same routine: another performance, and afterwards another stranger sitting in the passenger seat of Margaret's car, chattering away about something, and then gone again. Comedians, Shakespearean actors, motivational speakers. And now chess players. Funny. She liked him actually, the young man with the braces. Her mistake about him being a little boy, that was embarrassing, but he made a joke of it, which she liked. Slightly awkward, of course: those high-IQ people usually are. Although, she thinks, leaving the restaurant, buttoning her raincoat over her cardigan, he was still a lot more polite than the others, especially that officious man Oliver Lyons, who was basically quite rude. In the chess player, she thinks, you have an example of a friendly likeable person, perhaps lacking in some of the finer social nuances, whereas Ollie Lyons is a man who simply relishes the modicum of authority that he believes attaches itself to his captaincy of the local chess club. It's raining outside, water spilling from the gutters overhead, and Margaret fixes her scarf over her hair. Funny the feeling she had, talking to the two of them, as if she and the chess prodigy were in one camp together and Ollie in the other. Why: a sense of being outside the group, perhaps. Retrieving her keys from the bottom of her handbag now, she continues towards the office, nodding hello to that nice man from the bakery, what's his name again, Linda would know. She finds with her fingers the external key and lets herself into the building, pulling the door closed gently behind her. Rain drums on the roof, drips quietly from her raincoat onto the tiles, while she makes her way along a low cool corridor and, unlocking a side door, enters the hall.

Inside, all the lights are turned up bright, and thirty or forty spectators are seated in a tense, whispering silence. In the centre of the floor, a number of tables are arranged in a kind of squared U-shape, with the players seated around the outside. And on the inside of the square, the chess player, Ivan Koubek, is standing alone, leaning over one particular table, with one arm folded across his chest, using the other hand to rub his jaw. He looks very tall and pallid, looming there over the chessboard, while his opponent, an older man with a ruddy face, is sitting down comfortably in the chair opposite. Ivan moves one of the pieces – Margaret, standing in the doorway, can't see which – and then he walks around to the next table. Touching the pieces, his hands look precise and intelligent, like the hands of a surgeon or a pianist. When he's gone, his opponent starts scribbling something down on a sheet of paper. The spectators are sitting around on plastic chairs, watching, some taking photographs or videos with their phones. The next one of Ivan's opponents is a small child, a girl, who can't be more than eleven years old. She has golden hair tied up in a purple scrunchie. When Ivan reaches her table, his back to the door where Margaret is standing, the girl moves a piece, and he responds immediately, without taking time even to think. Margaret waits for him to move on to the next table before she slips inside, clicking the door shut behind her. Some people look up at the sound, but Ivan does not. He continues along the same path, sometimes standing wordlessly for ten seconds, twenty seconds, cradling his jaw, and then moving a piece and carrying on to the next table. Without taking her eyes from him, she sits down on one of the nearby chairs, hanging her coat and scarf over the back and drawing her bag onto her lap.

Surveying the tables, Margaret gathers that two of the games are over already. The players are sitting back sheepishly in their seats, and the boards in front of them are set up with a white king standing in the centre. Ivan's king, she thinks, since he's playing with the white pieces, and it even looks like him, tall and thin, which is funny. Do chess players think of themselves that way, as the king piece? But from what Margaret remembers of chess, the king is weak and cowardly, and spends most of the game hiding in the corner. At the next table, Ivan stretches his arm up over his head and places the flat of his hand between his shoulders, rubbing the base of his neck with his fingertips. Under his arms are two darkened circles of sweat. The room is not especially warm, though it is very bright, so probably he's sweating from the sheer force of concentration. At the back of the room, someone says something Margaret can't hear, and there follows a murmur of laughter. Ollie, who is seated at one of the tables, and whose game is still proceeding, turns to glare in the direction of the laughter, which drops away into silence. Standing at the little girl's table again, Ivan moves his queen, and in a toneless voice says: Checkmate. The girl turns to look at two adults sitting behind her, a man and a woman, who must be her parents. Margaret can see them smiling at the girl and putting their thumbs up, mouthing: Well done! The girl turns back to the board and writes something else down on her sheet of paper, and then she passes it over the table and hands Ivan her pen. He leans down to scribble something at the bottom of the sheet, and then straightening up he offers her his hand. With a broad beaming smile full of milk teeth she accepts, and they shake.

In silence the games continue. Another player seems to give in, shaking Ivan's hand, and then another: men from the chess club who were here arranging chairs earlier. Finally, the only one left is Ollie. He has put on a jacket and tie, Margaret notices – he wasn't wearing a tie earlier today, but now he is, a red one with a light stripe. Ivan Koubek hasn't changed clothes, he's wearing the same light-green button-down shirt and dark trousers. His sneakers are dirty, and Margaret can see that the sole is coming away from the body of the left shoe. Ollie looks up at Ivan now and gives a little nod, and Ivan nods back. Ollie writes something down on his sheet of paper, and so does Ivan, and they shake hands. The other players start to applaud, and then everyone is applauding. Margaret lets go of the handbag she's been holding in her lap to clap along. She gathers from the general energy of the ovation that Ivan has defeated Ollie and won all ten of the games. Ivan nods his head to acknowledge the applause, which is growing louder rather than fading, and someone at the back of the room gives a long loud whistle. Ivan stands there inclining his head, smiling politely without showing his teeth, bathed in the cheers of the spectators. Ollie gets to his feet from behind his table and slowly the applause subsides. He thanks everyone for coming, and thanks Ivan and congratulates him on a 'clean sweep', and after a little more clapping and thanking of various people, the event comes to an end. People start to get out of their seats, talking to one another, gathering their things, and one of the chess club men has propped open the main door to let the audience file out.

Rising from her seat, putting her coat on, Margaret sees that Ivan has gone back to speak to the little girl with the scrunchie. He has his back to Margaret but she can hear him talking. You played a really good game, he's saying. Do you know where you made a mistake? The girl shakes her head. Let me show you, he says, and that way you won't do it again. To her parents, he says: You don't mind, do you? It's going to take like one minute. She played a good game otherwise. He's setting the board up while he's speaking. Around them, the spectators are leaving, checking their phones, zipping up jackets. Margaret is standing by her chair, thumbing the strap of her handbag absentmindedly, her long raincoat hanging loose, unbuttoned. You remember this position? Ivan says. The girl nods her head, staring down at the board in front of her. After a few seconds, he asks: Do you see now why it was a bad idea to move that rook? She looks up at him solemnly and nods her head again. That's alright, you're learning, he says. You played really nicely. Maybe we'll have a rematch in a couple of years. Her parents are smiling, her father with his hand on the girl's shoulder. It's so kind of you to take the time, the mother says. I'm sure you're exhausted. Ivan straightens up from the table. I'm alright, he says. The father is looking behind Ivan now, at Margaret, and Ivan follows his gaze and sees her standing there. She smiles, and he looks back at her without speaking. She can see that his forehead is still damp.

Congratulations, she says.

Oh, he replies. Well, whatever. Thank you.

He wipes his forehead with the sleeve of his shirt: noticing that she noticed, maybe. The room around them is emptying out, the girl and her parents saying goodbye and leaving. Inattentively Ivan says to them: Okay, bye.

I believe I have the honour of giving you a lift home, Margaret says.

Ivan looks her in the eyes, a very direct look, even, she thinks, intense: with that feeling, again, of their belonging wordlessly somehow to the same camp. Right, he says. I think the others are going for a drink now. But I can skip that, I don't mind.

Would you like a drink? she says. You deserve one after what you've been through. I'm astonished you're still on your feet.

He smiles at her, showing his braces again, the new white ceramic braces that young people have now. Yeah, there's a lot of walking around, he says. That's what people say, forget about the chess, practise the walking. Were you— He breaks off here, with a look that is shyly proud. Were you watching, or? he asks.

Margaret feels suddenly very kindly towards him, a rush of kindly feeling, to see him look so proud of himself. Oh, I was spellbound, she says. Not that I had any idea what was going on. What do you think, would you like to go out and celebrate?

He's still looking at her. Sure, he says. I'll get my things.

She goes to join the group at the door. Ollie tells her they're going for a drink in the Cobweb and she says she'll come along. She knows one of the men vaguely from town, the retired chemist Tom O'Donnell, and another man says his name is Stephen, and another Hugh. When Ivan joins them, they all leave the hall together. The men are talking about chess, using vocabulary of which Margaret has only the vaguest comprehension, gambits, sacrifices, and in the long corridor their voices echo off the walls and ceiling. Though the conversation seems to be directed towards Ivan, he isn't speaking, only walking quietly with his small black suitcase. The case has wheels but he isn't wheeling it, just carrying it by the handle. Before they go out onto the street, Margaret turns the lights off and then gets up onto a little step-stool to set the alarm, while the others wait, while Ivan waits behind her. He's watching her, she thinks, but how does she know without looking? And she doesn't look, she just knows, as if his eyes are sending out little needles in her direction and she can feel the needles pricking painlessly on her skin. She feels for him, surrounded by these blustering middle-aged people, men who admire him and at the same time fear and perhaps resent him, men who want to impress him but also to intimidate or slight him. And yet she seems to feel that Ivan is well aware of the dynamic between himself and the other men, and that this awareness has something to do with his watching Margaret now while she sets the alarm. But how to know, how to interpret the watching, when he doesn't say anything to her or even seem to want to?

Outside, the rain has softened into mist, and the streetlights are on. The chemist Tom O'Donnell is putting up his umbrella.

Tell us, the man named Stephen says, where is that name 'Koubek' from?

Slovakia, says Ivan.

You don't sound Slovakian, Stephen replies.

No, yeah, Ivan says. I'm from Kildare. My dad was Slovak, but he moved here in the eighties. And my mother is Irish. O'Donoghue.

They are walking across the car park, passing Margaret's car, and she unlocks it so that Ivan can leave his suitcase in the boot. The other men go on talking. Her hair is getting wet, and she takes her scarf off and knots it over her head again while Ivan closes the boot down quietly and says: Thank you. She feels for an instant a strange urge to turn to the other men, saying something like: I said I would drop him back to his accommodation. This would be, she thinks, a bizarre remark. No one is wondering why Ivan is so quietly and obediently placing his suitcase into the boot of her car. To offer an explanation would suggest that something is in need of explaining, raising the spectre of other, alternative explanations, which have as yet occurred to no one. A terrible thing to say. She says nothing. They all keep walking together, through a little paved alleyway to the Cobweb Bar, and Ollie holds open the door for Margaret to enter first.

Inside, the bar is warm and quiet. Along the walls are padded benches with tables in front of them, and old advertisements, dimly lit. Margaret unties her scarf from her hair, letting her eyes half-close, inhaling the warm familiar atmosphere. It's Friday, she thinks, the working week is over, it's not so bad to sit in a bar with all these men for just a little while, to be for a while the only woman in the warm enclosed room. Let me get you a drink, Ollie says. Margaret says she'll have lemonade. And Ivan? Ollie asks. I presume you're of legal age by now, are you? Ivan gives an embarrassed laugh at that, and answers: Yeah, I'm twenty-two. Ollie asks what he would like to drink in that case, and he asks for a glass of Italian beer. Slipping her coat off her shoulders Margaret finds a space to sit on one of the soft leatherette benches, with a low table between herself and Ivan. One of the other men asks her if she watched the games and she says: Oh yes, what a performance. Ollie goes up to order at the bar, and the others get up to help him, or to insist on paying for their own drinks, leaving Margaret and Ivan alone in the corner. The fact that they have been left alone together is present to her with a kind of insistent intrusive feeling, and wanting to make light conversation she says aloud: So, were you ever in trouble?

For a moment he says nothing. You mean like, in the chess just now? he asks.

Yes, I'm sorry. That's what I meant.

Selfconsciously he smiles, and he's rubbing at his shoulder with his fingertips again. Right, obviously, he says. No, I wasn't in trouble really. I mean, I do draw games sometimes, if it's a lot more people or the players are better. But with these local club players I wouldn't worry about it. He swallows now, glancing back at the bar, and then says in a friendly voice: Ah, but you won't tell them I said that, maybe.

She smiles also, at the backward glance, his friendly tone, almost conspiratorial. No, don't worry, she says. But don't you ever lose games?

In an exhibition? Not too often, because I'll only play people below a certain rating, which would be a lot lower than mine. I lose competitive games, though. All the time. I'm like, not actually that good at chess.

She starts laughing then, and he smiles along with her, which she finds sweet: his unfeigned pleasure at being funny. That's hard to believe, she says.

He glances down at his hands. His fingernails are bitten, she notices. Well, I mean relatively, he says. Still examining his hands, frowning, he adds: We don't have to talk about chess, by the way. I know you don't play.

No, but it's always interesting to hear people talk about things they're passionate about.

He looks up at her again. Is it? he says.

Uncertainly, smiling, she replies: Don't you think it is?

I don't know, he says. Being honest, I've never thought about that. But I will think about it, now that you've said it. I suppose it depends what you mean: 'passionate'. I find some people can be very boring when they talk, but maybe it's because, actually, they're not passionate enough. He gives another smile now. I don't know if I even am that passionate about chess, he adds, but I suppose everyone probably thinks I am.

What do you think you're passionate about? she asks.

At this, he blushes. She can see him, even in the dim light, blushing, and he says something that sounds like: Hm. Alarmed, she says with forced cheerfulness, too loudly: Never mind, you needn't tell me. Then she regrets saying that too. The other men are coming back from the bar, finally. Ollie leans over to hand Margaret a cold damp glass, saying: A lemonade for the lady. They're taking seats around the table, drinking, talking, but Ivan is not talking, only looking at the side of her face, while she avoids his eye. Maybe he's watching her because he doesn't know what else to do, she thinks, because he feels awkward or ill at ease. Maybe he wants to catch her eye because he has something particular he wants to say, and by avoiding his gaze she's only prolonging the interval during which he feels it necessary to keep looking. Or maybe – the idea intrudes forcefully into her thoughts – maybe he's looking at her for sexual reasons. It is not possible for Margaret to exclude such thoughts completely from her life, however much she might in certain circumstances like to. Ideas intrude which are shameful, sad, even obscene and immoral. Most of the time she can go through life interacting pleasantly with the people around her, pleasantly and superficially, never thinking or wanting to think about the profound and so carefully concealed sexual personalities of others. But it is not possible all the time to be so unconscious of other people, the disguised aspects of their lives. This young man with the braces on his teeth, who spends his weekends visiting arts centres to play chess in front of spectators, carrying a cheap black suitcase around and leaving it in the corners of rooms, this young man also has sexual thoughts and feelings, almost certainly, almost everyone does, especially at the age of twenty-two. He's still looking at her even now. Why did she say the word 'passionate' to him when they were talking? And why did he repeat it so many times, three or even four times? Is the word 'passionate', or is it not, basically an obscene item of vocabulary? No, it isn't. But is it like a small bandage placed over an item of vocabulary that is in fact obscene? Maybe, yes. A word with blood running through it, a red word. In casual conversation it's better to use words that are grey or beige. Where did it come from, then, this word 'passionate'? She knows where. From that so firmly suppressed feeling, present all along, that when he looks at her, when he speaks to her, he is addressing not only the superficial but also the deep concealed parts of her personality – without meaning to, without knowing how not to. Looking at her, his eyes communicate: I know that you are a person with desires, and so am I, even if I am helpless to do anything about this knowledge. Has she, unconsciously, half-consciously, been enjoying the little interplay between their respective roles? His repressed but perceptible impatience with the other men, his attentiveness towards her, his quiet searching looks, the colour that rose to his face just now. Beside them the other men are talking about a famous chess player from the nineteenth century. You know he was Irish, Ollie says. His father was an Irishman. Murphy. The others disagree about that. Ivan sits drinking from his glass and looking at Margaret, she can feel the pressure of his eyes on the side of her face still, while she goes on pretending to listen, pretending to smile. Finally she turns and meets his gaze. They look at one another without speaking. Belonging, it could not be clearer, to the same camp, separate from the rest. And he puts his glass down on the table. Clearing his throat he says to the others: Listen, thank you. I'll see you in the morning. They all want to congratulate him again, and slap him on the back, and Margaret needs a minute anyway to put her raincoat back on, and to find her scarf hanging over the back of a chair.

Out of the bar together and into the dark street they walk with the rain falling around them. For a while, not speaking, not even looking at one another, they walk side by side, and this is simple, and correct. Margaret asks Ivan where he's staying and he takes out his phone to show her the address, down in the holiday village by the lake. In the car park she unlocks her car and they get inside together, closing the doors, and all her acts and gestures are just the necessary things that follow after getting into a car: putting the key in the ignition, and turning the lights on, securing her seat belt. These actions more or less perform themselves, ritually, and she has no decisions to make, nothing at all to do, except to feel and observe herself checking the rear-view mirror, reversing out of her parking space. Ivan sits with his hands in his lap saying nothing. Outside, the car park is glowing with the skeletal orange light of the streetlamps, the paved surfaces dappled and glistening. She turns on her wipers and they click and scrape rhythmically over the windscreen. It happens all the time that she drives someone home like this, or drops them to the station, and they sit in the car together this way, chatting about something. It's just work. And if Ivan doesn't want to chat, if he wants to sit there looking at his hands and then looking at her and back at his hands again, that's okay – he's only twenty-two, and very gifted at one particular kind of board game, and after all there's no formal etiquette for the situation. Finding yourself in the car of an older woman after a presumably strenuous public event, being driven to your accommodation with your little black suitcase, no one ever teaches you how to behave under such circumstances. If he wants to sit in silence, looking at his bitten fingernails, that's alright, no problem. She, too, of course, is sitting in silence, and has nothing to say. They come off the main road and down onto the small lane to the holiday cottages, the gravel crunching noisily under the tyres of Margaret's car. She has done nothing wrong, has done nothing at all, in fact, beyond what is required for the purpose of driving Ivan from the bar to the holiday village. If she made a little error in the conversation earlier, if she used one little dubious word or phrase, asking him what he was passionate about, that was excusable, even in a sense deniable, because subjective. She pulls up outside one of the houses, a white bungalow with peeling paint and darkened windows.

This is you, I think, she says.

It's the first time either of them has spoken since they got into the car, and inside the sealed environment her voice has a compressed sound. Ivan looks out the window at the bungalow.

Thank you, he says.

She tells him it's no problem. He nods his head, and once more he looks at her.

Would you like to come inside? he asks.

Doubtingly, he goes on looking at her, as if to say he's sorry to ask, and he waits for her to answer. There's something so vulnerable in his look, in his tone of voice. Is there anything she can say to explain? About her job, and how much older she is, and her life situation. But her explanations will only sound like lies. Nobody when they're rejected believes it's really for extraneous reasons. And it almost never is for extraneous reasons, because mutual attraction – which even makes sense from the evolutionary perspective – is simply the strongest reason to do anything, overriding all the contrary principles and making them fall away into nothing. She lets her eyes drop down for just a fraction of a second to his hands, which are resting in his lap: fine-looking, sensitive hands, she noticed that earlier, when he was playing chess.

Okay, she says.

The house is damp and chilly, and all the rooms are dark. Ivan is carrying his suitcase, and Margaret finds a light switch in the hall. Overhead a bare bulb comes on, with no lampshade, and in the corner by the door the wallpaper is mildewed. In a friendly conversational tone of voice, she says: Not what I'd call luxurious. It's the chess club that booked this for you, by the way, not us. He smiles at that, showing his braces again. I've seen worse, he says. Sometimes I just have to sleep on someone's floor. She hangs up her coat and scarf and he puts down his suitcase. They go along the hall together into a living room with a kitchenette. He turns the light on this time. There's a red cloth sofa, and a small dining table, and a sliding glass door leading into the back garden. Margaret goes to look in the kitchen and Ivan follows after her. On a shelf above the microwave is a box of tea and a tin of instant coffee, and someone has even put milk and butter in the fridge.

I wonder if Ollie came in and stocked the kitchen personally, she says. I think he might have a crush on you.

Ivan laughs at that, looking gratified. I could tell he was happy with how his game went, he says. Which is kind of sad, because he actually made a lot of mistakes.

You're not a professional, are you? she asks. I mean, you don't play chess full-time.

He says no, but he does get paid for exhibition games, and for coaching. Then he clears his throat and afterwards says nothing. She remembers when she was nervous around men, as a young person – though, of course, it's different for women. Impossible to imagine a girl of twenty-two behaving as Ivan has behaved tonight, as he is behaving even now. Not that he seems more powerful or domineering than a girl, not that at all: rather, that he seems to have taken on exclusive responsibility for what appears to him a very difficult task – the task, unless she is mistaken, of seducing an older woman he has just met – and he appears to feel frustrated with himself for not knowing how to accomplish this task, frustrated and guilty. These feelings would not arise in a young woman. Different feelings, equally unpleasant, but different. At the same time, isn't Margaret herself playing her part in these feelings, in this drama? Is it not, after all, a drama with two principal actors? She is not offering, she notices, to accept any shared responsibility for the accomplishment of the task Ivan has set himself. She has indicated, by entering the holiday cottage, that she may well be available to be seduced; but she is not helping him along towards success in that respect. To help, however, would be obviously injurious to her dignity, far more than the present situation is to his. She asks him if he's in college, and he says he just finished a degree in theoretical physics. Another silence falls. The house is cold, her back is cold against the fridge door.

Sorry I'm being so awkward, he says.

I don't think you are, really.

Well, I'm definitely a lot more awkward than you are, he replies. You know, when you're talking, everything you say sounds so normal and like, smooth. I can never get words to come out that smoothly. You're the type of person who can just go up to someone and start a conversation. It's very— He breaks off, and then after a pause goes on: I was just going to say, it's very attractive, but maybe I shouldn't say that.

She turns her eyes away, oddly flustered now after all. Ah, she says. Well, I don't know.

He's looking at his hands again, examining the little pink stubs of his fingernails. I'm sorry, he says. Just because you're being nice to me, it obviously doesn't mean—you know. It went through my head, or whatever, but it's stupid. Like, yeah, Ivan, I'm sure she thought it was really cool and sexy when you beat all those elderly guys at chess.

She feels a strange, light, amused sensation at his words: as though, concluding that the negotiations have fallen through, he wants only to show how nicely he can take defeat. Not only elderly guys, she says. You also beat a ten-year-old girl.

He gives a little laugh. Yeah, she wasn't too bad for a ten-year-old, he says. Although she made one serious blunder. I actually had to go back and talk to her afterwards. It was three or four intelligent moves and then a horrible mistake.

I guess you only make good moves, she says.

I don't make horrible mistakes, he answers.

I do.

Looking over at her, he starts to smile again: revising, she thinks, the presumption of failure. Under the dim ceiling light she can see the wire of his braces wet and gleaming. Okay, he says. Interesting. That's very interesting to me.

Are you sure you're twenty-two? she asks.

Yeah, I'm sure. Do you want to check my ID?

Would you mind?

He puts one of his hands into his pocket, and takes out a wallet to show her an age card. She notices the hand trembling a little.

The photograph is not too nice, he says. Or I don't know, maybe that's just what I look like.

She removes the thin plastic card from the wallet and studies it under the light. Born in 1999, she says. Jesus. I started college in 2004.

Really? You're what age, then? Thirty-five.

Thirty-six, she says. She's still looking down at the card, at the small image of Ivan's face, grave and sombre. You know, I actually did think it was impressive when you won all those chess games earlier, she says. I thought you were glamorous.

He gives a sweet, foolish smile. Ah, wow, he says. That's nice of you to say. I definitely don't feel glamorous. But that's cool of you to be so nice.

She hands the card back and he puts it in his wallet. Do your parents play chess? she asks.

Well, no, not really, he says. My mother, not at all. And my dad did play a little bit, but actually, uh— he just passed away. Very recently, like three or four weeks ago. Four weeks, I guess it is.

Oh God, she says. Ivan, I'm so sorry to hear that.

Yeah. He had cancer for a long time. So it wasn't unexpected.

She's looking at him, but he's looking at the floor. She says: My dad— Not that it's the same, I'm sorry. But my dad died a couple of years ago. I can imagine how you must be feeling.

He looks back at her now, dark quiet eyes, and she feels him very close. It is kind of hard, he says. And like, weird or whatever. I don't know if you felt that.

Of course.

My parents were split up as well, he says. And I lived with my dad mostly. Not to give you my whole life story, I'm sorry.

Don't be sorry. Do you have siblings?

An older brother. Who's a lot older, like ten years. But we're not close or anything. Before she can respond, Ivan clears his throat and adds: He actually— Just that you were asking if the other people in my family play chess. My brother does, but he's not very good.

Tentatively now she smiles. Ah, she says. Compared to you, I suppose not.

Right. Although, if you want to know something sad, I already hit my peak like four years ago. I was playing really well for a while, I mean, really well. But I'm not able to play like that anymore. I don't know why. It makes me depressed when I think about it. You have all these dreams that you're going to keep getting better and better. And then in reality you just start getting worse, and you don't even understand why. Is this boring to hear about?

Margaret says no, it isn't. He's looking down at his hands again.

I don't know, he says. The one thing I said to myself in the car was, if she comes inside with you, don't start talking to her about chess. It takes up too much of my life already, to be quite honest. Like to say the absolute truth, I spend too much time on it, because I'm not even that good. Although it makes me really sad to admit that. You know, a lot of people told me I was letting it take up too much time, and I just thought they didn't understand. But now I think, maybe I've really wasted a lot of my life. Like when other people were out having fun, getting girlfriends or whatever, I was at home basically reading. You have to read a lot of opening theory – that's the beginning of a game, the first moves. Which have all been played before, so you just have to learn them. It's not even that interesting, but it has to be done. So you have all these openings that come from books, and you have all these endgame strategies, which can be honestly kind of formulaic. And you're learning all this for what? Just to get to an okay position in the middle game and try to play some decent chess. Which most of the time I can't even do anyway. Sometimes I think, if I could go back to age fifteen, I would just give up. I was already pretty good then, I haven't gotten much better. And I could have used that time to get more of a social life. I don't lie in bed every night just thinking about chess, you know. I won't go into detail on what I do think about, but I can tell you it's usually not related to chess at all.

She's smiling, listening, nodding her head, and yet his words give her a strange feeling, a feeling in the pit of her stomach.

But don't you think you enjoyed it? she says. All the time you spent practising, don't you think it made you happy sometimes?

With a pained expression, picking at his thumbnail, he answers: Yeah, there is that side of it. I did win a lot of games. And I played at big tournaments, I beat some good players. I have played some very nice chess. One or two games, I would say, better than just nice. That's the other side. You're right. And if I gave up when I was fifteen, and I tried to be more social and talk to girls more, it might not have worked anyway. You know, I don't think I would have become this really popular guy just from not playing chess. You can drive yourself crazy thinking about different things you could have done in the past. But sometimes I think, actually, I didn't have that much power over my life anyway. I mean, I couldn't give myself a new personality out of nothing. And things just kind of happened to me.

She is silent after he finishes speaking, and her eyes are turned towards the floor, bare yellow linoleum.

Are you really bored now? he asks.

After a moment she replies: Not at all. It's true, you can drive yourself crazy thinking about different things you could have done in the past. I drive myself crazy in that way too.

He's looking at her, she knows. Yeah? he says. Why?

When I was your age— That's not right, a little older than you. In my twenties, I met someone. And later we got married. Legally we still are, because it's all so complicated. But we don't live together anymore. It's like you said, you can drive yourself crazy thinking about these things. The other lives you could have had. And the life you did have, after it's over – where did it go? I mean, what are you supposed to do with it? Anyway. It's lucky you're thinking about all this now when you're only twenty-two. When I was that age my life hadn't even started happening to me yet. I hardly remember anything from before then, honestly, that's the truth. You know, everyone in their twenties has these problems you're talking about – feeling left out, and thinking people don't like you. Those aren't serious problems at your age, even if they feel that way. Maybe you're on a different wavelength from some of the girls you've met in college. But I can tell you, you're very attractive. You really are.

Women are going to fall in love with you, believe me. That's when the problems start.

She looks up at him now, and he's looking back at her, an intense silent look. She tries to laugh, and her laughter has a helpless sound. Margaret, he says, can I kiss you? She doesn't know what to do, whether to laugh again, or start crying. Okay, she says. He comes over to where she's standing against the fridge and kisses her on the mouth. She feels his tongue move between her lips. Drawing away slightly he murmurs: Sorry about my braces, I hate them so much. She tells him not to apologise. Then he kisses her again. It is, of course, a desperately embarrassing situation – a situation which seems to render her entire life meaningless. Her professional life, eight years of marriage, whatever she believes about her personal values, everything. And yet, accepting the premise, allowing life to mean nothing for a moment, doesn't it simply *feel good* to be in the arms of this person? Feeling that he wants her, that all evening he has been looking at her and desiring her, isn't it pleasurable? To embody the kind of woman he believed he couldn't have – to incorporate that woman into herself, and allow him to have her. Pressed against her, his body is thin and tensed and shivering. And what if life is just a collection of essentially unrelated experiences? Why does one thing have to follow meaningfully from another?

In the bedroom the windowpane is wet with condensation, and Ivan has to kneel up on the mattress to pull down the blind. The ceiling light is off but the light in the hall is still on, the door half-open. Margaret gets onto the bed beside him, they lie down together. The sheets on the bed feel cold, maybe damp, or maybe just very cold. He unbuttons her cardigan, her blouse, and she helps him to unhook the clasp of her bra. He can feel himself sweating: his underarms, his forehead, a hot feeling. With her mouth she finds his mouth and they kiss once more. Her right breast in his left hand, her nipple raised under the tip of his thumb, hard, touching. She lets out a little breath almost into his mouth, a little sigh, as if she likes to be touched that way. Who can explain such a thing, and why even try to explain: an understanding shared between two people. Her breath warm on his lips when she sighs, and when he kisses her again, a muted sound from her throat. He moves his fingers to her zip and she lets him, lifts her hips from the mattress to help him take off her skirt. Lying on her back now she's wearing only a pair of black briefs. You're really beautiful, he says. I mean, obviously. I presume people tell you that all the time. She gives a kind of laugh, shrugging her shoulders. Well, no, she says. But then I don't do things like this a lot. Kneeling upright on the mattress he looks at her. Right, he says. Me neither. With eyes glittering soft in the almost-darkness she looks back at him. You're not a virgin, are you, Ivan? she says. I hope you don't mind me asking. Swallowing, he laughs and the laughter catches in his throat. No, he answers. I'm actually not, but it's okay. I guess I probably seem kind of nervous. Softly she smiles. That's alright, she says. I'm a little bit nervous myself. A certain feeling rises inside him when she says this: like a pleasurable form of anxiety, a strange anxious anticipation of pleasure. He touches with his fingers the black cotton of her underwear, damp, and she makes another high moaning sound, closing her eyes. What are you nervous about? he asks. Laughing breathlessly she says: Oh God, I don't know. I don't know what you must think of me. The same anxious thrill moves through him again, and he finds himself without conscious thought answering her, rapidly and almost unintelligibly: No, don't worry. I really like you. Don't worry about that at all. Inside her underwear, his fingers, wet, and her hand is clutching at the pillowcase. At this moment, touching her, watching her eyes flutter closed, he wants her so badly, feels such a wrenching almost painful wave of desire, that even the increasingly likely prospect of having her, of being inside her, within only a few seconds or minutes, feels like it might not be enough to relieve this desire completely. Her mouth, wet, open in that way, he wants, and to make her come, to feel it like that when he's in her, he wants so much, Jesus Christ. He really is sweating a lot, he has to wipe his forehead with his wrist, and his upper lip is wet, which makes him nervous again, like maybe it's disgusting to sweat so much, or even at all. She isn't sweating, although she's very very wet where he's touching her with his fingers, wet inside, and moaning from her throat. Do you have a condom? she asks. The idea of her asking, oh God. He goes on touching her still. Yeah, he says. In my suitcase. After a second he adds: I guess it's been there for a while. Like a year maybe. But that's okay, is it? She lifts her hand to her head, touching her hair, half-smiling. I'm not an expert, she says. But there should be an expiry date, I think. He takes his hand out from her underwear, wet, and she kind of groans. Ah, he hears himself saying. Sorry. I really love touching you like that. She makes the same noise again and covers half her face with her hand. It's so good, she says. If she brushed against him even really lightly now, just brushing him there with her hand, he probably would come. Oh no. What if he can't even do anything to her, imagine, and she would be awkwardly nice about it, probably. He gets off the bed and goes out to the hall, where his suitcase sits on the floor under the coat rack. It's very bright out here with the light on: quiet also, and cold. He unzips the front pocket of the case and takes out a serrated foil square he got for free in college like two years ago, unbranded. In small black dotted print the expiry date reads: 07/25. He puts it in his pocket and goes back inside, saying: Yeah, I checked, it's okay. When he gets on the bed she starts to unbutton his shirt, and her breasts are rising and falling with her breath, light, shallow. How much she liked it when he touched her, he thinks: and what if it's different now, and not as good. Quietly, quickly, he finishes undressing and rolls the condom on. She helps him to take off her briefs. Dark curls, damp, and she rolls her head back on the pillow, saying softly: Oh. To disappoint her like that, he thinks. One of her arms she has laid across her body. He gets on top of her, finding her mouth again, open. Yeah, I really want you to like it, he says. I mean, that's kind of concerning me a little bit. Just the idea, you know. Looking up at him as if amused she smiles. Mm, she says. But that's a nice normal thing to be concerned about, isn't it? He laughs, hears himself laughing. Is it? he says. Okay. But still, I feel that. Like even if it is normal, I would still be concerned. She puts her hand down between their bodies, and with the palm of her hand, warm, she touches him, saying: It's okay. And it is okay, he thinks. The story of human life. All of their ancestors, his, and hers also. Life itself, the passing mystery. Very easily in the end he moves inside her. She lets out a little gasping sound, her hand grasping his arm, and she whispers something. His name. He hears her. Closing his eyes quickly now not to see. And her hips lift a little off the mattress, wanting what he wants. Jesus Christ, he says. Fuck. So close almost already feeling her so wet and her high breathing. Deeper inside she wants him and when he gives it to her like that she likes it better, he can feel. Try to remember everything, he thinks. Every breath exactly. Her mouth on his neck, mumbling again: Ivan, oh God. Because she likes it so much. He bites on his tongue for a second. Saying his name for instance. And so wet like this and breathing. Because she does. Yeah, he says. I feel like, kind of worried that I might, uh— They look at one another, her face all flushed and hot, like his, and she says: It's okay, don't worry. It's nice. Throbbing inside her and wet she says this. Closing his eyes he can hear himself crying out kind of and feels light-headed, pinpricks behind his eyelids, a fainting sort of feeling, and he says again: Fuck. It's finished then. How long, like a minute probably. Her arms heavy around his neck he feels. I'm sorry, he says. Just, uh. I guess it felt like, a little bit too good. Not to blame you, obviously. She's laughing now, sweetly, her face still flushed, looking up at him. You can blame me, she says. I don't mind. But you don't have to say sorry, it was perfect. A very strong feeling comes over him then: something inside himself warm and spreading, like dying or being born. He has no idea what the feeling is, whether it's good or dangerous. It's related to her, the words she's saying, his feeling about her words. She said it was perfect. And she meant what he did to her, even though it was over too quickly, she liked it, or more than liking. You're being nice, he says. She's smiling, lying in his arms, her eyes closing, sleepy, and the feeling is so strong, powerful, like he could lift an entire building in his hands. No, I mean it, she says. It was beautiful. Thank you. Is this how it feels, he thinks, to get what you want? To desire, and at the same time to have, still desiring, but fulfilled. It was beautiful, thank you. Ah, I feel really happy, he says. Or, I don't know, that's not even the right word. Her eyes are closed then. Me too, she murmurs. He's nodding his head, feeling for no reason a powerful sense of protectiveness over her. Sensing that she wants to sleep, he draws away, and she turns over on her side to face him. He leaves the condom on the carpet beside the bed, he'll get it in the morning, and pulls the duvet up over them both. Other people might experience these feelings all the time, whatever they are. Strong, powerful feelings of happiness, satisfaction, protectiveness. It could all be very ordinary, in the aftermath of mutually pleasant episodes like just now. Or even if it's rare, to have a few times in life and no more, still worth living for, he thinks. To have met her like this: beautiful, perfect. A life worth living, yes.

In the morning, Margaret wakes alone in the holiday cottage to the sound of her alarm: Saturday, 8.30 a.m. After finding the phone and fumbling to switch the noise off, she lies back down in solitude, empty of thought, hearing a faint humming noise elsewhere like a fridge or a dishwasher. The ceiling is finished in stippled plaster, the peaks and dimples casting small irregular shadows in the light from the window. Weak watery morning light. The minutes pass. She sits up and finds her clothes on the floor, damp, crumpled, and turns yesterday's underwear inside out to put it back on again. With something like detached curiosity, with a pale inward blankness, she thinks about Ivan, who has gone now, who has left her in bed alone – she remembers him the night before, very deep inside her, saying: Ah, fuck. Well, that's what boys his age like to do at weekends. Why not with her? She's not bad-looking, so they say, not old yet, no longer really married, and then she failed to put up the resistance he seemed to expect. Her lack of resistance, so unusual, fascinated and stirred him. Also, he was grieving over his father, she thinks, and in grief people do uncharacteristic things, behave irresponsibly, get drunk and sleep around. Not that he'd been drunk last night. He had, if she recalls correctly, had a single glass of beer. Will he tell his friends about her, she wonders? The chess prodigy, Ivan Koubek. Almost nothing about him was really explained. Quietly he seemed to observe other people, and to perceive a great deal, and when he spoke, his words conveyed a sort of loneliness she found touching. He was very nice to her in bed, she remembers: so nice that it's difficult for her, even now, to regret completely the whole ludicrous episode. She has never in her life spent the night with a stranger before. But then Ivan did not, at the time, seem to her like a stranger: he seemed, all too consciously, to belong to her own camp. Yes, that again – and what does it even mean? Simply that he was tall and good-looking, that he wanted for the usual animal reasons to get her into bed, that she for the same reasons wanted to let him. Maybe. Now, in any case, her life will return, unexplained, to whatever it was before. But no, she thinks, because its shapelessness has been exposed to her now, the old values and meanings floating off unattached, and how can she go about reattaching them? And to what? In another room, the whirring noise comes suddenly to a halt, and she can hear something like a curtain hissing along a rail. Oh, she thinks. Oh Christ: he's been in the shower. Frantically she gets to her feet, finishes dressing, and with darting hands makes the bed, hearing his footsteps now along the hall.

When Ivan enters the room, his hair is wet, and he's wearing a clean grey sweatshirt. Ah, he says. You're awake. I was wondering if I should wake you. He coughs and continues:

Anyway, this is awkward, but they only gave me one bath towel and it's wet now. I hope that's not really annoying. I'm sorry I didn't ask first, but you were sleeping, like I said.

She stands at the bottom of the bed with her arms folded. Her face feels tired and swollen, her eyes swollen, hot. It's no problem, she replies. I'll shower when I get home.

Right, he says. Right, that's what I thought. Sorry.

By his ear he has a small thin cut, where she supposes he has cut himself shaving.

Do you need a lift to your workshop? she asks. I don't mind driving you.

Oh. That actually would be cool, if it's alright.

She's toying with a button on her cardigan. Sure, she says. And look, if you don't mind, I would be grateful if you didn't tell people at the event today. About last night. I'm sorry to ask, but I think it would be difficult for me at work, if everyone knew.

He gives a strange little laugh. No, obviously, he says. I mean, I get you, but that's not the kind of thing I would tell people at a chess workshop anyway. The conversation doesn't really go there. For like, a lot of different reasons.

Without looking up she nods her head and says: Are you going— She breaks off, smiling, wiping her nose with her fingers. I was going to ask if you were going home today, she says. But I don't even know where you live.

Oh, I live in Dublin, he says. And yeah, I'm going back today. On the bus.

Her eyes are hot, her face is hot, she's nodding, pretending for some reason to button up her cardigan.

I probably have to go soon, he says. To be on time for the thing.

Sure. I'm ready.

Right, I just want to say something to you first.

She looks up at him, and he's looking back at her – a very direct and intense look, like yesterday evening, when the games were finished, and everyone else was leaving, the same look. Can I give you my number? he says. Like in case you ever think about me. I could just put the number into your phone and then it would be there, you wouldn't even have to look at it again if you didn't want to. What do you think?

With her fingers she dabs at her eyes. Let me think about it, she says.

Outside, a wet chilly morning, the branches of trees dripping overhead. They get in the car together and drive back the same way they came the night before, and again they're not speaking, again the windscreen wipers scrape back and forth. Once she has parked outside the building, she says: You can give me your number. But I don't know if I'll get in touch or not. Okay? And if you don't hear from me, it won't be because I haven't thought about you. I will think about you. I just have to figure out what's best. He says he understands, and he keys the number into her phone. The time on her dashboard is 8.56 a.m. He gets out of the car and she watches him walk up to the main entrance of the building, carrying his black suitcase. One of the wheels on the case is hanging askew, broken – she can see that now. That's probably why he carries it, instead of using the wheels. At the entrance, he turns back and looks at her over his shoulder. Then he's gone, the door swinging shut behind him. The door of her own workplace, with its flat rectangular handle, with one glass panel broken at the bottom and repaired with brown tape. She has been contained before, contained and directed, by the trappings of ordinary life. Now she no longer feels contained or directed by these forces, no longer directed by anything at all. Life has slipped free of its netting. She can do very strange things now, she can find herself a very strange person. Young men can invite her into holiday cottages for sexual reasons. It means nothing. That isn't true: it means something, but the meaning is unfamiliar.

# 3

A purring mechanical tone tells him the call is ringing while he sits on the sofa unlacing his shoes. Home from work late, Tuesday night, awkward time to call, and never texted beforehand, almost as if, yes, hoping no one will answer. Duty discharged in that case. Diphenhydramine with a glass of red wine, see what people are saying on the internet. Fall asleep with the lights on for an hour or two if he's lucky. Wake up again and try something stronger. Watch in claustrophobic dread the passing of hours, scorched feeling in his eyelids blinking. Three in the morning, four, another Xanax, open a new browser tab to type out: insomnia psychosis. psychosis average age of onset. can't sleep going insane. About to hang up when with a dropping sound the call connects and the voice of his brother is saying: Hello? Oddly normal the way he says that when answering the phone. Makes him sound so adult and reasonable. But what does Peter expect him to say: nothing? Just pick up without a word and breathe audibly into the receiver? Hey, says Peter.

What's up? Ivan asks. Is this about the dog?

Peter, remembering, massages his forehead with his hand. No, he says, I haven't heard anything from Christine. Have you?

Oh. Yeah, she's been texting me. A lot, actually. Complaining.

I see. I'm sorry about that.

Ivan's voice more familiar now: flat, affectless, and yet communicating at the same time somehow a wary distrust. You haven't thought of anything we could do, he says.

No, not yet.

Funny thing is that people used to say their voices were alike. Home for the weekend, picking up the old landline with the rotary dial: Is that Ivan? Put me on to your dad, good man. Laughing then: Peter, actually. No, no, don't worry, I'll take it as a compliment.

I feel like the texts are getting kind of threatening, Ivan goes on. Like, she is talking a lot about trying to give the dog away, if I can't take him.

We'll figure something out, Peter says. Leave it with me.

Ivan is silent for a moment. Then he says: Cool, okay. Is that it?

Sorry?

I mean, are we finished talking now?

Peter closes his eyes. Is this not a good time? he asks.

Uh, says Ivan. Well, for what?

To talk on the phone.

Yeah, I get that. But about what?

Inhaling deeply Peter holds his breath a moment and then releases. Nothing, he says. I'm just calling to say hello.

After a pause Ivan answers: Oh. Then he adds: Okay.

So how are you?

I'm fine.

How was your chess thing, at the weekend?

Again with the note of wariness: Who told you about that?

Sylvia did. Why? Was it supposed to be a secret?

No, obviously. That makes sense she told you. I just didn't remember us talking about it.

Smoothing his hand over the arm of the sofa, crease in the faded cloth, Peter asks: It went okay?

Yeah.

What was it, a simultaneous?

Right, says Ivan. Ten games.

Ten wins?

Yeah.

Peter smiles now: My brother, the genius.

Hm, says Ivan. Thank you.

Where was it, down the country somewhere?

Yeah, in Clogherkeen. In Leitrim.

Town hall job? asks Peter.

Yeah. It was a nice place actually, like an arts centre. I guess they do different kinds of events there. I don't know, cultural things. Music or whatever. Some of the staff came to the event, they seemed pretty cool.

Peter's eyes open again now. Corner of the fireplace, grey against white. Go on, he says. What were they like?

I don't know. I guess kind of artistic. We went out for a drink afterwards, with the chess people as well. It was fun.

Any ladies present?

Ivan pauses. You mean when we went out afterwards? Ivan says. There was one woman, but the rest were men.

Well, I'm glad you had a good time.

Another pause. Yeah, she was pretty cool, actually, Ivan adds. The woman.

Peter falls still a moment: touched, even pained by this remark, delivered in his brother's flat monotonous voice. To think I sound like that, or ever did. Also I sang the tenor part in school and he was baritone. That's nice, Peter says. Ivan gives no further reply. Wonder who she could have been. Local graphic design student on ecstasy, maybe, attending a chess event as a joke. Trapped in conversation with Ivan afterwards, saying aloud: No, yeah, wow, that's so interesting. Signalling to her friends with her eyes: Save me. Trust him not to notice. She was pretty cool, actually. In silence, Peter gets up and goes to the window. Dark out now, he could let the blind down.

So how are you? Peter asks. How are you feeling?

You asked already. Like a minute ago, and I said I'm fine.

The row of houses opposite with the upstairs windows lit like picture frames. People you can see sometimes. Couple used to live there and that was their kitchen, but empty now he thinks. Made eye contact with the woman once. At night, with the dark street between them like that. Okay, says Peter. Well, I'm glad. Ivan says nothing. A little rain, there must be, because of that man on the street out walking with the umbrella. No marks on the windowpane though. He looks into a streetlamp to see: yes: slow falling mist in waves through the lighted air. Always tell by the streetlamp. Way the water holds the light in falling.

I know things must be difficult at the moment, Peter adds.

Right.

Another silence. Peter unhooks the cord and lets the blind down. Did you and Dad talk on the phone much? he asks.

Sometimes. If I wouldn't be home for a while, or whatever. He would ask what I was up to. Or we would talk about the dog, things like that.

He wanders back to the sofa while his brother is speaking,

leans half-standing against the arm. In silence he waits, they wait, each for the other.

You must miss him, Peter says.

Yeah, I do.

No idea what to say. Feeling cowed. And by what. Honest answer to a simple question. Needle him to say what he feels and then what, shrug your shoulders, too bad. What's the point. Can't help you there. Not that Ivan expects help. Doesn't feel himself to be asking anything, to be giving anything away. No need to conceal what isn't a weakness. More normal than he is, in that way. Straightforward. Yeah, I do. Miss him. Of course, says Peter. I'm sorry.

Are you okay? says Ivan.

Peter feels the phone hot, glassy against his face. Sure, he says. Do I not sound okay?

No, I mean, I'm not saying if you do or not. I'm just asking.

Well, I'm fine.

Cool, says Ivan. I just realised, you asked me if I was okay, and I didn't ask it back to you. Or if I did, I don't remember. I probably wouldn't have listened anyway. I do that a lot. Like, I'll remember to ask a question, but then I won't listen when the person answers. Or I'll just go the whole conversation not asking anything.

That's alright.

Yeah. It's bad manners, though.

I wouldn't worry about that, Peter says, we're family.

No, right. I just mean more in general.

Never really know what he's talking about, do you. Pointless even to try. No idea what he makes of it all, what he thinks you're talking about, what he's trying to say, never have any idea. Like talking to the dog. Big intelligent eyes looking back at you, uncomprehending. If a lion could talk, we could not understand him.

Well, I know you're probably busy, Peter says. I won't keep you.

Okay.

Glances over at the window again, forgetting he let the blind down. Just a blank white square now, no idea why he did that. Suppose Ivan the lion, or I am. Makes no difference which, or does it.

Listen, do you want to have lunch together at the weekend? he asks.

Hesitation drawn out by the vowel sound: Uh. Then: Yeah, okay. If you want. Nowhere expensive, though, because I'm waiting to get paid still.

Don't worry, I'll pay.

And there's no reason for this, is there? Ivan asks. You're not like, wanting to tell me some big news in person or something.

No.

You're not getting married, or anything like that.

Who would I be getting married to, Ivan?

He pauses, and then: No, I don't know. It was just an example.

Peter for his part also pauses. Well, it's nothing like that, he says.

Right.

I'll text you about lunch. Let's say Sunday. Okay?

Yeah. Bye.

They hang up. Why lunch? Wanting to make an effort, to tell Sylvia, probably. Picking her up from the hospital on Thursday, give them something to talk about while the sedatives wear off. You're not getting married or anything. After the funeral, when she stayed, he must have thought. Not that anything happened. Not nothing, but not that. They lay in bed together, that was all. He held her in his arms. A certain feeling, yes, but nothing in reality. Can hardly expect Ivan to understand that, considering Peter doesn't understand himself. Ivan anyway observes and reaches his own mysterious conclusions as usual. The first time he met Sylvia he was, what, nine or ten years old. The selectively mute days. He can talk, Peter told her beforehand, he just doesn't. At the house: peeling paint, damp carpets, smell of drains. Clothes drying over the range. Ivan's eyes watching. Don't mind him, Sylvia, said their father, he's just shy. Peter chewing and swallowing slowly a slice of dry roast beef. Vinyl-coated tablecloth with a pattern of pears. After dinner, on the cleared table, a game of chess. She had the white pieces. Everyone grateful not to have to talk. My brother, the genius. To this day she still receives every year on her birthday a card in the post with a neatly handwritten greeting inside. Dear Sylvia, Happy birthday to you. I hope you have a great day. Best wishes, Ivan. And the card will have a picture of a bird on it or something. His idea of friendship.

On screen now, a new message from Naomi.

NAOMI: hey handsome
NAOMI: you free?

He taps the banner to open the message and types back quickly.

PETER: Not tonight
PETER: In court in the morning

PETER: Everything ok?
NAOMI: yeah. . . . .
NAOMI: well except this lol

To the second message she attaches a screenshot from her bank account showing that she is seventeen euro in overdraft. Their relationship a kind of moral dilemma. Like right now, his reluctance to talk to her on the phone, difficult to specify, and he can't go over and see her at this hour, but nonetheless there is something it seems to him unnameably wrong with just wordlessly transferring her some money. Why does he get into these moods, irritable at the idea of having to talk to her, bordering on actually bad-tempered? Why has he only twice ever and both times under the influence of substances invited her to the flat where he lives alone without roommates and could theoretically entertain her whenever he wants?

PETER: I see
PETER: I can make a transfer now if that works
NAOMI: ahhhh thank you
NAOMI: im really sorry, i just need to renew a prescription
PETER: 200 ok?
NAOMI: literally youre a lifesaver
NAOMI: thanks

She plays it out with such consummate skill that he does have to wonder sometimes if he's even the only one she does this to. Which is funny. To be the only idiot showering her with money he has to work to earn: not much of a distinction, and yet preferable to the alternative. When he was out of town, for instance. Though at least she told him afterwards. Expert in self-preservation. Lazy too.

NAOMI: are you around tomororw night?
PETER: Not sure yet
NAOMI: ok cool

An effort to emphasise that he expects nothing in return for his money, thinks nothing of it, and may not even be available in any case to collect on the debt his money very pointedly does not incur. Then on a purely human interpersonal level she feels hurt and rejected by his coldness, maybe. Someone just seems like they have to be exploiting someone here. But who, and how? He her, financially, sexually. Or she him, financially, emotionally. It can be exploitative to give money; also to take it. Money overall a very exploitative substance, creating it seems fresh kinds of exploitation in every form of relationality through which it passes. Greasing with exploitation the wheels of human interaction generally. Now he feels bad, and actually does want to call her, to hear her gossiping about her friends, or describing what she's reading for college, to interject occasionally with unsolicited advice or commentary, that kind of thing, but it's too late. Why does everything have to be so complicated? He knows why. Flashing eyes of two animals through the undergrowth. Yes: what they want from each other.

In the morning, hiss of the iron, buttered bread roll, milligram of alprazolam, blue tie or green. Stands at the dining table rearranging his papers while the coffee cools, thoughts running rapid with broken phrases, details of argument, streams diverging and recrossing, hands clammy touching the pages. The point of law. To raise the question of. His briefcase then, bitter aftertaste, overcoat, and outside the chill wind of October moves through the leaves of trees. Wide grey streets around the Green, buses slowing to a stop, wheel and cry of gulls overhead. Leaves rustle over the park gates. Barred windows of Ship Street then and the vans reversing. Blue clearing in the white clouds, rain-washed cobbles. River dissected by the glitter of sunlight, Grattan Bridge. Copper stepped saucer dome over Portland stone balustraded parapet, dirty green cap in daylight, the Four Courts. Feels the effects by the time he's inside, dressing: slow serene feeling beginning in the hands and feet. Breathing settles. Thoughts grow orderly and sequential, facts arranged in place, stately procession of claims and counter-claims. That's not actually recreational, Naomi told him once. Like, you can get a prescription if that's what you're using it for. Along the corridor, scent of cleaning fluid, overheard voices. Even medicated he feels it: the white light of his own righteousness. Clear luminous certainty. In the courtroom, flow of speech unhurried, precise, inexorable. Admitting no contradiction. Familiar command almost perfect, yes, and pleasurable even, and then over. Changes his clothes again, eats lunch, answers a few emails. Something to do with the dog, he remembers: leave it with me, he said, and seemed to mean. Walking under sunlight by the river alone. Classes in the afternoon. Satisfaction of performance wears off with the milligram. Judges idiots anyway. Whole system corrupt, the Gonzaga cohort, revolving door. Death of his own illusions: desire to fight for something, all his sacred rage directed and useful for once. Late nights drafting and redrafting, visions of triumph, vindication, clients crying and embracing. His purpose in life recuperated.

Six months later gets back some three-page irrelevant judgement full of errors. I'm sorry. I don't know what to say. And his colleagues. The men frantic with insecurity, rehearsing the same old jokes in increasingly strained voices, desperate to catch the senior's eye. The women, nearly worse: giggling along. Oh my God, *lads*, you cannot say that. The meaningless lives people live. And afterwards, oblivion, forever. Futile rage at nothing. Directed one way or another, what's the difference. On the boardwalk by the river a little girl wearing a leopard-print hat, eating an ice cream cone. Thought rises calmly to the surface of his mind: I wish I was dead. Same as everyone sometimes surely. Idea occurs, that is. Remembering something embarrassing you did years ago and abruptly you think: that's it, I'm going to kill myself. Except in his case, the embarrassing thing is his life. Doesn't mean he wants to really. Or even if he does, not as if he would do it. Just to think, or not even think, but to overhear the words inside his own head. Strange relief like a catch released: I wish. Deepest and most final of desires. Something bitter in it too, luxuriously bitter, yes. And why not. Why doesn't he, that is, if the idea is so consoling. Oh, for other people, of course: to protect them. Other people prefer you to suffer.

Through the damp cool quiet now of the front arch he passes. Inside, the open square: golden sunlight, autumn. Birds circling. The sky a glass bowl struck and resounding. The old life, here. Carrying on without him always. Young people with books in their arms, laughing. First taste from the world's full cup. Everything beginning again. Aesthetic splendour he remembers: evenings in the back dining room, dusk settling over the tennis court outside. Voices through the windows. Lamplight. Walking her to the library under the trees. Live again one day of that life and die. Cold wind in his eyes stinging like tears. Woman much missed. She could be around, he thinks, might run into her. Drop by one of her lectures. Sexuality and the Origins of the Novel. Seeing her tomorrow anyway. Tell her he talked to Ivan after all. Upstairs in the toilets now he swallows another pill with a mouthful of water from his bottle. Sour. Overheated classroom. Out the window, thin white edge of the campanile. Students yawning, sipping from paper cups, fingernails clicking on keyboards. Laughing politely at his jokes. Dressed up in tweed and satchels. Clothes so new they're still creased where the shop had them folded. Himself too, once. Live again one hour of that life.

Back across the river then for a meeting. Expelled from the warm somehow private interior of the college, his mind and body unprotected. Raw feeling. Ordinary drab greyness of the city. How weary, stale, flat and unprofitable. Gary wants to know is he around, get a drink, dinner. Naomi texts him: plans tonight? To go on like this, just for the sake of other people, and anyway who. Not her, God knows. Better off if he actually did it. Nor Sylvia. She wouldn't want him to suffer on her account. Principle of her life, practically: to demand nothing of anyone. Least of all him. Long low mirror behind the bar reflecting silver the passing traffic on the street. Typographical errors he notices silently on the printed menu while Gary is telling an anecdote about the Workplace Relations Commission. Broccolli. For Ivan, probably, he thinks in the end. Couldn't do it to him, in reality. Propriety rather than affection. First your dad and then your brother: no. Even if you didn't really like the guy, still. Convincingly now he laughs aloud at a punchline he has not heard. Classic, he says. A few others arrive, another glass, two, and gradually the feeling softens. Thoughts wash slowly in and through, lap of water on shore. Not a bad lot, Gary and the others. Doing their best. Tired and frustrated as he is. Give each other a hand when they can. Ray asks if Costigan is around and Gary says no, he's in London. You know his wife's pregnant again. Didn't know actually. Must drop him a line. Sent a nice card for the funeral, decent of him. You having another? Drink too much and he'll be hungover tomorrow at the hospital. Embarrass her in front of the nurses. Slips phone from pocket: after nine already. He swipes a text and hits send, finishes his drink. Heading off, are you? Tell the lovely Naomi we said hello. Coat buttoned. Cold dark air of the river carrying him through the streets. Eyes wet again in the wind. To go on living just for Ivan's sake, imagine. Too depressing to think. Every morning waking up, every hour spent at work, every miserable meal prepared and eaten alone. All for a younger brother he hardly speaks to. Not as if he asked. Nor anyone else either. Delusional perhaps to think anyone cares whether he does or not. Not their fault. His own failures, mistakes he has made, people he has let down. Self-disgust. Defeat. Making bank transfers while she's in the shower. Forget about it. Her all-destroying pain. That suit at the funeral. And his father. Final agonies. Inevitability of death. Meaningless existence, false scaffold of morality assembled around nothing. The final permanent nothing that is the only truth. Sliding doors open up before him, the Spar on James's Street, and in the bright interior he feels his head pounding. Light chattering noise of the radio. Taps to pay for a bottle of whiskey and a tray of donuts wrapped in plastic. Thank you, thanks.

Outside, he texts from the corner. Sees the light in the door as it opens. Hand on the frame, dark nail polish. Not hers: Janine's. Plump pretty face smiling. Come on in, she says. Oh my God, did you bring donuts? Down the hallway together. Bright sweet scent of her perfume. Yeah, I didn't know what the vibe would be, he says. On her cheekbone a small dark mark in a heart-shape: silver sticker. We love you, Peter, she says. In the kitchen, bare limbs glistening, thick fragrance of smoke, spilled alcohol. Naomi on the countertop in a leather miniskirt, laddered tights, legs swinging. Her supreme desirability. Every man she passes on the street, he thinks. Helpless fantasies of doing what she lets him do to her. Friends by her side, laughing, as always. Low lights, loud shudder of music. She catches sight of him now across the room. A look exchanged. Sucks her lower lip, smiling, friends forgotten. Slips down from the counter as he approaches. Hello lover, she says. Semi-sheer blouse she's wearing, thin under his fingers as he leans in to kiss her. Taste of vodka and lemonade. Her back against the counter. Carelessness of youth. To see her so beautiful and so happy: sentimental feeling. Wonders sometimes what her friends must think of him. Competent, intimidating, the grown-up. Or lonely, desperate: the absolute cringe, imagine. Male friends jealous maybe. The sheer blouse, her perfect pointed breasts. She's talking to him now, her voice garbled and swallowed by the noise. What? he asks. Exaggeratedly she pronounces: How was court. He lifts his eyebrows. Oh, it was fine, he answers. Thank you. Her fingers in his hair, the back of his neck. Did you win? she asks. Feels himself smiling, his hand on her hip. For today, yeah, he says. She laughs, pink tongue, flash of silver. So sexy, she replies. The tray of donuts is opened, passed around, and she pulls one apart with her fingers. Her friends are talking about undercover guards. She swallows one soft sugared piece of donut and offers him another, which he eats. When you ask them if they're undercover, do they have to tell you? her friend Seamus is asking. Peter feels the others looking to him. No, he says. They don't. One of the girls, Leah, says: I thought it was in the law they had to. Eating another piece of donut he answers: There are no laws. Seamus laughing. What do you do for a job, then? he says. Smiling, tired, Peter answers: I tell lies. Naomi playing with his fingers. Music throbbing like a migraine. Drunk enough to dance with her, he wonders. Life perfect and everlasting until the end of the song.

Hand on Naomi's elbow, Janine is saying: Did you tell him about that letter?

What letter? Peter says.

Get him to look at it, will you?

Naomi pulls her face down into a grimace. It's in my room, she says.

Strangely her room is empty. Bed unmade, noise vibrating the floorboards. His coat he takes off, hangs up on the wardrobe door. Walls revolving gently in slow circuits around his eyes. Sits down on the bed while she looks through papers on her dressing table. Yeah, we got another one of these, she says. His head pounding as she hands him an envelope. It doesn't matter, she adds. I just told the others I'd tell you.

Blinking in the half-light he lifts the torn flap. Court order instructing vacation of property. Dated 22/09.

Right, he says.

Sitting down cross-legged beside him, long glossy hair thrown over one shoulder. Is it bad? she asks.

He screws his eyes shut and opens them again: text wriggles and darkens on the page. Yeah, it's bad, he says. I don't know. I'll read it properly tomorrow.

She takes the letter back and looks it over herself. Drunk, or you're back on the Xanax? she asks.

Eyes closing again he lies down on his back, saying: Both.

He feels or hears her looking at him. You're not supposed to do that, she says.

Pointlessly he lies: It was just a half, I took it ages ago.

Her hand he feels on his forehead, pushing back with gentle fingers his hair. You want to sleep it off? she says.

So close to her he feels she is somehow himself, same person, both down in the dark together. No, he says. I can't stay.

She lifts her hand away. Why not?

I have something on in the morning.

Work?

No, he says. I'm seeing a friend.

Soft click of her tongue detaching from the roof of her mouth. Your friend Sylvia, she says.

Opening his eyes he sees her looking down at him. Yeah, he answers.

You're always seeing each other.

Are we?

Bright and cool Naomi's eyes. Do you fuck her? she says.

He looks up at her a moment longer. No, he answers. A long time ago, but not anymore.

Slowly as if in a mirror she nods her head, looks down at the letter again.

Do you care? he asks.

Without looking up she laughs. Well, I'm not trying to get chlamydia, she says. So yeah, to that extent, I care.

He turns his gaze up the ceiling. Bare unlit lightbulb. Don't worry, he says. If you get it, it won't be from me.

Toying with a folded corner of the letter, her fingers. Are the two of you getting back together or something? she asks.

Why, he says, are you worried you might have to find a job?

Without hesitating she lets out another cackling laugh. Yeah, because right now I'm surviving on, what is it. Two hundred euro you've given me in the last six weeks?

Despite himself he smiles. Okay, he says. Point taken.

I don't know why I bother. You're not even nice.

You don't like nice people.

With a thin banging noise the door of her room comes open and her friends appear: Janine, two girls he doesn't know, some guy. Are we interrupting? one of the girls says. Your phone's ringing, Janine says to Naomi. Tosses the lighted screen to her quick nimble hands catching. Yes, you're interrupting, says Peter to no one. Naomi answers the phone, standing up from the bed, turning away. Hey, she says. What? Say again. Music louder with the door open. Naomi paces around, covering her other ear with her hand. Voices shrieking laughter outside. Janine sitting down on the mattress beside him, if you don't mind, picking up the folded letter. I can't hear you, Naomi is saying into the phone. Wait one second. And through the cluster of people in the doorway of her bedroom she weaves an exit without looking back. Did she show you this? Janine asks. Peter looks down at the letter. Head aching. Yeah, he says. I haven't read it yet, I'll look at it tomorrow. Guy leaning against the wardrobe door, lighting a rollie, smiling. So how do you guys know each other? he asks. Peter, apparently addressed, looks at Janine, who presses her lips flat. Back at the guy then. Sorry, who are you? Peter says. Everyone awkwardly laughing. I live here, the guy says. Jesus Christ. And what to do now, just wait until Naomi decides to get off the phone and come back, if she ever does. While around him her friends go on laughing: at him, presumably. Tremble of futile anger. *How do you guys know each other*. Know of course what he's talking about. One of her fans. Spent enough money maybe to level-up to real life. Girlfriend experience. What they must think, laughing. Actually we met in a bar one night after Christmas, he could say. She asked for my number. Walked her home afterwards, talked about her living situation, profile she had up on the website. Harmless flirtation, that was all. I was seeing someone else anyway. Just enjoyed the attention. Exchanging looks. Text messages afterwards, meeting up now and then on nights out. Nothing happened. I told a friend about her at the time, showed her some of the pictures, she said I was playing with fire. I thought it was an overreaction. I guess we danced together, maybe I bought the drinks. Complicated little game. Intelligence in her eyes. All the other men who wanted to talk to her, ignored. Kind of intoxicating the sense of power. Like a drug. Contest for dominance: each to make the other give in, confess. On the doorstep one night she asked me to stay. Shivering in her fake-fur jacket. She asked me. What do you want me to do, I said, break up with my girlfriend? She said yes. I told her I would think about it. Stupid situation. Let things get out of hand. Became kind of infatuated with her, or whatever. I mean, for God's sake, she was twenty-two. Also legally homeless, and borderline what you might call a sex worker. Obviously when you put it that way, yeah. Peter, I told myself, you're a lawyer, you're in your thirties. Your dad is in cancer treatment, you have responsibilities. Don't wreck your life for this girl. She doesn't care about you, it's just a game. Think for a second. What would people say. Your friends, family. Your reputation. Useless to reason by then of course. Blood no longer reaching the brain. Mouth just wet for the taste of her. So anyway, yeah, I ended things with the girlfriend. Good-looking woman, by the way. Mount Anville girl, associate at a consultancy firm. Her dad's a judge,

I often see him around. Not to worry. Colleague of mine she's seeing now, engaged any time I expect. House somewhere off the South Circular maybe. Meanwhile I'm lying here on a mattress in a filthy illegal squat beside the hospital while Naomi is taking a phone call in another room. That's it, that's how we know each other. Oh no, the cancer treatment was unsuccessful, thanks for asking. He died.

Where are you going? says Janine.

Putting his shoes on he answers: Out.

You're only after getting here.

Takes his coat from the corner of the wardrobe door, says nothing.

What will I tell Naomi? Janine asks.

Upstairs and outside alone. James's Street in the dark. He hails a taxi, climbs inside. Twenty past ten. Baggot Street, please, he says. Thanks. And taps at his phone: Can I drop by? He's had worse ideas. Head to the hospital together that way and he can wait with her during the thing. The epidural. Makes sense now that he thinks of it. Put off for a while the inevitable grim silence of the flat. Involuntary recollections. Do you fuck her. I wish. Passing the stone portico of St Audoen's, the quick light vibration of her reply: Sure, I'm home. First taste of peace he has had all day. Affecting suddenly. Wants to close his eyes into the feeling. Idea of her there, in tranquil solitude, reading a novel maybe. Pays in cash, with tip, clambers out onto the street. Key he finds in his pocket, up the staircase, linoleum marked with bicycle tyres, and with the second smaller key he opens her door.

In the dim hallway, warm scent of cooking oil, a little music playing quietly. Emperor Concerto, he thinks: the nocturne. Entering the main room he sees her, standing over the sink, with her back to him. The music and hiss of the tap. In the doorway he stands and watches: her straight shoulders, small hips, hair golden-coloured under the fan light. Her quiet well-organised existence. Sure, I'm home. Drunk and chaotic he intrudes as usual. And why. Are the two of you getting back together. Just me, he says aloud. Without turning she answers in her low beautiful voice: How did the hearing go this morning? He summarises briefly the oral argument. Pleasant, amusing. Begins to feel almost sober. She's drying her hands on a tea towel, smiling. Grey lambswool sweater. Tortoiseshell clasp in her hair. The confusion and noise of the other place dissolving, kind of bad dream you have when delirious. Waking into the peaceful quiet of her presence he feels himself at rest.

How are you feeling about tomorrow? he asks.

Hanging up the towel, she faces him. Fine, she says. Nothing to worry about.

Quietly they look at one another. Love at times indistinguishable from hatred. What they represent to one another: unsatisfiable desires. And yet she held his hand through the funeral. And tomorrow at the hospital he'll be there, bored, nervous, as always, checking his phone. Yeah, that's me. I mean, no, sorry, not her husband. There isn't. Like, I am with her, but we're not. Relationship mutilated by circumstance into something illegible. Platonic life partnership. Living separately of course. That way he can chase after other girls, piss money up the wall, embarrass himself, get home drunk at four in the morning without waking anyone. And she can get some work done without the distracting physicality of his body in her small apartment, sheer size of him, his too-carnivorous appetites. Perfect team they were once before everything, he remembers. Made it look easy. Voices resonating precisely in the air, glittering with the pace of thought, light free leaps over covered ground, each clause catching and deepening again the argument, yes, made him laugh sometimes for sheer joy. To be in the presence of her intellect: lifted into finer air. Still feels that way. Admires her in that way still, beauty of her mind. Not only that. It was for her he called Ivan last night, he thinks, dragged himself through the conversation, whatever use that was. For her, wanting her approval. Cases he takes on to impress her, difficult thankless unpaid work. To earn her respect. All the good in him, what little there is. Trying to be loved by her. His morality. Principle of his life. She looks back at him. He touches her hip with the palm of his hand. Despite everything. Death, nothingness. For a moment longer they look at one another, knowing without speaking. Finally he kisses her. Warmth of her mouth accepting. Draws her closer, weight of her frail slender body cradled against his. She can tell of course that he's been drinking, knows probably where he's been. Must wonder what he's really here for: repentance, maybe. Bless me for I have. Not like that, he wants to tell her. Why then. Terror of solitude. Pissed off with his girlfriend. Delusion of time regained: young again, and in love, promise of happiness, don't speak. No, not that, not only. Simple need to be with her. Broken and defeated, wanting the consolation of her nearness. To be closer and closer he thinks until no longer separate. Her back against the kitchen countertop. Last time he ever talked with his father, in the ICU. Nurse in and out keeping an eye on the oximeter. Late hot afternoon in August. How is Sylvia? She's good. Asking after you all the time. She'd love to be able to visit herself. Ah, she's a great woman. Tell her I'm thinking of her. He lifts off her sweater now: thin t-shirt, soft white cotton bra. Kisses gently her throat. Frightened of his own clumsiness. Hands too large and brutish-looking.

Takes pleasure in it usually. Terrible to think. Her mouth he kisses again. Fingertips under her t-shirt. Her eyes closed, she says faintly: You know I can't . . . He answers: Yeah, I know. Pauses. Her face flushed. I'm not hurting you, am I? he asks. She lets out a helpless breath, half-laughing. No, she says. It's nice. To give her so little, he thinks. Simple almost innocent pleasure of affectionate touch. That she would let him. And for what reason: his desire, or her own. What lives they have been leading. You're not getting married, or anything like that. Not too late, he thinks, is it. To try after all. Life they could live together. Not the one they wanted, but the one they have. Waking at night to feel her familiar weight beside him sleeping. Is that not enough. To say when the nurses ask: Yes, that's me. A sigh at her lips. Young and radiant he remembers her, in some hot curtained hotel room overseas. Lying naked with her chin in her hand, reading poetry. Where you would wait for me: yes, as I knew you then. When life was perfect. It was once. To let go of her now better for them both maybe. Sylvia help me. I'm sorry. His name she murmurs and called to her without thinking he answers for once honestly: I love you. I love you too, she says. He closes his eyes. Exhausted, drunk, ashamed. Wanting forgiveness. Take back everything. Live the right life.

# 4

On Thursday afternoon, Margaret is making her way along the low tiled corridor to the studio room upstairs. The door has been left ajar, and she can hear the tinny sound of the portable stereo from inside, and Alannah's voice talking over the music: Now into second. Elbows up, girls. Looking good. As Margaret approaches, the music jolts to a stop, rewinds, begins again. Alannah's voice counts aloud: And two, three, four . . . Margaret knocks gently with the knuckle of a finger before opening the door halfway and looking in. Pale white light from the window. Skinny teenage girls in their leotards, soft ballet shoes, hands on the barre; their faces pink and formless, long limbs like fawns. Alannah, compact and muscular, hair pinned back, comes to the door, smiling, and Margaret hands over the keys. You're a star, Alannah says. No problem, Margaret replies. Turning back, Alannah addresses the girls again: Remember your turnout. Margaret closes the door, quieter now, and walks back down the corridor alone, her shoes clicking softly on the tiles. Downstairs the coffee shop is busy. Women with babies and pushchairs, Mrs Harrington in the corner with her pot of tea, the espresso machine clanking beside the sink. Margaret orders the usual afternoon coffee and waits at the counter, leafing through a newspaper. Pages thumbed already and greasy, brown-grey. The steam wand hisses in the jug of milk and Doreen in her apron asks: Are you back in tonight? Margaret looks up from the Letters page to answer: Mm. Cello. Supposed to be very good, the guy. Doreen lays her cup and saucer on the countertop. There you are, sweetheart, she says. Folding the paper, Margaret lifts the saucer, saying: Wonderful. Thank you. Back up in the office, Linda is on the phone, and Margaret sits at the other desk, wakes the computer, opens her email inbox. Outside in the street below, brittle brown leaves drift over the parked cars. When Linda hangs up, she and Margaret exchange some conversation about the new vouchers, David's idea; the ticketing software, impossible; and David himself, their executive director, whom they haven't even seen since Monday. Margaret sips her coffee, hot and velvet bitter, while out the window the dry leaves scatter and fall.

That evening after work, in the garden behind her friend Anna's house, Anna refills the bird feeders and Margaret sits on the bench watching. Early October. Anna is talking again about genetically modified mosquitoes, which she says are being released into the wild somewhere in the United States in order to kill off – or maybe just render infertile, Margaret isn't sure – the old classic mosquitoes, God's originals. Margaret watches Anna hanging a little wire feeding contraption up on the branch of a tree and listens to her talking about the mosquitoes, though she has already explained about them before. To play devil's advocate, Margaret says, I think malaria does kill a lot of people. Anna is refilling another feeder now, a lock of hair falling forward onto her forehead. Obviously, she replies. But this isn't in a medical lab they're doing this, it's an ecosystem. The sun comes out from behind a low cloud and Margaret screws one of her eyes shut against the cold white light, the other eye shaded already by the foliage of a tree. Hey, she says. I meant to tell you something. Anna hangs up the second feeder and sits down beside her on the bench. Margaret doesn't look at her, but she can hear her moving, feel the weight of her body on the thin wooden slats.

What's that? Anna asks.

You know the chess club had this event in the hall at the weekend.

No, I didn't. What kind of event was it, a competition?

No, says Margaret. Well, I don't know. They invited a chess player down from Dublin to play ten people at once.

Wow, really? Did he win?

Margaret gives a half-smile now, answering: Mm.

All ten of the games?

Right.

That's amazing, says Anna. How did he do it? Was he playing them all off against each other?

Margaret wriggles her back against the bench to sit up straighter. No, she says. After a moment's thought, she adds: He couldn't have won all ten if he was doing that, could he? I mean, if you think about it, he could only have won five.

Oh. True. But there must be some trick to it. I mean, I doubt he was ten times better than everyone else.

Well, the other players were just random people, from the chess club. And one of them was a ten-year-old. I don't think it matters.

I'm just saying, I'm sure he had a system, Anna says.

A cloud draws over the sun and the garden grows darker. I think his system was just being really good at chess, says Margaret.

I would have told Luke if I'd known it was on. He plays a little bit.

Margaret turns to look at her, saying: Does he?

Yeah, online. You know, it's an incredibly complicated game. I mean, people study for their whole lives to get good at it.

Right, I know that, says Margaret. This was one of those people. The guy.

A grandmaster?

I don't know. Something like that. I feel like we're getting very immersed down into the chess aspect of this story.

Anna gives a little shivering shake with her shoulders, and indeed, Margaret thinks, it has grown perceptibly cooler outside. I'm sorry, says Anna. I thought the story was about chess. Please go on.

It's okay, says Margaret. She feels herself exhaling, feels on her hands and face the gathering cold. I didn't know Luke played chess, she adds. Do you want to go inside?

The little back kitchen has grown dim now, and Anna turns the light on. Anna and Luke live with their ten-month-old son Henry in this small terraced house, ex-council, with a garden where they grow crab apples and potatoes. Luke is a woodwork teacher and Anna is a visual artist and also gives art classes to children. She cannot drive, and used to be well known in town for cycling around in eccentric clothing, carrying her shopping in a wicker basket. For Margaret the last twenty years have passed this way: Anna on her bicycle at the age of sixteen, in school uniform, laughing, heedless of the vulgar shouts from the boys; then at twenty-six, coloured scarf flying out behind her, skirt spattered with dirty water, bag of oranges in her basket; now at thirty-six, happy, tired, more often walking than cycling, pushing a second-hand pram with a mismatched wheel. Of course, from Anna's point of view, Margaret thinks, these years must have passed the other way: watching her, Margaret, growing older. Easier to perceive the way the years accumulate in others. For Anna there must be such a Margaret, who has been one thing and is now another, while Margaret looking at her own life sees only the onwardly flowing blur of all experience. Anna is putting the kettle on, talking again about the mosquitoes, and from the front of the house they hear Luke's key in the door. A moment later he appears, carrying Henry in his arms. Margaret says hello, and Luke greets her, old friends, lifting the baby's fat hand in a simulated wave.

I won't intrude, Margaret says. I was heading off anyway.

Anna has started folding some of Henry's clothes, which have been left on the countertop. When will I see you? she says to Margaret. Are you around at the weekend?

Sure, Margaret says.

Come for dinner, says Anna.

On the street outside, Margaret's car is parked. A single sycamore leaf of rich yellow colour has drifted onto her windshield. Along the gutter of the street, many more leaves, red, brown, have been lifted by the wind and left to settle. Margaret gets into her car and pulls the door shut, starts the engine, touches for no reason the mirror. Dinner at the weekend, Anna said. That will be nice, and Margaret might make something for dessert. She could have said to Luke: Anna was telling me you play chess. But why? To revive the conversation, to work her way around to telling Anna after all about what happened. In that case to bring it up in front of Luke would have been a bad idea, since Margaret doesn't want to tell Luke about what happened, and isn't even sure if she wants to tell Anna. Anna is a person of firm and occasionally unpredictable beliefs: maybe she would judge Margaret harshly. Also, Margaret thinks as she drives out of town, Anna has the baby now, she doesn't see as much of her as she used to, and, in any case, she was never really the type of friend who liked to gossip about people's sex lives. Probably she was not going to be the ideal interlocutor for that particular conversation. But then the ideal interlocutor – a friend with no rigid moral beliefs, few or no competing demands on her attention and perhaps a taste for faintly scandalous anecdotes – does not seem to be available to Margaret at present. Her friend Joanie, maybe, but she's away in Lisbon. There's Corinne, but then Margaret has never been so close with Corinne as to tell her things she hasn't already told Anna, so the whole interaction would probably feel strange for both of them. She could email her friend Rosalie, owes her an email anyway in fact. But what is it that she actually wants to say? And once she has said it, what does she hope or expect to hear in response?

Outside town now, the evening gathers. Past the garden centre, past the old graveyard, having taken a left off the main road and under the railway bridge, Margaret manoeuvres her car through an open gateway, tyres crunching down the overgrown drive. Behind the hedgerow is the low stone facade of the cottage she has been renting since last year. When she kills the engine and gets out, birds start from their branches and together flicker through the air as if mechanised. Margaret lets herself in the front door, turns the lights on, picks up and looks unseeing at the post on the front mat. Her name, address, a magazine subscription. She takes off her coat and scarf, hangs them up and goes into the kitchen, yawning, opening the fridge. On a milk carton in the door, a black line of type reads: OCT 11. She takes out a sealed plastic package of raw chicken thighs and closes the door again. Is there even a reality left there, something that in fact did happen? The way a dream, untold, vanishes, never having taken place to begin with. Better perhaps in this case: a dream, attached at the corners to no reality, shared with no one, vanishing into nothingness. Tonight she will drive back to work for a cello recital, and stand in the lobby taking tickets, making polite conversation, directing people to their seats. Afterwards, another stranger in her car, a cellist this time, looking out her passenger window at the passing town. Like the chess player. His number in her phone still. His hands she remembers: bitten fingernails. *I really love touching you like that*, he said. His almost innocent tenderness. They talked, she thinks, as well as everything else. He told her about his father, his disappointments, regrets, and she confessed herself also disappointed, regretful. It was easy then to make love, easy and pleasant, a relief. Is there anything left of that now? And where? In that room, in the cold little bungalow with the damp curtains. Or in the contact between their two lives, touching.

At the kitchen table, she sits and eats alone, knowing that after she's finished eating she will have to wash up individually each utensil she has used to prepare and eat this meal, and to wipe down also each surface involved: the sink-side countertop, the fridge-side countertop, the cooking surface, and the kitchen table itself. Afterwards she will ring her mother to discuss the new dishwasher that Margaret has offered to buy for her, a process that has become mystifyingly lengthy and complicated, so many phone calls about the dishwasher, which to buy and where, and whether the man who installs it will be able to take away the old one at the same time. Margaret already, in advance of the awaited transaction, finds herself silently lording over her two siblings and their increasingly elderly mother the ultimately inconsequential expense of this dishwasher: evidence of Margaret's essentially dutiful personality, her reliably self-sacrificing fulfilment of filial obligations. It's only going to cost a few hundred euro. Margaret, though of more limited means than her siblings, can't even think of anything she would rather do with the money. She has nowhere to go, no one to visit. Maybe she would like a new pair of winter boots, she thinks; but the boots from two years ago are fine. The upcoming expense of her mother's new dishwasher is in practical terms irrelevant. And yet she lords it over her siblings and mother secretly, which is terrible. Eating, perceiving the flavour and texture of the food she has prepared, sweetish, salty, she rehearses in advance the conversation she will have on the phone with her mother in just a few minutes' time. I saw Ricky in town today, her mother will say. She is bound to say this, or something like it. He was looking well, she might add. He was asking after you. And he would too. No stopping him. Ricky Fitzpatrick: Margaret's ex-husband. Margaret Kearns: Mrs Richard Fitzpatrick, once.

That night, Ivan is in the kitchen of his flat, eating a bowl of instant noodles and scrolling through a page of search results matching the query: need a temporary home for my dog ireland. Once again, however, after five or six attempts using different keywords, the results consist of links like 'How to Foster a Dog' and 'Dogs Available for Fostering Now'. To take a dog out of the fostering system, into one's home, appears to be very simple, and yet Ivan cannot find a single website explaining how to put a dog into that same system. No process, obviously, can consist exclusively of output, without any corresponding input. The dogs are coming from somewhere. But how to make his own dog one of them, Ivan still has no idea. How often in his life he has found himself a frustrated observer of apparently impenetrable systems, watching other people participate effortlessly in structures he can find no way to enter or even understand. So often that it's practically baseline, just normal existence for him. And this is not only due to the irrational nature of other people, and the consequent irrationality of the rules and processes they devise; it's due to Ivan himself, his fundamental unsuitedness to life. He knows this. He feels himself to have been formed, somehow, with something other than life in mind. He has his good qualities, kind of, but none of them have much to do with living in the world that he actually lives in, the only world that can be said in a fairly real way to exist. Anyway, it's not going to matter, because Peter said he would take care of the dog situation. Leave it with me, he specifically said on the phone. For Peter, social systems are never confusing, always transparent, and usually manipulable to his own ends. He is someone who not only knows a vast number of people, but through knowing them can somehow make them do things he wants them to do. He won't be sitting in his apartment typing 'dog foster ireland help' or whatever into a search engine. He'll be in a big room somewhere surrounded by people who think he's really smart and interesting, and one of them will probably be like the CEO of a dog fostering charity. Peter could even at this moment be regaling the CEO with a story about his loser younger brother who can't find a temporary home for their dog, and they're laughing together. However: let them laugh. If it means the dog will have somewhere safe and caring to stay for a while until Ivan finds a new flat or house-share where dogs are welcome, laugh it up, as far as he's concerned.

The dog, Ivan's dog, Alexei, is six years old. His photograph serves as the lock screen on Ivan's phone: Alexei's slender black-and-white body curled on the sofa, forming an O-shape, eyes closed in blissful sleep. Ivan put a lot of work into training him as a puppy, taking him out endlessly for toilet breaks, even during the night, and teaching him to sit on command and to walk nicely on the lead and not pull. After long, unhappy days at school, Ivan would return alone to the small semi-detached house where he and his father lived together, and each afternoon, without fail, the tiny body of Alexei would bound up to the door to greet him, wagging the tail delightedly. It did not matter to Alexei that Ivan was considered by his peers to be a loser; that, due to his insectile physique, people at school called him 'Spider' Koubek; that one of the popular girls in his year had once asked him, on a dare, if he knew what a blowjob was, and that he had, for reasons he still doesn't understand, answered 'no', even though he obviously did. As far as Alexei was concerned, Ivan was the most charismatic and loveable person alive. In the evenings after dinner, they would lie on the sofa together, Ivan playing online chess against adult opponents in foreign countries, Alexei with his long thin face burrowed lovingly in Ivan's shoulder. Beside them, Ivan's father sat in the armchair watching television, shaking his head when the news came on. After Ivan moved away for college, his dad gave him regular updates about the dog over the phone. Much of the conversation that passed between father and son in recent years concerned Alexei: his little antics, his moods, visits to the vet, and so on. Periodically, Ivan's father would text him photographs, and Ivan would reply: Ah he's so cute! The photograph on the lock screen of his phone, in fact: that was one his father sent him. A year ago now, or more. My home help, his dad used to call Alexei as a joke, because he sometimes would bring him his slippers. And now his dad is gone, and the dog is living in Ivan's mother's boyfriend's house in Skerries, and his mother is sending hostile text messages saying things like: It's been over a month now sweetheart. I'm not running a dog shelter you know! xx

Through the second page of search results he goes on scrolling, when out of nowhere a voice behind him says: Ivan. Starting up, dropping the fork he was still holding distractedly in his right hand, Ivan turns and sees his flatmate, Roland, standing behind him. Jesus, says Ivan. I didn't hear you there. His face feels hot, and he fumbles to pick his fork back up. Roland watches impassively. Okay, he says. I was just going to ask you, are you around at the weekend? Ivan feels his heart palpitating still from the shock of Roland's presence, even though it's not shocking anymore, it's just Roland, standing in the kitchen of the flat where they both live. Oh, says Ivan. Around here, you mean? Roland answers: I genuinely don't know what else I could mean by that. Ivan swallows. Yeah, I'll be here, he says. I mean, I think so. I don't have firm plans. Roland nods his head slowly and then goes to the fridge. Cool, he says. Roland's girlfriend Julia appears in the doorway now, wearing silken pyjamas, with a towel around her shoulders. Sensing that the kitchen environment is no longer hospitable to his presence, Ivan gets up, lifts his laptop from the table and in the other hand takes his half-eaten bowl of noodles. Averting his eyes from Julia he mumbles: Hey. Julia answers brightly: Hey, Ivan. Turning to Roland, she says: They can't stay with her sister, by the way, I asked. Ivan makes his way quietly towards the door, eyes lowered, while Roland, who appears to be making himself a sandwich, answers: God, they're so annoying.

When Ivan re-enters his bedroom, he can see that his phone is ringing on the bed where he left it. The screen is lighted, displaying an incoming call from a mobile number he doesn't recognise. The phone is on the vibrate setting, but the vibration is almost soundless, the noise absorbed by his mattress, so he didn't hear it from outside. Also the charger is plugged in still, because the phone was on two percent battery when he left it here to make himself the noodles. He is conscious of an extreme sense of urgency, a frantic urgency to answer this incoming call, not knowing how long it has already been ringing. Shutting the door behind him, dropping his laptop on the bed and setting his bowl of noodles down on the bedside table, he taps the green icon and answers, realising too late that the phone is not sufficiently charged to unplug it from the wall yet, so in order to hear anything he'll have to crouch on the floor beside the nightstand, holding the charging phone, which is also really hot, up to his face. Arranging himself in this way, crouching down on the carpet, he says into the phone: Hello? For a second, nothing happens. Then a woman's voice says: Hello. Hi. Is this Ivan?

With a feeling of frightened exhilaration he recognises, or rather remembers, or thinks that he remembers, this voice. Hi, he says. Yes. This is Ivan speaking. Hello.

Hi, says the voice again. This is Margaret Kearns. We met last weekend.

Quickly he answers: Oh, I remember. It's cool. I mean, it's nice to hear from you. I hope the call wasn't ringing for too long or anything. I just had my phone left on charge because it was running out of battery.

He is conscious that he says all this very rapidly, too rapidly, and she pauses before she replies. His pulse is so fast and loud in his ears that he wonders for a second if it's even audible on the other side of the call, or is that medically possible, to hear the sound of another person's heartbeat on a phone call: probably not.

That's okay, she says. It wasn't ringing for long.

Carefully, quietly, he takes an inhaling breath and then breathes out again, slightly away from the phone, not wanting her to hear any loud breathing noises. Is it his turn to begin talking again now, or it's still her turn? Another second passes in silence. Maybe it is his turn already and he's coming across as rude and standoffish.

I just remembered that you said I should call, she says, if I ever thought of you. And I've been thinking of you, so.

Ah, he says. I've been thinking about you too. A lot.

She pauses again. He manoeuvres himself down into a sitting position on the carpet, his back against the bed. At the chess workshop last Saturday morning, when they were waiting around for latecomers to arrive, one of the men from the chess club called Margaret 'a fine woman'. It was only other men there at that point, no women, and Ivan felt that the remark referred to Margaret's good looks. This provoked an unfamiliar feeling in him, a hot stirring of something like defensiveness, as if there was something derogatory about the man's words: and maybe there was, in a sexist way, valuing a woman only on her appearance and so forth. But at the same time he also felt in himself a private feeling of triumph and excitement, knowing that he had secretly spent the night with the woman in question, and that the two of them had even made fun of the other men a little bit. She was so attractive that people actually talked about it behind her back, and he had gone to bed with her, and afterwards lying in his arms she had said it was perfect. Oh dear, you're making our guest blush, Ollie said then. And everyone turned to look at Ivan, who swallowed, not really aware that he had been blushing but confusedly feeling his face getting hot even at the idea that he had been. Maybe we should just keep the conversation to chess, he said. All the men laughed at that, so heartily that it unnerved him slightly, and then the conversation did after all go back to chess. Probably they just thought that Ivan had developed a little crush on Margaret the night before, at the bar, which was, though obviously kind of true, not the whole truth. And now he crouches on the floor of his room waiting for her to start talking into her phone again, to say anything at all.

I had to drive a cellist home from an event tonight, she says finally. That reminded me of you. Although he wasn't staying in the holiday village.

Nervously he feels himself smiling. Yeah? he says. I guess they got him a hotel room or something.

In her voice also he hears a little smile when she answers: Yes, they did. Or rather, we did.

Nice. Maybe I should get good at cello instead.

He can hear her laughing now, beautiful sound. I suppose you probably could, if you put your mind to it, she says.

Why, do you like musicians? Because I actually can play a little bit of piano. Although not very well or anything.

Now in a low private kind of voice between the two of them she murmurs: Multi-talented.

Foolishly he hears himself laughing. Yeah, big time, he says. No, I wish I was. Actually I'm not even, like— whatever the singular form would be. Uni-talented.

Oh, I think you are. I should know, because I'm really not.

That's not true, he says. You know, uh— He pauses, nervous again, and the phone is very hot in his hand. I was going to say, he continues, I can think of a few talents of yours.

Sounding amused, she answers: Aha. Dare I ask, like what?

He swallows, thinking for a second, and then he says: Well, I don't know if you know this, but you have a very beautiful speaking voice.

Thank you, Ivan. I'm not sure that's a talent, though. Strictly speaking, I think it's more like a quality.

Okay. I see. And being very beautiful to look at, I guess that's more of a quality as well.

She's laughing again. He sits up with his back straighter against the bed. I think so, yes, she says. It's very kind of you, but I don't think it's a talent.

Mm, he says. I do have some things I could say about you that are more into the realm of talents, but, you know. I don't want to make you hang up on me.

In a gorgeously sweet humorous voice she answers: You're being very funny.

He puts his hand behind his head, irrepressibly smiling. Do you think that? he says. To tell the truth, I sometimes find myself pretty funny, but no one else ever says that about me.

You must not have met the right people yet, she says.

For a second he thinks of saying: Well, I have met one of them.

Meaning her. But in these situations you have to be thoughtful and not go too far with your remarks, making the other person feel that you have a one-track mind. In her voice he hears a kind of purring which he personally finds unbelievably erotic, but possibly that's just how her voice sounds and she can't help it. On the other hand, he has actually slept with her, and she said at the time that she liked it, and now she's calling him on the phone a week later nearly, telling him that she's thinking of him. These are probably the kind of circumstances where you can make flirtatious remarks and it's normal. He already has flirted a little bit anyway, telling her she's beautiful, and hinting at other things, and she has been laughing and apparently having fun. Suddenly he starts saying: Do you— Then he breaks off and, awkwardly, goes on: I don't know. What do you think about seeing each other again, maybe?

She's quiet for a second, or at most two. Well, she says, we're at very different stages in our lives.

He answers: I get you. They both fall silent again. It was the wrong thing to ask, he thinks. If he had just said nothing. Or if he had said something irrelevant, like going back to the cellist she mentioned, and asking what kind of music she likes. But no, he thinks: talking about music is never interesting. It doesn't matter now. The reality is that he did ask, and she said in a doubting voice: We're at very different stages in our lives. Why did she call him then? Just to get compliments from him, or what? Now, having had this thought, he feels terrible, because even to be liked by her to the small extent that she enjoys his compliments would be okay, but she probably doesn't like him even that small amount. What does it mean, different stages in our lives? It means the age thing, obviously, but he thinks most likely it's nothing to do with that. Most likely that's just a way of saying, I don't like you, sorry. However, just in case she seriously does mean the age thing, he adds: I just think – from my perspective – I don't personally care about that, at all.

When she answers him she has a sad smiling tone in her voice, like a sad rueful smile. Maybe I should be the one who cares about it, then, she says.

Ah, he says. Okay. They're being quiet again now. He wonders where she is at this moment: at home, he would guess, but where does she live? House, apartment? And where in her home is she: kitchen, living room, or in her bedroom maybe, like the way he's in his. He would like her to be there, in the room where she sleeps. Well, I'm happy you called, he says. Like, if I'm honest, I didn't think you were going to. I suppose it doesn't matter to say all this now. But after I got home again at the weekend, I started getting kind of anxious, like maybe I did something wrong, or, I don't know. Do you ever go back over things in your head, and you're thinking, why did I say those things, or why did I do that? I guess you probably don't, because everything you say is interesting. But I do that all the time, going back over things. And getting kind of mad with myself. Anyway, it doesn't matter. I was just saying, I'm happy you called me. Because I guess, it makes me feel a bit more like, you probably don't hate me after all. Or maybe you do, I don't know.

Quietly, without hesitating, she answers: I don't hate you, Ivan, of course not. And you didn't do anything wrong the other night. Not at all.

Well, I know I was really awkward, he says. Like the way I talked so much about chess, I honestly don't know why I did that. I think I was just a little bit nervous, because I'm not too experienced at those situations or whatever. But I wouldn't be like that again. If we saw each other again, I mean. I would be a lot different.

Still in the same quiet voice she says: I wouldn't want you to be different.

He feels so embarrassed and stupid that he starts laughing for no reason. Okay, he says. That's good, because actually I don't know if I would be. Even though I just said I would. But if you don't want me to, it's better. Are you really definite that you don't want to see each other again?

She pauses, and then: No, I'm not definite, she says. Actually I do want to. I just think it might not be wise.

Because we're at different stages in our lives?

Yes, because of that.

He looks at the screen of his phone. The battery is on twenty-three percent now, which he thinks is high enough, so he takes the charger out. Well, he says, maybe we could see each other and just talk, what do you think? Nothing would have to happen. And if we were just talking, I don't think it would matter about the life stages being different.

She lets out a kind of helpless exhalation into the phone. Oh God, she says. I don't know. Do you really think it's a good idea?

For a moment he considers this question: whether it is a good idea for them to see each other again. Is it different, to want something, and to think the wanted thing is a good idea? Yes, it could be different, he thinks, if the long-term consequences of the event were foreseeably worse than the short-term gratification involved. And indeed, the long-term consequences of seeing someone again who you like very much, who doesn't really hand on heart seem to like you in the same way, while unrelatedly you're still grieving and feeling distraught about a recent death in your family, those consequences could be pretty bad, devastating even, in the long term, if you got to like her more and more and she understandably, due to your bad personality and looks, did not experience the same thing on her side. A lot of negative feelings could follow on from that: sadness, low self-esteem, anger at yourself and the other person, despair. People probably have lost their minds over less, and gone actually crazy from the misery. And yet, at the same time, it seems incredibly possible now, tantalisingly possible, that he might once again hear her voice murmuring his name in a low pleasurable satisfied tone while he makes love to her. And for this, he thinks, whatever: despair, heartbreak, even losing his mind and going insane later on, anything. Literally, anything, any price. Yeah, he says. I think it's a good idea. I do.

At thirteen minutes past nine on Saturday night, Margaret is in the car park beside the bus stop, waiting for the arrival of the Sligo service from Dublin. The car heating system is turned up to the maximum setting and absentmindedly she holds her hands over a hot-air vent, thinking: What if someone sees me? She is sitting here alone in her car, long after the shops and businesses in the vicinity have closed, very clearly waiting for something. Anyone could be passing, and knocking cheerfully on her driver's-side window they would say: Hello there, Margaret. What brings you into town? And she would have to roll the window down and reply: Oh hello, how are things? Right at that very moment, of course, the Sligo bus would pull up, and probably only one solitary person would alight. A more suggestive scenario Margaret struggles to imagine. Worse than suggestive: sordid. She, an older woman, approaching middle age, is waiting in her dusty overheated car in a poorly lit car park for the arrival of a young man, hardly past adolescence, on a night bus from Dublin. Not even the kindliest, most trusting and well-intentioned of passers-by, observing the scene, could conceive of a wholly innocent explanation for these events. The sexual element would simply leap forth with explanatory power. And, inevitably, people would come to hear about it. Her mother, Anna, the gang at work. Even Ricky. And what would he say, she thinks, if he knew? Would he laugh, to see her humiliating herself like this? Would it infuriate him, that after all her preaching and scolding she could do such a thing? Or maybe in confusion, bewildered, he would refuse to accept the truth. After all, despite everything, he still believes in her decency. Which she, too, believed in once: her own decency, a rag to clutch at, amid the squalor of their life.

On the phone, Ivan told her that she was beautiful, and that he wanted to see her again. This was flattering, and therefore pleasurable: the pleasure of flattered vanity. Margaret disapproves of her own vanity and knows that Anna, above all a decent person, disapproves of it also, Margaret's and her own. This is probably why Margaret never told Anna about Ivan the other day even when given the opportunity, even in the garden, when she seemed to be about to tell her. And also why, when letting Anna know that she wouldn't be coming to dinner this evening after all, Margaret didn't explain what she would be doing instead. Because Anna deplores in Margaret, as in everyone, the vanity that is gratified by the flirtatious attentions of others. But then Anna has a husband, and now even a baby, both of whom offer her in different ways the love and devotion that supersedes and makes irrelevant the pleasure of praise and compliments. It seems hard in Anna therefore to condemn Margaret's vanity, which has been so painfully starved in recent years, when Anna's own is fed by the incomparably hearty nourishment of unconditional love. In the short time since Margaret met Ivan, he has provided, why not be honest, the only mouthful of desirable flattery she has tasted in a very long time. It is wrong to be vain: obscurely, warming her hands over the air vent, Margaret knows and admits to herself that it is wrong. But wrong in what way? Who is the victim of the wrongness: just herself? Or, somehow, other people?

Headlights appear now at the brow of the hill, and trundling slowly the bus makes its way down to the stop and whines to a halt. The door is released, and the luggage door also, lifting mechanically out and upward to display a lighted compartment containing a small number of coloured suitcases. From the door of the bus a young woman emerges, looking at her phone, and goes over to the luggage compartment. For a second or two, nothing else happens; and then she sees one more person alighting. Ivan. He's wearing a dark jacket and carrying a backpack over one shoulder. Margaret before she knows what she's doing feels her hand fumbling for the door-release handle, and the inrush of the cold October night over her face; she's getting out of her car. Ivan, looking around, sees the car park, and then sees her: recognises her, and approaches. He doesn't shout out enthusiastically: Hello, Margaret! or anything like that. He just comes over silently to the car, carrying on one shoulder the strap of his backpack. Under the artificial orange light of the streetlamps, he looks tall again, as she remembers. A polite distance away from her he stands, and says: Hey. She feels herself shivering in the cold. Hey, she says. Do you want to hop in?

They get into the car and she starts the engine. Her hands

are shaking, although the car, she notices now, is stiflingly warm. Turning the heating system down, she asks Ivan how his journey was, and he answers: It was okay, thanks. Those buses aren't too bad. They stop a lot, though. You don't have a train station in town, do you? She is reversing out of the parking space, looking in the mirror, everything visible only in shades of orange and black darkness. No, she says. The closest one is over in Carrick. He's nodding his head. His backpack is resting in his lap. On the phone he said they would see each other just to talk, and nothing else, which perhaps was a genuine suggestion and that really is all they're going to do. At the moment, however, they are not even doing that: they are sitting in silence together while Margaret pulls out of the car park onto the road.

I live in the middle of nowhere, by the way, she remarks.

Like outside town, you mean?

Right. I'm just renting a place out there for the moment.

Cool, he says. I've always wanted to live in the middle of nowhere myself, but it hasn't worked out like that. Clearing his throat, he adds: You live alone, I guess.

She laughs, a little nervously. Yes, she says. Indeed I do.

Yeah, I thought that, he replies. I live with roommates.

After a pause, unable to think of anything else to say, she asks: Do you work from home?

Oh, says Ivan. I guess we didn't talk about work before, did we? He looks around at her, waiting for an answer.

No, she says, I suppose not.

He starts nodding his head again, looking out the windscreen, and he even seems to take a deep breath, as if to prepare himself. Okay, he says. Well, to be honest, I don't totally have a job at this exact moment. I had this idea to take some time off after I finished college, to focus more on my chess. That was just this summer when I finished. But obviously I have to pay rent and everything, so I've ended up doing a lot of freelance work anyway. Data analysis, which I hate. And I also used to work as a delivery driver for one of those apps, but that was actually so bad that I quit.

That's interesting, says Margaret. Driving a car, or cycling?

Cycling, he answers. I can drive, by the way, I have my full licence. I could drive my dad's car if I had to, but in the city it's not worth it. He glances over at her here, as if to make sure she's listening, before going on. Anyway, he says, it was kind of funny sometimes, the delivery thing, because of the weird stuff people would order. And it was good to get the exercise. But on the other hand, I almost got killed a few times, so that aspect put me off.

Oh God, really?

Yeah, on the roads. People who drive cars are psychopaths. Sorry, I mean – no offence. Not you, obviously.

Smiling now she says: That's okay. I have a friend who cycles everywhere, and she says the same thing. That drivers are insane.

It's so true, Ivan says. After a moment he adds: So that's kind of the work situation, to answer your question. I don't exactly have what you would call a job.

Because you're focusing on your chess.

Well, that was my plan. But I'm not really playing too well right now, as it happens. I don't want to bore you too much with all that. The way I'm playing at the moment, I'll just say, I might as well get a job.

Do you want one? she asks.

In her peripheral vision she can see him frowning, his

brows knitting together. That's a good question, he says. Do I want to have a job? I have a lot of thoughts about that, actually. Putting the whole chess aspect aside, I would like to be doing something, rather than nothing, yeah. But what would be something, compared to nothing? Or maybe that's too abstract. For example, I do a little bit of data analysis, like I was saying. For tech companies mostly. They'll give me a lot of data – say user experience data, like how long users spend on each section of a website – and I'll spend a few hours making graphs and whatnot. Say it takes me – I don't know, four hours to make these graphs, and I'll pretend it took me ten hours, to get extra money. He glances over at her again, and adds: You might think that's immoral, I don't know. But anyway, never mind that for a second. The four hours that I actually spend making the graphs, and the ten hours that I get paid for: what is that? Like, any of that: what is it? At least when I worked as a delivery driver, I knew what I was doing. Someone wanted a Big Mac, and I brought it to them, and the amount I got paid was like, what it was worth to that person not to have to collect their own burger. The amount they will pay, not to leave the house, is the amount I will accept, yes to leave the house. Minus whatever the app is taking. If you get me.

I get you. You're making perfect sense.

Oh good, he says. Because in the data analysis example, my question is, what is the money that's being paid to me? It's the money that the company will pay, to have their own information explained back to them in a graph. And how much money should that be? Clearly no one knows, because at the end I'll make up a number of hours and they'll just pay me for that number. I guess the graph is supposed to make the company more profitable, in theory, but no one knows by how much, it's all made up. Briefly Ivan pauses here, and then goes on in the same tone: For my dissertation in college, I don't know if you care about this, but I was working on climate modelling. Which is a big area in theoretical physics. And the more you work on that type of thing, the more you start seeing the economy in terms of, what we would call, throughput. Like, uh – resources, you know. Say, for example, concrete, or natural materials like wood. I'm not explaining this too well. I guess I think of the economy in terms of: what does everyone actually need, to be able to live, and then, where are we going to get all that stuff? And at the moment, you know, it's messed up, from the climate perspective. Am I talking way too much now?

No, she says. Not at all, go on.

Well, obviously, the way it is now, not everyone has what they need. In terms of world poverty, and all those problems. And then a lot of people have way too much, to the extent that they're just throwing money around for no reason. Paying people to make graphs, and the graphs could cost anything. The number comes from nowhere. It's not related back down to any real resource value. You have— Not to get too politicised about it, because I'm not saying it from that side. But you do literally have people going hungry, I know that's a cliché. Food shortages, it is a real thing. And then you have these tech companies paying me to make a graph. Why? It comes from the wrong distribution of resources. I mean, including the resource of labour, my labour in this case. That would count as a resource, in terms of total throughput. Because in theory I could be doing something else. You know, building a bridge, or working in a science lab or whatever it might be. My dad was an engineer, for example. But it doesn't have to be that. I mean, even if you're just delivering a burger to someone's house, at least you understand your role in the economic system. Maybe it seems kind of stupid that people won't collect their own burgers, but I guess not everyone might be able to. Whereas data analysis, I don't know. It's a lot more money for me, obviously. Especially if I exaggerate my hours, which, to be honest, I always do.

They're driving in darkness now, and she turns on her full-beam headlights. She finds herself reviewing these remarks, combing back through them as if with her fingers. It's interesting, she says. But then I suppose my job is more like the example of data analysis. I mean, whatever I get paid, it's sort of random. It's not as if my work adds a certain amount of profit and I get some of the profit back in my wages. It's just an arts centre, we're subsidised by the state.

He's looking over at her. The turn-off for the cottage is approaching on the left, and she taps the indicator, which starts ticking quietly. Oh no, that's not what I meant, he says. I'm so bad at explaining myself when I start talking about this stuff, I'm sorry. In itself, I think profit is actually sort of an inefficiency. For different reasons, I won't go into it too much. But say if you take the example of a teacher, they go into work every day and like, teach children to read. The school isn't making any profit, obviously, because it's free to go there. But I think we all agree, the children should learn to read, so we better pay someone to teach them. Since that person needs to eat, and so on. If we organise everything in view of profit, we get things happening in the economy that make no sense. Like in this example, no one has a direct profit motive for teaching children, but the whole economy will collapse if people can't read. You get the same problem with infrastructure, and all kinds of things.

Margaret turns the car, and they make their way along the

narrower road, its surface perceptibly uneven under the tyres. But I don't teach anyone to read, she says.

No, but what you do— Well, I only know from meeting you in your job last weekend. So you can correct me. But you helped to run the event, as I remember. And you gave me a lift to my accommodation afterwards, as part of your work.

Smiling to herself, looking out the windshield at the approaching gates, she answers: Right. Yes. Although I clocked off at that point.

He gives a sweet, kind of goofy laugh. I would hope so, he says. But putting that aside— I don't know, it's more interesting, so I don't know why I'm putting it aside. Just to say that your work has value, from my point of view. What do you call it, by the way? Your job title, I mean.

Oh, I'm the programme director, she says. Managing the artistic programme. Booking events, basically – music, theatre, things like that. And trying to get an audience in. But there are only three of us on staff full-time, so we all do a bit of everything.

Cool, he says. I guess you see a lot of interesting shows then, at your work.

You know, I really do. I'm very lucky, I love my job.

She turns the car through the gates and slowly they make their way up the darkened drive, under the trees. Inside the cottage the lights are on, the windows glowing dimly yellow. Together they get out of the car and Ivan stands looking at the low darkened facade of the house for a moment, the left half partly covered by trailing ivy. Then Margaret opens the front door and they enter the hallway. A small brown moth circles the overhead light while they take off their jackets and shoes. She asks if she can offer him anything: coffee or tea, or something to eat. He says he has eaten already, but he would like to refill his water bottle if that's okay. They go into the kitchen together, the terracotta tiles cold underfoot. He takes a silver water flask from his bag and refills it from the tap.

Your house is really nice, he says.

Oh, it's not mine, it's just rented.

Yeah, but I just mean it's a nice place. Plus it's cool you get to live alone.

She opens the kettle to look at the water level inside, and then shuts the lid again. Right, she says. I suppose— It wasn't what I had planned for my life. To be living alone. But it's okay.

He looks over at her. Oh, he says. I'm sorry. That was stupid of me, to say that.

No, don't worry. I mean, you're right, there are worse things. I spent a few months living with my mother last year, that was much worse.

He goes on looking at her. You don't get along too well? he asks.

Margaret feels constrained in her response now, as if the conversation has become somehow hazardous, though she doesn't understand why. With my mother? she says. I don't know. I suppose we both do our best. It probably just didn't suit us, to be living together.

He's nodding his head thoughtfully. I get you, he says. I had to live with my mother sometimes, like off and on, and that never really suited us either. You know, partly because she lives with her boyfriend, and he has his own children as well. Who, honestly, I believe she prefers.

Margaret is listening, half-frowning, curious. You think your mother prefers her stepchildren? she says.

Yeah, I think so. They suit her more, with her personality.

They're both like, super normal and they have good jobs and everything.

Ah. You think she would prefer if you had a full-time job?

Definitely, says Ivan. It's a fact, she would prefer that. She brings it up a lot. At the funeral even, last month. Again she brought it up about the job, why don't I have one. I don't know what you think of that, but to me it seemed a little bit on the harsh side. To be bringing that up at my dad's funeral, I don't know.

Margaret finds herself trying to picture this woman, Ivan's mother, trying to imagine in what tone of voice she could possibly have said this, and even what she looks like, how she was dressed. That does seem harsh, says Margaret.

Does it? I'm glad, because I thought that myself. But sometimes I pick up on things the wrong way.

And what about your brother?

Yeah, Peter, says Ivan. You mean, what does he do for a job? He's a barrister.

That's interesting. But I suppose I meant, does he get on with your mother?

Oh, I see. No, not really. They don't actually like each other too well. Although he does have a good job, in her opinion. But it's not about that. It's more like a personality clash between them. I guess I would say, if you're interested, they're both kind of dominant personalities. Who like getting their own way. So my mother trying to be the authority figure, that never went down too well with Peter, if you get me. Because he wouldn't be a great fan of getting bossed around.

I see, Margaret says.

Ivan is looking at her. Yeah, he says. Whereas with me, I

guess, my mother can be the authority more. But with no great results, because she's never happy with me.

Margaret smiles despite herself. I'm sorry, she says. My mother is never happy with me either.

He smiles back at her. It's weird, he says. I feel like if I created a new human being out of nothing, I would be very happy with them. Just that they were alive, even. You know, that's my dad's attitude. Or it was. He was always happy with us.

Touched, pained, she lays her hand over Ivan's, where it rests on the countertop. I'm sorry, she says.

Thank you, Margaret, he answers. It is really weird, definitely. That he's gone. And I have my regrets, you know. Like not being better towards him. Not that I was really bad. But say, even the stupid way I acted when I was a teenager. I wish I apologised for more of that stuff while I still had time. I don't know, I'm sorry. I know that you lost your dad as well.

She's nodding, feeling a kind of tightening in her throat. Yes, she says. I remember feeling that way at the time – regretful. But I don't feel it so much anymore.

Oh, really? That's good to know. Maybe that will happen for me as well, that the regret will fade. I guess feelings do change.

They do, she agrees.

She can feel him looking at her while she looks down at the countertop. Sorry, he says. I don't know how we got onto such a sad topic.

Smiling with her eyes averted, she says: That's okay. You know, life can be sad. It's no good pretending to be happy all the time.

He pauses. Yeah, he says. I agree with that. Not that I really pretend to be happy, but I just don't have anyone to talk to about these things. He swallows, and then continues: A lot of the time when I try to talk to someone, I feel like I must be really boring. Because I'll notice that whoever I'm talking to is just zoned out and not interested in what I'm saying at all. That's why I don't talk a lot usually, I guess. I mean even with my friends, I don't. Something might come into my head to say, but then I'll just imagine how boring it would be from the perspective of everyone else, and I won't say it. But when I'm talking to you— I guess, to be honest, you seem kind of interested. And then I probably get carried away a little bit, wanting to tell you things.

Well, I am interested, she says.

He's nodding, looking down at his water flask on the countertop, saying: Honestly just being near you, I feel really good. Or— I'm sorry, maybe that's weird.

Quietly she answers: No, it's not.

He looks at her, not speaking. In this look she sees his question, and silently she gives her answer. Still without speaking he comes closer, he touches his hand to her hip. Closing her eyes, she feels his lips on hers, slowly. She lets her mouth come open. A long and deep kiss, with her back against the countertop. Not nervous or hesitant his gestures now but slow and thoughtful. A feeling of pleasure this gives her that seems more than vanity. Deep sensation like an opening outwards, inside. He, this person – his braces, bitten fingernails, ideas about resources, the delivery job he quit, sadness he has been unable to express – he wants her, and she wants him. To give him the feeling that he wants. She hears herself in a low voice saying his name.

Afterwards they lie quietly in bed, and he's holding her in his arms, her head resting against his chest. When he tried looking on the internet last night, the advice was so confusing and contradictory, different things you had to do, and a lot of the websites were also trying to sell you certain products, like electronic toys or whatever, kind of making it seem like it would be impossible without these products, which he didn't know how to use or even have time to purchase, until eventually he felt so confused and anxious that he just stopped looking. And then in real life, just now, everything was simple and easy. They got on the bed together, lying down, kissing like before, and in the light of the bedside lamp he started to undress her, taking off the sort of rough woollen jersey she was wearing, and unhooking her bra. She was smiling, lying there half-undressed, and when they looked at one another, she laughed, touching her face, and there was no need even to say anything, he understood completely, and he started laughing as well. They were both embarrassed, he thinks, but happy at the same time, and there was a pleasant feeling of foolishness between them that made them want to laugh even though nothing was funny. They kissed again, and he put his hand inside her underwear, feeling her breath kind of high and catching, because she liked that, and quietly he said that he wanted to make her come. She was flushed, nodding her head, and she said if he wanted that, then maybe when he was inside her, she could touch herself a little bit. Shyly her eyes were half-closed, not looking. I don't mind, she said. It's not the most important thing. The idea of it, that she would touch herself while he was doing it to her, and he could watch, made him even more excited, and he said: No, let's definitely do that, if you want to. He got a condom from his bag, and she went on top of him. He could see she was getting really shy then, blushing, and she said she hoped she wasn't very heavy. No, you're not at all, he said. Which wasn't completely true, because she was kind of, but he liked it. Then he was inside her, and she was clutching at his shoulder with her hand, because he could tell she loved it so much when it was deep like that, and her bare white breasts moved softly with the motion of her body. Slowly at first, and it felt so good that he wanted actually to stay just like that, watching her, holding her hand, maybe even for a long time, doing nothing else, and then it was faster and he heard himself mumbling: Fuck. From nothing this word formed in his mouth and was spoken, and she started to touch herself, looking down at him, and her tongue was at her lips, wet, and then he could feel that she was coming. She said his name in a crying voice, Ivan, oh God, and her eyes were closed, and he finished as well at the same time, not completely meaning to, but it was better anyway, and actually it was perfect. Now she lies on his chest maybe sleeping, and he moves his hand slowly over her back, thinking with satisfaction and happiness about how good everything is at this moment.

Many times in his life, he has experienced intense feelings of desire. In itself, he thinks, it's not all that pleasurable a feeling: maybe a small bit pleasurable, but mostly frustrating and embarrassing, and also anxiety-inducing when you have to see the girl or interact with her, and you're so anxious to come across well and not be creepy, even though it's really obvious that she doesn't like you in that way and never will. And on the other side, a few times in his life, he has even, supposedly, been an object of desire for someone else, like that girl Claire, who was in a younger year at college and a member of the chess society. In that experience there was almost no pleasure at all, just a lot of awkwardness and bad feeling, trying to avoid seeing her, and then sometimes getting caught in conversation with her, and everyone would be looking. She was always praising him loudly for being so good at chess and then deprecating herself and talking about how bad she was in comparison, which was kind of hard to disagree with, since he was literally one of the top-ranked players in the country and she was just some random unrated girl hanging around the college chess club. But sometimes he could see from her face that the way he spoke to her was hurting her feelings, which made him feel bad and guilty. No, the experience of being liked by her was basically just unpleasant, although she wasn't ugly or anything, and some people even considered her to be pretty. Maybe in some small part of his brain – for instance, when one of the other guys said to him, *that girl Claire seriously wants to suck your dick, Ivan* – maybe there was a certain amount of good feeling in that. Because it was said in an offhanded way, as if it wasn't really surprising, and other girls overheard, without seeming shocked, as if Ivan were more or less an averagely attractive guy and why shouldn't some girl from a younger year want to do that to him, it was imaginable. However, other than this minor and temporary improvement in his self-image, there was nothing really enjoyable about being the object of another person's desire, per se. And aside from these experiences, of wanting and being wanted, he has also had encounters with women which really involved neither category, as for example when at parties in college he would end up kind of drunkenly messing around with someone he didn't know. He attended many parties in the hopes that this scenario might unfold, and then on a very few occasions it did, but never in a satisfying way. If he got to touch the girl, for instance, she definitely wouldn't be moaning and writhing around or anything like that, actually she would just lie there, and he would be asking anxiously: Is that okay? And she would be like: Yeah, it's fine. Then if he ever had to see her again in day-to-day life, his entire face would turn red and he would start stammering, and his friends would be like, Ivan, what's wrong? Because he had just seen some girl who once gave him a handjob at a party or something, who probably didn't even remember or care at all. Not that this happened frequently, because in fact he had only had like three of these encounters ever, and one of those was basically just kissing. The one time he actually succeeded in having full penetrative sex with someone, it was so awkward and bad that he walked back to his apartment afterwards and literally cried tears, hating himself more at that moment than maybe ever before in his life. Anyway. Nothing he has done or felt in this regard before has prepared him remotely for this new experience, with Margaret: the experience of mutual desire. To feel an interpenetration of thought between the two of them, understanding her, looking at her and knowing, yes, without even speaking, what she feels and wants, and knowing that she understands him also, completely. In her eyes, the look of warmth, the flickering kind of amusement, acknowledging: and this relates he thinks to her beauty, her thick dark hair in its loose unravelling braid, her full expressive mouth, the supple roundness of her arms, her breasts. Even her clothes, rumpled and softened, the careless way they drape over her figure, all of this is given life by her understanding, her complete personhood, which in a single look he senses and knows. The way she said his name in a crying voice, with her face and throat all flushed. To know that life can be like this: his life. Moving his hand over her back, he says aloud: Can I ask you— Then he remembers no one has been talking for a while, so he adds: Or maybe you're asleep already, I'm sorry.

She lifts her head to look at him, and her face is dreamy, her eyes bright and glazed-looking. No, she says, I'm awake. What were you going to say?

Did you— It's pretty stupid. But I'm just curious, did you always plan that you were going to call me? The other night. Or did you go back and forth on it.

She rests against him for a few moments longer in silence, and then she rolls over onto her back. He watches her, the bed-linen all white and tousled around her, like clouds, and her dark hair tumbled on the pillow.

To tell you the truth, she says, I told myself I wouldn't. Because it didn't seem to make any sense. I mean, with the age difference, and then we don't even live anywhere near each other. And it was kind of crazy anyway, what happened. I actually felt shocked with myself when I thought about it, because I met you at a work event. And I never, never do things like that, never. I started thinking: I don't know what came over me. I can't imagine what kind of person he must think I am. And then, after a day or two, I started to wonder if maybe I should call, just to say: nice meeting you, and best wishes. Because I hated the idea of making you think— I don't know, it's silly, but I didn't want you to feel that it didn't mean anything to me. And I thought it would be nice to hear your voice again, actually. But that's all. I just called to say thank you, and goodbye. Supposedly. I don't know if I really believed that.

She's looking up at the ceiling, not at him, while he lies in silence watching her.

My life isn't very happy at the moment, Ivan, she says. Things are still difficult, with— the man I was married to. You know, he doesn't really accept that we're— Sorry, he does accept that we're not together. But he doesn't want to accept it. And my mother, I think, feels the same way. About my marriage, I mean. It's complicated. I suppose I don't have many people I can talk to. I know you were just asking me if I was planning to call you or not. And the answer is, I tried not to, and I told myself what a bad idea it was, and then eventually I started to think – what's the point? I mean: what's the point in pretending my life makes any sense anyway? Maybe it did once, but it doesn't anymore.

She turns to him then, looking at him, and he looks back at her, nodding his head, to show that he understands.

I'm sorry to hear about that, he says. About your ex-husband.

She lowers her eyes, saying quietly: It's okay.

Well, I'm sure it will be okay. But it sounds— to be honest, pretty bad.

She laughs now, looking up at him, and he can see that she's sad, her eyes even looking almost tearful. It is pretty bad, isn't it? she says.

Is it, like— Does he want to get back together with you?

I don't know, she says. Sometimes I think he just wants to make me miserable. But that's not true either. I suppose if you asked him, he would say yes, he wants to get back together.

And you don't, says Ivan.

She shakes her head quickly.

That's hard, he says. I'm sorry.

Oh, I don't know, she replies. I'm not giving you a very good impression of him. He's a decent person, you know, he just has his own problems. And I married him, after all.

He looks at her for a second or two, her face all pink and white like a flower, and her dark hair. I guess you're probably not supposed to ask questions like this, he says, but were you in love with him?

I was once, she says. And after a pause she asks him: Have you ever been in love?

Ah, he answers. I thought I was, at different times. But it was never mutual or anything.

She nods her head, understanding without further explanation. After a moment she asks: Is it okay that I called you? You don't think it was the wrong thing to do.

He pauses. No, he says. It wasn't wrong, definitely not. I'm very happy. Or like— It's weird to say I'm happy, because in a lot of ways I'm not at all. You know, because of the grief and regret that we were talking about before. But I feel really good being here with you. And I think it's right. I know you're not a great fan of the age difference, but I don't think it matters. Or living far away. It's not even that far. Not that I'm presuming you'll want to see me again, I don't know. But I'm very happy that I met you. And even knowing that you're alive, I feel like my life will be a lot better. Just being able to remember – being with you, and having such a nice experience together. I don't mean that in a weird way. But no, I think it's the right thing that you called me, definitely. Yeah. And I'm thankful. Did I say that already? Or I don't know if I did. But if I didn't, I want to say thank you for calling me, and seeing me again. Because to me it means a lot.

She comes to him now and buries her face in his shoulder, and he puts his arms around her and touches her hair. He can feel that her jaw is moving a little, like maybe she might be crying, but if she is crying he thinks it's okay. Her feelings about her ex-husband are obviously difficult, and about her mother, and her life has become senseless, and she also feels for him, Ivan, the situation that he's in, and she likes him, even though she thinks he's too young, and she feels confused about the sexual aspect of things, he can tell. But he thinks it's okay for her to have these confusing feelings. It doesn't mean that he has done anything bad, or that the sex wasn't good. Dimly he even feels that she's confused because in fact it was so good, and maybe she wants it again, the same way he does. How to make sense of these feelings in such a context? For him it's not so difficult, but for her it seems to be very difficult and even makes her cry. About the crying, however, he feels calm, not panicked. Perhaps because as soon as her tears began, she came to him and put her face in his shoulder. And whatever she's crying about or thinks she's crying about, this still seems to mean something: that she wants to feel his arms around her, which is the same thing he wants. Whatever complicated circumstances may account for the situation, there is still this ultimate reality, that they are two people, a man and a woman, and the woman wants to lie in the arms of the man when she's upset. And that reality has its own meaning. Ivan has never been such a man before, and had probably even thought that he never could be, that he would just get anxious and flustered, worrying that he had done something wrong, needing the woman to reassure him that he hadn't done anything, or whatever, but now that the right moment has arrived, he finds it's very easy. Just to hold her in his arms and feel her warm tears against his shoulder, and to touch her hair, and even say to her: Margaret, it's okay. Don't worry. It's alright.

The next afternoon, a Sunday afternoon, they go walking together along the laneway behind the cottage. The sky overhead is pale blue, and the leaves of the trees are light and brittle, falling now and then in golden flurries through the air when the wind touches the branches. Margaret is walking with her hands in her pockets to keep them warm. Clear days she finds are colder, because on overcast days the clouds are like a blanket, like the sky is wearing a white woollen blanket keeping in the heat. Whether this is true or not she doesn't know. Ivan might know but she doesn't ask him, only walks beside him along the laneway, where indeed anyone might see them, but no one does. This morning they ate breakfast together, talking a little. She made him coffee in the cafetière and he said the coffee was good. Last night she thought: he's too young, too much in grief over his father, it has to stop. We can be friends, but nothing more. Already he had started asking about her marriage, her life situation, and to confide in him about that would be the act of an insane person. Going to bed together was one thing, foolish maybe, but not sinister. Telling him about Ricky would be different. Contaminating his life, conscripting him into her own private misery. Pathetic, besides. No one believed me, Ivan. But you believe me, don't you? If he had any sense he would run a mile. Terrible: and worse again if he didn't. No, she thought, for his sake, for both of us, it has to stop. Then this morning they lay in bed together, and he talked to her about chess, how he first began playing, and his more recent feelings of disillusionment, not being able to take much enjoyment in the game anymore. She said that she would like to play chess again sometime, out of interest, not having played since she was a child, and for some reason this made him very happy, and he kept saying how much fun it would be for them to play together, even though he had just been talking before about how chess no longer gave him any pleasure. She could perceive then that along with his painful feelings of disillusionment, he still felt, maybe even unconsciously, an almost childlike enthusiasm for the game of chess, both at the same time. He was in a good mood, and he wanted to kiss her, and for a while they kissed, and then without talking any more he made love to her again. It was obvious then that it was not going to be enough that he was too young and going through a bereavement. Those were solid sensible ideas, powerful enough for the surface of daily life, but not powerful enough for the hidden life of desire shared between two people. They ate breakfast together afterwards and had the coffee, and now they are walking in the laneway, quiet, contented, and the feeling between them seems good and somehow wholesome. As they turn the corner around the low stone wall, the lane dips down ahead, and rainwater has pooled in the hollow, reflecting the clear blue of the sky, and around the water she can see little birds, drinking and preening themselves. At the sound of the approaching footsteps, the birds lift themselves into the air, and there are more of them, many, starlings, with dark iridescent wings, and they lift themselves in one cloud into the blue air, rising, all together, while Margaret and Ivan both stop and look. All as one the birds move together, a dark cloud beating with the loud muscular sound of wings, ascending towards the overhead telephone wire, and strangely it seems now the cloud parts, one half rising up above the wire and the other half falling below, cut cleanly, and then together the two clouds combine once more into an edgeless and mobile arrangement, which is called a murmuration, Margaret thinks. Wow, says Ivan under his breath. Down by the pool of water a few smaller birds of a different kind are still bathing themselves, little sparrows, or finches. And the pale blue air all around them is still and silent, the leaves of the trees are silent and still. Margaret touches Ivan's hand and he smiles and they go on walking. The other birds dart off through the air as they draw near. He begins talking again about the game of chess they're going to play together, which he says they can do 'over the board' or online, and she's laughing, thinking about this game of chess she has for some reason agreed to play with him, and then his phone starts to ring.

One second, he says. Sorry.

He lets go of her hand to take his phone from his pocket. Glancing at the screen, Margaret can see that the person calling is named Peter. Still looking down at the phone, Ivan says: Oh, wait a second. This is my brother calling me. Is today Sunday? Fuck. I might have to pick up, is that okay?

Sure, says Margaret. Don't worry.

I'm sorry, he says. One second, it won't take long.

As he says this, he's already picking up the call, sliding the icon to one side and lifting the phone to his face, saying: Hello? He turns a little away from her, standing in the grassy verge at the side of the laneway. She can hear a voice on the other end of the call, buzzing faintly, but she can't make out the words. Hey, listen, Ivan says. I'm really sorry about this, but I forgot. Again she can hear the buzzing. Yeah, says Ivan. Well, no, I can't. Because, the thing is, I'm sorry about this, but— I'm actually not in Dublin right at the moment. He pauses, biting absently at one of his fingernails, while she waits with her hands in her pockets. Then he says: No, it's not that, I'm just— I'm, uh— He turns to Margaret, pointing at the phone as if to say: What should I tell him? Bemused, she shrugs her shoulders. It seems his brother is saying something, because Ivan is nodding his head, turning away, looking down at the grass. Yeah, he says. Yes, that's right. He glances back at her. Well, kind of, he says. Basically, yeah. Smiling now, looking relaxed, he kicks at a piece of grass with the toe of his shoe. Look, I feel bad, I'm sorry, he says. I can see you in the week if you want, like for dinner or something. Yeah. Okay, I'm going now. I'm sorry. Bye, sorry again. Goodbye. He hangs up the call and puts the phone back in his pocket, looking at her.

That was my brother, he says. I actually was supposed to meet him for lunch today, like ten minutes ago. But I forgot about it. He was there at the restaurant waiting for me and everything.

Oh, I'm sorry, Margaret says.

No, no, don't be, says Ivan. He didn't mind. No, he was very surprised I wasn't there at first, because I'm usually the punctual one. But he figured out I was with someone. And then he was like, oh, forget about lunch, it doesn't matter at all. Have fun. Yeah. He's weird. He's kind of funny. He really likes women, I don't know if I said that before.

She stands there smiling, folding her arms, tucking her hands into the crooks of her elbows. No, you didn't say that, she says. What does it mean, he likes women?

You know. He has a lot of girlfriends.

All at once?

With a funny kind of shrug Ivan walks on, and Margaret walks beside him. I don't know, he says. We don't talk about things like that. I've just heard from other people that he goes out with a lot of different girls. He did have a more long-term girlfriend once, when I was younger, but they broke up. Which was sad, because she was really great. And now he seems to have new girlfriends all the time. Not that it's any of my business.

Together they go on walking, shadows short and dark over the gravelled path ahead. When you told him just now that you were with someone, Margaret says, did he ask who?

Well, he asked if I was in Leitrim. Because he knows that I was here last weekend, for the chess thing. And since I'm here again, I guess he worked out that I met someone the last time. But I never told him anything.

What do you think he would say if he knew?

If he knew what?

She swallows. That I'm thirty-six, she says. Or that I used to be married.

Oh, says Ivan. What would Peter say? I don't know. He's in his thirties as well, I think I told you. Around your age.

She says nothing. He looks over at her while they walk.

I guess you're thinking about what different people in your life would say, he remarks. If they knew about me, or whatever.

You're right, I suppose I was thinking about that.

Your ex-husband, and so forth.

Yes, she says.

You don't think he would be too happy.

With a kind of laugh, frightened, not knowing what to say, she answers: Ah, no, Ivan, I don't think he would.

But it's your life, you know.

She nods her head, looking down at the ground. It's difficult, she says. I don't know. Ivan says nothing, just goes on walking beside her in the cold bright air. From the field beside the laneway, behind the low stone wall, a small sturdy sheep watches them passing, its dirty fleece silvered with rainfall, its face velvet black. Golden-green fields stretching out into the faint blue distance. Limitless clear air and light everywhere around them, filled with the sweet liquid singing of birds.

# 5

Ten past seven Monday evening he's just crossing O'Connell Bridge, late as usual. Red tail-lights in the blue dark, silhouettes of buildings. Bus making a yawning left at the quays as he waits to cross. Wanting to tell her about the judgement: phrases he already has memorised to recite back. *Such a concatenation of careless errors must call into question the extent and quality of the Minister's review of information*. Crossing at the lights, he makes his way up Westmoreland Street, hands in his coat pockets. Desire almost to begin whistling to himself, opening theme of the Concerto No. 24. *The Minister acted unreasonably in this regard and arrived at a clearly erroneous conclusion.* Message he received from Ivan this morning, tell her about that too. Hey. Sorry again about yesterday. If you still want to see each other, how would this week suit? I understand if you're annoyed. Really got a laugh out of her last night, the story. Dark horse, she called him. They were eating together, takeout from the Japanese place she likes. I think he's starting to look like you, she said, did I tell you that? Seeing him at the funeral, it made me think. He's so grown-up-looking. Laughing out in shock Peter heard himself. Are you serious? he asked. I thought he looked atrocious. Lying stretched out on the sofa for her back, dipping her tempura carefully in the little bowl of sauce. The suit, you mean, she said. But I just meant in his face, I could see a resemblance. He's getting very handsome. Raised an eyebrow, though really he felt pleased. Handsome: well, maybe. Hard to imagine all the same who the girl could be. Teenage chess enthusiast, poster of Magnus Carlsen over her bed. Funny to think of Ivan playing the seducer. Flat monotonous voice on him. And the braces, diabolical. Not remotely annoyed, Peter wrote. Looking forward to catching up. How about dinner on Thursday night? Approaching the gates now, his stride lengthens, brisk, cheerfully impatient.

Since last week, their unspoken arrangement. Morning he waited at the hospital while she had the procedure. Nurse came in to tell him when they were finished with her. Recovering from her sedative under the bleach-white lighting she looked thin and tired. Tea they had given her in a plastic cup, and dry toast. Now, you know she can't drive for forty-eight hours, the nurse was saying. Felt overcome looking. Small and frail in her patterned gown. Remembering everything. She, his father. Clinical air quality, sterile light. Yeah, he said. They took a taxi back to her apartment. All went well she told him. Took turns that night brushing their teeth, filling water bottles at the tap. In her room he found her in bed already. Neatly on her chest of drawers he folded his sweater. Got into bed beside her, turned off the lamp. In quiet and darkness the sweet slow measure of her breath. Since then he has spent his days working, attending meetings, drafting reports, and in the evening he calls round to her apartment for dinner. Small and clean her kitchenette under the yellow glow of the fan light. Books and papers in the living room, old comfortable sofa. Over the fireplace, Braque lithograph she picked up in Paris, *Nature morte oblique*. While they eat he asks her advice about work, she talks about a paper she's reading on philosophical logic and natural language. Something about a liar who says all of his hats are green. Does that mean he has some hats, all of which aren't green? Or maybe he has no hats. Would it still be a lie, if he didn't have any? Afterwards, television, cloud of steam from the kettle boiling. Nights he no longer has to spend trapped in claustrophobic solitude, self-medicated, panic attack or am I dying how to tell. Instead the deep replenishing reservoir of her presence. A chaste kiss, cold mint taste of her mouth. And in bed the low familiar conversation before sleep. Latest available translations of the Gospels, literary merits thereof. What Jesus meant when he made that remark to the Canaanite woman about giving the children's bread to the dogs. It's challenging, Sylvia said. It's hard for me, because I don't understand it. Her sincere and transcendent love of Christ, his ironic sort of joking but then at times terrifyingly real and serious fear of Christ. After weeks of sleeplessness he wakes now only to hear her turning on the coffee machine in the morning, low pummelling sound through the wall. Peace so intense and complete he could weep. Just to inhabit lightly the space that is cleared for him by her tactful silence. Questions she doesn't ask. Hasn't heard a thing from the other, hasn't texted her either. Icing each other out. Why are they even annoyed with one another, he hardly remembers, or wants to. For the best, he thinks. Let her come crawling. The usual game, not to break first. While she's out spending his money on ketamine and eyelash extensions. Is there someone else, he wonders: guy in her room the other night lighting a cigarette, how do you two know each other. Doesn't bear thinking about. Whole thing patently insane. In the meantime he's getting some sleep for once. Eating three meals a day, answering emails. Even laying off the Xanax. Just as well, now that his dealer's not speaking to him. Suffering, yes. Tormented often, regretting everything, sick at heart. Endurable however. Can be borne, has to be. Call it what it is. You're grieving, she's always telling him. Closes his eyes at times as if in prayer: and it's peaceful somehow. Recalling senselessly the old familiar words, worn smooth by childhood repetition. Blank tokens now, long since expired, exchangeable for nothing. Consoling merely to weigh and handle once again, yes, thy kingdom come.

Taking the staircase two at a time he at last reaches the room, late, and short of breath. Cluster of bodies around a draped table of hardbacks, voices talking. New anthology of contemporary critical perspectives. One glance discloses her, standing by the window, slim and immaculate in black cashmere. Amber tone in her lifted gaze. Without approaching he smiles at her and she, listening absentmindedly to the conversation going on around her, returns the smile. Tacit acknowledgement of a certain shared privacy. The others, her students, colleagues perhaps, friends. Competing all for her attention, he thinks, while she magnificently listens and inclines her head. Resplendent among her disciples. He makes his way across the room towards her and seeing his approach she turns to him: arresting the attention of the others before she even speaks. Hello, stranger, she says. Voice low and smiling. Have I missed your speech? he asks. Light gesture of her fine white hand. Oh, it was nothing, she says. Never mind that, let me introduce you. Her students, a teaching assistant, all young women. Peter's an old friend of mine, she says. Looking up at him she adds: He could have been a very fine academic, but sadly he decided to become a human rights lawyer instead.

At that he laughs, easily. Ah, you're flattering me, Sylvia, he says. Not that I object. He breaks off, and adds with exaggerated politeness: Or should I call you 'Professor' in front of your students?

Innocuously she answers: First names I think are fine. Though let's not go any more informal.

With the same easy amused feeling he replies: In public? I would never. Turning to the students he says: You're all in the English department?

Their laughter giddy, almost frightened. Too awed it seems to speak aloud. He and she collaborate instead to supply the dialogue: stories of their old debating triumphs she pretends to find embarrassing. Undergraduate antics remembered, presentations on books they had never read. Yes, you would bring that up, wouldn't you? You're making me look bad in front of the young people. Enjoying herself, he can see. He also. Their power to captivate, dusted down again, given a little run-out, why not. Feel them staring. His own desirability enriched by its close but mysterious relation to hers. Cerebral her glamour and at the same time sensuous: fine lustre of her golden hair, small and soft her breasts under dark cashmere. Vision of a life before him, to walk over from work through the dim blue evening, tired, satisfied, and to stand by her side in an overheated seminar room. Her consort and protector. How she holds herself gently apart from everyone but him, how they in the discreet gestures of their mutual privacy set themselves apart together. Around half past eight she turns to him in all simplicity and says: Shall we head off, do you think? And he has to restrain himself from laying a hand on the small of her back as he answers: Yeah, let's.

Down the steps and out onto Nassau Street, Dawson Street, exhaust fumes and streetlights, they're laughing together. That was fun, he says. It's nice to be around you at these things, I get some of that reflected glow. Hands in the pockets of her tweed coat, her breath a wreath of mist. Oh, you don't need any reflected, she says. You're very magnetic. Did you get that judgement this morning? Leaves like dried paper underfoot. St Stephen's Green. Reminded of his victory he gathers her arm against him, small firm pressure, and starts telling her: concatenation of errors, extent and quality, the Minister acting unreasonably. Her delight, her quick intelligent questions, walking with their heads together in absorbed discussion, their usual shorthand. Did he— Yeah, they were— But you must both have been— Right, exactly. Oh, they must have been sickened. I wish I'd been there. Pleasure of his success redoubled, deepened, meeting with her approval and pride, yes. Together they climb the bright staircase of her building. Clink of her keys in the dish and he takes his shoes off in the hallway. We still have some of that ragu from the weekend, she's saying. If you're hungry. In the kitchen he boils the pasta while she sets the table, and sitting down together they eat. Talking, tearing pieces off a loaf of bread with their fingers. Debriefing on the daily papers. Did you see that horrible piece about. Oh Jesus, awful. How do they publish that stuff. Still talking by the time they're getting ready for bed. Feature in *The Irish Times* about the rising popularity of cosmetic procedures. Perfectly attractive young women. Nineteen, twenty-year-olds. Huge expense. Not to mention the risks. Ominous sign for the culture it must be. Gender relations, I don't know. Seated on the side of the mattress she's taking out her hairpins. I mean, it's a normal experience, she says. You're unhappy with your body. Your breasts aren't perfect, whatever. That used to be considered normal.

Finds himself smiling, watching her. Shaded light of the bedside lamp. You think your breasts aren't perfect? he says.

With a look of repressed amusement she replies: I was speaking sociologically.

Ah, I see. My mistake.

In her striped cotton nightdress, bare arms, she gets into bed beside him. The room is cool, almost cold, the duvet crisp and soft over their bodies. It's not something that keeps me awake at night, she says. Not having perfect breasts. I've made my peace with it.

I think they're perfect, he says.

Free and handsome her laughter. How would you know? she asks.

I'm just giving my subjective opinion.

Casting your mind back, are you?

He's laughing now too, foolishly, looking at the ceiling. Well, feel free to refresh my memory, he says.

Amused, indulgent, her look. Don't you have a girlfriend? she asks. Even if you're not speaking to each other.

Turns over to face her. The fine delicate filigree of lines at the corners of her eyes: moving he finds and beautiful. Oh, I don't know, he says. I think that might be on the way out.

You still haven't heard from her?

No, he says. But it's not strictly monogamous anyway, you know.

I should hope not.

These words, this tone of voice. Her hand on his arm he recalls, you're very magnetic. And as if carried forward quite naturally by the same momentum he reaches his fingertips under the quilt to brush her arm. How intriguing of you, he says.

She gives at this a funny embarrassed smile, still lying on her back: but doesn't draw away. Well, you have been known to kiss me goodnight, she answers. Which might be enough to make some people jealous.

Damp softness inside the crook of her elbow he touches. Oh, they always get jealous of you in the end, he says. I suppose I talk about you too much.

She's quiet a moment, allowing him to trace with his fingertips a whispering line from her elbow to wrist. Don't you tell them there isn't anything to be jealous of? she asks.

He pauses. Weighing his terms. Parrying briefly, waiting move, he answers: Well, I'm not a very good liar.

Still the same uninflected voice. You know what I mean, she says.

Meeting her now, he answers simply: No, I've never talked about that with anyone.

For a few seconds she gives no reply. Then she says: Why not?

It's your private life. I don't have any business discussing it with other people.

She goes on looking overhead. In a gentle tone, she replies: I'm only asking out of curiosity. I've never really talked about it with anyone either. Obviously my friends know I'm in pain a lot. They might suspect there are difficulties. Emily probably has an idea. But I've never told her outright. It's hard, because it's a big part of my life, in a way, but I find it very difficult to discuss. You're the only person I've ever really told, as such. And obviously it's not something we talk about.

Watching her, careful, he answers: We could, if you ever wanted to.

She gives a kind of shrug. I don't know if there's much to say, she replies. It's not getting any better. Which for a long time I thought it might, or I hoped it would. I suppose I still find it difficult to accept that that part of my life is over.

He goes on watching. Pulsing sensation in his throat. Cautious he thinks, and cautiously says: Does it have to be?

A little pause, not looking at him but straight up at the ceiling, frown in the crease of her forehead. Well, what most people are talking about, when they talk about sex, she says, that's not something I can do anymore. Not in any kind of normal way, or not without a lot of pain. So yes, in that sense, it is over.

His fingers at her hipbone. Above all not to be tactless. I understand what you're saying, he says. But sexuality, speaking broadly, it's more complicated than that. I mean, it's not just the one physical act.

She breathes out between her lips as if considering. In theory, she says. But practically speaking, people have expectations about what an intimate relationship will involve. She breaks off here a moment, teeth at her lower lip, and then adds: I suppose it's my personality as well. You know, if I can't do something properly, I don't want to do it at all. Maybe that's part of the problem, I don't know. I think I would find it humiliating, having to negotiate all that with another person. I would feel I was offering something very inferior.

Palm of his hand resting low on her belly under the hollow

of her navel. Soft warmth through the cotton nightgown. Quietly he says: But just from your own perspective, there are still certain things you find— pleasurable?

Strangely she laughs at that. Her ear he sees pink, her throat. Yes, she says.

Low kind of aching sensation he feels, her closeness, heat of her flushed throat. Right, he replies.

Lowering her eyes, speaking in a shy humorous voice. I mean, I have the full range of sensations, she says. On my own, I can still— you know.

For a moment he closes his eyes. Hot scalding feeling in his eyelids. Aha, he says. And opening his eyes to look at her he adds: But then, I would go so far as to say, that part of your life isn't really over at all.

Shyly in the dim enveloping radiance of lamplight she's smiling. The back of his hand she touches with her fingertips under the quilt. When you're resting your hand like this, she says, it's nice.

Quietly he watches her. In that way? he asks.

Nodding she says only: Mm.

Warmth of his hand low on her belly, between her hipbones, heavy. It turns you on? he says.

Very quietly she answers: A little bit.

Hot pleasant throbbing sensation, deep. Me too, he says.

Turning her face away, hiding under her hand, but her voice still smiling. You don't have to say that, Peter, she says.

His palm resting warm on the soft shallow dish of her belly. What, you don't believe me? he asks. You can find out for yourself if you'd like, but I won't insist.

She falls silent a moment. Then in a low dark voice says: Would you like that?

Flood of luxurious pleasure he feels, deep, heavy. Ah, he says. Yes, if you're offering. I would like that very much.

Covering her eyes with both hands, she groans, guttural sound he loves. I don't know, she says. I'm sorry. Her voice constrained, she adds: To want what I can't have, you know, it's difficult.

Low on the flat of her belly he stills his hand. Wrongfooted, a little, or just cautious. Well, I know there are certain things we can't do, he says. But that's okay, there's no pressure. Even just to talk, it's nice.

Moving her fingers and he realises she's wiping tears away. Crying. The shock of it, wrench of pain inside himself: tenderness, distress, compassion. Sylvia, he says, don't. I'm sorry. Don't get upset.

Glistening wet her eyes and face through her fingers, nodding, unheeding. Her voice thin as thread. I just want you to remember me the way I was, she says.

Terrible feeling. Tight in his throat. Oh God, he answers. Jesus.

Shaking her head, her hidden face. When they. Yes: the way she was. Perfect, everything. The life they wanted. Her pride in that remembrance worse than touching. Pity he feels and despises himself for feeling. Her pain, the impassable territory between their bodies. Sees her receding behind its monumental heights. Remember me the way I was. Hard to breathe thinking. Dashing tears from her eyes now, however she seems more angry than sad. With herself, with him, both probably. Exhausted he hears himself apologising and she also, crossly, not looking. No, no, I'm sorry. Never mind. No, it's my fault. It's alright. Her head shaking. I'm just tired. Let's forget about it. In a dull deadened voice he asks if she wants him to leave and she clips back: No, of course not. Don't be dramatic, Peter. Angry at herself for crying, he thinks. And at him for touching her, drawing from her certain soft words and looks, now regretted. She props herself up to turn off the lamp and in the darkness lies down again on her back.

Look, she says. I know you're grieving, you're finding it hard to cope. I want to help. But there are certain things I can't do for you. And you know that.

Feeling heat in his face that could be either shame or indignation he answers: I wasn't asking you to do anything. I thought we were just talking.

She allows her tone to rise, high and tensed. I don't even know what you want, she says. Whatever I do, it's not enough. It has to be the one thing I can't do, suddenly that's the only thing you want. It's like you're trying to make me suffer, just because you're suffering.

He passes a hand down slowly over his face. Well, you're making yourself very clear, he says. I wasn't trying to make you suffer, but obviously I have, and I'm sorry. It won't happen again.

Defeated by the inexorable calm of his dejected apology she has nothing to say. Turns over on her side with a tug of the duvet. And what is there for him to feel. Tired, very. Ashamed of himself, as usual. Everything spoiled and debased, which earlier seemed golden. Triumph, partnership, the private treasure of mutual admiration. A nice evening, almost. In the dark he lies quietly for long enough that she can pretend to be asleep. Gets up then to find the foil sheet of tablets in his wallet, swallows two with a handful of water from the bathroom tap. Crying she said to him: I want you to remember me. Too painful to contemplate. Staring into the sun somehow: agony intense enough to annihilate. Even without looking he finds it brightens. For a little while, in bed beside her again, he too feels like crying. Pointless, and anyway he wouldn't dare. Slowing and congealing the formless language of his thoughts, until released into medicated sleep.

By the time he wakes she's gone already. Bar of white daylight fluorescing under the blind. Back to his flat now, he thinks. Alone again in the claustrophobic silence of his failures. Why did he have to do it: deluded optimism, maybe. Thinking after all these years it could be smoothed over with a little conversation. Or just self-sabotage. His life in danger of becoming tolerable for a minute, why not go out of his way to aggrieve and distress the only person who could put up with him. In the end however perhaps inevitable. Couldn't go on that way, virtuous partnership, sharing meals, discussing theology. Lying in her bed alone after she goes to work, imagining certain scenarios. To undress her, and she's happy, laughing, her white throat. The wet warmth of her mouth. Idea of that, yes. Get in the shower then and go to work. See her again in the evening for dinner. What did you get up to today? Oh, nothing much. No, it was absurd. Brute force of his appetite had to confront eventually the fact of her living body. Stop making excuses, come here. I want you to remember me, she said: to be loyal she meant to that remembered woman, her happiness, beauty, promise of a future. Forever warm and still to be enjoyed. Forsake therefore the injured and angry person she has become. He too of course. Himself as he was then, the young idealist, aflame with righteousness. That person she wants perhaps, not this. And yet she said she liked it: his hand resting. Palm heavy between her hips, the catch in her breath. Took her by surprise perhaps, the feeling: to be touched again, desired, caressed. When last did anyone in tenderness lay a hand on her, he wonders. Her high cold austerity, her palisade of personal space. Too much excitement, panic, spilling over inescapably into tears. His existence an affront to her dignity it seems. And what about his dignity: consigned again to pleading and fumbling at her. Just give me your hand, it's only going to take a minute. Oh, leave me alone, can't you? Her high rare refinement, her disgust at his crudeness, the obtrusion of his body. Each in the end angry and humiliated. Better for both of them if he. Yes. No. What was it she said? Don't be dramatic, Peter.

Swings his legs out of bed finally and plugs his phone into the wall. In and out of the shower, thick soft bath towel, wet footprints on the kitchen tiles making breakfast. Late morning light through the Turkish curtains. After eating he rinses the dishes, hers also. His clothes hanging over the back of the chair in her room. Clean underwear in the zip pocket of his bag. Powers up his phone and pulls his socks on waiting. Home screen finally. Lifts the device and starts scrolling through notifications. Work mostly. New text he sees from Janine's number. Strange. He thumbs to open.

JANINE: Check the news. Shes in Kevin St. They took her phone

He scrolls up, must have missed something. No. Last text received in July: She says to tell you were in workmans!! Sent to the wrong number this morning, he thinks, must be. Pointless to reply. Hasn't heard from her in nearly a week. You're always seeing each other. Her friends sniggering at him. Looks at the message a few seconds longer. Two taps, hits send.

PETER: ?

Instantly Janine starts typing and he waits, sitting on the mattress.

JANINE: Hey we got evicted this morning. Security people trashed the place and then the guards arrived and Naomi got arrested
JANINE: Pretty sure shes at Kevin St station but no one has heard from her bc she has no phone

Sound of his own breath leaving his mouth in the silence of the room. Letter they asked him to read and he didn't. Closes his eyes and opens again. Finally the resigned padding of his thumbs on the screen.

PETER: That's terrible news, Janine, I'm sorry. I'll head over to Kevin Street now. Do you know why Naomi was arrested? And is she ok?
JANINE: Yea I dont think she got hurt or anything. No idea why they arrested her, it was so chaotic
JANINE: Dont tell her I text you lol. Your the only lawyer I know
PETER: Thanks. I'll be back in touch as soon as I've seen her.
PETER: In the meantime, are you ok? And everyone else?

JANINE: Yeah we're fine. . . . well we're homeless but otherwise 100

The 100 emoji. He stares down at his phone until the screen goes dark in his hand. Letter he never read. Dont tell her I text you lol. He drops his phone on the bed and buttons his shirt up, muttering aloud for no reason, heard by no one: Fuck, fuck, fuck.

# 6

Cab rank across the street there under the trees. When he gives the address the man says: No trouble, I hope. Smiles wanly without answering. Out the window the passing facades of buildings, painted brickwork, stickered windows, laundry while you wait. Anyone might see him. Why is he even doing it. Don't you have a girlfriend? Even if you're not speaking to each other. Should have ignored Janine's text, he thinks, taken it as a sign. Find some other young one to hang around with, maybe even a well-adjusted girl from a nice family this time. Would feel guilty though, if she ever got to like him. Naomi at least never. All this madness for what: some transient satisfaction, flattery, probably insincere. To normalise once more his relations with the other, the relevant energy spent elsewhere. Does he need all that so badly. And is it anyway in such short supply. Must be any number of girls out there tolerably pretty who just want to get fucked a couple of times a week. No hard feelings. No text messages from the best friend: Shes in Kevin St. Stupid bitch. No, I'm sorry. Pressing down the roller button for the window, cold wind stings the side of his face. Okay if I pay with card?

Inside: grim waiting room with broken chairs, noticeboard, woman in an ugly synthetic raincoat filling out a form. Garda behind the Plexiglass. Grey eyebrows. Member in charge. Is she in custody here, yes. Arrested on suspicion of what, may I ask. See it in the man's face of course: here we go. Kids these days pretending to be homeless, crying about illegal evictions, hardly in the cells five minutes before Daddy calls the lawyers in. Go home to Donnybrook why don't you. If that's what he wants to think, let him. Probably better for her if he does. You the solicitor? No, but I'm happy to call one. And I'm sure he'll want to know why exactly his client has been arrested, so why don't you tell me? Garda asks his name and Peter as usual has to spell it, K for kilo. Catch the split-second pause. Not many Koubeks on the Ailesbury Road are there. So what then: just some cheap little tart after all and her Polish boyfriend. Want to risk it though. Fairly well spoken isn't he, never know these days. Okay, the man says, I'll be back to you. Disappears then behind the greenish glass. Notice on the wall Peter reads about passport renewal. K for kilo. Woman in the raincoat gone already. Minutes elapse.

Clanking of a door somewhere inside now, and he turns, looks down the cool grey corridor. Walking towards him, dark hair piled up glossy on top of her head. Garda beside her. The lovely Naomi. Tear in her black tights, scraped knee, bleeding he can see a little. In her leather jacket, chewing gum. Lips he has how many times kissed. In fondness, frustration, irresistible desire.

Hey, he says.

And she answers: Well, look who it is.

Outside, the sun dazzles through parted clouds, flattening the streets with light. Released without charge, the man said. It's your lucky day. Rage pounding in his blood even thinking. Thirst for violence. Go back inside, rip a chair out of the wall, fuck it into the guy's head. Your lucky day. Jesus, God. Don't think. Anyway she said she just wanted to get out of there. Don't make a scene. It's pointless. What do they care what the law says. That's for a court to decide, later on, years later, after your life has been wrecked already anyway. Find out the eviction was illegal after all. Very comforting. Snapped her chewing gum between her teeth murmuring, don't make a scene. Windshields flashing past now. Cold wind at the same time carrying rain. Together they walk away from the station towards the Bishop Street flats. Canvas bag over her shoulder bulging, sleeve of a sweatshirt hanging out like a pink cotton tongue.

Who told you? she asks. Janine, I bet.

Ignoring the question, pointing down at her knee, he says: How did that happen?

She stops walking and looks. Oh yeah, she says. Security guy tried to drag me up the stairs. Is that legal?

Closes his eyes again briefly at the thought. Is it legal, he repeats. Jesus, I don't know. It's insane. Did he hurt you?

She shrugs. I'm alright, she replies.

Where are all your things?

Looks away from him, down the street. One of those pricks took my phone, she says. I was filming him, it was stupid.

I think Janine has my laptop. She swallows, looking down at the concrete pavement. I have my wallet, she says. And my prescriptions. Some clothes, not everything. They threw a lot of stuff out on the street.

Where are you going to stay tonight? he asks.

She shrugs again. I'll find somewhere, she replies. Rubbing her eye, tired. After a pause: You didn't have to come.

Right. You're welcome.

She makes a face then, looks up at him. Acting the big man, she says. Fuck off.

Despite everything he smiles. Cut of her in her little jacket, telling him to fuck off. You could stay at mine, he says.

She pretends to laugh, averts her eyes. That place, she says. What if your cleaner sees me, would you not be mortified?

I don't have a cleaner.

She really laughs then. Flash of chewing gum white between her teeth. Seriously? she says. I thought you did.

Maybe you're thinking of a different boyfriend.

Looking up at him, chin lifted. Or maybe I don't remember your flat too well, she says. Seeing as you've only invited me back once.

Twice, I think.

No, the second time I actually invited myself.

Holds her gaze a moment longer. Up to you, he says. Sunlight white on the wet road surface. Alright, she replies. Go on. He hails a taxi passing. Get inside together, middle seat between them. Click of her seat belt. Upset, he thinks: that's natural. A year she lived there nearly. And was happy. Time of life at an end. Dragged up the staircase screaming. Feels for her, of course. While impassively she gazes out the window at the traffic. Doesn't want to feel like a charity case, who would. Resents him no doubt for being out of touch. But was she glad at all to see him, he wonders. Or wished it could have been someone else. One of her own friends. Feel more at ease. Coming with him in the taxi out of grim self-preservation maybe: roof over her head, in no position to say no. Dreading the thought of what he'll want to do with her later. Sleep on the couch in that case, figure something out. Someone else after all maybe. Lad in her room the other night. Or that guy online who posts the peach emoji under all her pictures. Peter naturally unable to be thirsty on main, he has a career to think about. Prominent junior barrister faces questions over use of 'smiling devil' and 'droplets' emoji on social media website. Anyway maybe there is no one else, maybe she's just bored of him. She stares out the window, not looking, and he at least declines to pay her the ignominious tribute of looking at her.

Once parked she climbs out and leaves him to settle up. He follows her up the front steps, opens the main door, worried they might run into someone, but they don't. Inside his apartment it's cold and the air is stale. He turns the heating on, goes to the living room window to pull it open, selfconscious, while she waits by the sofa.

You didn't sleep here last night, did you? she says.

He turns to her. Oh, he answers. Yeah, no. The last few nights, I haven't been.

Airily she touches the arm of the sofa, as if expecting dust. Staying with your friend Sylvia, were you? she asks.

Stunned for a moment by his failure to anticipate the question he falls silent. Finally answers: Right.

She stares at him a moment longer. Cool, she says. Very interesting. So are you back together then?

He clears his throat. No, he says.

She laughs: high musical sound. He shuts his eyes briefly and opens them. Why not? she asks. She's not interested?

I don't think her feelings are any of your business.

Raises her eyebrows. Terrible, he thinks: as if to play them off against each other. But what else can he say. His weakness, feeling of loyalty, confused. Defending himself, and worse, more painfully, defending her. Her angry miserable tears, I want you to remember, oh Christ. In an arch tone of voice, sarcastic, Naomi says: Okay . . .

He nods his head. Avoiding her eyes. Do you want to eat something? he asks.

She gets in the shower while he looks around in the kitchen. Milk still usable. Stick of butter in foil, packet of bacon. And in the bread bin, half a stale loaf. Box of eggs. He turns the fan on, heats some butter in a frying pan, beats the eggs with a fork. She sings in the shower usually, but not today. Nice sweet voice too, mezzo soprano. Soft sizzle of the dipped bread on the pan. Whitish foam of frying butter. Wonders what the others will do: find sofas to sleep on. Hostels maybe. Go home, some of them. Not she, of course. Father not in the picture, and the mother's a headcase, drinker, in and out of rehab. Only forty-four. He's heard them on the phone together: Naomi the grown-up, her mother the child. Yeah, I know, but drinking isn't going to make you feel better, Mam. Pain in his chest thinking about it. From the bathroom, the sound of the shower door unsealing: open and then shut again. Something like a sigh he can hear. Spots of bacon fat sticking to the pan. Spitting. Closer to his own age, the mother. Not, but feels that way. In the kitchen doorway Naomi reappears, smaller now in bare feet, adolescent-looking. Old white bathrobe fraying at the cuffs, gold embroidered hotel logo. Peers into the pan, her eyebrows raised. And he can cook, she says. What a catch. He lifts a slice of fried bread on a spatula and slides it onto a clean dinner plate for her. This isn't really cooking, he says. Turns a piece of bacon fried side up, the fat crisped and amber, translucent. Holding the plate expectantly she casts an eye. Is the bacon not for me? she asks. Feels himself again despite everything smiling. It's for you, he says. It's just not done yet. Sweetly she laughs. And coffee?

In the living room they sit at the ugly glass dining table together. With her mouth full, eating, she tells him she needs a new phone. He's peeling an orange onto a small white saucer. I can get you one, he says. She nods her head, swallowing, lifting another forkful to her lips. Cool, she says. Nothing fancy, obviously. Just need to let people know I'm alive. The peel splits and he deposits it onto the saucer, begins peeling again. To see her eating wholesome, relaxing. Wonders what he would have done if he had been there. Not impossible. Lying in bed with her maybe sharing a cigarette when they broke the door down. Tried to drag me up the stairs, is that legal. Tear in her black tights.

I'm sorry I haven't been in touch the last few days, he says.

She's mopping the butter from her plate with a crust of bread. Yeah, she says. Janine told me you stormed off the other night when I was on the phone.

He divides the orange in half, the half into sections. Well, I didn't know where you went, he says. You didn't seem too pleased with me.

I wasn't.

Hands clumsy. Pith yellowing the white of his fingernails. Okay, he says. Look, I suppose I haven't been feeling great lately. Or behaving very well either.

You're upset about your dad, Peter. I get that. But I think you could communicate better. If you want to stop seeing each other, you have to actually say it.

He doesn't look at her. I should have read that letter for you, he says.

That wouldn't have made any difference.

Shrugging he answers without looking up: Still, I could have tried.

I can take care of myself.

He wipes his nose with his fingers, swallowing again, half-smiling. Okay, he says. Next time you're arrested, I'll just let you sort it out, shall I?

She starts laughing. You didn't even do anything, she says. Three hours I was in there screaming my head off. And then you show up in your nice suit waving your dick around, and it's oh yes sir, of course sir, your friend is free to go.

Sheepishly he laughs also, separating a segment from the orange with his fingers. Your lucky day, he says.

She falls silent for a time. He eats a piece of orange, soft pulp in his mouth, and then another. Finally she asks: Does she know about me? Your friend Sylvia.

About you being evicted? Not yet. I'll tell her.

Funny expression on her face when he looks up at her. I meant, about me and you, she says.

What, that we're seeing each other? Of course she knows. It's not a secret.

Pleased now, she looks down into her coffee, trying not to smile. Talk about me a lot, do you? she says.

Chewing and then he swallows, smiling back at her, and says: Complain about you, you mean. All the time.

Gratified, he can see. Thought he was lying about her.

Letting on he was single. Showering afterwards and transferring her some cash. Listen, thanks again. Dinner with Sylvia, sorry I'm late, darling, you know what it's like at work. Feels guilty for letting her imagine. She lifts a hand now to her hair. Can I lie down on your bed? she asks.

Yeah, of course.

Quietly she rises from her seat, empty plate left on the table. Thinking quickly he finds himself. Uncertain. Glancing up at her as she passes him. You want me to come with you? he asks. Touching his sleeve she nods her head without speaking. Dissolving effect on his train of thought, sort of darkening down, and he follows. First night they spent together, he remembers: the way she trembled when he touched her. So young she seemed suddenly and innocent, all her brazen looks and words forgotten. At the foot of the bed now he unties the sash at her waist, lets the robe fall from her shoulders. Pink softness of her smooth full figure, heavy breasts. Her open waiting mouth he kisses. Eyes lowered she says: I really need it. Everything in him aching to give it to her. Animal stupidity of desire. Get on the bed, he says. She lies down and he kneels up, still dressed, looking down at her. Graze stinging pink on her knee he sees where she washed it clean. Sound of her high breathing as if only to be near him. You can do whatever you want with me, she says. Anything you want, you can do. Tracing her cheekbone he smiles at her irresistibly. You're so pretty, he says. His hand between her legs then, and she shuts her eyes. Wet and open her cunt. You can do anything you want, she repeats. And he could, he thinks. Turn her face-down, hurt her a little, make her take it, tell him how it feels. Degrading. Shock her out of thinking about anything else. Afterwards, though, remembering, the door broken down, dragged up the staircase:

distressing probably, and not funny anymore. I know, he says. Like this, alright? And moves with his hands her legs, open, her knees bent. Drawing away then he starts to undress him-self. She waits, watching, glassy her eyes and lips parted. He moves his hand down over her jaw, her throat. Heat of her body under his palm. Gets on top of her and she opens her mouth to be again kissed. Taste of her tongue, her soft passivity, deep. Closing her eyes as if ashamed she says: Just use me, just do whatever you want. You can hurt me, it doesn't matter. Inside her now slowly very deep and tight until she cries out. Soft sinking feeling so peaceful it's like sleep. Contentedly his eyes close and for a moment he rests still. Says nothing, not moving, feeling only the rapid flutter of her breath beneath. In a tight-ened voice she whispers: Is it okay? So docile she always gets and anxious. He smooths her hair back from her cheek. Kisses her lips. It's good, he says, don't worry. When he moves inside her she cries out again. Raw almost wailing sound. Oh God, she says. Thank you. The openness, the receptivity of her body, the flush on her cheeks, her throat. Allowing herself to be used like this, wanting, needing it, and he for a moment has to close again his eyes. That she, trusting, wanting only to please, is letting him, giving herself into his power, to be caressed and played with like a doll. Frightened only of disappointing him. Pleading for reassurance, is it okay. Just use me, you can hurt me, any-thing you want. Her breath shallow and once more he looks at her. Do you like that? he asks. Look of desperate gratitude she turns towards him. What he feels also and can't express. I love it so much, she says. I feel really safe. I don't know. When it's like this, I get this feeling. I feel so safe, I can't explain. All over himself a strange rising intensity like heat looking down at her. To give her that feeling, yes. Naomi, you are safe, he says. Completely, I promise. Everything's going to be okay. For a moment longer just looking at one another. The same desperation they feel, the same terrible gratitude, tender painful vulnerability, depth of pleasure. Gasping contractions of her breath. Peter, she says. Fuck, I'm sorry. He also then. Wet inside her, which she loves. Hears her dazed voice under him mumbling: Oh, it's so nice. Her irrepressible love of life, he thinks. Pulling fried chicken apart with oily fingers. Last sip of soft drink rattling in the straw. Or trying on a new dress, the way her body luxuriates in tactility. Pleasure of her own gorgeousness in the mirror. Deep complete joy she finds in being alive. No job, no family support, no fixed address, no state entitlements, no money to finish college. Owner of nothing in the world but her own perfect body. Men, and even other women, and systems, bureaucracies, laws, intent it seems on breaking her, forcing her to accept misery. And here she is laughing, drinking sugary coffee, begging to be fucked. He loves that in her. Wants to protect her at times even from himself. Her freedom, wild animal that she is. Both finished they lie in silence side by side. He thinks of her staying a while, however long, her underwear drying on the clotheshorse, dishes in the sink. Sees himself cooking dinner while she sits with bare feet on the sofa recording some interminable voice note for her friends. I literally can't believe he even said that. Undressing her for bed at night, kissing fondly her unresisting lips. Far away here from anything that could harm her. Object only of idiotic desire and love.

Was that okay? he asks.

Feeling silly now perhaps she laughs. Yeah, she says. You didn't do anything bad.

Don't sound so disappointed.

Looking sleepy, happy even, she rolls over beside him. He

puts his arm around her. Can you believe they fucking evicted us, she murmurs.

Moving his hand over her back he says: Do you want to stay here for a while?

For a moment she says nothing. Then asks simply: Are you sure it's okay?

Yeah, I'm sure.

Thanks.

In silence they lie together for a time. Sense of them both having dropped a long pretence. Wants almost to say more. Tell her everything, what happened, is still happening, the agony, hatred he wakes up with every morning, wishing he was dead, fear of losing her, both of them. I can't go through it again. I'm sorry. There's someone else. I think it would be better for everyone if I. No need however he thinks to speak. In the quiet of their breath and the slow grey sounds of the passing traffic on the street she touches his hand. To have her here with him enough. Bathed, fed, satisfied, half-asleep. Out of harm's way. I have to teach a class this afternoon, he says. Alright? You can take the spare keys if you want to go out, they're on a hook by the door. She says that's fine. Do you need some cash? he asks. Her eyes closed, no answer. I'll leave some with you, he says. Without looking she answers quietly: Okay. He touches her hair. She lifts her gaze finally to meet his. The feeling however futile and senseless is in its own way mutual. Something understood between them that can't be expressed. Thank you, she says again. He kisses her forehead, salt damp. See you later.

# 7

On Thursday evening, Ivan is waiting for his brother in a dimly lit restaurant. Elsewhere he can see rich people eating expensive meals, and soon his brother will arrive, another rich person basically, and they will eat a meal together also. Why not? Peter, though overly motivated by the acquisition of personal wealth, Ivan thinks, and often obnoxious, and not as smart as he thinks he is, nonetheless has talked sense about a couple of things down the years. At least on a few significant points, in fact, Peter has been right, and Ivan himself has been wrong. On the topic of women, for example, when they used to argue about that, Peter, always a fan, was as it turns out broadly speaking correct, and Ivan mistaken. Just today, or was it yesterday, when that pregnant woman boarded the tram at Smithfield and Ivan got up to offer her his seat, and they smiled at each other and she sat down, saying thank you: this was the kind of thing he would have argued about with Peter in former years, and from the wrong side. It had once seemed to Ivan absolutely no business of his if some total stranger happened to be pregnant. That makes her so important, he thought, just because she's going to have a baby? Isn't the wealthy global north overpopulated already? And how can feminists say they want equality, if what they really want is to be considered biologically more important than men? Feminists, it seemed to Ivan, were campaigning for a world in which men, far from being equal citizens, in fact had to give up their seats on public transport whenever any random woman decided to get pregnant, which happened constantly. That really was his view, at the time, which his brother had never been shy about denouncing and describing as 'fascist' and so on. Later, in college, Ivan came to feel more like: okay, whatever. I'm not that tired, and I guess if the woman is so tired, she can sit down. It's not one hundred percent fair, since it's not as if I made her pregnant, or have ever had the opportunity to do that with literally any woman, but whatever, I'm not going to make a big point out of it. And on the one occasion during his college years when this hypothetical situation arose in reality, he did give up his seat, but not with any great feeling of camaraderie; rather, with a slight feeling of awkwardness and irritation still. Now, today, or actually no, yesterday afternoon, he smiled at the pregnant woman on the tram with a very genuine smile, and she looked up at him with eyes of gratitude, saying: Thank you. Ivan perceived in himself at that moment a completely different attitude towards the whole situation. He no longer felt annoyed or imposed on; rather he was filled with kindly and even tender feelings towards the woman who was pregnant. These feelings seemed, when he thought about it, to be connected with recent developments in his own life: his new understanding of relations between women and men. How certain things can happen, resulting in such situations, even unintentionally, which is something he has always understood on a literal level, but now understands with personal sympathy and compassion for all involved. This particular weakness of women, in regards to their desire for men, strikes him as beautiful, moving, worthy of deep respect and deference. And these are probably the same feelings, really more sentimental than ideological, that have also motivated Peter through the years to care so much supposedly about the oppression of women: because Peter has always at any given time had at least one girlfriend he could imagine in the role of the oppressed. It's easy, Ivan can readily see, to become upset and angry on behalf of a woman who likes going to bed with you. Such a relationship by its nature excites feelings of protectiveness and even a sort of awed reverence on the part of the man towards the woman. But on a number of other points too, Ivan thinks, his brother has long been a person of good sense. On the subject of how to deal with their mother's boyfriend Frank, for instance. Or how to tell a waiter politely that they've brought the wrong food. Ivan has even observed Peter doing this. Looking down at the plate, he will say in a friendly offhanded kind of voice: Ah, I think it was the tortellini for me. He doesn't hesitate before saying it, he just says it right out, completely normal. This is not a skill Ivan urgently needs to cultivate, considering how seldom he frequents restaurants, considering that he has almost literally no money, but he would still like to have this skill in his pocket for the rare occasions on which a waiter brings him the wrong dish, to be able to say nonchalantly: Ah, I think it was the tortellini.

Ivan had planned to spend this week studying opening theory, but instead he has had to devote his time to calling and emailing a small tech start-up, trying to get them to pay an invoice he sent them in July. Hello, he writes in his emails, just sending another reminder about this invoice, sent 08/07. I am still awaiting payment on this. Thanks again. Best, Ivan Koubek. His rent is due in ten days and, for several reasons, not only his own failings, but also the time he had to take off for the funeral and so on, he has no other outstanding income due. He has called the phone number on the company website so many times that by now when he reaches the automated voice message on the other end he actually finds himself mumbling along with the words, like some kind of insane tuneless karaoke, pacing around his tiny box room with the streaming wet window. *You've reached EduFocus One. Thank you for calling. Please leave your name and number and a member of our team will reach out to you.* It's a female voice saying these words, a kind of robotic accentless voice, and then a tone sounds. One important thing Ivan has learned about leaving these messages is not to become aggressive, because he did that once before with a different start-up, not screaming but using an angry tone of voice, and then he got an email saying that protecting the dignity of staff was the organisation's top priority and that he had made the work environment feel unsafe, and then he didn't get paid. Also the email scared him and made him feel like he was going to go to jail. He has, relatedly, been looking for new work during the week too, sending emails, making calls; even, through half-closed eyes with his mouse pointer poised over the red x button, looking at graduate jobs listed online. Trading Technology (Trainee Scheme). Graduate Financial Services Engineer. Junior Software Analyst. These words sort of roll and slide over his consciousness, adhering to nothing, rolling away again as soon as he clicks the x. And his mother this week has been sending the usual guilting text messages about the dog, about Ivan's failure to visit the dog, and implicitly also about

Ivan's failure to visit her, his mother, whom he doesn't want to visit, because she'll ask him about his career, which doesn't exist, and her stepson Darren will probably be there, wearing ugly brand-label clothing and talking about his sailing club. On the bus this morning, Ivan received another such text from his mother, saying: I thought you couldn't bear to be parted from this creature? And attached to the message was a picture of his dog Alexei looking mournfully up at the camera, his thin face pointed down but with eyes upturned in melancholy. Sitting on the crowded morning bus in his jacket, the air too warm and humid with other people's breath, his shoulder pressed against the shoulder of the person beside him, Ivan felt bad about his dog, and missed him, and started to think he really should visit, even all the way out in Skerries, in his mother's boyfriend's house, with the photographs of boats on the mantelpiece. He remembered then about the unpaid invoice, about the rent due at the end of next week, the graduate jobs he had seen listed on the website, the opening theory he hadn't studied, the eulogy he hadn't given at his father's funeral, and then, before his thoughts could sink down any more deeply into debilitating dark regret and misery, he thought about Margaret. For each of the last two weekends he has been with her, and this weekend he's going to be with her again. And bringing this to mind on the bus, he closed his eyes just briefly and felt the proximity of that approaching peace and restfulness, a sense that he was even now proceeding there, that time was moving ahead in that direction, towards the weekend, when he could be near her, and he thought about all the things he wanted to ask her about herself. What kind of books she likes to read, was she popular at school, does she like her sister better or her brother, does she believe in God, did she have a lot of boyfriends before she got married or only a few. Some of these questions he could ask her over dinner, and some he could ask her in bed, holding her in his arms, kissing her intermittently on the mouth. Of course, whether or not there is a beautiful woman in his life who enjoys being kissed by him, he still has to pay rent: he accepts this. Nonetheless, it is better to feel hopeful and optimistic about one's life on earth while engaged in the never-ending struggle to pay rent, than to feel despondent and depressed while engaged in the same non-optional struggle anyway.

Now, from behind a curtain near the restaurant entrance, Peter appears in person, seven minutes late, wearing a long navy-coloured overcoat. In his hands he's carrying a briefcase, and also a rolled-up umbrella and a folded copy of a newspaper, as a server shows him to Ivan's table. Hello, says Peter. Hey, says Ivan. The server goes away again and Peter takes off his coat and puts away the items he has been carrying, pretty much effortlessly, like he doesn't have to think for even a few seconds about where all these various objects will go. Then he sits down opposite Ivan at the table, smiling to himself.

What? says Ivan.

Nothing, says Peter. Am I late, or you're early?

Ivan says he's early. Peter checks his wristwatch, a heavy-looking gold-rimmed watch face with a leather strap, and remarks: That's nice of you, but I'm also a little bit late. Looking up then, he asks: How was your weekend?

It was fine, says Ivan. How was yours?

Peter fills their water glasses from the carafe. Same as usual, he says. You were back in Leitrim again?

Right, Ivan says.

You're seeing someone over there.

In response to this remark, Ivan feels himself draw in a cautious breath between his teeth. Well, he says, yeah, kind of.

With a pleasant, interested expression, Peter looks at him. Kind of? he says.

I mean, yeah, we do see each other. But that's not to put labels on it.

In a smiling voice, Peter says: I see. Keeping things casual.

This could be interpreted as mocking, Ivan thinks, but from the tone he doesn't believe it's meant that way. Thinking it over, he swallows a mouthful of ice water from his glass. Then he says: It's more just, that it's still early times. But no, it's, uh— He breaks off here, not having prepared in advance any phrase with which to close this sentence, and not finding now any appropriate one to hand. Embarrassed, he smiles, and says nothing else.

Peter has meanwhile started examining the menu politely, as if not to make a big point of the fact that Ivan just randomly stopped talking mid-sentence, which Ivan can acknowledge is basically kind of nice of him. Without looking up, Peter says: A fellow chess enthusiast?

Sorry? says Ivan.

Your friend in Leitrim, does she play chess?

Oh, I get you. No, she doesn't.

At this Peter looks up from the menu with a curious, still pleasant, but noticeably different expression. Oh, he says. So the two of you met . . . ?

We met at the exhibition game, yeah, says Ivan. But she wasn't there watching, she works at the arts centre. Where it was on.

How interesting.

Ivan now also picks up the menu and looks at it, although he already had plenty of time to decide what to eat before Peter arrived, and in fact he had already decided before then by looking at the restaurant website. Yeah, I like her a lot, he says.

That's nice, Peter answers. I'm happy for you.

The server returns then to take their orders, starters as well as main courses, and Peter talks Ivan into sharing a bottle of white wine, and then the server goes away again, taking the menus with her. Ivan knew in advance that Peter would want to know what the situation was with Margaret, and he had even felt some anxiety about how the discussion would unfold, what Peter might imply or say about Ivan or about the relationship, but now that this section of the conversation has concluded, he actually feels it went well. Peter was courteous and tactful, he thinks; and he himself was okay, a little awkward, but fine, not a complete embarrassment. Practically flush with the success of this exchange, he asks Peter how work is going, and they are still talking about Peter's work when the starters arrive. Peter has ordered some kind of bruschetta dish, while Ivan has ordered French onion soup. They both begin eating, and the soup is so hot and rich and flavourful that Ivan feels his mouth watering even as he eats, remembering how hungry he is, the two plain slices of white bread he ate for lunch, his face growing damp now in the steam rising appetisingly from the soup bowl. It's not everything I thought it might be, Peter is saying. But at least I'm keeping busy. You know, you come in with all these high ideals, it's the same for everyone. Actually, let me correct myself, it's not like that at all for most of them. The majority of these people don't have any ideals in the first place. But even if you do, to finish my point, you still have to take the work you can get.

Ivan wipes his mouth thoughtfully with the cloth napkin and puts it back down in his lap again. Do you have ideals? he asks. Peter looks at him across the table with such a funny expression – hurt, and at the same time baffled and kind of alarmed – that Ivan immediately adds: I mean, sorry, I'm sure you do.

I do, Peter says, yes.

Right, right. But such as, for example?

Peter still looks puzzled. What do you mean? he asks.

Ivan can feel himself communicating poorly, and in order to smooth over the situation, he tries to smile. Like, what would be one of your ideals? he says. You don't have to say, I'm just interested.

In a gentle tone of voice now, Peter answers: It's a figure of speech, Ivan. To have ideals, it just means to be motivated by something other than your own self-interest. Of course, speaking personally, I would like to live in a more equitable society. And I do get quite a bit of work in that area. Equality, employment rights. But for the moment, as I was saying, my professional life still has to revolve around making money.

No, I get you. A more equitable society. It's interesting. I agree, I'd like to live in one as well.

Peter sips his wine and puts the glass down. I suppose more or less everyone would like to, in theory, he says. Are you thinking about a future career?

Yeah. Thinking of becoming an eco-terrorist.

Peter glances up and, perceptibly seeing in Ivan's face that he's joking, smiles. I respect it, he says. Give me a call when you need a lawyer.

In Ivan's mouth, the wine has a cold, enjoyably acidic taste. Honestly, he says, the big obstacle would be that I'm a coward.

Peter laughs so genuinely and spontaneously at this remark

that he has to cover his mouth, which is full of food. Coughing a little, and then swallowing, he says humorously: Ah, and I thought we had nothing in common.

Ivan feels consciously pleased at making him laugh. What do you mean, you're a coward as well? he says. I wouldn't have thought that.

Wouldn't you?

Well, the way you go into court and give your arguments to the judge. I think if you were cowardly you wouldn't want to do that.

Peter appears to think about this, and answers: Not if you were good at it. No. It's easy to do things you're already good at, that's not courageous. Trying to do something you might not be capable of doing– He breaks off here, apparently thinking again, chewing a crust of bread. We're being hard on ourselves in a way, he remarks, because both our lives involve some voluntary exposure to what other people might call defeat. Which I think requires a certain degree of courage. Even if just psychologically.

Ivan listens, letting the wine get warm in his mouth before swallowing. You mean like when I lose at chess, he says.

A lot of people probably wouldn't be able to cope with it the way you can.

I don't know. I don't think I cope with it all too well. It bothers me a lot to lose.

It bothers me a lot too, says Peter.

Ivan looks at him across the table. Yeah? he says. I wouldn't have thought that either. Like when you lose at a court case, it bothers you?

Peter nods his head, looking down at his plate, moving his cutlery around. Absolutely, he says. I find it very aggravating.

No way. It's funny. I don't remember you getting too annoyed when you would lose at debating.

He glances up with a kindly smile. I didn't lose very often, he says.

Yeah, true. At the time it made me feel like debating must be kind of fake, compared to chess. How you would win all the time and never lose.

Well, there just wasn't anyone good enough to beat us.

Ivan considers this, and then answers: I wanted my life to be like that.

Me too, says Peter.

They go on eating their food for a time in silence. Ivan feels he is learning something interesting from this discussion, although he can't say what exactly. Of course, he and his brother both wanted their lives to consist of winning all the time and never losing: this is presumably true of everyone. No one ever wants to lose. And yet for both Peter and Ivan, this particular feeling has perhaps been more important, more intense than for other people: the desire to win all the time, and also the naive youthful belief that it would be possible to live such a life, now soured by experience. There seems to have been in both their lives a period of exuberant repeated triumph, for Ivan his final years at secondary school, for Peter his time at college, which in both cases came to a disheartening close. After leaving school, Ivan struggled to focus on his chess, and his dad got sick, and everything started to get extremely depressing. What happened to Peter after he graduated from university is less clear to Ivan, but there certainly was a turn in his life, even in his personality, which happened around the time of Sylvia's accident. It's something Ivan doesn't understand too well, since he was just a child at the time. Or like sixteen, but close enough to childhood still. It seems to say something about Peter that when Ivan actually was a child, the two of them were good friends, but when Ivan became a thinking person with his own individuality, Peter didn't like him or want to spend time with him anymore. And what it says, Ivan thinks, is that Peter likes people he can dominate and feel superior to, and he's not such a great fan of people who talk back to him and disagree. Once Ivan got to the age of sixteen, seventeen, that's when he and Peter started getting into arguments, fights even, about politics, history, whatever, pregnant women on public transport, and Peter would call Ivan all kinds of names, a misogynist, a loser. That was sad, because they really had been friends before. If Peter and Sylvia had stayed together, Ivan thinks, everything would have been different, because she had a good effect on him. It was after they broke up that things changed. But this thought is obscure and confusing, since it's not like Sylvia went out of Peter's life, they're still best friends, and it's something Ivan doesn't know a lot about or understand. Peter is refilling their glasses now, and the server is bringing their main courses to the table. Ivan has ordered the salmon: a glistening pink fillet topped with delicate dissolving flakes of salt, surrounded by buttered green peas and asparagus and baby potatoes.

That looks good, Peter says.

Ivan, submerged in a pleasant warm vaguely confused feeling induced by the conversation, the ambience, the food and wine, his own thoughts, agrees that it looks good. It's a really nice place, he adds. I've never been here before. This, he thinks, sounds like something a person who habitually goes to restaurants would say. In his mouth, the salmon melts hot into an abstraction of flavour: salt savoury fish and the bright sparkling taste of lemon juice, melting together on the palate. It is extremely flavourful, Ivan thinks, extremely good to eat. Peter asks him if he's been back to their father's house since the funeral, and Ivan says no. For a while they talk about the house, which now belongs legally to their mother, because it was purchased jointly and their father never bought out her share. Christine has not yet revealed whether she intends to sell the property, and neither Peter nor Ivan can be bothered to ask her about it anymore, since, they both agree, she actually seems to enjoy keeping them in suspense. Personally I don't care what she does, Peter says. But maybe you'd prefer her not to sell. Ivan, after a pause, says it's hard to know, because it would be sad never to be able to go back to the house again, but he also doesn't like to think of it sitting empty and no one living there. An expression crosses over Peter's face, a difficult expression to describe, and then immediately it's gone again, and he answers: I know what you mean. I suppose with the transport situation, it wouldn't be practical for either of us to live there. Ivan agrees it would be impractical, and Peter after a pause asks: You're still living out in Ringsend, aren't you? Ivan says yes, for the moment.

And you're working? Peter asks.

Well, yeah, freelance, Ivan says. Data analysis. Only part-time.

But you're getting by okay.

Ivan chews a mouthful of his food, thinking, and then swallows. Mostly, he says. At the moment it's tricky, because I didn't get a lot of work done in August or September. With the funeral, and all that.

Right, Peter says. When you say tricky, you mean . . . ?

Ivan pauses again, and then answers carefully: I'm just waiting to get paid. And my rent is due next week. You know, if everyone would pay me on time, I wouldn't have a problem.

When he glances up, Peter is nodding his head, using his knife to construct an intricate forkful of pasta. Well, listen, he says, if it gets to next week and you don't have the money, just call me. Alright? I'd be happy to help, it's no big deal.

For a moment Ivan says nothing, watching his brother eat. Then he says: Cool. That's really nice of you, thanks. After a pause, he adds: Hopefully I'll get the money before then. But if I did have to borrow, I would pay you back, obviously.

Sure, I know. But no rush.

With a strange feeling, Ivan goes on eating, unable to think of anything to say. The idea of borrowing money from Peter has never occurred to him before: maybe because Peter's aura of wealth has always seemed more like a personality trait than a transferable item of property. Asking to borrow his money would have been like asking to borrow his sense of humour: it wouldn't even have made sense as a request. Ivan can see now, however, that Peter's money is not a personal characteristic, but literally just money. And although Ivan would still prefer not to have to do it, he has to acknowledge that it's soothing to his nerves, knowing that he can pay his rent next week no matter what happens, and he doesn't have to worry about it every minute. He feels touched by Peter's generosity: and even more so by his pretence of being offhanded about his own generosity, like it's no big deal, a pretence which serves only to make the situation less awkward for Ivan. He's trying to be nice, obviously. The whole thing, taking Ivan out for dinner, being tactful, making sure he's not in need of money: this is Peter's way of trying to be a nice person, a good brother. Ivan finds this so touching that it's actually sad, a sadness that seems to be related fundamentally to his brother's personality. It reminds him of Sylvia again, of her role in Peter's life. Like when their dad was in the hospital, and she would come and sit by the bed, doing newspaper puzzles: crosswords, letter wheels, sometimes even the chess problems. Peter himself did not have much patience to sit at their father's bedside. He liked to be up and about, visiting the vending machine, making phone calls, trying to get information from the doctors. Filling out the insurance forms, things like that. He was not someone to hang around reading slowly through smudged newsprint. Incline, four letters. R something something P. That was more for Sylvia and Ivan, who would sit on the uncomfortable chairs together looking over the back pages of the paper until his father felt tired enough to sleep. All three had their parts to play, however. The insurance paperwork was also important, and from the vending machines Peter would bring back some little snacks for Ivan and Sylvia, cups of coffee, a Twix bar, and fresh water for their dad. It wasn't like Peter was off somewhere else, having fun, letting Ivan handle everything alone. But you felt at the same time his need of Sylvia, as if he relied on her to supply certain things that went beyond him. It's all connected somehow, Ivan thinks: even right now, the dinner they're eating together, Peter trying so hard to be nice to him, it goes back to a certain sadness, a certain deficiency in Peter's personality. After the funeral last month, Ivan remembers, Sylvia stayed over with Peter, in his room. Is that why he has invited Ivan out for dinner, talked him into sharing a bottle of wine, offered to lend him money, and so forth? The server comes back with the dessert menus now, and when she's gone again Peter pours the last of the wine into Ivan's glass. Watching him across the table, thinking, feeling something almost like a gathering of courage inside himself, Ivan says aloud: So, what's going on with you?

Peter puts the empty bottle back in the cooler. What do you mean? he asks.

I don't know. Like, you're seeing anyone, or?

Looking over at him, Peter raises his eyebrows. Ah, he says. Well, it's like you were saying before. It's not always a straightforward question.

Ivan pauses, and then ventures: You're not back together with . . .

Peter waits a moment for Ivan to complete the sentence, and when he doesn't, he says simply: With Sylvia, you mean.

Right.

You can say her name, you know. It's allowed.

Ivan nods his head, knowing that the conversation has become different now, and more serious, and he has to try to find the correct words. Yeah, you're right, he says. I guess I just didn't want to be intrusive.

No, that's okay. It's not intrusive. I hope you know she really cares about you.

I do know that, Ivan says. It's the same for me, I care about her. After a brief pause he adds: I actually miss seeing her.

Peter looks down at the menu, even though he doesn't seem to be reading it. Sure, he says. I think she feels that way about you too. He seems to swallow, and then looking up he adds: She says we're starting to look alike. You and me.

Ivan finds himself laughing then, feeling a little drunk. Oh, he says. That's funny. I don't think that.

Well, I don't have your youthful charm, obviously, Peter says. But I don't think she meant you any offence. He turns around the dessert menu to look at the list of hot drinks and spirits. Sylvia's very important to me, he remarks. You know, she's a big part of my life, she always will be. But it's been a long time since we broke up, and now I suppose we both have other things going on. It's difficult. There are a lot of feelings there. I mean, to speak honestly, I still love her. Very much, yeah. But it's complicated.

Ivan is nodding his head. He senses that, for the first time in his life, Peter is speaking to him as an equal, someone who understands the complexities of life and intimate relationships: which, he thinks, is exactly what he is, someone who has come to understand those complexities for himself. There are a lot of feelings there, Peter said, and Ivan knows exactly what he means. With Margaret, when she cried, and he was holding her: there were a lot of feelings then, too many. To think of his brother and Sylvia in a similar situation strikes Ivan as strange and sad, although why it should be so sad he doesn't know exactly. He wants strongly to communicate all this somehow, how much he understands, how similar he feels in a way their circumstances are, and looking down at his own menu, almost unconsciously affecting the same offhanded manner as Peter, he says: I get you. With the woman I'm seeing, she has this ex-husband who she's separated from. So that makes things kind of complicated, as well.

After a moment, though he himself is still looking at the menu, Ivan can perceive that Peter is staring at him: another strange feeling. Looking up, he confirms that indeed his brother is staring, with a vague frown on his face.

I'm sorry, she has what? Peter says.

Feeling less confident of himself now, and wondering whether in fact he might be drunk, Ivan repeats uncertainly: She's separated from her husband.

Peter, still staring at him, says in an oddly quiet voice: What age is she?

Ivan senses himself swallowing. Thirty-six, he says.

Peter just nods his head neutrally for a few seconds. Still speaking quietly, he asks: Does she have children?

No.

Peter rubs his eyes with his fingers, looking tired now and depressed. Slowly he says: Don't take this the wrong way, Ivan. But the woman is nearly forty. She's been married already. You're twenty-two, you're hardly out of college, you don't even have a job. I'm not trying to be disparaging, but do you think a normal woman of her age would want to hang around with someone in your situation?

A prickling Ivan senses at the back of his neck, and also under his arms, prickling in his blood. What are you saying? he says. She's not normal?

I'm raising the question.

You don't know her.

For that matter, neither do you, says Peter. You've met her what, twice?

With a hot kind of trembling feeling all over his body, Ivan pushes his chair back from the table and rises to his feet. Fuck you, he says.

Peter sits there with a weary smile on his face, saying: Can we be civilised, please?

In a deliberately quiet almost hissing voice Ivan says: I actually hate you. I've hated you my entire life.

Without stirring, without looking around to see whether the other diners or the staff are watching them, Peter just answers: I know.

Outside in the night air, Ivan walks with long brisk strides, stepping into the street when he has to avoid oncoming pedestrians. He can feel his back teeth grinding against each other, can even hear the horrible grinding sound in his ears. Do you think a normal woman, Peter said, as if the idea were laughable. But Margaret is, whatever Peter might think or say, in fact a normal woman. Even if she weren't, it wouldn't matter to Ivan, since unlike his brother he doesn't assign an idiotically high, practically moral degree of value to the concept of normality, which phrased in another way means conformity with the dominant culture. But it so happens that Margaret is what Peter would consider normal: intelligent, cultured, at ease in social situations. What kind of abnormality was Peter even hinting at? That she might not be mentally all there? Or she's just using Ivan to get back at her ex-husband or something. Whatever. She's actually not like that at all. Gradually, making his way more slowly among the voices and bodies of other people, Ivan feels the heat in his face begin to dissipate, absorbed as thermal energy by the surrounding atmosphere. The extreme ferocious anger that provoked him to leave the restaurant so suddenly is now subsiding, he can sense, and the overwhelming intensity of bad feeling that remains inside him is not really anger anymore, but something else. He is beginning to feel that it was not a good idea – that it was, on the contrary, a shockingly awful idea – to tell Peter about Margaret's age and marital status in that way. Firstly, he can see that he never should have trusted Peter with that information to begin with. But secondly, if he were going to make that mistake, he should have taken pains to introduce the information in a careful and appropriate manner. He can see that now. It's so obvious. Margaret herself just the other day expressed anxiety about what Peter would think of her if he knew, because she understands that the situation might appear unusual and be open to misinterpretation. In saying what he said to Peter – not only the literal words, but the careless tone, the lack of forethought – Ivan realises that he has done something Margaret would not have wanted him to do. He has in fact brought about, of his own volition, the precise situation she was worried about, vis-à-vis his family and what they would think of her. Peter now actually does think badly of her, just as she feared he would, and it's all because of Ivan. This thought strikes him with such a forceful blow that he stops walking and stands still in the street, staring down at the wet cracked paving in an abyss of extreme despair and mortification. Can it be corrected, he wonders. Would it be possible, for example, for Ivan to contact Peter and somehow rectify the misunderstanding between them regarding Margaret's personality and moral character. But no, he thinks: not really. Because everything Ivan said at dinner was true, and Peter's judgement of Margaret, while incorrect, is based on correct information, and it's difficult to see what further mitigating information could reasonably be supplied to Peter to change his mind. At that, Ivan has to acknowledge, with distinct discomfort, that Margaret's marriage is not something about which he himself is immensely well informed. He does not actually know, for instance, what her ex-husband's name is, what he does for a living, how long they were married or why their relationship came to an end. Margaret has not to any meaningful degree, despite his confiding tone over dinner just now, opened up to Ivan on the subject. Do you think a normal woman, Peter said, and the memory of this remark instantly renews in Ivan a sufficient degree of anger to jolt him into resuming his walk. Just because he, Ivan, behaved stupidly and said things he shouldn't have, that doesn't mean that he, Peter, was justified in reacting the way he did. He could have shown some open-mindedness and sensitivity instead of leaping to condemnation and ridicule. Fundamentally Peter is a bad person, Ivan thinks, and Ivan's own life would be in no sense worse and arguably a lot better if he never had to see or speak to him ever again. From now on, he will block his brother's number from his phone and refuse to acknowledge him if they ever pass one another on the street. These thoughts, the image for instance of blanking Peter in public, embarrassing and offending him, can however only temporarily distract Ivan from the much more painful contemplation of his own remorse. Trying to be perceived as grown-up and sophisticated by a patronising older sibling, he has behaved stupidly, and worse than stupidly, he has betrayed the confidence and trust of a woman he likes very much and who might even like him. What could be worse than that? His resolution never to see his brother again is, he thinks, a paltry solace for the consciousness of his own wrong. As he makes his way across the canal, it begins to rain, at first faintly, and then more heavily. Bareheaded under the open sky he continues his walk – hair flattened to his head, dripping cold rainwater into his eyes – hating his brother, hating himself, and feeling extremely sorry.

# 8

On Saturday afternoon, Margaret finds herself once again sitting by Ivan's side, driving to the coast. They have been in the car for an hour already, and in the distance now, under the low grey sky, the sea forms a shifting slate-blue line on the horizon. When she collected him from the bus station last night, Ivan seemed withdrawn, and in the car he didn't speak much. At the cottage she asked him if everything was alright and he quickly answered: Yeah, I'm sorry. I'm very happy to see you, believe me. They were taking their coats and shoes off in the hall. Do you know the expression 'a sight for sore eyes'? he asked. Smiling, amused, she said yes. Well, that's you, he replied. Folding her gloves up into her handbag she asked why his eyes were, metaphorically speaking, sore, and after a pause he said: Different reasons. Nothing big. He was still unlacing his sneakers. Thank you for collecting me again, by the way, he said. I'm sorry to ask. I could have got a taxi, but I guess with the town being so small, the driver might know your house. She found herself surprised by the remark, by what it conveyed about his awareness of her situation, and for a moment said nothing. Finally she just said: There is that, I suppose. He left his shoes side by side on the shoe rack, neatly. It's cool, he said. If you don't mind collecting me, I mean. I'm grateful. She said it was no problem. He straightened up to his full height then and kissed her on the lips. The overhead light was switched on, bright and buttery yellow. She looked up at him, his clear almost lustrous skin, his long dark eyelashes, and before she could say anything he had touched his hands to her hips and kissed her again, tenderly. A sight for sore eyes, he repeated. I know it's a cliché. But it's so relevant to the situation, you have no idea. Now he sits quietly at her side, looking through the CDs in her glovebox, while she navigates the familiar bends of the coast road.

Have you ever had a dog? he asks.

Actually no, she answers. Although I like them. Did you have one growing up?

He clicks the glovebox shut and sits back in his seat, rubbing his jaw. Yeah, I still do, he says. Well, it's tricky. Because he lived with my dad before. And you know when you're renting, landlords can be pretty strict about pets, so I can't take him to live with me. My mother is looking after him right now, but she's not a great fan of dogs. Actually she hates them. So it's not a permanent thing. I'm just having a lot of trouble figuring out where he can go.

Margaret glances over at him, and then returns her attention to the road. Oh, I'm sorry, she says. I didn't know that. That sounds like a tricky situation.

I know. You'd really think the whole thing would be easier.

Like there would be a service where you could give your dog into care for a short time. I don't think there is, though. Unless you know of one.

She says she doesn't think so, but she'll ask around. Turning off the main road and down a gravelled lane towards the shore, she says: What kind of dog is it?

He's a whippet, Ivan replies. Like a smaller greyhound. I can show you a picture, if you want.

Please do.

He takes out his phone and starts scrolling, while she parks the car in the small flat gravel area overlooking the beach. Here, Ivan says. She looks down at his screen now to see a photograph of a slender black dog in a sunlit garden, its posture upright and graceful, eyes large and liquid dark.

Oh wow, Margaret says. How elegant.

Looking down at the picture, Ivan agrees sadly: He actually is really elegant. Yeah, I miss him a lot. With his finger and thumb he zooms in on the dog's face, a long narrow face with a white crest between the eyes. His name is Alexei, Ivan adds. He can give the paw and everything, I taught him that. And he doesn't even bark, he's silent. Maybe if he's really excited he gives one or two little barks, but that's it.

Margaret watches Ivan looking at the photograph. Does he like to run? she asks.

He smiles down at the screen. Oh yeah, he says. You should see him. Let me get a video, I'll show you. Returning to the photo library, Ivan starts scrolling again, while Margaret takes the keys from the ignition and finds her sunglasses in her pocket, although the day is overcast. Look at this, he says. He taps the play button. On screen, apparently in the same garden from the photograph, the dog is poised on all fours, his ears pricked up, watching something off-camera. The sun is shining, and the grass in the garden is vividly green, the sky blue overhead. In the background of the video, she can hear Ivan's voice saying: Okay, you can go. Then, from off-screen, a tennis ball appears in the air, making a long bending parabola over the garden. In one movement, the dog takes off in pursuit, his powerful body compressing and then flashing out full-length, soaring, hardly touching the earth.

Laughing, Margaret says: He's so fast, oh my God.

With the tennis ball in his jaws, the dog races back across the grass, and the camera moves briefly to show a bearded man in a grey cardigan bending down to pet the dog's head. The footage comes to an end then, the last frame frozen on screen. Oh, Ivan says. That's my dad, actually. By the way. I forgot he was in the video. Margaret, unthinking, reaches to touch Ivan's arm. It's okay, he says. It's nice. He really loves Alexei, as you can see. No, it's nice, it's a happy memory. Ivan goes on looking down at the screen. Anyway, I really need to figure out what to do, he says. My mother is talking about giving the dog away. If she would really do that, I don't know, it seems extreme. But she definitely wants him out of her house.

Could your brother look after him for a while? Margaret asks.

Ivan takes such a long time to answer this question that she wonders whether he has heard her. He goes on staring down at the screen of his phone, half-darkened now, still showing the faint image of his father with the dog. Then he answers: No.

Ah, she says. He's renting as well, I suppose.

Again, this question triggers a long silence. She watches Ivan, who is still gazing impassively down at his phone, running his tongue over his braces. Finally he locks the screen and pockets the device, answering: Right. Nothing further appears to be forthcoming, and after a few more seconds of quiet they get out of the car. The cold northerly sea wind blows Margaret's hair back over her face as she swings the door closed. She takes her straw bag from the boot and together they walk towards the steep stone staircase leading down to the shoreline. It's really beautiful here, Ivan remarks. They make their way down the steps together now, the worn stone treads crusted with sand and dried pieces of seaweed. Without turning around, he asks: What do you think, is it too cold to swim?

Watching the back of his head as he walks ahead of her, she answers: I don't mind. I'm used to it. You decide.

I don't mind either, he says. We can try, if you want.

Taking an elastic tie from her wrist she wraps her hair behind her head to keep it off her face. Ah, she says. Very brave.

Hand on the iron stair rail, he turns now to look back at her. Why, because it's cold? he asks. I don't mind that. But it's not dangerous, is it?

Are you scared?

Shyly he smiles now. Not for myself, he says.

Smiling back at him she replies: Don't worry, it's not dangerous.

Down on the empty shore the cliffs stand tall and sheer around them, and the wind whistles, the sea beats down on the flat reflective sand. Not afraid for himself, he said: as if to say, without saying it, that he was afraid for her. Some sort of masculine protective instinct, she thinks; foolish, of course, but then men and women are foolish about each other. The tender chivalry he seems to feel towards her: it gives her a strange sensation to think about that. Maybe he doesn't need to know about her life, she thinks. And if he wants to tell her about his life, she's happy to listen. Is that so wrong? To spend a little time together, liking one another, even very much, and nothing more. Over the rocks at the end of the beach, saltwater crashes with a hissing fracturing sound, and sea spray rises glittering against the grey sky, droplets suspended trembling in the air before they fall. Are we going to try our luck? she asks. Ivan answers: Yeah, okay. Let's do it. Is there somewhere I can change? Or maybe, if there's no one here, I don't know. Rooting in her bag she takes out an old green beach towel, handing it to him, and he thanks her. Under a smaller pink towel she changes herself, with some difficulty, tugging the glossy synthetic swimsuit up her legs and over her shoulders with one hand, holding the towel wrapped around her in the other. Discreetly they each avoid watching the other. If it's too cold, we'll just come back, she says. We don't want to get hypothermia. With a nervous laugh, putting his folded clothes into his backpack, Ivan agrees they don't want to get that.

Smiling with effort into the hard wind, they walk together down to the water's edge. Under her bare feet Margaret feels the cruel thin cold of the water and closes her eyes as the sensation crawls up over her toes and ankles. Her teeth start chattering. Don't go too quickly, she says. Let yourself acclimatise. Beside her Ivan mutters: Oh God. Moving further into the water, the cold becomes perceptible in her nerve endings only as a penetrating shock, bordering on pain. Slowly she continues up to her thighs, her hips, and she's swallowing, stuttering involuntarily aloud. Fuck, says Ivan beside her. Opening her eyes she sees the dark fragmented sea surface grey-green and the sky above grey-white. At her breasts now the water forms a line pure and piercing. Breath gasps hard in and out of her throat. If it's too much, we can go back, she repeats. Behind her, Ivan says: No, I'm okay. Are you? She says yes. Up to her shoulders, the delicate skin of her throat, her chin. Closing her eyes, she immerses her face and head. Seeing nothing, hearing only the gigantic noise of the sea pounding her eardrums, she feels all over her body now an almost unendurable assault of cold. Stiff, uncoordinated, she tries to move her limbs, forcing her blood to circulate. Her eyes screwed shut underwater, something brushes against her: slick, like the cold smooth hide of a seal, Ivan's body. She raises her face to the air again, breath heaving, and opens her eyes. His lips pale, his skin white and pearlescent wet, shoulders above the line of the water, teeth chattering. She can hear in the bones of her skull the sound of her own teeth also. Out of sight and weightless her arm floats itself to him, tips of her fingers she feels at his navel. Are you okay? she asks. He nods his head, swallowing, dark eyelashes dripping. Do you want to try swimming? she says. With effort they both swim a few strokes, parallel to the shore, hardly breathing it seems, everything grey and lapping up over them, crashing down. For a time, under the water, she experiences a numb kind of radiating pleasant sensation, but breaking the surface for even a moment lets in a new rush of bitter abrading cold. Salt stinging in her sinuses, limbs aching, eyes and nose scalded, running over. Finally, she raises her head to call out: Okay, enough for me. Ivan, beside her, nods again without speaking.

Wading back slowly to the shore, lifting her stiff waterlogged limbs, Margaret feels immensely heavy and ancient, numb, exhausted: solid artefact dredged wet from the sea floor. Following after her, Ivan says nothing. As they reach their belongings, she hears how heavily they are both breathing, how loud the noise of their breathing even over the sound of the sea. She hands him the same green towel from her bag. His face is no longer white, but flushed pink and healthy-looking, his lips parted, panting. They dry themselves roughly, quickly, peeling off underneath the towels their wet swimsuits, tender damp skin exposed again to the hard wind, and then dress once more with what gorgeous relief in their dry warm clothes. An old plastic bag she unfolds for their wet things, puts hers inside, and offers it to Ivan. After adding his own, he looks down at the wet black tangle of their swimsuits together inside, still breathing very hard, she can hear. Are you alright? she says. He nods again. That was fun, he says. Or actually it was horrible, but now I feel great. She smiles, towelling her hair. Right, she says. Same for me. He's nodding his head still, looking at her, his face pink cold almost sunburned-looking. Yeah, you're amazing, he says. You're honestly the most amazing person I've ever met. Can I kiss you? It's okay if you prefer not, since it's kind of in public. Although I don't think anyone else is here. Holding the towel in one hand she finds herself saying: That's alright. I don't mind. Touching her with his hands, drawing her close to him, he kisses her lips. Why with him is it like this, she wonders. The touch of his hands to her body, his voice when he speaks, his particular looks and gestures. Parting her lips she tastes the salt wet of his tongue. Feels his hand in her hair. The miracle of existing completely together in this way for even one moment on God's earth, she thinks. If never again in her life another, only to be here now, with him. Drawing away from her, he says politely: Thank you. Touching her lips she answers: Oh, well, thank you. I must say, I don't want to embarrass you, Ivan, but you kiss very nicely. I don't know if I've ever enjoyed being kissed so much in my life. He starts laughing his kind of goofy laugh, looking down at the ground. I'm happy, he says. Me neither. Although, the first time we kissed, I was really nervous. What with the braces and everything. I was scared you wouldn't like it. They start to walk back up the stone staircase together, Margaret buttoning her jacket. Well, I did, she says. Gallantly he takes her straw bag and puts it over his shoulder. Yeah, that gave me confidence, he answers. I remember that. It was special. The way we were talking about our lives at first, and then when we kissed, the way you liked it. He breaks off here to laugh again. I'm being really embarrassing, he says. I'm sorry. I think the cold water made me kind of delirious, can that happen? She says she feels that way too, a little. Retying her hair more securely behind her head, she asks if he would like to get dinner somewhere before they go home. For a moment he looks at her in his quiet observing way, and then he answers: Yeah. I would like that a lot.

On the way back, they stop at an old country hotel in Knocknagarry. Margaret doesn't think anyone will see them, it's too unlikely, there's no use being paranoid. And indeed, when they enter, the dining room is almost empty: a young family near the entrance, an elderly couple by the closed piano. Margaret and Ivan are shown to a small table, set with white linen, heavy silverware, a lighted wax candle. In her exhausted satisfaction after swimming, she smiles at him without speaking, and he smiles back. They order, the waitress brings their food, and they eat. When Margaret rests her arm on the tabletop, Ivan reaches over and touches the back of her hand lightly with his fingertips. No one else takes any notice, the staff, the elderly couple, the young family with their noisy children, and why should they. Margaret is reminded of the way she felt when she first met Ivan: as if life had slipped free of its netting. As if the netting itself had all along been an illusion, nothing real. An idea, which could not contain or describe the borderless all-enveloping reality of life. Now, in her satisfied exhaustion, with her hand resting on the white linen tablecloth, the touch of Ivan's fingertips, the candle dripping a slow thread of wax down its side, the glossy closed lid of the piano, Margaret feels that she can perceive the miraculous beauty of life itself, lived only once and then gone forever, the bloom of a perfect and impermanent flower, never to be retrieved. This is life, the experience, this is all there has ever been. To force this moment into contact with her ordinary existence only seems to reveal how constricting, how misshapen her ideas of life have been before. When the waitress returns to ask if they are enjoying the meal, Margaret does not move her hand, and neither does Ivan. Politely they both answer that the meal is very nice, while on the table the tips of his fingers brush her thumb. After they finish eating, they pay together and leave through the lobby, Margaret taking her keys from her bag to unlock the car.

That was nice, Ivan says. I like those old type of places.

Opening the driver's-side door, yawning, Margaret answers: I do too.

On the drive back to town, they sit in companionable silence for a time, Margaret watching the road and Ivan looking out the passenger window. Between them she seems to feel a deep animal contentment that goes beyond words. In the darkness they drive together past houses, villages, supermarkets with lighted windows. Finally Ivan says aloud: Can I ask you something?

She pauses, without knowing why, and then replies: Sure.

Well, I'm curious to know more about your marriage, he says. But we don't have to talk about it if you don't want to.

Hands on the steering wheel, she swallows. Having told herself, having known. And what: to say nothing. Thank you, I'd rather not. Is that even possible. Trying to resist something heavier and stronger than herself somehow, she feels. What about it? she asks.

I guess I wonder what happened. Like, why you broke up, for instance. But you don't have to tell me.

Feeling of breath passing down her throat, and up and out again. I think, when it comes to things like that, she says, marriages breaking down, there are probably always a lot of reasons.

That makes sense, says Ivan.

She wets her top lip with her tongue. In this case, there was one particular issue, she adds, which made things very difficult. But I'm sure there were also other things.

I understand.

Silently once more her breath fills her lungs and empties out into the closed interior space of the car. Trying to speak in a measured tone of voice she says: My husband— The man I was married to, I'm sorry, his name is Ricky. I won't go into the whole story. But he has a drinking problem. Not just, you know, drinking a little bit too much. I mean he has a very serious problem.

Ivan is quiet for a moment, and then he says only: Oh.

Mindlessly she nods her head, watching the empty road before them. I don't want to sound like I'm blaming him, she says. It's an illness, I can see that now. I couldn't always accept that before, but now I can. I understand, it's not his fault. She dips her lights at the sight of an approaching car, and then returns her hand to the steering wheel. I wish I had been able to help him, she says. But he just kept getting worse. You know, in and out of hospital all the time. It was very chaotic. And frightening, to be honest, it did frighten me. Turning the headlights back up, Margaret adds: I'm sorry. I don't want to make myself out to be some kind of saint. I'm not, at all. In the end, I just couldn't live like that anymore.

Ivan sits unmoving in the passenger seat, looking at her. I'm sorry, he says.

Distractedly she pushes her hair back off her forehead. It's such a horrible mess, she says. I feel guilty even telling you about it, to be honest. I didn't want to. Or I mean, I wasn't going to. I don't know.

You have nothing to feel guilty for.

She is conscious of the soothing effect of these words on her conscience, a false soothing or a true soothing, she can't tell. Everything about Ivan in this moment – his tone of voice, the quiet way he watches her when she's speaking, even the mere fact of his still, calm physical presence so close beside her – gives her a powerful feeling of consolation, too powerful. Thank you, she murmurs.

Do other people know? Ivan asks.

For a long time they didn't, she says. But it's gone beyond that at this stage. Half the bars in town won't serve him anymore.

Quietly Ivan answers: Ah, okay.

She slows the car down as they approach the roundabout outside Frenchtown. But I suppose not everyone knows how bad it's been, she adds. You know, they haven't been there with him like I have. And he can be very skilful in how he presents himself. He'll say he's changed, he's not like that anymore, I'm just dragging up the past. And then people don't necessarily want to get involved. My mother would say, you know, you have your story and he has his, I'm not taking sides. Which I do understand, in a way. It's not that I want anyone to turn against him. That's the last thing I would want, honestly, because life is hard enough for him as it is. But it's difficult, when you've been through certain things, and people in your life don't necessarily believe you. Or they just don't want to know.

Ivan is silent for a moment. That is crazy, he says then. You have your story and he has his? About someone who's an addict? That's a crazy thing to say, excuse me.

She lets out a high nervous exhalation. Well, she says, I can only give you my side of the story, remember. If you were hearing this from him, it would all sound very different.

In a sort of frowning intelligent voice Ivan answers: Obviously, since he's the one who has acted badly, he has the incentive to lie. What incentive do you have?

Tightening and loosening her hands on the steering wheel, she answers: I don't know. I suppose when a marriage breaks down, maybe there's an incentive to make the other party look responsible. I'm sure that's part of it. Not that I've been going around town complaining about him, by the way. I'm just talking about my own family and friends. But maybe I want them to think it wasn't my fault.

Because it wasn't, says Ivan.

Her shoulders jerk upwards in a kind of shrug. I don't know, she repeats. I do feel guilty, I can't help that. I wish there was something more I could have done. It's the kind of thing you do worry about. You know, if I had seen the signs, if I had tried to intervene earlier, I don't know. I don't want you to think that

I blame him. He's not a bad person, he's just very unwell. He's not hurting anyone other than himself.

Again Ivan pauses before he replies. I know what you're saying, he says. But it must have been very hurtful for you, as well.

She has a desperate apprehensive feeling now, wanting somehow to ward off, before it's too late, the sentiment he is expressing, and why, because it's too comforting, too close an embrace. Swallowing, she says: Of course. But you have to remember that it's an illness. You know, my friend Anna would say, it's almost like a kind of psychosis. If you were married to someone who started having psychotic hallucinations, you wouldn't blame the person. Maybe if they refused to get help, you would have to leave, okay, but you couldn't really say it was their fault. If you see what I mean. It's natural, when things go wrong, you want to blame someone. Yourself, or the other person. But in this case, there isn't anyone to blame.

She can see Ivan frowning, dark line of his brow drawn. Well, okay, he says. You know more about the situation than I do, obviously. If he's going around telling people that he's changed and it's not true, I think that shows a malicious side. But I don't want to argue. If you're saying he's not a bad person, I believe you.

Yes, a dangerous feeling, she thinks: the relief that reaches out to her from his words. To sense herself wavering on the brink of that relief. Helplessly, hardly even hearing her own words, she goes on: I used to pray that he would stop. I mean, I really would pray to God. Not that it ever worked.

For a time, Ivan falls silent. Briefly she rubs at her nose with her fingertips. Then he says quietly: Yeah, I used to pray sometimes. That my dad would get better. Which never worked either, obviously. It does put a question mark over the whole thing, the way people can get sick, and God does nothing to help them. It's hard to understand. But I don't think it means there's nothing there.

Through the darkness, the headlights throw out a long beam of silver light, illuminating the road surface as it disappears beneath them. You believe there is something? she asks.

I try to, yeah, Ivan answers. Some kind of order in the universe, at least. I do feel that sometimes. Listening to certain music, or looking at art. Even playing chess, although that might sound weird. It's like the order is so deep, and it's so beautiful, I feel there must be something underneath it all. And at other times, I think it's just chaos, and there's nothing. Maybe the whole idea of order just comes from some evolutionary advantage, whatever it is. We recognise patterns when there are no patterns. I don't know. I'm not explaining myself very well. But when I experience that sense of beauty, it does make me believe in God. Like there's a meaning behind everything.

Listening to him, she feels herself nodding her head again. Uncertainly she says aloud: I don't really think of God in that way. In terms of beauty. I suppose my idea of God is more to do with morality. What's right and wrong. She pauses, and then adds: It's not something I feel very sure of. But I do take it seriously, at the same time, or I try to. I want to do the right thing.

While she speaks, she can sense in her peripheral vision that he's watching her attentively. I get you, he says. To me, it seems like it might all be related. Like, I don't know, to find beauty in life, maybe it's related to right and wrong. But I haven't thought it out too fully. Sometimes I just have a feeling. Like a sense of being loved by God, almost. But it's not really something that can be explained.

She lets out a trembling kind of laugh. Well, if there is a God, she says, I'm sure he loves you very much.

He lowers his eyes. Yeah, I can feel that sometimes, he says. Like when I'm with you, I can. If you don't mind me saying that.

Her voice sounds strange to her, lighter or thinner than usual, when she replies: I don't mind, of course not. It's a nice thing to say.

They sit in the car together not speaking. In darkness they pass silent houses, television screens flashing blue in the windows. People have been very kind to her, she thinks. Last year when Ricky started ringing the office, trying to talk to her, and Linda learned to recognise his number so she could answer the calls herself. No, I'm afraid Margaret's in a meeting at the moment. I'll let her know you were in touch. Take care now. Doreen dialling upstairs to murmur in an undertone: He's on his way up. Giving Margaret time to hide in the staff toilet, keeping her breath low, overhearing his voice. She never seems to be in. She still work here, does she? Crying in Anna's kitchen while Anna fixed her a cup of tea. He's very sick, Margaret. He doesn't know what he's doing. Yes, people have been kind, even if they haven't always understood. It's not as if Ivan is the only person in her life who has treated her with dignity and respect: on the contrary. She only met him, what, two weeks ago. And yet his power to calm her with his words, with his presence, is so intense and strong, seemingly equal to, even greater than, the powers of people she has known for many years. It does put a question mark over the whole thing. The way people can get sick, and God does nothing to help them. Yes, she thinks, yes it does. To remember that God is not the nice man Jesus, who liked everybody and went around healing the sick; that God is, on the contrary, the one who makes people sick, who condemns people to death, for incomprehensible reasons. Jesus the healer, the listener, teacher, friend of sinners, seems in Margaret's mind to be practically on the brink of murmuring: Sorry about my dad . . . Jesus is easy to love and God much harder. Jesus also has his own reality, his place in history, whereas God is like a dim point of light in a dark room, visible only as long as you don't try to look directly. In the corner of Margaret's mind he is there, the sense of his presence, but when she tries to catch the sense it vanishes into nothing. If there is a God, what does he want from her? For what reason has he introduced such a person as Ivan into her life? Surely it can't be right for them to keep seeing each other in secret, telling lies to their family and friends, entangling themselves in deceit and dishonesty. But would it be right for Margaret to end things now, never to see Ivan again? Alone, he would return to the life of which she knows little, his thoughts and feelings closed to her forever. Is that the right thing, what God would want? She seems to feel obscurely that the day she met Ivan, they brought into existence a new relationship, which is also a way of being. And their fidelity to that way of being has taken on now a certain moral quality. Ivan's grief, his extreme youth, his liking for her, these facts exert their own pressures on the situation, yes, but only because of the basis of this relation. Some other young man, becoming for whatever reason infatuated with her, would not exercise any special claim on her as a result, would be entitled to nothing beyond the ordinary tact and politeness she owes to anyone. To Ivan, plainly, she owes more than that. But what exactly? Loyalty, understanding, some measure of honesty. At least that much. And maybe, in the eyes of God, much more: maybe everything, her pride, her dignity, her life itself. What she tried and failed to give to someone else, once.

Finally she says aloud: When I was your age, Ivan, I was still very young. I don't know if it would have been a good idea for me to get involved with someone so much older than I was. Especially if the person had been married before, and we were seeing each other in secret. I'm only speaking hypothetically, but I think I might look back later on and feel that this person had taken advantage of me.

She senses Ivan looking at her again as the car draws nearer to the lights of town. A haze of orange luminescence hangs in the dark sky, his face silhouetted against the window. Okay, he says. I get where you're coming from. But I think it's different.

What's different? she asks.

Well, I think you're comparing a scenario you made up in your head with a situation that has real people in it. You know, you're imagining some creepy older guy, maybe someone who went around preying on young girls or whatever. But that's not the situation we're in.

She feels herself shrugging, desperate. Why not? she says. Because I haven't had a younger boyfriend before? I don't see what difference that makes. I don't want you to be looking back when you're my age and thinking about all the suffering I caused you.

She can see Ivan looking down into his lap, and he lets out a long low breath like a sigh. If you don't want to see me anymore, you can just say, he says. You don't have to make out that it's for my own good. I would prefer if you were honest.

I am being honest, she says.

She sees his head shaking. Okay, he says. If that's what you think of me, what can I say? It's embarrassing. You're saying I'm so immature that you could be taking advantage of me the whole time and I wouldn't even realise. And you wouldn't realise either, we both wouldn't, until whatever, years into the future. It doesn't even make sense, I'm sorry. Taking advantage for what purpose?

She feels a hot unpleasant tingling in her nose and throat. Maybe for my own vanity, she says. To make me feel good about myself.

Once more he looks over at her, as she indicates to turn left off the main road. What does that mean? he asks. You don't care about me, but you're flattered that I like you?

She completes the turn, switches off the indicator, and drives more slowly now along the smaller winding road to the cottage. Of course I care about you, she says. But yes, to speak truthfully, I am flattered that you like me.

And what's wrong with that? he asks. It's not like I'm so innocent, I have no ego. Obviously it's nice for my self-esteem if you think I'm attractive, or whatever. If you do. Why should that be bad?

She parks the car outside the cottage while he's speaking. Lifting her hands from the steering wheel, she wipes at her eyes. I don't know, she says.

Out of politeness, or perhaps pain, he looks away, out the darkened passenger-side window. You've had enough sadness in your life already, Margaret, he said. You don't need me making you sad as well. And I don't want to, believe me.

Confusedly, she answers: I just want you to be happy.

He looks down at the handbrake between them. Well, if that's the case, there's no problem, he says. Because you can make me happy very easily. If we can keep seeing each other,

I'll be happy. Glancing up at her, he adds humorously: That's maybe a bit manipulative, but it is true.

Exhausted, feeble, feeling a powerful desire to be embraced by him, to feel herself held in his arms, she takes off her seat belt. Okay, she says. I'm not going to stop us from seeing each other. Shall we go inside?

In the kitchen, she unfolds the clotheshorse and hangs up their damp swimwear while he puts on the kettle. Her impression of the day they have spent together seems dimly to envelop her, succession of images, slender black dog racing across a green garden, taste of sea salt on her lips, glittering warmth of the hotel dining room. Idea of God as an aesthetic principle, you have nothing to feel guilty for. He makes the tea as she draws down the kitchen blinds. Depth of consolation she finds in his presence. Why this, why anything. Moving behind her now, he kisses gently without speaking the back of her neck.

On Wednesday evening, Ivan is over at his friend Colm's flat with some of the others, watching a Champions League game, Tottenham playing Sporting Lisbon. When he arrived earlier, some amused remarks were made about how no one has seen him lately, he's never around at the weekend, etc., which he, secretly pleased, pretended not to hear. Now the football is on and people are eating crisps and talking about other things, controversies from the internet, someone they know moving to London. While one of the players is down injured, Ivan goes out to the kitchen to get himself a bottle of beer, and inside, he finds Sarah pouring herself a glass of water from the tap. Hey you, she says. We missed you at Liam's last weekend. Ivan nods his head to show that he's listening, while he takes a bottle from the vegetable crisper and closes the fridge door. Because his friends had seemed concerned at first by his absence from successive weekend social events, texting him with nice messages saying they hoped he was okay, he may have dropped some small hints about the true explanation, not wanting them to worry, but also not really wanting to explain the whole thing. Looking at him now, Sarah adds: Everyone's saying you have a girlfriend. Ivan pauses for a moment, opening the cutlery drawer and taking out a bottle opener. Then he says: Okay. Sarah has a funny expression on her face, watching him. And have you? she asks. Opening the bottle, he answers: No comment. Playfully she gives him a little shove on the arm. So mysterious, she replies. When they go back into the living room together, she says in a loud announcing voice to everyone: You were right, he has a girlfriend. They all start laughing, talking, trying to get his attention, while Ivan sits back down in his seat, ignoring them, although he actually does think they're being funny.

What's her name? Colm asks.

Ivan takes a drink from his bottle, pleasant cold effervescence expanding in his mouth. After swallowing, he answers: I have no idea what you're talking about.

They all go on chattering and laughing, and someone throws a scrunched-up piece of paper at his head.

What's her FIDE rating? says Emma.

Ivan goes on feigning ignorance, looking at the television, trying not to smile, and eventually they all settle down and start talking about something else. Everything conspires to put him in a happy mood: his friends, the football, the enjoyably cold beer, the kind of glowing internal feeling of his secret, which is not really a secret, the way everyone is cheerful and throwing paper at his head. The gathering takes on in his mind a fun celebratory feeling, like a birthday, and he can see himself sometime in the future telling his friends about Margaret after all, and they'll be pleased for him and making silly jokes. Will they care that she's older than he is, or was formerly married? No, they attach no significance to meaningless social conventions. Will they be impressed at how beautiful and elegant she is? Probably not that either, since they're not really the sensitive type of people who crave beauty in their lives, but that's okay too.

After the football ends, one-all with a last-minute Spurs goal ruled offside, people start heading home, saying goodbye, and Colm asks Ivan if he wants to stay on for their usual friendly game. The others play a little bit of chess too, online blitz and that kind of thing, but Colm and Ivan are the only two serious titled players who still compete at classical tournaments. Not that Ivan has been competing recently: not since April, when he lost three consecutive games in Limerick and then literally the next day found out that his dad's final round of cancer treatment had been unsuccessful. Since then, Colm has earned the International Master title, IM Colm Keenan, and Ivan is still just an FM, even though he has a positive record against Colm in classical, four to one with five draws. When they first met, on the Irish junior circuit ten years ago, Ivan was considered the far better player, the strongest in their age category, practically a 'star'. He got FM when he was sixteen, two full years before Colm did. There was always mutual respect between them, mutual liking and friendship, but also a tacit acceptance of Ivan's superiority over the board. Colm was the one who had more of a social life, even played sports, while Ivan was the one who was better at chess: everyone knew that. When Ivan found out in June that Colm had made IM, he texted him to say congratulations, and Colm texted back: Thanks bud. Your turn next. And he added a thumbs-up emoji. Ivan well remembers receiving this text, the mixed feelings that it provoked in him, painful jealousy, self-loathing, sickening despair. Now, waiting by the window while Colm sets up the board on the dining table, Ivan cannot say that the memory of the text message has completely lost its sting, because in truth it still does sting, but it's more tolerable, a normal emotion that anyone could feel, nothing that makes him want to start crying or throwing up. At the weekend he was telling Margaret how badly he had played at almost every competition for the last two years, and she made a gentle frowning face and said: Oh, but your dad must have been very sick then. Which was true, of course. It's not as if Ivan never made the connection before, he just doesn't like to make excuses for himself, using his dad as an excuse for playing bad chess, practically blaming his dad, and anyway a lot of people play the best games of their life while some personal tragedy is going on in the background, that's a matter of historical fact. Nonetheless, when Margaret said it that way, Ivan could see there was sense in it, despite his former objections. It was actually difficult for him to get into the competitive mindset when his dad was very sick and dying. Even to get his college degree seemed like a lot of work, since he was driving up and down to the chemotherapy sessions every second week, and he felt tired all the time and depressed, and then he felt guilty for being depressed, since he should have been trying to make happy memories for his dad, not sad ones. Looking back, okay, maybe it wasn't too surprising that his chess had suffered. All his friends had told him not to be so hard on himself, but he always thought that was just the kind of thing you had to say to someone who had lost almost one hundred rating points over three years. Now he thinks he probably has been too hard on himself, which isn't at all what his dad would have wanted. No: his dad loved him, and wanted him to be happy, he knows that. And if he can be happy now, it's not betraying his dad's memory, as he has sometimes felt, but in fact abiding by his strongest wishes, his wishes for his children's happiness.

So go on, Colm says, who is she?

Looking out the window across the river, Ivan can see Liberty Hall, big and sturdy, with the crinkly roof on top. You wouldn't know her, he replies.

Ah, says Colm. I get it, she goes to a different school.

Smiling, Ivan answers: Right, I met her at Irish college.

It's not that girl who replies to all your tweets, is it?

Ivan returns from the window and sits down at the board. No, he says. And that's not just me, she does it to everyone.

Colm holds his two closed fists outstretched and Ivan chooses the left one: black. Colm opens with the English, his new thing, and they go into a Reversed Sicilian. Through the opening, Ivan feels a pleasant mental lightness, a sparkling feeling, intelligent moves just rising effortlessly to the surface of his mind. He thinks about the way Sarah shoved his arm in the kitchen, and how stupid everyone was acting, because, he could tell, they were happy for him, and he also was happy; and while he entertains these thoughts, the position on the board grows clearer and clearer before his eyes. Colm plays a small inaccuracy coming out of the opening, pushing f4 and allowing Ivan to capture in the centre, and Ivan not only recognises the weakness this creates in Colm's position but seems to understand instantly how best to exploit it. The mistake is like one little window left ajar, and with ease, with almost no effort, Ivan finds he can lever the window all the way open and climb right inside. Feeling all the time the same free lightness of touch, he forces a resignation in twenty-three moves. It's all very friendly: after shaking hands, they talk over the inaccuracies together, Colm should have captured on d5 that time rather than playing f4, and then he missed a few attacking chances later, Nf6 and so on. Colm isn't sour about losing, he enjoyed the game. After they tidy the pieces away, Ivan gets to his feet and starts getting ready to leave.

You coming to the norm event in December? Colm asks.

Ivan is zipping up his backpack. I registered, he says. But I don't think I'll go. I should email the guy.

Colm gives a little shrug and says: Whatever you think.

Ivan pauses, considering, and then asks who else has registered. Briefly, the two of them discuss names. Although Ivan had previously made up his mind not to attend the norm event at Christmas, and the idea of going had passed out of his brain, such that he had even forgotten that the event was still happening, he begins at this moment – under the influence of the elegant little miniature he has just won, and also the bottle of beer, the absurd header ruled out in added time, the company of his friends – to reconsider.

I'll think about it, he says. I don't want to miss the last bus, alright? See you again.

Out on the quays he walks alone to the bus stop, hands in his pockets. To attend the event after all, and possibly even make his second norm: the idea is sorely tempting. To play beautiful chess again, to regain the respect and admiration of his rivals, maybe to call Margaret from his room that night saying hey, guess what, I just won a chess tournament. Overheard no doubt by Roland and Julia in the next room, and why not, since he has to overhear all their conversations, and everything else as well, why shouldn't they overhear him bragging on the phone about his accomplishments. Crossing the bridge with these thoughts in his mind, life itself seems to glow all around him, and he finds himself thinking again about the weekend, when he and Margaret were swimming in the sea together, and everything was beautiful. The green water, the grey-white daylight, coarse sand, vast and silent cliffs, all complete and perfect in themselves. In nature, he thinks, there is no such thing as ugliness. It's like he tried to tell Margaret in the car, beauty belongs to God, and ugliness to human beings, although he couldn't explain himself very well. They had just had dinner together, in that old hotel, and Margaret had let him touch her hand on the table, not minding who saw them, as if he were her boyfriend. Ivan had never been with a woman in that way before, in front of people, and there was a certain special feeling to it, even if no one was really looking: a feeling of self-respect, somehow. In the car afterwards, he asked her about her marriage and she told him. He understood everything better then, why it was so hard for her to talk about, why she didn't want anyone to know she had started seeing someone new, and he could see how guilty and confused she was feeling. To watch a person you care about become very sick, right in front of you, just getting worse and worse, and there's nothing you can do: Ivan understands all too well the feelings that go along with that. Between himself and Margaret in that moment he felt a closeness that could never be joined by anyone else. Looking at her he wanted to say: I love you. Instead he swallowed and said nothing, not because it wasn't true, but because he knew it would make things more complicated. What she wants is for the two of them to spend time together with no commitments, to have interesting conversations about life, to show each other affection and understanding. She doesn't want to receive insane declarations of love from someone she only met a few weeks ago. Ivan understands completely. Still it can be difficult to hold the words back, and there's a feeling of sadness with it, for some reason. Vaguely it seems to relate to his father, though he's not sure exactly how. It was the last thing they said to each other before he died, I love you. A different kind of love, obviously, completely different, and yet the words are the same, with something of the same meaning. As if Ivan feels inside himself a moving force, coming from inside himself but directed outward, wanting to find a home for itself elsewhere. At the bus stop now across the river he can see Colm's building, squat and featureless, stained with patches of grey. Does it make sense to think this way, in terms of moving forces? Like the feeling Ivan had for his father has nowhere to go anymore, like it's lodged inside him, unexpressed. In the weeks since his father died Ivan has not heard these words from anyone, I love you, or said them to anyone either. Does this explain his intense longing to hear and say them again, to relieve the pressure of this confined force inside his body? Even to think of Margaret with love gives a little relief, to allow the feeling of love into his thoughts, like a flower opening outwards inside his mind. When he showed her the video of his dog running in the garden, and she said he was elegant. He remembers the day last summer when he made that video, when his dad was still living at home, still well enough to go for walks every day, to play with Alexei in the garden, and the sun was shining. Afterwards they went back inside, back into the kitchen, which was cool and airy with the window open, and

Ivan cooked dinner for both of them, he remembers, it was pasta that he cooked. Thinking about that day, the dog running for the tennis ball, the pasta that they ate together, the feeling wells up inside him painfully. Wanting to say and hear the words again, that can never again be said or heard. To return to the house once more, and not find it dark and empty, but airy and bright again with open windows. To spend an afternoon together, playing with the dog, eating dinner, doing nothing, only being together, just once more.

# PART TWO

# 9

Day of the eviction he'd texted her. Weeks ago now. On the bus out to Belfield then for Introduction to Contract Law, condensation beading grey on the windows of the upper deck. Sent a link to the news story and a three-dot ellipsis. Reply arrived almost instantly.

SYLVIA: Oh God! Is Naomi okay?

Strange feeling of peace that gave him. After her cold angry tears the night before, don't be dramatic, Peter. Renewal of ordinary discourse: his always eventful personal life, her good sense and dependability, their partnership retrieved.

PETER: Thankfully yes
PETER: They arrested her but she was released without charge
SYLVIA: ?
SYLVIA: Why was she arrested?

PETER: Unclear
PETER: I suspect they just wanted her out of the way
PETER: Wouldn't mind discussing the legal side with you when we get a chance actually
SYLVIA: Yes, let's do that
SYLVIA: In the meantime, does she have somewhere she can stay?

Typed and deleted. I told her. I couldn't think. It's all kind of. Finally his teeth raking his bottom lip he tapped send.

PETER: Yeah, I've said she can stay at mine for a bit
SYLVIA: Oh that's good, I'm glad

Out the window, dried brown leaves eddied through white air. Avenue of trees. Old stately red-bricks with painted doors. Pale bedraggled faces staring out from bus stops. His thumb tips on the screen. Image of Naomi an hour before, lying in his arms, sweat cooling on her skin. Oh that's good, I'm glad. Never let on that it bothered her: to witness from a polite distance her own replacement. Updated model, full functionality. Not like that, he wanted to tell her. What then. Whole thing getting out of hand. His life, widening black emptiness from which he could only avert his eyes. Frantically inventing distractions. Breathing out between his lips he typed.

PETER: Can I see you this week?
SYLVIA: Of course

Crossing the Dodder then, Anglesea Bridge. Nothing prepared for the seminar either. Supposed to spend the morning putting the handouts together. Above in Kevin Street instead spelling his name aloud. Half of them probably absent anyway, other half on their laptops scrolling their social media time-lines. What did it matter. What did anything. It was nice being with you last night. Felt like myself again. Remember me that way. Downstairs the hissing pistons of the mechanised doors, fresh damp air from the stairwell, noise of footsteps. Change dropped clinking into the machine.

Lunch with Gary after a hearing on Thursday morning, talking the case over. Usual pack of lies from IPAT, it's like they don't even bother, and the clients had to sit there listening, imagine. Now just wait and see. Judge not the worst, likes to think himself independent-minded. Could go either way. God I hate them all, I really do. After lunch, back upstairs to the gallery of the Law Library, laptop open in front of him, white light from the windows crossing slowly the room below. Reading up for a case on the Sectoral Employment Order. Sixteen tabs open and a draft email full of half-sentences. Just to get some work done: not to start thinking. All this for what. Handing his hard work over to the senior in the end and watching him make a hames of it, probably. Take the blame when it all goes wrong, name hardly mentioned when they win. What did he expect. Fundamentally, everyone either in one camp or the other. Distinction expressed in the answer to a single question: normal parents, or rich? Gary's alright, Gary's dad is a geography teacher in some little town in Cavan. And Sylvia's, a technician with the ESB. His own, the humble assimilating immigrant. Why does your dad talk like that. You're not from around here I take it. The sad truth is, these Eastern Europeans, they don't want to integrate. Not that Peter is prejudiced, sorry. Some of his best friends have rich parents. PJ, and the Davis-Clarke girls, Matt Kelly. Didn't Simon Costigan grow up on an old Anglo estate somewhere in Galway? Highly sophisticated people, some of them. Practically raised on the Linz Symphony and the novels of Colette. Still there is something, just a little hard nub of something, underneath it all, which can never be smoothed away. They are what they are, and he is what he is. Work they get from friends while he has to look out for himself. Unwritten dress codes, rules of speech. Oh, we have a house out there, lovely part of the world. And where did you go to school. Living at home in Ranelagh while he pays half his earnings in rent. What they were born to, he has to work for. Taste, manners, culture. On foreign holidays they slept off hangovers and he queued alone outside museums. In Florence, Botticelli's *Madonna of the Pomegranate*. Radiant crowding beauty of angelic faces. Twenty-two or twenty-three he would have been, solemnly pressing the audio guide to his ear, mouthing the Italian vocabulary. Later, in Rome: cool grey afternoon in the empty courtyard of the Doria Pamphilj. Pillars of stone enclosing a grove of orange trees. Overhead in the silence a single opened window. Moved almost to tears. Not to inherit but to earn. Magnificence of classical statuary, yes. Late style of Henry James, sumptuous tactility of crêpe de chine, Sarah Vaughan singing 'April in Paris'. What they would never understand. Mere privilege he thinks can't touch what he has so richly acquired. Beauty, culture: yes. Can't be bought. Reactionary, people call that now. Master's tools and the master's house, what would Bourdieu have to say. And perhaps it is just a delusion. Fantasy of making them feel as inferior as they try to make him. He doesn't want after all for others to be poor, doesn't even want to be rich. No. He only wants what he has always wanted: to be right, to be once and for all proven right.

That was the night he had dinner with Ivan, or tried to. Paid up afterwards, smiling at the waitress, leaving a stupidly large tip. Walking home in the dark. I've always hated you. Naomi was out seeing friends that night, didn't get back until one in the morning. He was in the kitchen washing up their breakfast dishes when she let herself in. Hey, he called out. She came in behind him, opened the fridge to look inside, letting out a puff of breath. Hey babe, she said. He asked how her friends were doing. Everyone's depressed, she answered. To be honest, I think Janine's pissed off with me. I don't know. She lifted a corner of tinfoil off a plate of leftover pizza. Why? he asked. Glancing over, seeing her inspecting the plate, he added: You can reheat it if you want, I had the other half yesterday. She took the plate from the fridge and peeled the tinfoil away. Thanks, she said. I don't know, I feel like she thinks I'm abandoning her.

He watched her turning the dial of the microwave. Cropped sweatshirt she was wearing and a yellow miniskirt. What does that mean? he asked.

You know, because I'm living here. It's like I'm choosing you over her. In her mind, I mean.

He pulled the plug and let the dishwater out of the sink while she went back out to the hall. Heard her taking her shoes off. I didn't realise she was so possessive, he remarked.

It's okay, she answered. It's not the first time we've been through it.

Paused, but she didn't reappear. Then he asked through the doorway: What, you moved in with someone before?

She was silent. Her former relationships until then a managed blank. Never asked, never volunteered. He hesitated, thought of taking back the question, and then from the hallway she answered: Kind of. A few years ago. But yeah, it turned out he wasn't a very nice guy.

I'm sorry, he replied. I didn't know that.

She came back inside then in her stocking feet. No, it's cool, she said. Don't worry.

They lapsed into mutual quiet. Bell of the microwave dinged and she lifted the plate out, padded away into the living room. Not a very nice guy: that could mean anything. She could say the same about him, probably would one day. Janine would, at least. While Naomi squinted remembering: Who, Peter? He wasn't that bad. Hey, he actually bought me this jacket. In the silence he wiped down the countertop beside the sink. Cheated on her maybe, though it was hard to think she'd care. Hard of course to see her caring about anything much. Had she loved him, he wondered, this other person. To think of her in love: bizarre, and somehow sad.

Naomi's voice calling back through the doorway: How was your dinner?

Tired, remembering again the dinner, he squeezed the sponge out in the sink. Yeah, fine, he said. Or actually, not fine. You know, my brother and I, we don't get along very well.

Poor Ivan, she replied.

Struck him as strangely touching she had remembered his name. Yeah, he said again. He told me he's seeing someone. When this prompted no response, he added: Apparently she's thirty-six. She's separated from her husband.

From the living room, a cackle of laughter. And her voice saying: You never told me your brother was such a legend.

Next day at lunch he'd walked over to her office, two weeks ago now or is it three. Paper bag with the usual two sandwiches inside. She would ask how things went with Ivan of course. I've always hated you, he said. And was that true? As a child, surely not: used to idolise him. Family photographs of the two together, Ivan's small pale face gazing up in wondering admiration. But that kind of feeling for an elder sibling perhaps contained some germ of hatred too. From the time Ivan was in his teens, in any case. After the accident, not exactly a font of consolation was he. Offended in fact by the idea that anyone might experience an emotion in his vicinity. Like I get it, you're upset, what do you expect me to do. Sixteen or seventeen then, sullen, withdrawn, staying up half the night reading forums, watching video clips. College Professor Destroys Feminism in 3 Minutes. Facts DON'T Care About Your Feelings. The arguments they started to have about politics, about women, excruciating. And now this married woman he was seeing: how had that started? She gave him the story of her life, maybe, poured out her grievances, cried on his shoulder for a bit, and one thing led to another. Having intentionally conceived of this scenario in order to disgust himself, Peter instead felt an unexpected pang of sympathy for the fictitious woman he had just invented. Imagine her crying on Ivan's shoulder, and one thing leading to another. Dear God. If that was all the solace she could gather at her time of life. Pathetic, of course, but hadn't he himself often felt pathetic, typing 'hey, any plans tonight' into an online messaging interface? Didn't human sexuality at its base always involve a pathetic sort of throbbing insecurity, awful to contemplate? He tried with effort now to return to his previous feeling about the unknown person: distrust, even condemnation, a middle-aged woman taking advantage of a naive youth. But taking advantage in what way: sexually? And considering that Ivan was nearly twenty-three, what would rise to the level of taking advantage in that sense? She was too old for him, obviously. But if he liked that kind of thing? Peter did finally succeed in feeling some disgust then, but he wasn't really sure anymore where the feeling was directed: at Ivan, at the woman, or just at himself. Maybe he should have been happy that his brother had found someone who seemed to enjoy his company. Even if she was thirty-six and basically still married. Living in some hole of a town in Leitrim, half-dead for the want of a little excitement. Slim pickings no doubt. Good Lord.

Upstairs in the arts building he knocked and heard Sylvia's voice answering: Hello? Creaked the door open, small neat room, familiar drab and brown. She was sitting very straight, chair rolled up to her desk. Just me, he said. And she smiled at him, tired-looking, saying: Hello there. Her smile he thought gentle, somehow apologetic, and he felt apologetic too. Atmosphere of awkward friendliness, like when the bill arrives and you both insist on paying. Hadn't seen her since that night, remember me the way I was. Don't be dramatic, Peter. The usual routine now, she moved the keyboard off the desk and they laid out their sandwiches on the paper. He hung up his coat. She asked how Naomi was doing and he said she seemed okay. Talked a little about the eviction, the arrest. Various legalities.

You're fond of her, Sylvia remarked.

He gave an uncomfortable smile. You're always saying that, he replied. You're right, I do like her.

You do, said Sylvia.

I'm agreeing with you.

She was looking at him but he busied himself eating, avoiding her eye. And why. Not wanting. Not wanting not. Pointless to deny of course, not because the other would care, but because she already knew. Still there was something he didn't like in it. Insisting at last a bit too hard. Admit it, confess, confess. You're the one who won't let me touch you, he thought. Then briefly allowed his eyes to close, despising himself.

How did you get on with Ivan last night? she asked.

Deep already in self-despising, he even laughed. Ah, not great, he said. Not too well. Told her of course: where they met, what was said. About the house, about work, about rent. Tried to recall what they had been saying when Ivan brought up the girlfriend and then remembered with a strange feeling almost too late that they had in fact been talking about Sylvia. I still love her, he himself had said, or something like that. Jesus Christ. Passing over that particular interlude, he went directly to the denouement, separated from the husband, I've always hated you, and the door of the restaurant swinging shut. Oh good God, Sylvia murmured. What do you think I should have said? he asked. They looked at each other again, more directly now, the awkwardness forgotten, and she gave a frown. Wiping her fingers on a paper napkin. I don't know, she said. I understand the instinct. He's your little brother, you've always been very protective of him. And he's grieving, he's vulnerable. But at the same time, he is a grown man.

In stature, sure, he replied. But psychologically?

She gave him a funny look. What do you mean? she asked. He's twenty-two.

Right, but he's hardly what you would call normal.

Leaning back in her seat then, an interested sceptical expression in her eyes. And who is? she said. Am I?

What, normal? Of course you are. I mean in terms of social skills. Ivan can't talk to people, literally.

By which you mean, he can't talk to you.

Felt his face changing, frown tugging at his mouth, his brow. What's your point? he said. With me, he's a dour little weirdo, but when I leave the room he transforms into Cary Grant?

She laughed at that, head lifted. I'm just saying, it's possible you have an inhibiting effect on his conversation, she said.

Why should I?

Oh, I don't know. Maybe he doesn't like talking to people who think he's developmentally stunted.

Rose from his seat distractedly then and went to the tiny strip of window overlooking the square. Raining. Glass dotted with refracting droplets. Coloured umbrellas bobbing and weaving below. Hm, he said pointlessly.

Have you been in touch with him since? she said.

No.

You could text him.

And say what? he asked.

I don't know. That you're thinking about him. Which, evidently, you are.

Close enough to the glass that his breath was condensing. Heard himself saying aloud: Look, I see your point. He's an adult, it's none of my business.

In a curious tone of voice she asked: When did I say that?

He paused, thinking. I don't know, he said. Did you not say it?

No.

Turned around to look at her. Calmly she sat there behind the desk. Well, what are you saying, it is my business? he asked.

Why do you think he told you about it?

I don't know, why does Ivan do anything?

With knowing eyes she gazed back at him. I imagine he wanted to tell you about this relationship because it's important to him, she said. And he wants you to be involved in his life.

Exaggeratedly blew out a breath between his lips. Is that right? he said. Because oddly enough, I never hear from him. The only time we ever talk is when I make the effort to get in touch. You have this sentimental idea that he looks up to me or whatever, but the reality is that he doesn't have the slightest interest. He doesn't even know what I do for a living. I don't think he could name a single one of my friends. He doesn't care. I could be kidnapped and held to ransom and Ivan would just say, well, that's your problem, it's nothing to do with me.

Conscious of feeling a little flushed after saying all that. Tried to smile, shake his head, disclaiming the dramatics. She sat there watching him. I didn't know that, she said after a time. That you never hear from him. Have you ever talked to him about it?

He exhaled something like a strained laugh. What, have I ever gone crawling to my little brother begging him to be my friend? he said. No, oddly enough, it's never come up.

Maybe he doesn't realise you would appreciate it, she said.

As I was saying. Lack of interpersonal skills.

They looked at each other again, old familiar look, fond, indulgent, and she started to fold up the greasy brown sandwich paper on the desk. Anyway, you can hardly object to him having an older girlfriend, she said. Naomi is twenty-three.

I knew you were going to say that, he answered. But I'm not thirty-six, am I?

With the side of her hand she was brushing crumbs off the desk onto the folded paper. Oh, come on, she replied. We're not far off.

That was how she put it: we. He went on standing at the window, looking at her. Come to think of it, he said, maybe that's why I find the whole thing so disturbing. Some kind of Freudian nightmare about you choosing Ivan over me.

As if reluctantly she laughed at that. No thank you, she answered. One Koubek brother is enough trouble for this lifetime.

He paused, still looking, smiling, and then said: You did say the other day you thought he was handsome.

Lifting her keyboard back onto the desk, pretending not to be amused. Do you want me to tell you you're handsome, Peter? she asked.

I wouldn't object.

You're ravishing, she said. Now go home to your girlfriend and let me get some work done, will you?

Stupidly pleased he laughed. Thanks, he said. Left her to it then. Swamped presumably with the usual uncorrected essays, unanswered emails, departmental meetings, while he with nothing in particular to do wandered down South Leinster Street. Reaching the park he found a bench empty among the low branches of the trees, leaves curled dry and dangling as if singed. Not cold yet, though nearly Halloween. Took his phone from his pocket and started to draft a text message. Hi Ivan.

I want to apologise for what happened at dinner. I suppose as your older brother I sometimes forget that you're an adult now with a life of your own. Your situation at the moment sounds complicated and I'm here if you want to talk about it. Having typed all this he took a moment to review the sentiment, and found it, broadly speaking, generous. Practically even convincing. Was he there, if Ivan wanted to talk? The prospect was not without some moral satisfaction: image of himself listening, sage, unshockable, dispensing sound advice. Being as usual the bigger person. Yes, he thought: why not. Thumbed his way through the text once more and hit send. Instantly a single checkmark appeared beside the message to indicate that it had been sent. Stared down for a time at the screen thinking after all the bench a little damp or was it starting to rain. Traffic passing unhurried outside the gates. No second checkmark.

Three weeks have passed since. Nearly four. Sylvia says she's heard from Ivan in the meantime, so obviously he's just blocked the number. Well, if he doesn't want to talk, God knows Peter has enough to be getting on with. Mistake the solicitor made last week and no one noticed until after. On the phone to the client, ten o'clock at night, trying to sound reassuring. Man practically threatening to kill him. Yeah, no. Absolutely, I understand. But I'm afraid, the fact is, I can't discuss that without your solicitor present. Meanwhile his accountant sending emails about the tax deadline. Making up the balance from last year, payment a little larger than expected. Quite a bit larger when he looked at it. Wait, sorry, run that by me again. Queuing up at the bank on a grey Tuesday morning to move money between accounts. Cancel a few of those direct debits. Time to find some work. Vultures most of his colleagues, probably telling the solicitors he's still off on bereavement leave. Koubek, is it? I don't know, I've heard he's taking it very hard about his dad. I'm run off my feet myself, but I could try to have a look at it for you. Inventing scenarios to infuriate himself. Compensating for his own failings, laziness, poor sleep hygiene, overuse of alcohol and drugs, irrational bitterness, directionless and therefore immobilising fury. No. Nice interesting case is all he needs. Somewhere to aim his outrage. Where's a bit of sexual harassment in the workplace when you need it? Employees not being wrongfully dismissed anymore or what? His mother ringing him to give out about the dog, Christ, and he lies that he's working or just rejects the call. Drops by Sylvia's office with coffee, sits there complaining about work, the dog, Ivan, union meetings, tax deadlines, judges, landlords, the demoralising idiocy of various named individuals. Stop, you're terrible. How am I wrong? Feeling he gets when one of her colleagues puts their head round the door, asking for something, and he's sitting with her, the two of them bickering together. What is that: to be witnessed, yes. To be mistaken for someone happier than himself, and better. Ran into her friend Emily one afternoon in Hodges, stopped to chat. Didn't mention what Sylvia had told him about her latest woes at work. Wondered what she was refraining from saying to him. Heard you tried it on again the other night. When will you get the message. No, instead they talked about a new book everyone liked which they had both thought terrible. Relish of mutual mean-spiritedness and high discernment. She blew her nose in a handkerchief before saying: How are you and your brother getting on? I know it can't be easy for you. Startled for a second thinking Sylvia had told her about the dinner, about everything: but no, of course, she only meant about their father, it can't be easy. Yeah, it's difficult, he said. It's sad. Dad was sick for a long time, you know. But we miss him. Strangely she hugged him before leaving the bookshop, brief pressure of their bodies, all five foot two of her. To have produced such clichés he felt embarrassed, it's sad, it's difficult, and prolonged for no reason his loitering, examining various hardback non-fiction titles he would never buy or read. He was sick for a long time. But we miss him.

After dark he gets home to find Naomi's clothes all over the place, bath towel discarded on the carpet, noise of the hairdryer on full blast. Perversely relaxing he finds picking up after her, cooking dinner, while she relates some long confusing anecdote about one of her friends saying something to one of her other friends. Exaggerated pleasure she takes in his cooking, eyes rolling back in her head, oh my God, so good. Lie on the sofa together then eating gummies and looking at YouTube. She wants to watch a compilation of snooker shots you'll never believe, and he wants to watch Alfred Brendel playing Mozart's Sonata No. 14 in C Minor. Settle instead on an eight-minute video about how elastic bands are made. High out of his mind watching rubber extrude in glistening cylinders through heavy machinery. You know he's blocked my number. Ivan. I know, you said. You mention it like a lot, actually. Had some friends over the other night for a drink, Gary, Matt, that crowd. She the unspoken centre of attention. Laughing delightedly at everyone's stories. His friends of course falling for it, imagining themselves special, practically jostling for her attention. After they left she curled up in his lap, tired, while he, privately gratified, finished his glass of wine. Flirting with my friends in front of me, thanks very much. Sinful he always thinks her smile. I only wanted them to have fun, she said. You don't have to worry about me, I'm a happy woman. Happy, yes. And if she is. In bed that night he wanted her to say it again. Sometimes wonders how much of his capacity for pleasure is just vanity. Please, I need it. Oh God, it feels so good. He loves that. Happy woman. Compliment deeper and more intense, to make her. Tightening kind of throbbing feeling inside him just thinking about it. Are you happy, Naomi, he said. And looking up at him she answered yes. Didn't even laugh about it afterwards: too weird maybe. Is that what you're into, Peter, you like the girl to pretend she's happy? Instead she lay with her head on his shoulder, talking about which of his friends she liked the most. Felt so in love with her then he could hardly speak. Pain in his throat like crying. Am I annoying you, she asked. He moved his hand over her hair, swallowing. Not at all, he said. Go on. Light touch with the cash in the morning, don't worry about it. Watching him get dressed for work the other day she said from bed: Honestly, very dilf-coded. Alright, he replied, I changed my mind, I'm taking you back to jail. She, the calculating liar, the exploited innocent, yes. Whole thing getting a bit fucking Marcel Proust. Waits until she's out of the house to vacuum the carpet, wipe down the bathroom surfaces. Haul the laundry up and down from the basement. Not wanting her to see: and why. Awkward to make her thank him maybe. Or trying to maintain the fiction of his own dominance, when in truth she has become effortlessly the mistress of his household, he at times something more like a live-in servant, washing on the delicate cycle her favourite underwear.

Monday evening he and Sylvia had booked tickets for a screening of *The Thin Man*. Cold solitary walk to Temple Bar, taxis and buses streaming past, coloured lights already for Christmas in some of the shops. In the foyer of the cinema she was waiting, idly reading a printed programme, her luxuriously huge tweed coat buttoned to the throat. Foolish lift of his heart to see her there, her simple self-possession. Hey, he said. And looking up she smiled to see him: smiled, reflexively, at the sound of his voice, the sight of him, yes. Sitting beside her in the dark then, rapid chatter of dialogue, laughter, music, clink of refilled glasses. Flickering silver light over her hair and face. Afterwards they went for a walk together, out along the quays towards the docklands. She told him about a paper she was preparing for an Austen symposium. Enough familiarity to keep up his end of the conversation. Even made her laugh, stupid joke about Darcy having his pen mended. Cold dark winter air, the lights on the water. Literature in the Regency period they talked about. Significance of the Napoleonic Wars. Napoleon, the man. Toussaint Louverture. Bolívar, Garibaldi. Romantic appeal of various historical figures. Eleanor of Aquitaine for some reason he's always thought. Cultural differences between Protestant and Catholic nations of Europe. When you visit their churches on the continent, the way they always make you listen to an audio guide rhapsodising over Martin Luther, and it's creepy. But they probably think we do that with the popes. Mutual digression then on the most difficult teachings of Jesus: she said it was turning the other cheek, and he said it was the thing about looking on a woman to lust after her being the same as committing adultery in your heart. Her hand on his arm, she was laughing, the lines around her eyes he thought so beautiful. Oh, I forgot that one, she said. That does seem hard on you. He too was laughing then. The inexchangeable pleasure of her conversation. Just to walk the streets saying things, anything, just the act itself, walking together at the same speed, and talking, purely to amuse and please one another, to make each other stupidly laugh, for no further accomplishment, no higher purpose, to let their words rise and disperse forever in the damp brackish air. Why then leaving her at her door that night did he want so much to kiss her. Simplest of all instincts. Brief contact involving no one else, demanding nothing further. In itself, affecting, a gift at once bestowed and received. What does it mean? Desire by its nature resisting reason. The will to survive, appetite for life itself. These days, yesterday, last night, this morning, I've wanted everything. Well, goodnight, he said. Quiet the street and cool under the lamplight. His lips to her cheekbone. Take care. She touched with involuntary fingers her face. Pleased, or confused, replying: Tell Naomi I said hello.

Back at the flat he found her lying on the couch in shiny yellow gym shorts, eating from a family-size bag of Doritos. One earphone in, listening back to an online lecture on her laptop. How was the film? she asked. He moved her legs to sit down. It was good, he answered. I don't think you would have liked it. She stretched her legs back out over his lap. How's Sylvia? she said. His hand around her ankle. Prominent the bone there, white, smooth. She told me to tell you that she says hello, he said. Flexing and pointing her toes, the muscles contracting under his palm. Clean the soles of her feet now: because the floors are. Nice of her, she said. Does she mind me staying here? He said no. Has she ever been here? she asked. He nodded. But you hang out at hers mostly? she said. That's enough questions, he replied. Slyly she was smiling. I guess I'm not allowed to meet her, she said. Even though I've met your other friends. His thumb moving over the smooth obtrusion of the ankle bone. It's not a matter of being allowed, he said. I'm not planning to arrange an introduction, if that's what you're asking. She settled herself against the armrest, put her other earphone in. Hand rustling into the Doritos again. Unclear whether you're cheating on me with her, or you're cheating on her with me, she said. Absentmindedly he considered the proposition. Either option preferable he thought. Dignity of good old-fashioned faithlessness. Neither, he answered. Sylvia is a very dear friend of mine. And you're just a homeless college student who lives in my house. That made her laugh. The actual disrespect, she said. Crunching a corn chip between her teeth. Coloured salt dust on her fingertips. He allowed his eyes to close. Their laundry he had taken that morning from the downstairs dryer. His t-shirts, underwear. Her leggings and sweatshirts. Smoothed and folded into two matching bundles on the bedspread. Iconography of a relationship. Tell her I said hello.

Thursday in the Law Library, desk that isn't even his, while around him falling rain patterns the windows. Decision in that discrimination case this morning. Handshakes all round. Client on the steps outside afterwards, blowing her nose into a tissue, talking on the phone to her husband. Nice woman. Bastards will probably drag her to the Labour Court now. Oh well. Money in his pocket after all. Clammy her hand holding when she looked up into his eyes. I'm so grateful, Mr Koubek, I really am. Not at all, my pleasure. And it was, wasn't it. To feel for a time his own untouchable righteousness, supreme command, the Olympian, to feel them all stilled around him into silence, his pleasure, yes. White flame bright and trembling. Back in July the tribunal was. His dad in and out of the High Dependency Unit. Well, it's an interesting case, actually. It's about work uniforms, different rules for the female employees. Making them wear high-heeled shoes and that kind of thing. Diskriminácia žien. Yeah. We'll see. Only now they have the decision. Never did see. Oh well. I'm so grateful, I really am. Phone vibrates now against the desk and he checks it. Message from Naomi: do i look cute? Picture attached. He glances around, make sure no one's looking. Everyone else with heads down making notes or paging through documents. Unlocks his screen then and opens the image, a photograph Naomi has taken of herself in the full-length mirror in his bedroom, wearing a red velveteen mini-dress. He types back: I take it the job search is going well.

NAOMI: is that your way of saying i dont look cute....?
PETER: I'm at work

Sensing someone behind him he locks the screen. Chris Hadley approaching, poorly cut jacket, sleeves too short. Few years ahead of him, Hadley. Pausing by the desk now for some reason. Phone screen lights up again and Peter reaches quickly to cover it with his hand. Listen, says Hadley, I just wanted to say, I was very sorry to hear about your dad. Screen light bleeding between his fingers Peter feels bad, tries to give a smile. Ah, thanks for that, Chris. That's kind of you, I appreciate it. Goes away again, but Peter can see the faces around him lifted now, looking. Pretending not to see he checks the phone again discreetly.

NAOMI: ok........ you left your eyes at home or?

He lifts the phone to type a reply. Part of the image still visible in the thread above, hem of the dress, her bare smooth legs.

PETER: If you want to be fawned over during business hours I suggest you find a boyfriend who is less employed
NAOMI: cool, i'll do that then :)

He puts the phone face-down on the desk. Has to wake up his laptop, re-enter the password. Find his place in the draft again, half-sentence hanging at the end of a paragraph. Cursor blinking. One more glance around the gallery. No one watching.

PETER: The only drawback would be that you wouldn't have any money or anywhere to live
NAOMI: yeah youre right
NAOMI: that would be the only drawback

Shuts his eyes briefly. Opens them again and taps his trackpad to keep the laptop screen lighted. Am I insane how to tell. Online free insanity test multiple choice. Does she mean it, he wonders. Only in it for the money after all. Taking pleasure perhaps in being brazen. Showing her friends the messages, laughing. Wishes briefly they were both dead, and then, terribly ashamed, tries not to think at all. Just to sit at the desk and think nothing, empty mind. On the library floor below, people entering and leaving, taking phone calls, carrying boxes of documents. On screen in front of him the cursor silently blinking.

Private Law Remedies in the afternoon. The kids with their serious faces pretending to listen. Baby solicitors. Ten years' time they'll be his age, dressed in polyester-blend officewear, braying down the hall at the new trainee. Where are my photocopies,

Joanna? Text swimming in front of his eyes to think. I'm sorry, where was I? Statute of Frauds (Ireland) 1695. Suddenness and finality of November evenings. Dark cold midnight by six o'clock. Packs up his laptop in his briefcase, puts on his coat, gloves. Outside, buses trundling frills through standing water. Said he would swing by Matt's birthday. Thirty-three. Age Jesus was when he. So Barbara says. Is that right? Above in the Hacienda, bending his head to try and hear. And it actually says that in the Gospels, or? Must be getting old, can't make out a thing she's saying. Laugh when she laughs. Gold earrings fluttering. I hear congratulations are in order. Wasn't that your case today? Backwards in high heels. Right, right, he says. Grinning at him. Hope you're proud of yourself, profiting off our misery. She's joking. Smile back at her. Damned if you do and all that. Drinks for the birthday boy and then he'll head off. Is that right about Jesus, do you know? That he was thirty-three. What's that, mate? Never mind. Listen, happy birthday. Thanks for coming, good to see you. Cold air outside. Dry at least. Used to live around here, before. When she. Hardly know the neighbourhood now, so different. And himself of course: different also. Remembering he takes his phone from his pocket and in the search bar enters: jesus age at death. By tradition yes thirty-three apparently. Before he pockets the phone he texts the other: On my way, let me know if you want anything from the shops. Conciliatory, he thinks. Messaged Ivan again the other day, just on the off-chance. Not delivered of course. Humbling himself to appease him and still rebuffed. Dear Ivan, I take back everything I said. On reflection I think it's wonderful that, driven mad by grief, our father hardly cold in the ground, you have taken up with a married woman twice your age. Perhaps you should ascertain where she stands on the issue of family planning though, because at this stage the old clock might be ticking. No, never mind. Fog over the river. Lights in the distance suspended in nothingness. No reply, she's out probably, or ignoring him. That would be the only downside. Cloak of grey quiet lending to the streets a melancholy dignity. Empty the city feels, desolate, dimly beautiful. Ten minutes, twenty, and he's crossing the canal. Feels his nose streaming, cold. Tired he thinks, staring at a screen all day. Stinging in his eyes. Exhaustion, that's all. Overhead the beams of streetlamps cast glowing bars through the mist. Finally he lets himself in at the large heavy front door of his building, climbs the stairs, unlocks the smaller door of the flat. Inside it's warm, unexpectedly, and all the lights are on. Humidity in the air, sweet scent of soap, cocoa butter.

Hey, is that you? her voice calls out. I'm in the bath.

Tingling feeling behind his eyes and nose. You should hope it's me, he answers.

Faint splashing sound like she's lifting a limb from the bathwater, while he bends to unlace his shoes. Come in for a minute, she says.

Feel his face and hands throbbing warm again after the cold. Unhurried, he crosses to his room, takes off his cufflinks, tie, gets a hanger for his jacket. Knocks on the bathroom door then and enters. Clouds of scented steam inside, mirror fogged. Surface of the water all dense white froth. Her arms and shoulders glistening pink, her hair heaped up on top of her head.

Did you text to say you were coming home? she says. My phone's in the other room.

Distractedly he gazes at her soft full mouth, dark eyes, line of the water moving with her breath. Then, belated, answers: Oh, did I, uh— I texted you, yeah. Do you want your phone now?

Smiling she licks her lips. It's alright, she says. You want to get in?

Hears himself give an uncertain laugh, still looking at her. In the bath, you mean? he says. I'm not sure if there's room.

Touches a wet hand to her face, affecting amazement. Yes there is, she says. Are you telling me you've never shared this bath with anyone before? I would have thought you had girls hopping in here with you every day of the week.

Smiling, foolish feeling, he shuts the door behind him. Me? he says. No, I was actually a virgin before we met.

Sound of her high laughter echoing on the tiles. Same, she says. Get in, will you?

Pleased despite himself. Non-committally he begins to unbutton his shirt. You're making me selfconscious, watching me, he remarks.

Okay, I'll close my eyes.

When he looks, she has closed them: grandly, below raised eyebrows. He finishes undressing. Lap of the water, her breasts wet beneath a delicate lace of blue-white foam. One of her knees raised, pink. You want me to get in behind you? he asks. Without opening her eyes she shifts forward. Flat of her back, nape of her neck. Gracelessly he climbs into the tub, water sloshing up to the rim and over, scalding hot on his feet and calves. Lowers himself to sit behind her and she settles back against him, lifts his hand to her soft wet breast. He moves his thumb over the point of her nipple, weight in his palm. He can hear and feel her murmuring: Mm. In the enveloping heat of the bathwater he closes his eyes. This is nice, he says. Thank you. She takes his left hand to her lips and kisses it. Can we get in bed after? she asks. Tracing the shape of her mouth with his fingers he answers: Yeah. Soft her lips and warm. And you'll tell me what to do? she says. His other hand moving over her round belly. Is that what you want? he asks. With a smile in her voice almost shy she answers: Yes. Under the water he moves his hand between her legs, touching the inner surface of her thigh, silk soft. And you like it? he asks. For a second she says nothing. Then turning or half-turning as if to look back at him, small and delicate her pink ear. What do you mean? she says. Feels himself exhaling, his face hot, his scalp, steam rising scented from the water. I mean, do you like it, he says. I don't know. Her fingertips finding the back of his hand, tracing. As in, do I like going to bed with you? she says. Don't be funny. I like it so much it's embarrassing. Smiling then painfully he feels himself. Well, I'm glad, he says. If you do like it. You know. I really want you to. She goes on touching his hand under the water and in her voice he hears a funny tone. Where is this coming from? she asks. Whenever you put your hands on me, I start talking like a crazy person. Saying you can do whatever you want with me. What do you think, I'm putting it on? He tries to laugh, uncomfortable, shrugging his shoulders. No, he says. I hope not. Her hair lustrous and dark against the radiant pink purity of her skin. Fingers linked through his, wetted, warm. I guess you're just used to it, she says. I always think, Peter is such a stallion, every time he lays a hand on a woman she probably starts gibbering like an idiot. Half the little lawyer girls in Dublin are probably in bed right now with their ears burning, remembering things they've said to you. Laughing now, he's shaking his head. Do your ears burn, when you remember? he asks. Turns as if to look back at him again. Are you joking? she says. My entire head is scalded. I'm not an easy person to embarrass, but if you went around telling people about that stuff, I would literally have to leave the country. Gratified, feeling somehow pleasantly evil, he bends his head to kiss the side of her face. Don't worry, he answers. I'm very discreet. She gives a little groan, and he finds with his fingers the hard half-circle at the centre of her collarbone. Anyway, you'd be surprised, he goes on. I don't have quite the same effect on other women. Turning all the way around now, craning her neck to look at him. Really? she asks. Hesitating a moment, he answers: Yeah. Her eyes widened, lips parted, she affects a look of amazement. You don't boss other girls around in bed like you do with me? she says. Frowning vaguely, trying to look dismissive, he says: Look, it's different for your generation. You're all going around getting strangled and spitting in each other's mouths or whatever. I'm thirty-two, okay, we're normal. Delightedly laughing she puts a hand to her face. You've never spit in anyone's mouth before? she asks. Flatly he answers: Like, other than yours? Apparently satisfied she settles back against him, resting her weight, hot and damp. I don't mind, she says. It's just funny. I mean, it's what you like, isn't it? His hand he rests at her throat, feeling her voice when she speaks, faint beat of her pulse. With you, he says, I like it, of course. And maybe in the past I've had fantasies. You know, where the girl is really begging for it, or whatever. But who doesn't fantasise about that? It never occurred to me I could go out looking for that kind of thing in real life. You know, I've been with girls who were a bit more experimental, or whatever. But the thought didn't cross my mind that I could start bringing my personal fantasies into it. How weird would that be? You go home with a woman and you're like, great, so now we're here, you might get down on your knees and plead with me, if you don't mind. Just act desperate, sort of humiliate yourself. In his arms Naomi is laughing, high and bright the sound. Well, I didn't need to be told, did I? she says. Irrepressibly, foolishly, he feels himself smiling again. No, yeah, he replies. That's what's so nice about you. They sit for a time in silence in the hot water, damp with steam, lather of soap crackling faintly on the surface. Look, I hope you know I'm grateful, she says. That you're letting me stay here, I mean. And everything else as well, cooking for me, helping me out with things. It means a lot to me, how decent you're being. In my life, to be honest, people don't do things like that for me. You know, in my childhood, I didn't grow up in that kind of situation. And with relationships, I won't even go into all that, but let's just say it has not worked out that way. You're going to think I'm reading too much into it now, and I'm not. It's not like I think, oh Peter must be really serious about me, he's in love with me, or whatever. I'm not stupid. But I just want to say I appreciate how decent you've been. And I am actually grateful, although I probably don't act like it. He allows his eyes to close, hot, stinging. I don't want you to be grateful, he says. I just want you to be happy. At first she gives no answer. Rests still against him, the weight of her, fragrance of her dark hair. Then she says: Wow, I think that might be the nicest thing anyone has ever said to me. He exhales stupidly. Well, whatever, he says. His hand in hers still holding. You don't want me to be grateful, you just want me to be happy, she repeats. I'm actually touched by that, like emotionally. Smiling, his throat tightening. Hm, he says. Slowly she lifts his hand once more from the water, lifts it to her lips, kisses slowly the tips of his fingers each by each. To think, not to think. After the funeral: crying alone in a locked bathroom cubicle. And now the blocked number, I've always hated you. Cold desolate emptiness of the city outside. And in here, in the apartment, all the lights turned on, hot bathwater. Warmth of her body against him, sound of her voice, her laughter. Why didn't you tell me my picture was cute this morning, she asks. As if having expected the question he answers with no hesitation: Why did you tell me the only thing you wanted from me was money. Her tongue at his fingertips he can feel and somehow almost taste. If your friend Sylvia sent you a picture, I bet you would tell her it was cute, she says. Eyes still closed he answers: Don't start that. Softly her mouth browsing over his knuckles. I'll tell you what I think, she says. I think you've had your feelings involved with someone else all along. So every now and then, you just act cold with me for no reason. Or randomly stop speaking to me. To make sure I don't get too attached. Eyes closed, he swallows. Right, he says. Or to make sure I don't. Half expecting in the silence that follows to hear her again laughing. Glitter of her teeth. To make him come crawling at last, as she has wanted, as she has always planned. Instead she murmurs: Can we go to bed now. Catch in his throat trying to swallow. Mm, he says. You want that? And her head is nodding. Yeah, a lot, she says. Like, a lot, a lot. Rich fragrance of her unwashed hair. And will it make you happy? he asks. Again her head nodding, sweetly, her hand holding his, small firm pressure of her fingers. Yes, she says. I can promise, I can tell you for certain. It will make me very happy. Okay? Please. Opening his eyes damp and stinging. Oddly bright the lights seem, condensation on the tiles. Parcel of her breathing body small and wet in his arms. To make you happy: yes, I want to. Stay, please. Let me. Anything, I'll do anything, whatever you want.

Next morning she's out at her lectures and he's sitting alone at the dining table, answering emails. Rain streaming in rivulets down the window, sound on the roof tiles overhead he can hear. Sorry about the delayed response. I see I'm late responding here, I'm sorry. Apologies, just seeing this now. Beside him his phone starts ringing and he glances: Christine again. Looks back at his laptop, hesitant, and then picks up. Hello, he says. I'm just in the middle of something, can I call you back?

Where have I heard that one before? his mother says.

What?

At the weekend you told me you would ring me back, and you never did.

Oh, he says. Right, I'm sorry. Is there something up?

In a kindly tone of voice she answers: Just checking in. If there's a time that suits you better, you can say.

Abashed frustrated feeling. Pushes back his chair from the table. No, he says. Now is fine, I was just looking at emails.

How are you?

I'm well. Thank you.

Any news? she asks. How is work?

Glancing back unwillingly at the still-lighted laptop screen, half email unfinished. Good, he says. Busy.

Nice article in the paper today about that case of yours.

Relenting now he reaches to close the laptop lid. Oh yeah, he says into the phone. The hearing was in July, I've no idea why it took so long.

God forbid anyone should have to look smart at the office, she says. You'll have us all in matching grey overalls next.

A lifelong ambition of mine, as you know.

Funny that your women friends are always so well turned out.

Feels himself reluctantly smiling. As a matter of their own free will, yes, he answers. But we won't relitigate, Christine. I'm afraid you'll find the courts are on my side.

She laughs into the receiver. Cheeky little devil, she says. How are your women friends these days?

What, all of them?

How many are there?

He pauses briefly. Of my friends, who happen to be women? he says. Plenty.

I see, she answers. Well, in that case, how is Sylvia?

Retracting now he answers in a cooler voice: She's fine, thank you.

I saw Denise Lanigan the other day in town, she was asking me if you had a new girlfriend. After she saw the pair of you together at the funeral. I had to tell her, no, no, that's just a good friend of his.

Quiet for a moment. Finally answering: Right.

I think it's nice you've kept so close.

Massaging his brow with the tips of his fingers now he gives no reply, and she also is silent. Three seconds, four, five.

Are you there? Christine asks.

Clears his throat to answer: I'm here, I just didn't have anything to add.

Have I said something wrong?

No.

The same ritual he thinks each time. She tries to extract from him some valuably hurtful information and he tries to conceal from her any aspect of his life in which he suspects she might gain a foothold. Her fake innocuous queries and his studied evasions. Screens her calls whenever Naomi is home. Why does his mother even want to know: why does he want her not to. Contest for dominance. Story of his life.

Anyway, she says, I want to ask you. What are your plans for Christmas?

Oh, he answers. I don't know, what are you doing?

Well, we're supposed to go over to Frank's sister in Edinburgh this year. You know Pauline. Now, you're welcome to come along, there's plenty of room. Or if you like, I can stay in Dublin, and yourself and Ivan can do Christmas with me.

Automatically, and even with an unexamined feeling of relief, he answers: You don't need to stay on my account, I'll be fine. But I don't know what Ivan's plans are.

She gives a kind of exaggerated sigh into the phone. That makes two of us, she says.

Once more he pauses. Whether to ignore, or take the bait, find out what she knows or doesn't. With studied offhandedness he asks: Why, what do you mean?

Oh, he's very busy this weather. No more than yourself. He tells me he's back at these chess competitions.

Is he, says Peter. Okay, I wasn't aware.

Scrabbling noise on the other end of the call and something like whining: the dog. Aha, his mother says. Do you hear that? That's the hound of the Baskervilles speaking.

I don't hear anything, he lies.

Do the two of you think I'm running an animal charity?

We're trying to figure something out.

Noise like a door opening and then closing again. Mar dhea, she says. You never even answer my calls. And Ivan is off playing his chess, supposedly.

Feeling of caution, tentative. Rising from his chair he replies: Well, if he's back doing tournaments, it's not surprising he's busy. You know, he's probably focused, he's trying to get the rating back up.

Lofty the tone in her voice. He told me last weekend he couldn't come out to us for dinner because he was at a competition in Cork, she says. And like the loving mother I am, I went looking for the results online afterwards. What do you think I found? There was no competition in Cork last weekend.

Stops lightly at the doorway of his room. But it might have been one of these small invitationals, he says. They don't always advertise them online.

Doubting he detects in her hesitation. You don't think he might be lying? she asks.

Why would he lie about attending a chess competition?

More quickly now she retorts: I think you know more than you're letting on.

Affectation of innocence. Me? he says. I've never exactly been au courant with Ivan's personal affairs, have I?

You don't think there might be a girl on the scene?

Well prepared now to deliver the awaited reply: If there is, I don't see why it's any of our business.

I'm worried about him, Peter. His poor father is only dead a few weeks, you know.

His father, he repeats. Okay. He was also my father, I believe. Unless you have some surprising news for me.

Crackle of her breath. God help me, she says. How did I raise such insolent children?

Out the window of his room, the yellow leaves of Herbert Street. Rain smearing the glass. If it's any consolation, he says, you didn't really.

Noise of her laughter now, angry. Oh, here we go, she says. I suppose your father raised you both on his own, did he?

He did his best.

So did I.

Staring down at the carpet. Beige, smudged-looking. In a

lowered voice he says into the phone: You left when Ivan was five years old, Christine.

Marriages break down, Peter. I know that's difficult for you to accept. But I didn't leave my children.

Right, of course. And Ivan was always made to feel so welcome out in Frank's house, wasn't he?

Wavering now with the tone of self-righteousness, her voice. I see what kind of mood you're in, she says. Blame Mother for everything. Okay, Ivan never fit in with Frank's pair. Whose fault was that? He never fit in at school either, if you remember. Maybe he's not the type to fit in.

Pacing back out to the living room. Ugly recessed lighting he hates. Cheap flat-pack furniture. That's a nice way to speak about your son, he says.

After a pause she says in a different tone: And you're his best friend all of a sudden, are you?

He falls still, facing the bookcase, closes his eyes. I didn't say that, he says.

You're at each other's throats half the time. You were hardly even talking to each other at one stage. And now you're accusing me of neglecting him. Where is all this coming from?

It's not exactly comparable, he says. I'm not his mother.

Well, seeing as I am, why don't you tell me what's going on?

Opening again his eyes the dim sealed interior of the room encloses him, claustrophobic. I can't, he says. He's not speaking to me.

What? Why?

It doesn't matter, he says.

Looks down at the lighted screen and taps the red icon. End call. Pinpoint of pain he feels behind his right eye. In the kitchen he pours himself a glass of water and drains it down in two mouthfuls standing at the sink. Paracetamol somewhere. And something for his nerves. Why did he bother giving out to her like that? Not for him to play the role of her conscience. First time they visited the house in Skerries: Peter was what, sixteen, and Ivan six. Excruciating. Sitting in the kitchen together while Frank's pair played some rugged healthy game out the back, Darren and Caitriona, nine or ten years old they would have been. Sound of shouting through the window, glance of a ball flying past the glass. Christine tried to get Peter and Ivan to join in. Imagine. Feeling of disgust he experienced at that moment. That she would do that to them: pretend they were the same. When the other two came inside, she made up glasses of orange dilute, put out a plate of biscuits. They were children. Peter, the adolescent, ironic and literate, felt himself remote, untouchable. While Ivan, white as a sheet, stared wordlessly at the biscuit plate. Yes, that. Well, and what could Peter have done? Not as if they made it easy for him either. Harder if anything, because of his nonchalance, because he lacked the courtesy to be cowed by them. But he was off to college within a year or two. Sharing a flat in Rathmines, austerity era, rental market at rock bottom. Couple of hundred quid and you were half an hour walking into town. The good old days. College Historical Society. PJ, Cawley, the rest of the gang. Rolling cigarettes in the Committee Room. Dressing up on weekday evenings for the chamber debates, audience up on their feet. Sylvia Larkin radiant in a dress of grey silk. Everyone was in love with her then. And only he. He only. Strap of her dress slipping down from her shoulder, down her slender arm. You never told me you had a brother. Oh, yeah. Ivan, he's just a kid. Who could think about such things. Their father alone in the kitchen making up the packed lunch, Nutella sandwiches, an apple wrapped in kitchen roll. Lumpy linoleum floor. No, Peter had a world to conquer. Continental victories, all-time records, academic scholarships. Weekends Ivan spent in Skerries, ashen, speechless, Peter was accepting prizes in foreign countries. Gigantic drive of his determination. Very proud, revengeful, ambitious. With more offences at my beck than I have thoughts to put them in. Take it out on Christine, why not. His own guilt. Also hers. They each had their own happiness to think of. Striving restless spirits, both. Ivan and their father different. Acceptance in their nature: yes, mute bewildered acceptance of life's inexplicable cruelties. And now not even that. Pointlessly he takes his phone from his pocket again and taps the Contacts icon, scrolls to Ivan's name. Taps again. For a moment the screen darkens, connecting, and then the signal drops. Call unsuccessful. What does he have to tell him anyway. I just want to say, I'm on your side. I know I've never done anything to help you, Ivan, but in principle, in spirit. I've been on your side all along.

# 10

On Saturday morning, Margaret is sitting alone in the living room, reading the newspaper, while Ivan is in the shower. Faintly through the walls she can hear the motor running, and the plash of hot water. And absently she allows her eyes to move over the paper, yesterday's, brought home from the office last night. Columns of cramped newsprint, photographs with colours misaligned, oversaturated greens and reds.

The passing weeks have seen autumn into winter. Sunlight on the treetops falls cold and clear now over loosening leaves. Weekday mornings before work, Margaret remembers to fill the bird feeders, and over breakfast watches from the window: goldfinches, four, five of them, powerful thrum of wings, and sparrows, greenfinches, coloured plumage flashing. The tiny precise gestures of their beaks. She chases off magpies with a knock on the glass, clink of her silver ring. Noisy flutter departing. After rinsing the dishes, she drives into town, and in the dim quiet building unlocks the office, the community arts room, studio upstairs, checks the radiators. Linda arrives at ten, catching up, gossiping, and the phone starts ringing. Town waking up outside the window. Shutters rolled back, steam curling in grey tendrils from heating vents. Schoolchildren in their uniforms then, splashing through puddles, and teenage girls in black tights, schoolbags slung heavy over one shoulder. On rainy days Margaret watches them huddle in the walkway opposite, crowding around each other's phones, laughing. Rivers of rainwater streaming in the gutters. Occasionally from the street she hears the sound of a car horn, impatient, as someone stalls at the lights. Monday morning the national school were in, first or second class, making papier-mâché masks with Tina downstairs in the art room. Margaret checked in at eleven to see how it was going: the room lighted and warm, Tina's apron smeared with paint, and the children in their claret-coloured tracksuits huddled over the trestle tables, dabbing carefully. Aren't you all working hard? Margaret said. A little dark-haired girl held up her mask for Margaret to see: a sort of indistinct papier-mâché blob with a red painted mouth. In a serious tone of voice the girl said: I'm making a princess. Oh, she's lovely, Margaret replied. Through the high windows a glimpse of blue sky over Ellison Street, cold sunlight. On her way back up to the office, Margaret stopped in the coffee shop, ordered a cappuccino, chatted with Doreen. Christmas coming up now. Hard to believe the way the year has flown.

In these weeks the town has seemed more than ever to her eyes beautiful, the rich bronze tones of November darkening at night into deepest liquid blue. It has something to do, she thinks, with Ivan, with his way of looking out the passenger window of her car on Friday evenings and saying: God, it's so nice here. On their walks in the laneways around the cottage he likes to observe trees and other plant species, as well as the local livestock, heavy browsing cattle, nimble sheep. In her garden, the fat spherical brown rabbits with their beady black eyes. Last week in the car, he said: If I had my choice, I would live somewhere exactly like this. With a garden, to grow vegetables. Yeah, I went through a phase of learning all about growing vegetables, the different techniques. No dig, and all that. Which is kind of sad, since I might never be able to do it. It is interesting just to learn about, though. Margaret told him about Anna and Luke, the various small crops they cultivate in their garden, and Ivan was very curious, asking a lot of questions. Beyond the subject of crops, he was generally interested to hear more about Anna and Luke, their respective jobs, their friendship with Margaret, their baby, what age the baby is, what kind of motor skills a baby has at that age. One teacher and one working part-time, Ivan said. They can afford to live on that, with a child? Margaret was parking the car outside the cottage then. They live pretty modestly, she said, but they're okay. Thoughtfully Ivan was nodding his head. When they get to the house, they have something to eat, a dish of pasta or rice, and then they wash up together. Putting away the pots and pans the morning after Ivan has done the washing-up, Margaret finds them surprisingly clean to the touch, almost squeaky; whereas when she washes the dishes herself, tired and distracted after work, they retain a faint greasiness under her fingers.

In her room she and Ivan lie down in the lamplight, talking, undressing one another. While he unbuttons her blouse or looks for the zip of her skirt, he likes to ask her intimate little questions about her sexuality, and about female sexuality generally. He seems to appreciate how harmlessly idiotic some of his questions sound, and often he starts laughing at himself before he has even finished asking. Do women, or I mean— Like, say you, for example, do you— When you're in bed at night, do you ever touch yourself, or? In return, he will talk with bashful good humour about his own sexual experiences: mistaken ideas he used to entertain about girls, how awkward he feels buying condoms, whether he watches pornography. Well, it depends what you mean by a lot. I do look at it, yeah. Not lately, but I would have before. And when I was a teenager, more so. I saw too much stuff at that age, to be honest. You even start getting preferences about what you like, which is probably a sign that you should stop. They were both laughing then, lying side by side looking up at the ceiling. She asked if he would tell her what his preferences were, and after a second he answered: No. That made her laugh even more. Nothing too sick, he added. I don't know, it's all pretty sick, but nothing that would really freak you out. I did go through a phase— It's not as bad as it sounds. But did you ever see online any of the Japanese animation type stuff? Margaret was laughing so much she had to wipe her eyes. You mean the little cartoon schoolgirls with gigantic breasts? she said. Ivan was laughing as well, his face and throat flushed. Right, he said. I went through a phase of that. It's not all schoolgirls, there are different genres. And you can get full series, with plotlines and everything. I don't know why I'm saying that, it just sounds worse. Anyway, I don't look at any of that stuff anymore. Animated or real, I mean. She asked why not, and after a pause he answered: Recently I don't feel like it. He cleared his throat and then said in a funny joking voice: I have more interesting things to think about now. Inside herself, deep, a certain pleasurable feeling, and she turned over on her side to face him. On the quilt he lay stretched out, wearing a pair of light-blue cotton boxer shorts. Milky white his skin, and his figure slender and beautiful as a Grecian marble. Unknown youth reclining. So do I, she said aloud. He gave a kind of groaning sound then, smiling, shaking his head. Oh my God, he said. Margaret. Come here. Mint taste of his tongue in her mouth. His hand inside her underwear. A catching sensation in her throat. He likes to kiss and touch her for some time before they make love, to make her very wet, she thinks, to feel her breath hot, wanting, to feel her almost impatient. Do you like that? he murmurs. And when she says yes, he smiles. Cool, he says. I'm glad. I feel really good. You're sure it's nice? And again she says yes, yes, and he's happy, even laughing. Okay, he says. For me as well. You look insanely beautiful, by the way. Like, it's actually crazy. Do you want me to get a condom? To allow herself this pleasure. To be foolish and impulsive for once. To lie half-asleep afterwards, murmuring: I don't know, am I being foolish and impulsive? And to hear Ivan's thoughtful intelligent voice answering: Well, if you are being, is there anything so wrong in that? I'm not saying you are, but even if.

Yes, his intelligence, his thoughtfulness. His travel chess set with the embossed leather case. Sensitivity to beauty in inanimate objects. Generally sensitive, yeah. No, I don't like being around ugly things. You know, if something is really ugly, I can even get a bad feeling. Kind of nails on a chalkboard sensation. Which is weird, I know. Games of chess Margaret has played with him at her kitchen table, or on the sofa, with the board propped between them. His fine attractive hands moving the pieces, his voice analysing, cautioning, dispensing encouragement. Aha, okay. Let's just be a little bit careful with that rook. His refusal, environmentally motivated, to travel by air. Image of him alone on long-distance continental trains, reading books of chess theory, biting his nails. His clothing exclusively second-hand, preferably without any synthetic fibres. Not that I'm saying my clothes are so nice, by the way. Subjectively, other people probably think they're ugly. But to me, ugliness is something else. Yes, his philosophical theories. Enthusiasm for explaining concepts in physics – how a refrigerator works, what a 'water battery' is – by sketching out diagrams on scrap paper. His extremely broad and general love of learning. No, but I listened to a podcast about the Crusades once. For no reason, just interested. You can get a lot from podcasts, if they're well researched. His success in attaining the title of FIDE Master at the age of sixteen, and his subsequent failure, over the following six years, to qualify for the International Master title. His interest in everything about her: did she have a happy childhood, was she popular in school, was she always so beautiful or did she grow into her looks more. To reconstruct her life for him, the story of her life, her personality, to make herself interesting to him, to become in the process interesting even to herself. In school, bright but disorganised, a daydreamer, lover of books and music. Her friendship with Anna. Folk records they used to listen to together, French novels they would lend one another after school. Adolescent dream of attending university in Paris: sunlit boulevards, tempestuous love affairs, autumn afternoons at the Louvre. Went instead to Galway, hung around in poorly ventilated apartments smoking hash with boys who played acoustic guitar. The romance of those years. Her first boyfriend, the American, with his ironed shirts. His accent she thought glamorous. Fifteen years ago, more. Anna didn't like him, she said he was arrogant. Actually he was arrogant, but I liked that about him. I suppose it made me feel special, that he liked me. They were eating dinner together, and Ivan was smiling. It's a stereotype, I hope you know, he said. Pretty girls always go for the most arrogant guys. But go on, what happened? Crisp bedlinen, fragrance of cut flowers, cold winter sunlight. Her simple physical sense of being in the world again: renewed, as if after a long absence. Turning of the seasons. At work, the dim buzz of her phone against the desk.

Is it wrong, the relationship between them? Ivan says he's certain that it is not. His mother's brother, for instance, is married to a woman who's eighteen years younger than he is, and they have like four children together, is that wrong? Faced with the question, Margaret said that in this day and age a lot of people might actually say yes, and Ivan gave a scoffing sound, saying that people think all kinds of things these days. They were having breakfast in the kitchen then, drinking coffee, eating toasted soda bread with butter and jam. At least their marriage isn't a secret, Margaret said. Ivan shrugged his shoulders. If it bothers you to keep secrets, you can tell people, he replied. But I think the only reason you're not telling is because you think people would react stupidly. That has nothing to do with right and wrong. Margaret said that in fact she sincerely feared the judgement of others, and Ivan said that to fear judgement was not the same thing as believing that the judgement was valid. You're making yourself anxious, he remarked. What's the point? We have a nice time together, no one is getting hurt. Margaret fell silent then for some time, thinking. And finally she said: I suppose I'm afraid that someone will get hurt, in the end. Ivan gave no sign of shock or distress at this, he just went on refilling his coffee cup. Yeah, obviously, he answered. I mean, it's possible. It's probable, if you want to put it that way. But you still have to live your life, in my view. He swallowed a mouthful of the coffee then and put the cup back down. And if it's any consolation, if someone does get hurt, it will definitely be me, he said. Getting my heart broken in the end, let's be honest, it won't be you. With a horrified laugh Margaret said that was no consolation at all, and that it made her feel terrible. Ivan smiled then, looking at her, and replied: Oh, well, okay. Maybe it will be you. I doubt it, but you can think that if you prefer. She put her hands in her hair, and her head was shaking. I think you're going to meet a nice girl your own age, she said. Some beautiful nineteen-year-old, and she'll be able to play chess with you. He started laughing at that. Hm, he said. I was about to say that nineteen seems a little young for me. But maybe that wouldn't be tactful. They looked at each other, and they were both laughing, sheepishly, flushed. It's the brain, he added. It's not fully developed until twenty-two. Margaret said that actually she had read it wasn't fully developed until twenty-five, and Ivan frowned for a moment before answering: Well, I guess it varies by individual. Mine is done, for sure. I can tell. Last year, maybe two years ago, it was still going a little bit, but it's finished now. So if you're hoping I'm going to develop any further, you'll be disappointed.

Walking the laneways around the cottage on Saturday afternoons, Sunday mornings, Ivan often talks about his father. His illness, first diagnosed when Ivan was finishing school. The remission, the relapse, requiring further rounds of chemo and radiotherapy for two more years. The final months and weeks, the secondary infections, antibiotic cocktails, the spells in the ICU and the High Dependency Unit, the particular nurses and doctors who were nice and those who weren't. Now and then Ivan will repeat to Margaret a particular anecdote he has already told, prefaced with the remark: I know I said this before, but anyway. Sometimes, he has found something more interesting or revealing in the anecdote the second time around, and sometimes it seems he just wants to tell it again in exactly the same way, perhaps to relieve some of the pressure of keeping all these stories inside himself all the time. On their way back to the cottage Margaret may talk a little about her own family, her own father, or about the last several years in her own life, and Ivan will ask interested questions. What did her family do to help her when her husband was drinking? Well, there wasn't a lot they could do. But they were supportive when she decided to leave? Supportive, I don't know, it depends what you mean by that. But they would check in at least, and let her know they were thinking of her. Surely her sister Louise, after everything Margaret had done for her. I never put it like that. You're exaggerating now. And she paid me back that money, remember. Okay, he said eventually. I get it, you don't want to say anything bad about your family. And I won't either. I have my own opinions on what I think of them, but I'm keeping silent unless you ask. She was smiling then, embarrassed. They're not that bad, Ivan, she said. And mildly he would only reply: I never said they were. I said I'm not sharing my opinion.

On Monday evening, Margaret called round to her mother's house, dropping back an electric drill she had borrowed some time before, and they had a cup of tea together. Bridget sat peering down through her glasses, looking at a social media website on her tablet, while Margaret sipped slowly at her drink. Occasionally Bridget would read aloud a piece of news or a joke and Margaret would smile and say it was funny or interesting. Bridget is seventy-two now, widowed, retired. Her favoured children have long since left home, and only Margaret lives in town, the daughter with whom she has never been satisfied. If she had taken her mother's advice, she never would have married that poor man; and once she had done, she ought to have stayed married to him. On Thursday evening, Margaret looked dutifully at a series of pictures of her brother Stuart and his wife and their children on holiday. Bridget turned the screen of her phone to face Margaret and thumbed through the images one by one, and with restraint Margaret nodded her head instead of taking the device from her mother's hand and flinging it forcefully across the room. This is what you get, Bridget seemed to be saying, for being different. Well, it's true, after all, Margaret thinks. This is what you get. To work in a nice place with a few interesting people, to have friends with whom to discuss life and ideas. To attend the theatre, to hear live music, to arrange the use of the studio room on Monday nights for the local philosophy reading group. Oh, Kierkegaard, that'll be interesting. To exercise once again, for a little time, who knows how long, the power to charm and fascinate, to be the object of an intense and searching desire. And to feel inside herself the reciprocating force of desire, this is what she gets, a life of her own.

Last weekend, with the light coming through the curtains, she and Ivan lay half-awake in each other's arms: and when he looked at her, she seemed to feel herself understood completely, as if everything that had ever happened to her, everything that she had ever done, was accepted quietly into his understanding. Without speaking they made love, and the intimacy between them felt total and perfect, their ways of knowing one another passing out beyond language. In the moments afterwards he held her very close, and then said almost inaudibly: I love you. I'm sorry. You don't have to say it back. Tender, the feeling inside her, a warm immersive accepting feeling. It's alright, she said. I love you too. He made no reply, only held her in his arms, breathing deeply, his face in her hair. For the last four weekends, five, he has come to see her, and again this weekend; and next weekend once more, she thinks, until inevitably there is some reason why not. A chess tournament he has to attend, or a friend visiting from abroad. Then, another week, another reason, and gradually Ivan will stop calling and texting, she knows. He'll meet someone else, a girl his own age, just like Margaret said, and at first he'll feel confused and guilty, and then in time he won't. And Margaret will greet these events with acceptance, with loving fondness, sincerely wishing Ivan well, remembering always the beautiful purity of what seems to her his soul. Her life, after the interlude of their nearness, will resume as before, no worse, and perhaps even for his affection a little better.

Now, with the light streaming in through the window, and the sound of the shower still running at the end of the hall, she turns another page of her newspaper. Finds her hand pausing. Something tugging at her attention. Quickly she scans, and sees: yes, Ivan's name, it is. Not his, but his family name, Koubek, in the Crime and Law pages. A line reading: *represented by Peter Koubek, BL.* Her eyes flicker up to the headline of the piece: *Sales associate wins discrimination claim over 'sexist' uniform.* Ivan's brother, Margaret thinks, it must be, and with a funny distracted feeling of excitement she starts to read the article, almost at random, jumbling up the paragraphs.

> 'The complainant performs precisely the same workplace duties as her male colleagues, but is obliged to do so in uncomfortable, restrictive and implicitly sexualised apparel, because and only because she is a woman,'

> Mr Koubek told the tribunal. 'The disparity between the "male" and "female" uniforms serves no practical purpose, except as a visual advertisement of gender inequality in the workplace.'

Down the corridor she hears the bathroom door coming open, Ivan's footsteps on the floorboards, and she folds the paper flat, ready to show him. A visual advertisement of gender inequality: very oratorical. When he appears in the doorway, fully dressed, Margaret says smiling: Did you know your brother's in the news? Strangely, instead of answering, Ivan averts his eyes. Without speaking he walks to the other sofa, sits down, and then finally says: No, I didn't know. What is it, a legal case? She has been holding the paper out in her hand, expecting him to take it, but now she leaves it down in her lap. Right, she says. Something to do with gender equality. I assume it's your brother, anyway. Peter, isn't it? Without raising his eyes, Ivan gives the barest twitch of a nod. He has taken his phone from his pocket and is looking down blankly at the screen. Is something wrong? Margaret asks. Ivan glances up then and says: Oh no. Not at all. What do you feel like doing today?

You don't want to see the article? she asks.

Pensively he returns his attention to his phone. Not really, he says. It's not a big deal. I'm not too interested in law.

After a pause she asks: Has something happened?

No, he says. Something like what, what do you mean?

I don't know, she says. Is everything okay between you and your brother?

Without looking at her he shrugs his shoulders. Sure, he says. I mean, nothing happened, or anything like that. But we're not the best of friends. Actually, yeah, we don't really talk.

In surprise now, and in vague embarrassment at her own mistake, she says: Oh, I didn't know. I didn't realise.

Ivan locks the screen of his phone, she can see it turning dark in his fingers, but he still doesn't look up. Yeah, he says. It's whatever. You know, he told me once before that there's no point trying to talk to me, because I can't speak any normal language anyway. And that I have a weird accent. International Chess English, he called it. The way I speak.

She goes on looking at him, but he doesn't return her gaze. What a bizarre thing to say, she replies. There's nothing unusual about your accent. And in any case, he's your brother, I imagine his accent is the same as yours.

Oh, it's not at all, Ivan says. If you heard him, hand on heart, you would swear he was from South Dublin. He's so obsessed with fitting in with his lawyer friends, it's actually sad. Like, if he could change his name to O'Donoghue without anyone noticing, one hundred percent he would. Our mother's last name. Because he hates for anyone to think he's foreign.

Watching Ivan across the space of carpet between the chair and sofa, Margaret feels herself frowning, as if these pieces of information somehow don't fit together correctly. Well, you're right, she says, that is sad, if it's true.

At last Ivan puts his phone away, face down on the coffee table in front of him. Some time elapses during which he says nothing, but seems to be at every moment on the point of speaking. Finally he says: Just out of curiosity, is it always the eldest child who gives the eulogy at a funeral? Or it differs. In your experience.

She goes on looking at him. I suppose it differs, depending on the family, she says. Did your brother give the eulogy at your dad's funeral?

Yep, Ivan says. He told me it was always the eldest. Breaking off, he bites at his thumbnail, before going on: And he didn't even do a good job. It was just a speech, it was nicely written, but it had no feeling to it. Everyone afterwards said it was really good, but I didn't think it was.

I'm sorry, she says.

He starts picking at his nail then with his fingers. So am I, he says, because I would have done better. I was a lot closer with Dad than he was. And I understood him more. But Peter pressured me not to do it, saying it was always the eldest, which isn't even true. Like you said. He just thinks he's a better public speaker than I am, because he was this big debating champion in college. In reality, that's why he wanted to give the eulogy, to show off how good he is at public speaking. That's just the kind of person he is.

She waits for him to go on, but he says nothing more. I didn't realise you had such a low opinion of him, she says.

Well, I do. And it's mutual, by the way. There's not a lot of liking on either side.

He doesn't look back at her while he's talking, and again she waits for him to continue. When it's clear he has nothing more to say, she answers finally: But weren't you supposed to have lunch with him a couple of weeks ago? And then you missed it, because you were here. Remember?

Still looking at his fingernails, Ivan gives no response at all for some time. Then he says vaguely: Right. That wasn't a big deal.

But if you were planning to go out for lunch together, you must have some kind of relationship.

Well yeah, we're blood-related. He's my brother. That doesn't mean we have to like each other.

Carefully she answers: Sure, but you never gave me that impression before. At the time you just said something like, he's funny, and he has a lot of girlfriends. You didn't say anything about the two of you not getting along.

Ivan shrugs. He doesn't care about me, he says. I can assure you, he doesn't.

Do you care about him? she asks.

Ivan falls still, as if surprised by the question. He stares down at the carpet, and then at length says: I don't really think of it that way. As in, do I care about Peter. I guess the answer is, not really. I don't like his personality at all. His brows knitted, he rubs his palm against his chest. There is still a part of me that's like, the younger brother, he adds. Kind of looking up to him, or whatever, which is stupid. Maybe he has certain qualities I wish I could have, and it makes me jealous. Like the way he's so popular, and people think he's really witty. And when he's critical of me, it sticks in my head. What he said about my accent, that was like four or five years ago, maybe six years ago, and I'm still selfconscious about that, even now. But I don't think that means I care about him. Absently Ivan scratches at his chest with the tips of his fingers. I used to, more, he goes on. Say when I was younger, we got on a lot better then. You know, for a long time he had this girlfriend, who was like part of our family. I think I mentioned her before. Sylvia, we all loved her, me and my dad both. And I guess Peter would behave more friendly when she was there, so I started getting along with him better. You know, he would take an interest in my chess, and we would talk about different things. I definitely did care about him at that time. Or even kind of heroised him, maybe. But anyway, that had a sad ending, because Sylvia was in an accident. It was really serious, she was in and out of hospital for a long time afterwards. That was when they broke up. I was like sixteen then, and I guess we kind of drifted apart from that point, me and my brother. Because Sylvia wasn't there to smooth things over, probably. Even though he always stayed friends with her. And she's still in our family. You know, I see her, still.

Again and dimly Margaret feels confused, as if the story fails to cohere, as if some key details have been left out. To make sense of this person, the brother: to imagine the same information, she thinks, presented as if from his perspective. We all loved her, Ivan said about the girlfriend. And then something terrible happened, some dreadful accident, and everything changed, they couldn't be together anymore. Distractedly she murmurs aloud: Oh, that's very sad.

What is?

Looking up now she sees Ivan watching her. Somehow flustered, without knowing why, she answers: Sorry. I mean, that his girlfriend was in an accident, and then they broke up. It sounds like a sad situation.

Blinking at her, Ivan replies: Right. But I mean, he wasn't in the accident, he was fine. For her it was a lot worse, she could have died.

Margaret feels her face growing hot. No, I understand that, she says. But just to have a relationship break down in those circumstances, I imagine it must be difficult, that's all. Obviously I don't know the details, I'm just listening to what you're telling me.

Ivan looks up at the ceiling, breathing in slowly, as if in thought. Well, I don't know the details either, he says. Peter doesn't tell me things about his life, personal things or whatever. It's not something I think about a lot. She broke up with him, he told me that at the time. That it was her decision, not his. But apart from that, I know nothing. Briefly Ivan falls silent, and then adds: My dad was always encouraging us to get on better. You know, it really upset him when we would fight. I regret that. Now that he's gone, I don't care whether I ever see Peter again, to be quite honest. But I do regret the way it affected our dad. Even the last few times I talked to him, like when he was in the ICU at the end, he would bring it up with me. Your brother really loves you, and things like that. Which isn't true, by the way. I'm sure my dad thought it was true, but in reality it's not.

When he has finished speaking, Ivan wipes at his nose with his fingers, in a businesslike, almost dismissive way. What makes you say it's not true? she asks.

He shrugs his shoulders, wiping again at his nose. That Peter doesn't love me? he says. He doesn't show me respect. He's not even nice to me.

Well, I'm sorry about that. But I think, as sad as it is to say, I think people aren't always very nice to the people they love.

Ivan exhales now, a quick frustrated kind of laughter. Okay, he says. What does it mean to love someone, then? I'm curious. If you don't care about the person's feelings, and you're not nice to them, and you don't really want them to be happy, how is that love, in your opinion? Maybe we have different definitions.

Pained, she says nothing for a moment, only watching him. Then she says quietly: I'm not trying to make you angry, Ivan, I'm sorry.

He's shaking his head, drawing his sleeve across his eyes. I'm not angry, he says. It just feels like you're defending my brother against me. Saying his life is so hard, and why can't I be more understanding, or whatever.

The heat has not quite left her face, she feels. I didn't say that, she says. I didn't tell you to be more understanding.

But you're giving his side.

No, I'm not, she says.

He rests his forearm over his eyes, not looking. Okay, he replies. I'm sorry. It just makes me feel bad, talking about these things. You know, my dad wanted us to get along, and we don't get along, that upsets me. And I feel like you're saying it's my fault. Like I'm going against my dad's wishes. Maybe I am, I don't know.

Quickly she replies: I must be expressing myself badly if that's what you think I've been saying. I never meant to imply that anything was your fault, or that you're going against your dad's wishes, of course not. If you're telling me that your brother isn't nice to you, I believe you, and I'm sorry. And I don't think you should be selfconscious about your accent, by the way. You have a very pleasant speaking voice.

From behind his arm he gives a little smile, relenting. Well, I don't know, he says. Thank you. International Chess English, it's probably true to some extent. Not that I talk like that on purpose.

She rises from the chair and goes to sit by his side on the sofa, touching gently his hair, and he lays his hand on her knee. And he's right, she thinks. If being around his brother makes him feel bad, why should he have to do it? On the other hand it strikes her as some kind of imperative, perhaps even a law of nature, that people should do their best for one another in times of grief. Ivan and his brother have both lost the same father: surely the loss is something that should be shared, expressed, consoled, not kept separate and silent. But the situation remains unclear to her, she can see that. Much has been disclosed, a proliferation of new facts and details, and yet somehow she doesn't feel she understands Ivan's relationship with his brother any better than she did before. It strikes her that on the contrary she has become, during this conversation, even more confused, even more uncertain. Something has not been said, she thinks: there is something Ivan has not wanted to say. Does it relate to the girlfriend somehow, the one who was in an accident? And why did Margaret herself respond so strongly, with such a strong wave of emotion, on hearing that story? The hospital visits, the relationship destroyed, the terrible waste of it all. Dimly she wonders now whether she has been thinking somehow about herself, her own circumstances, and she feels her face again growing flushed. It is this, she thinks, her own sense of identification, that has thrown everything into confusion. She has lost sight of the brother Ivan has been describing, replacing him with herself, and therefore attributing to herself a greater understanding of his motives than she could possibly possess. Never having, after all, laid eyes on the man, whoever he is. And she can see in retrospect that Ivan, accusing her of defending his brother, was not entirely wrong, that she did feel defensive, that for some reason even now she still does. Wishing irrationally that Ivan might try, despite all his brother's faults, to care for him more. He, the older, disappointed, compromised person, who has made a mess of everything, who does not deserve Ivan's love.

On Thursday afternoon, Ivan is walking alone from Skerries train station to the housing development where his mother lives with her partner and stepson. The air around him is filled with an indistinct grey rain, like a very fine beaded curtain through which he has continually to walk, and in the absence of any head covering, his hair and face are growing faintly but increasingly wet. Passing through a small mixed-use commercial area and taking a right, he continues up a hill towards the housing development, towards the large engraved rock at the entrance, which reads in italic font: *Hazelbrook*. At eight o'clock this morning, he woke up to the sound of his alarm as usual, turned it off as usual, booted up his laptop and began some puzzle training he had planned for the morning. In the kitchen he made his coffee and ate breakfast without running into any of his flatmates, and everything was shaping up towards a good day. Then, after lunch, he received a new text message from his mother. Sweetheart I have done my best. But we just can't put up with this any longer. I'm sorry. I'm going to search online for a good home – I promise he will be well looked after. xxx. Attached to the message was a picture of Alexei chewing innocuously on a roll of toilet paper: as if this was evidence of some unspeakable sin against nature, as if no one could possibly be expected to live with an animal whose worst habit was occasionally chewing on safe and inexpensive household products when left alone for protracted periods of time. And now, instead of spending the afternoon as he would like to spend it, a valuable afternoon he had put aside only for chess, Ivan is on his way to his mother's boyfriend's house in Skerries to confront, in person, the issue of the dog.

The other day, without forethought, simply allowing the words to form and express themselves unimpeded, Ivan told Margaret that he loved her. And lying there warm and peaceful in his arms she said that she loved him too. All day afterwards he could feel himself smiling, irrepressibly, sort of stupidly even, although not, because the happiness was real. On the bus home he was still smiling, and even with his flatmates that night, in the kitchen, he could not disguise his good mood. Roland's girlfriend Julia was like, what are you smiling about, Ivan? And Roland said, he's met a nice little lady chess player for himself. With a somehow sympathetic feeling Ivan laughed at that. From the kitchen he took a yogurt and a clean spoon and then went up to his room alone. For a time without even opening the yogurt he dwelled on the events of that morning, telling Margaret that he loved her, and the simple accepting way she had said: I love you too. But rather than smiling this time he felt a kind of acute feeling, almost like pain, opening out inside himself, and his eyes were stinging. To love, and for his love to be accepted, yes. It was in fact painful, the relief of all that compression suddenly, to say the words aloud, and hear her saying them, to be loved by her, it was so needed that it actually hurt. Not even a feeling of unmixed happiness, but of happiness that was strongly and confusingly mixed with many other feelings. Sadness, missing his father, and a kind of shame somehow, because each passing day seemed to bring Ivan further away from him and the life they used to have together, a life that was receding increasingly into the past, into the realm of childhood and adolescence. The realisation that his adulthood, into which he was entering now so definitively, and which would last all the rest of his life, would have to be lived without his father. That he was becoming a person his father would never know. And he was thinking also about Peter, their argument, the blocked number, and how upset and hurt their dad would feel if he knew the situation. The sense that he was doing something to hurt his father, that he was disrespecting his memory, and yet the opposite and even stronger sense of wrong, of the wrong Peter had done. The need Ivan felt to protect himself from that, the contempt, the cruelty, and to protect Margaret also, to keep her from the terrible and pointless hurt of finding out the truth. Eventually, he ate the yogurt, and then opened up his laptop to play some chess. In time, getting into some nice positions, making intelligent moves, watching the online rating climb higher, he started to feel okay again. And by the time he went to bed that night, he could once more remember the words that had been spoken in the morning, I love you, with no pain, but rather with a deep radiant warmth that seemed to envelop his whole being, and nothing could harm him, he was happy.

That was before the incident with the paper, Margaret seeing Peter's name in the paper, and Ivan having to say some things to Margaret that were not one hundred percent truthful. Because, while he didn't tell any actual lies, he did give a false picture of events, which isn't something he feels proud of. But what else was possible? He should have told her about Peter's cruel words, do you think any normal woman, and so on? She didn't need to hear that. She's sensitive about these things. Anyway, all words can give a false picture, and who's to say what picture another person ends up with, even when the supposedly right words are used? Just the other day, to that point, Ivan got a text from Sylvia, asking if he would like to get a cup of coffee together, and he responded instantly, almost within the minute, saying yes. They met up near the college and strolled around together, drinking coffee, talking, and he felt good to be in her company again. There was a lot of liking between them, a lot of mutual respect and liking, and she didn't pry into his life or bring up difficult topics. Instead she asked him if he could explain a logic puzzle to her, and he said yes, of course. The puzzle was about a liar who always lies, and the liar says: All my hats are green.

Now, can we conclude that he has some hats? Sylvia asked. Or is it possible he doesn't have any hats at all?

Ivan explained that it was an established problem in formal logic. You have to think of it as a conditional, he said. Saying 'all my hats are green', it's like saying 'for all hats, *if* they are mine, *then* they are green'. And if there aren't any hats that satisfy the condition of being mine, it can't be a lie to describe them as green. You can say anything about the hats and it would be true, because they don't exist. That's called vacuous truth. So yeah, if the liar says 'all my hats are green', he has to have hats, otherwise it wouldn't be a lie.

Promptly, Sylvia replied: So if I said, 'all my sisters are right over there', it would be true? Because I don't have any sisters.

Ivan confirmed that it would, but only vacuously, and he reiterated again about vacuous truth, not to confuse it with a meaningfully true statement.

What if I said, 'my sister is right over there'? Sylvia asked. Just one sister, but she doesn't exist.

Ivan himself had to take a little pause then. Hm, he said. I think, in that case, that actually would be a false statement. Because you're not making a conditional statement, if x then y. You're giving what's called a definite description. In logic, it's different. If you say 'my sister is over there', you're claiming 'there is such a person as my sister' and also 'that person is over there'. So if the first claim isn't true, that makes the whole statement a lie.

Sylvia had a sort of interested innocuous look on her face.

It's a false statement if I just invent one sister? she asks. But if I invent more than one, it becomes true?

Ivan was frowning then, he could feel a frown had developed. A universal statement is conditional, he repeated. With the example of sisters, maybe it's different. But no, yeah. If it's one non-existent sister, it seems, I think, yes, you would be lying, because of the way the statement would be formalised in logic. But a universal statement, to include all your non-existent sisters – I don't know. It doesn't seem to make sense that one would be true and the other not, does it?

Sylvia was smiling lightly, mischievously. No, she said, not to me. But then, of course, I'm not a mathematician.

Ivan said he would look into the puzzle and get back to her. And he did try to look into it, later, but he couldn't find anything useful. If the liar says that all his hats are green, it means he has some hats. Accepted. But if the liar just says that his 'hat' is green, does it mean he has to have a hat? Yes, by the same logic: it can't be a false statement if he has no hat at all. And does that imply that it's not a lie if you say 'all my daughters are waiting for me', as long as you don't have a daughter? You can claim you're telling the truth, albeit vacuously? And if it's just one daughter instead? But why should it be any different? It goes to show, Ivan thinks, that the difference between truth and lying is complicated. You think you're fitting language onto the world in a certain way, like a child fitting the right-shaped toy into the right-shaped slot. But at times you realise that that's a false picture too. Language doesn't fit onto reality like a toy fitting into a slot. Reality is actually one thing and language something else. You just have to agree with yourself not to think about it too much. While they were strolling and drinking coffee, Ivan mentioned to Sylvia that he had been seeing someone, and she touched his arm and said: Oh, how nice. She didn't ask what age the woman was, or anything else, even her name. Yeah, she's actually an amazing person, he added. Who I think you would like a lot, if you ever met her. Sylvia said that she would love to meet her, and Ivan could feel a tightening inside his throat then, a feeling of emotion that was difficult to describe. Okay, cool, he said. It's still early times, obviously. But maybe one day, it would be nice if you could meet. Because she makes me really happy. Sylvia too was becoming emotional, he could see that, and she put her arms around him, saying he deserved to be happy, he deserved all the happiness in the world. And the feeling between them in that moment, wasn't that true? Doesn't the feeling between people have a truth of its own? Not in the sense of formal propositional truth-value, no. But then why does that word, 'truth', have a certain sensation to it, which is not exhausted by the formal definition?

As of this week, Ivan's online chess rating is within six points of his highest ever, a record achieved when he was only eighteen. Every time he begins a new game now, he feels a light buoyant sensation, like his brain is floating up above the game, up to a vantage point very high and refined, from which he can see everything clearly. When a move suggests itself to him for no obvious reason, he need only apply the slightest pressure to his intuition, a few seconds or minutes of conscious calculation, in order to feel the strength of the intuition asserting itself forcefully in response: because after the exchange, for instance – forcing his opponent to withdraw the rook and then taking with the pawn on g5, exposing the light-squared bishop, trading, after all that – then white's knight will be trapped. And this image, this idea of the trapped knight, was there in Ivan's mind, unexpressed, not even visualised, but present, folded into itself, preparing to be made real. There inside him, the trapped knight: the hidden idea that manifested its own reality, the idea that created itself. And after the game is over, pacing around his flat, or maybe walking the streets, breathing the cold winter air, breath of his body blossoming into mist, he feels impressed and humbled by the work his brain has done for him, humbled and impressed. Like, thank you, brain, whatever you are. A strange little room in his head where things happen secretly: which in fact seems so impressive it crosses over into being alarming. Of course, he thinks, all his other vital organs also perform their work without his conscious knowledge, carrying out all their various finely calibrated tasks. What makes the brain any different? It has always been Ivan's philosophy, at least in previous phases of his life, that the brain is indeed different, that the body is merely a sack of flesh and the brain an animating consciousness. But on his walks around the city lately – after long arduous chess games in which his brain has played a role he has not entirely understood – it has occurred to him that perhaps the mind and body are after all one, together, a single being. And that he should be humbled not only by his brain, but by his body also, a complex and beautiful system for the sustenance of life itself. When he and Margaret are together, for instance, the intelligence that animates instinctively his gestures, touching, is that not the same intelligence that suggests to him the move that will later trap the knight? It is the same, himself, his own intelligence, his personhood. And for this he feels a tender wounding gratitude, a sense of blessing, that he exists simply in this body, in this mind, that he is himself, this one person, rich in priceless resources which to his conscious mind remain almost infinitely unknown.

When his rent was due last month he was a hundred short, but they let him pay a week late, and he promised to be on time in future. Now he is assiduous about finding work, completing it on time, submitting invoices right away, and following up not aggressively but firmly until the minute he gets paid. The fact that he is playing such good chess, and that he spends the entirety of each weekend with Margaret, far from interfering with his financial stability, has given him unprecedented motivation in terms of income. He has for really the first time in his life worked out precisely, to the euro, how much money he needs in order to pay rent and purchase bus tickets and feed himself, and he is committed to making this much money in the smallest number of labour hours possible. It's kind of like a game, adding the hours together, and not going over, because his time is so important now. Each additional hour or even minute he spends compiling data or toggling between the R interface and an Excel spreadsheet, that is a golden hour or minute he could be playing chess, or reading theory, or lying on his bed thinking about Margaret, literally even just thinking and remembering. In the evenings he sees his friends, they hang out in Colm's flat or Emma's house, playing board games or FIFA or talking about the tournament coming up in town next month, which will be Ivan's first formal chess competition since the spring. He will finally have the opportunity to qualify for his second IM norm, moving him one step closer to the three norms he needs to secure the title, but he will also have the opportunity to fail, to lose rating points, to slip further away from his goal, perhaps even unreachably far, so far that the goal is no longer attainable. And in that case, rather than forging ahead to become a grandmaster, he would just drop out of the chess world in his early twenties as so many failed hopefuls do, with his sad little FM title more like an embarrassment than an accolade. But that won't happen, he thinks, not with the way he's playing lately. And even if it does happen: so be it. There is more to life than great chess. Okay, great chess is still a part of life, and it can be a very big part, very intense, satisfying, and pleasant to dwell on in the mind's eye: but nonetheless, life contains many things. Life itself, he thinks, every moment of life, is as precious and beautiful as any game of chess ever played, if only you know how to live.

Reaching the front door of his mother's boyfriend's house now, under the same hanging veil of tepid rain, Ivan rings the bell and waits. After a moment, he can hear the sound of footsteps, and then his stepbrother Darren answers the door. Ivan nods at him.

Hey, man, says Darren. Come on in.

Ivan enters the hallway and allows Darren to close the door behind them. Inside, the house emits its familiar synthetic smell of cleaning products and air freshener. Darren, who is three and a half years older than Ivan, is wearing a polo shirt with an embroidered brand logo on the front, and a pair of plastic flip-flops for some reason. Closing the door behind them as Ivan wipes his feet on the doormat, Darren adds: Your mam's just out at the shops. Be back in a minute, though. All good with you?

Ivan feels inside himself a strong unwillingness to answer this question, a sudden and extreme attachment to his own silence. With effort, however, he replies: Yeah. As soon as he pronounces this word, this single syllable, he hears a clattering noise from somewhere inside the house, a scrabble of paws, and at the same time a high whimpering whine. Where is he? Ivan says.

Oh, the little guy? says Darren. He's in the back.

Ivan, walking towards the sound, down the hall towards the kitchen, says: Where?

There in the utility room, Darren says.

Ivan crosses the kitchen, opens an interior door, and instantly the dog springs out, tail wagging, the entire back half of his body wagging madly. Three times Alexei runs in a circle around Ivan's feet, leaping, scampering, lifting his thin head intermittently to lick at Ivan's hand. He even bows down playfully like a puppy and lets out a kind of elongated howl of excitement, flicking his tail. Ivan crouches down on the tiles and embraces him, smoothing his palms over the dog's short silken coat. Burying his face in Alexei's neck, Ivan breathes in, smelling at first only a sweetish detergent fragrance, and then, underneath that, the kind of dark soil or sweat odour of his body, a smell which most people would probably consider kind of disgusting, but which at this moment fills Ivan with an overpoweringly strong, agonising feeling of love, and also a horrible guilt. Alexei, wriggling with delight, licks at his neck and ear with a dry panting mouth, dry nose. Ivan gets to his feet again and the dog looks up at him, tongue lolling. The door of the utility room is still open: a tiny room with a washer and dryer inside, releasing into the kitchen the same strong fragrance of laundry detergent that Ivan could smell in Alexei's coat. On the floor by the washing machine, Ivan can see the dog's fleece bed and two empty silver feeding bowls.

From the kitchen doorway, Darren says: Well, he's obviously happy to see you.

Yeah, says Ivan. How long has he been in there?

In where?

Ivan turns around to face Darren. In the utility room, he says.

Darren affects a thoughtful frown, answering: Couldn't tell you. I was in the office all morning, just working from home now this afternoon.

Ivan goes into the small room and takes one of the bowls from the floor, while the dog noses and licks at his hands. He happens to know that Darren lives at home and works for a corporate law firm, earning a massive salary and contributing zero, literally nothing at all, to human civilisation. 'Working from home', he said just now. How so 'working'? Is this work, standing around uselessly in plastic flip-flops? Do they pay him for that? Why can't Ivan get paid for standing around, if all this money is just sloshing pointlessly through the economy, spilling over into the bank accounts of people like Darren? Returning to the kitchen with the bowl in hand, he says: His water bowl is empty.

Ah, says Darren. He must have drank it all.

Ivan goes to the sink and refills the bowl. Alexei follows at his heel, beating his tail rhythmically against the door of a cabinet. When the bowl is full of cold water, Ivan puts it on the floor, and instantly with a wet lapping sound the dog begins to drink. In the silence, the drinking noise is so loud as to seem exaggerated, like a joke. Droplets of water spray over the tiles with the rapid energy of the dog's clamorous gulps. Ivan stands there, and Darren stands there, working from home presumably, while the dog goes on and on lapping from the bowl. Thirsty boy, Darren remarks. Ivan gives no answer. When the bowl is empty, he refills it from the tap, and the dog takes a few more mouthfuls before returning to Ivan and burrowing his nose, now cold and wet, into his hand.

So how's life with you? says Darren. How's the chess?

Again, and now even more strongly than before, Ivan feels a strong desire not to answer, feels his lips glued shut, his tongue sealed to the roof of his mouth, against this question, and any question that Darren might ask, any interaction that Darren might try to initiate. Darren knows nothing, as it happens, about chess. As a child Ivan was, for a time, actually prohibited from playing chess in this exact house, supposedly because it was 'antisocial', but in fact because his prowess at the game made Darren, why not be honest, feel insecure. When Peter came home from college at the weekends, he would make a big point of bringing a chess set with him, wanting to play, because he knew that although everyone could bully Ivan, no one would even attempt to bully him, and the chess would be allowed to proceed. Not that it was great-quality chess or anything, because Peter never practised, but it was a gesture anyway. Now, before Ivan has to do or say anything in response to Darren's palpably insincere question, he hears the front door opening, and Darren says: That must be Christine now.

Ivan's mother enters the kitchen carrying a woven plastic shopping basket, heavy with groceries. Seeing Ivan, she raises her eyebrows, making a funny shocked face, and then hefts the basket up onto the countertop. The prodigal son, she says. Come here to me. Approaching him, she wraps his body in a motherly embrace, smelling strongly of perfume and face powder. Drawing back then, she grips his arms and holds him out in front of her, as if to scrutinise his facial features. You'll have those braces off soon, she says.

Yeah, he answers. Next month.

You won't know yourself. You'll be so handsome.

Pausing, he answers: Hm. Then he says: Anyway, never mind that. I'm here because of the dog.

At this, she releases him again, throwing her hands up into the air. Well, it's good to see you too, my darling, she says. I have been trying to get in touch, you know.

Ivan watches her return to the shopping basket, which she begins to unpack. Dogs are supposed to have fresh water to drink, he says.

Excuse me. He's been given fresh water.

His bowl was empty when I came in. And he was really thirsty. Darren saw.

They both look at Darren, who gives an exaggerated shrug and says: Here, I know nothing about dogs.

You saw him drinking an entire bowl of water five seconds ago, says Ivan. You said yourself, he's a thirsty boy, or something like that.

I don't know, sorry, says Darren. He's not my dog.

Indeed he's not, says Christine. Nor mine. Are you staying for dinner?

No, Ivan says.

Christine goes on unpacking the basket. Alright then, she answers. Suit yourself. Ivan stands in dissatisfied silence watching her. She is wearing a cream-coloured woollen jacket, and her pale hair has a glossy and slightly rigid-looking texture under the ceiling lights. She has always been someone who sets a lot of store by personal appearance. At the funeral, for instance, she asked Ivan right out loud where on earth he had acquired such a 'hideous' suit. Did the question make him feel bad? Actually, yes it did, despite his being typically and with some conscious pride invulnerable to the opinions of others regarding his looks. Ivan is not a person who needs his mother, or the world in general, to approve of his sartorial choices, especially considering that for environmental reasons he stopped purchasing new clothes at the age of nineteen and has since then only ever shopped second-hand, except for underwear. Nonetheless, given the context of the funeral, his mother's remarks did give him a bad feeling, like maybe his suit was so hideous that it was drawing people's attention towards him rather than, as he hoped, quietly repelling their attention away; or maybe he even seemed to be making a mockery of the funeral proceedings, or of his father's memory, by looking so bad. His mother, by contrast, is a glamorous person who dresses in matching outfits and always wears strong perfume. This sensory association is so powerful in Ivan's mind that he experiences a mild feeling of unease even walking through the perfume section of a chemist or department store, like his mother might be lurking somewhere nearby, ready to leap out and catch him in the act of shopping.

I texted you about Christmas, she says. You never got back to me.

He lingers by the sink watching her put away the groceries. Oh yeah, he says. What's the plan, you're going to Scotland?

Looking up at him she says: You can come along if you like. Or I can stay.

He shrugs his shoulders. Lifts a thumbnail to his mouth and then drops it again, to avoid being seen chewing his nails. He finds it off the top of his head doubtful that he will go to Frank's sister's house in Scotland for Christmas, since he doesn't travel by air, and he doesn't like Frank or Frank's children, although the sister Pauline is actually okay. But he also finds it unlikely that he's going to personally ask his own mother to stay home from Scotland in order to spend Christmas with him: it's not the kind of thing he would do. The question of Peter's whereabouts naturally arises, to an almost obtrusive extent, but, for obvious reasons, Ivan isn't going to raise the subject himself. I'll think about it, he says.

Your wish is my command, she answers. I don't know what your brother's plans are, but I suppose that doesn't really put you up or down.

After a pause Ivan answers judiciously: No, yeah.

Seeing as the two of you have fallen out again, she adds.

Lurching sensation now in his stomach. Cold and at the same time hot: that Peter told. That she knows already about everything, and this is all a game, the whole thing, the text about his dog, because she already knows, and now Ivan is trapped here almost physically imprisoned in her kitchen and she's even standing between him and the door. In a toneless voice he asks: Peter said that?

Not that he would divulge the reason, she replies. Go on, what's he done this time?

While speaking, she hands Darren a box of eggs for him to put away, and Ivan involuntarily exhales in the direction of the kitchen tiles. Nothing, he says.

Blood from a stone, says Christine. I don't know which of you is worse.

Having put away the groceries, she hangs up the basket from a hook on the wall. Chewing after all on his thumbnail, Ivan can see that his moment of panic just now was unwarranted, because, for all his faults, his brother is not a rat. Though not, like Ivan, wary of Christine, Peter doesn't really like her, and has often even sided with Ivan against her in the past, from a combination of specific filial antipathy and the sort of free-wheeling belligerence he seems to have available to him at all times. In fact, Ivan thinks, if their mother had somehow found out about Margaret first, and had predictably tried to make life hell for Ivan as a result, the person most likely to take his side in such a scenario would be, there's no doubt about it, Peter himself. Making arguments about personal liberty and the hard-won sexual freedoms of the post-Catholic era or whatever. Yes, Ivan thinks, one of the only consistent principles in his brother's life is to become unbelievably partisan in every conflict he ever encounters and then to win the conflict using a barrage of extreme verbal force: a horrible personality trait, practically a disorder. But another of Peter's principles is, admittedly, that he's not a rat. Ivan drops his thumbnail from his mouth and, with an unexpected little jolt of sensory input, feels the wet nose of his dog once again touch his hand. In response he bends down a little to smooth his palm over the animal's soft silken head, thinking again about the empty water bowl, scent of detergent, the cream-coloured jacket, the plastic flip-flops, the lack of care shown once again by his family, who seem in this moment of contemplation like actual narcissists, wrapped up completely in pursuit of their own interests, caring nothing for the feelings and needs of those more vulnerable.

Does the dog get left in that room all day? Ivan asks.

Not this again, Christine says. Why don't you take him off with you if you're not happy?

Ivan looks down at Alexei, who is sitting obediently on the floor at his feet, gazing up at him with deep dark eyes of absolute trust and love. In this moment, looking into his dog's eyes, Ivan begins to feel a purity of sensation inside himself, a strong pure clear feeling. There is compassion and decency in this world, he thinks. He thinks about Margaret, about being alone with her, the way she says quietly: I love you. And the lifting sensation he feels at those moments, like being lifted up from the earth, which even now, remembering, is pure inside him and glowing. Her tenderness and compassion towards him, he thinks: and not only him, but people generally. The people at her work who she likes so much, her friend Anna, the husband and baby of Anna, college friends she keeps up with over email, the circle of her care and concern growing outward and outward, including even people who have let her down and hurt her, her mother, her ex-husband, and so on. Her loving and considerate attitude towards others. The way that, when Ivan complains about his own family, Margaret can be very much on his side while still showing a little bit of sympathy towards such characters as Christine and Peter, who after all are just human beings, flawed, okay, but not literally evil. Yes, the world makes room for goodness and decency, he thinks: and the task of life is to show goodness to others, not to complain about their failings. Bending down, he takes Alexei's body into his arms, cradling him like the little puppy he once was, and when he stands up again Alexei begins to lick his ear and jaw. Okay, Ivan says. I'll take him. Would you mind putting his things in a bag?

Christine and Darren stare at Ivan together. Where are you going to go? she says. I thought you couldn't have pets in your apartment.

I'll figure it out, says Ivan. He's my dog. You've looked after him for long enough.

His mother, frowning, looking almost anxious now, answers: He's far too big to be carried around like that, you look ridiculous. Why don't you stay for dinner? Frank can give you a lift back into town.

Although this suggestion is in fact sensible, and Ivan isn't totally sure how he's going to get Alexei back into town without the use of a car, he finds it in this moment more important to preserve the feeling, the strong radiating feeling of purity, which has driven him at last to decisive action, than to accept practical advice. No, thanks, he says. If you can just get his things together, we'll go. Thank you.

Finally, Christine and Darren exchange a glance, as if to confirm quietly that they both agree Ivan is a lunatic, and furthermore that they think he's too stupid to notice them exchanging this obvious glance right in front of him. But such a trifle cannot aggrieve or harm Ivan in his present state of mind, he thinks: in fact it doesn't matter at all. Okay, says Christine. Have it your way. We'll get his things.

The dog rests his thin head peacefully on Ivan's shoulder while they wait together for Darren and Christine to pack up his accoutrements: feeding bowls, red lead, blue extendable lead, waste bags, fleece bed, sachets of wet food, and so on. Then Ivan attaches the red lead to the dog's collar, puts the bag over his shoulder, and says: Cool. Thanks. Christine repeats that he's welcome to stay for dinner and Ivan again politely refuses the invitation. Walking out the door with the lead in his hand, Alexei trotting obediently at his side, Ivan says in a friendly tone of voice: See you again. Christine closes the front door and immediately he can hear her voice through the door, talking in a high exasperated tone to Darren, about Ivan, no doubt: and why not, he thinks. They have each other, their housing development with the big engraved rock outside, their synthetic fragrances, polished marble countertops, and he wishes them happiness and inner peace. Okay, they look at him as a weird unnerving person, in need of some explanatory neurological or cognitive diagnosis, which for some reason never seemed to be forthcoming. But he does not have to look at himself in that same way. And with the sense that, on the contrary, there is nothing really wrong with him, he does not need to nurse any bitterness towards his mother and step-family anymore. He even begins to suspect that he might be the normal one, and they might after all be kind of weird and unnerving: a strangely guilt-inducing thought, which makes him go back to wishing them inner peace and happiness again.

Out of the estate he walks with the dog by his side, back out onto the main street system, and towards the train station, Alexei glancing up at him with what looks like a delighted smile. At the side of the street, Ivan stops and takes his phone from his pocket to type into the search engine: dog on commuter train dublin. An information box appears, indicating that pets are permitted to travel on commuter trains if appropriately restrained. Okay, Ivan murmurs aloud. Then, looking down at Alexei, who looks back up at him panting happily, Ivan says: You have to behave yourself, alright? Walking back through a commercial area on the way to the station, Ivan notices people looking at Alexei, children for example, pointing at the dog and smiling. Alexei, relishing the attention, lifts his paws elegantly, cock of the walk, even holding his head at a jaunty angle while they make their way along the street. A young woman in a purple tracksuit looks down at him as she passes and says aloud: Oh my God, your dog is gorgeous. Alexei responds to the attention by straining on his leash to try and reach the woman, obviously eager to be petted and admired by a complete stranger, and smiling awkwardly Ivan mutters: Yeah, thanks. Only now, attempting for the first time in nearly a year to walk his dog through a busy urban environment, does Ivan remember what an embarrassing little showboat Alexei can be in front of people. Ivan shortens the lead by winding it around his hand, and eventually succeeds in manoeuvring the dog to the station and through the barriers onto the platform. The display board shows that the train is due in seven minutes. Time, he thinks, to consider the next phase of the plan.

Ivan has, in reality, despite his decisive behaviour up at the house just now, no precise next steps in mind. If quiet and well behaved, Alexei could probably stay in the apartment for a short time, but his presence would technically breach the terms of the lease, and Ivan does not want to cause conflict among his flatmates, with whom his relations are already to his mind strained. But okay, he thinks: a night or two at the apartment, considering that the flatmates did sign that card for him when they heard about his dad, two nights will probably be okay. And afterwards? As Ivan stands alone on the train platform, the dog urinating on the base of a lamp-post, the pure clear strength of feeling inside him seems to have subsided, and he now feels a more familiar gnawing anxiety and dread. Maybe this plan doesn't make any sense at all. He doesn't actually have anywhere for Alexei to live. And his dramatic behaviour may have made Christine unlikely to take the dog back again, meaning Ivan has not only not improved the situation but actually made everything worse. Suddenly, with a buffeting feeling of shock, he remembers that tomorrow is Friday. He's supposed to see Margaret at the weekend: what will he do with Alexei then? He looks down at the dog once more, and, seeking an outlet for his agitation, bends to stroke the soft downy coat between his ears. Along the rails he can hear the rhythmic sound of the train approaching, and Alexei turns to look up at him again with loyal and devoted eyes. It will all be okay, he thinks. Margaret will understand: she understands everything. As the train draws closer, threading through the grey of the late afternoon with its lights flaring ahead, Ivan feels strangely as if Margaret is in some way close to him, understanding and loving him quietly without words, and he knows that nothing is wrong. The dark mechanical body of the train comes clicking to a stop, and with a soft hissing sound the doors open. Together, Ivan and his dog enter the lighted carriage, the doors seal shut again, and the train begins its work of bearing them away.

# 11

Class in the afternoon. EU Competition Law. That's an interesting question, yeah. I think in a sense that goes more into the realm of jurisprudence. Afterwards, the dark carpeted corridors of the arts block. Three o'clock her lecture finishes. Could get another coffee downstairs and hang around, he thinks. Even just to lay eyes on her. Feel better then. Tell her about Christine, about Ivan, the phone call, dissolve his bad feelings in the familiar tonality of her conversation. Black, no sugar, paces the length of the concourse checking his emails again, sipping, too hot. Typing with one thumb: Thanks for this. Yes, that's correct. At ten to three the other doors start opening, students filing out, zipping up jackets, yawning, chatting amongst themselves. Loud undifferentiated hum of conversation. Waits outside to see her as the other lecture halls empty themselves, unspooling face after face. Door of her room still closed. On the hour. Then a minute or two past. Cooling coffee in his hand he hits the button, goes inside. Empty and silent the interior. Down all the rows of folded seats, a few discarded pens and pieces of scrap paper. Vacant lectern with its angled microphone. He walks back out letting the door swing closed behind him. Did he get that wrong, the hour. Check her office in that case. Odd he thinks the anxious feeling. Across the concourse again, drops the empty cup in the bin, and he's climbing the stairs. Turn right down the dark corridor to her door: PROFESSOR SYLVIA LARKIN. Reassuring specificity of the brown engraved nameplate, the little Max Beerbohm cartoon of Henry James snooping at a bedroom door. Knocks and gets no answer. Places like Henry his ear to the door, hears nothing. Shakes his head, knocks again, louder. Recognising in himself some dread feeling, something wrong. Woman coming down the corridor towards him, he turns, and dimly recognising says: Sylvia around? One of her colleagues, holding a lunchbox in one hand, unlocking her office door with the other. No, sorry, she says. Home sick today, I think. He nods, feels himself nodding, feels the various muscles that are required to produce this small gesture contracting and stretching as necessary. Ah, okay, he says. Thanks. The woman enters her office then, saying aloud as she leaves Peter's field of vision: No worries. The door closes. Once more alone in the dim carpeted corridor. Home sick: ah, okay. Silently in solitude he makes his way back down the windowless staircase.

Outside, he takes his phone from his pocket and lights the screen. Taps and taps again. Begins typing.

PETER: Hey, I hear you're out sick from work. Feeling ok?

PETER: If I can help at all, let me know

In the improbably blue sky over Dawson Street a small white cloud appears, alone. Cold sunlight. Don't worry, it was nothing. I just wanted to complain about my mother, brother, about my work, my personal life. I forgot again or studiously suppressed the certain knowledge that you are very often and presumably right now in excruciating pain. It's just something I prefer not to contemplate. No, I just feel kind of slighted by the fact that you're off work and you didn't tell me. Like some random colleague from your office knows that you're sick and I don't. Never mind, not that. Yes, I was looking for you, but I only wanted to see and be near you, and actually it wasn't going to matter what either of us said as long as we could be in physical proximity to one another, making eye contact, breathing each other's breath for a while, how does that sound.

SYLVIA: That's very kind thank you

Small white rounded cloud passing slowly and in silence over the sun. Change in the quality of light on the street, dimming, greying, the outlines of buildings less defined now, loss of contrast.

SYLVIA: Actually if you don't mind it would be very helpful if you could pick up my prescriptions for me and just leave them outside the apartment door
SYLVIA: If you're in town already but if not don't worry

Dread again and deeper in the pit of his stomach. Messages unpunctuated. Why at the door, why leave it at the door. Resting in bed perhaps and forgets he has his own key: but how could she forget. Only a few weeks ago. When every night he. Might be something contagious then, doesn't want him to catch. Begins to walk with long strides to the pharmacy, over the tram tracks, typing as he goes.

PETER: No problem. I'll be at your apartment in 15
PETER: Do you have covid symptoms? I can pick up tests if so
SYLVIA: No it's nothing like that
SYLVIA: Just in pain
SYLVIA: Nothing to worry about

Artificial bell of the tram passing. Sick feeling, his reflection flashing and vanishing in the darkened windows of the carriage beside, one hand in his pocket clutching his phone to feel in case it vibrates. Heart beating hard. Bright fragrant interior of the pharmacy like a migraine, shelves of plastic packaging, cosmetics, hair products. They know him in here, he's been before, collecting her prescriptions. Damp his hands and tingling sensation. Pays up and walks back with wide rapid step to the street, paper package rustling in his pocket. Pulse of his phone and he's lighting the screen, new message.

SYLVIA: You can just leave the medicine outside my door if you're passing thanks

Reading, he glances up, trying not to walk into anyone, and back at the screen. Why at the door. Because she doesn't want him to come near, he thinks. Because of what happened. And has no one else to help her. Feels as if rather than breathing he is swallowing raw the dirty urban air. To think of her in pain. And what is that thought. A way of provoking in himself merely a familiar suite of bad feeling. Guilt, self-hatred, something else, worse. Nothing achieved, no solace provided. Only alternative however is not to think, not to imagine or even try. Leave her even in his own mind alone and untouched in her agony. Perform unfeelingly the various duties, pick up the medicines, call by the hospital when she needs collecting. To her it would probably make no difference. Not to be thought of, since his thoughts accomplish nothing. Why think then. Why open that part of his brain, why gaze with such dread down into the bottomless emptiness that is the suffering of another person, emptiness he can never measure or touch. Like going along to his dad's meetings with the oncologist. Asking intelligent questions, remembering the right details, exact haemoglobin count at the last blood draw, 10.6 off the top of his head. What was it all for, the show of erudition, command of detail. Not as if it made a difference. Insurance against future shame. I was there, I served my hours, punched my time card, don't forget. I did everything that could be done. Don't blame me. I was there. While his father sat timidly beside him, embarrassed probably by his peremptory manner. Afraid of alienating the doctors. Why even think about that now. The suffering of another person. Which he failed to stop. False show of competence only disguising the fact of his uselessness, his failure to do anything, to make anything better, to make any difference at all.

Reaching at last the door of her building he fumbles with the keys, ascends two at a time the familiar staircase. Painted walls marked by trailing bike handles. At her door he knocks, swallowing, and says aloud: It's me. No sound from inside. I have my key, he adds. I can let myself in. Side of his face almost pressed to the door he hears a faint muffled noise. Then her voice, strained, calling out: No, it's okay. Just leave it where you are, thank you. In his grip the paper bag crumpled, damp. You don't want me to drop it inside for you? he asks. It'll save you coming out. She gives no answer. No sound, nothing. Sour taste in his dry mouth he glances at the other apartment door along the hall, closed, silent. I think I'll come in, if that's okay, he says. He waits and hears no protest. Slides his key into the lock, waits again, and hears nothing. Slowly turns the key and enters. Dim little hallway lighted only by the open door into her living room, white daylight leaking. He closes the door behind him, takes off his coat, his shoes. In a thin voice she says from the other room: I'm alright, there's nothing to worry about. He hangs his coat up on the hook, answering automatically: I'm not worried.

Entering the room he sees her lying on the floor, between the coffee table and the sofa. Not quite face down, half on her side, and with her hand she shields her eyes, hiding from him her expression. A white cotton t-shirt blotted with sweat she wears and a pair of grey sweatpants, the seam of one leg twisted the wrong way around her ankle. Beside her on the floor, her phone, and a plastic basin into which she has been sick. Bitter odour in his nose and mouth. She says without looking: I'm just in a lot of pain. And I don't feel like trying to get up right now. But there's nothing wrong. Controlled minutely her voice. The room he thinks hot. She has fallen on the floor and can't get up. Why she told him not to come in, he knows now. Not to see her like this. He stands there looking down at her. Okay, he says. I'll get you a glass of water and you can try to take your medicine. How does that sound? Still with her face in her hand she gives a kind of nod. He goes to the kitchen, lets the tap run cold and then fills a glass. Opens the cardboard packaging, creases two tablets from the foil. Crossing back to the living room he gets down beside her on the rug. Here, he says. Gives into one grasping hand the two tablets and then passes her the water. Lifting awkwardly her head she swallows once, and again. Blotchy her face he thinks. Rinsing the water inside her mouth she drains the glass. He straightens up, takes the basin from the floor and brings it to the bathroom. Hears her saying desperately from behind him: No, Peter, don't. Just leave it, please. Methodically he empties the basin into the bowl of the toilet, thin whitish yellow foam, and flushes. Cold churn of running water and the cistern refilling. Rinses in the bathroom sink the bowl, tapping on the rim, and then returns, leaving the door ajar. Places the basin back down saying: I'll leave it here for you. Are you just sick from the pain? Averting her gaze she answers yes. Tearful her voice. Why didn't you call me? he asks. For a moment she's silent and then says without looking: I didn't want to bother you. Hard feeling in his chest. Don't talk like that, he says. She gives no reply. Sensation of pressure inside his head, inside his ears, almost ringing. How long have you been lying there? he asks. She wipes roughly at her eyes with her hand. You can be angry with me if you like, she says. It won't change anything. He goes on watching her a little longer and then at last gets down on the floor, rests his back against the leg of the coffee table. Her hand gripping the edge of the rug he sees, tassels between her fingers. Skin stretched translucent over the bones of her knuckles. He lays his hand on hers and she doesn't pull away. Only lies there saying nothing. Ten minutes, twenty. Now and then as if against some blinding light she closes her eyes, contortions of pain moving through her face and body, and grips hard his hand hurting. Watching her he feels: what, nothing. Overwarm, sweating, mild discomfort of sitting on the floor, nothing else discernible. Only a kind of pounding feeling somewhere inside himself, a certain indescribable pressure. To see her like this. On the floor, drenched in sweat, sick, exhausted. Alone, not wanting to bother anyone. Her hand damp in his or is it his in hers. You just tell me when you're ready to try getting up, he says. And I'll help you into bed. Okay? She exhales a hard little breath. Jaw trembling he sees. And her eyes closed. Okay, she says. I'll try.

He gets up and she allows him to help her to her feet. Through the cloth of her t-shirt he can feel with his fingers the thin bands of her ribcage. Hissing intake of breath through her teeth, wincing, but she says aloud: I'm okay, I'm fine. Standing she bends almost double, clutching his arm with tight fingers, and says she'll go to the bathroom. He helps her to the door, lets her close it behind her. Sound of the tap running. A minute or two later she opens the door again, bent over, leaning her weight on the handle. Hand towel she has left crumpled beside the sink, and her toothbrush, wet now, and she smells of soap. He takes her weight on his arm again. In her room, the blind pulled down, the bed unmade, clothes discarded on the floor. Slowly, carefully, she lies down, and he sits on the side of the mattress. Do you want me to bring in that basin for you? he asks. She shakes her head. I'm feeling better, she says. I think the medication is starting to work. Thank you. Quietly he rests back against the headboard, stretches his legs out. His side of the bed. Filtrate of fading daylight through the blind. Feels the warmth of her body beside him. And thinks for no reason of being with her, before. When she would wake him in the night, unable to sleep, wanting to talk, to complain, to make love. Heaviness in his limbs he remembers. Fumbling half-asleep with her nightdress. Awkward at first and then easy. Her face hot in his neck. Regrets now every night they didn't. Drunk, or too tired, or whatever. Other things also he regrets. Kind of thing that can never be said, too much like an accusation, or just too painful. Beside him in the dark now he hears her breath catching. Soft sibilant sound of her crying, trying not to cry. As if she too has been thinking. Come here, he says. And puts his arm around her, draws her closer. Unresisting she rests her head on his chest, crying almost noiselessly. What's wrong, it's the pain? he asks. Gesture of her head shaking. Thick her voice answering: No, it's alright. It's not as bad as it was. His hand at the back of her neck, fingers in her hair. What is it, then? he asks. She just shakes her head again and says nothing. Strands of her hair light and fine between his fingers he feels and remembers feeling. Touching with his hand her head. As when she would wake him at night, wanting, and he would take her into his arms. Feel better then. Go back to sleep. I'm sorry, she murmurs aloud. He waits, and then asks: For what? His hand in her hair, his fingers caressing. Quietly she says: I don't know. I feel I've done everything wrong, I've gone about everything in the wrong way. Heavy like sleep the weight of her head resting. That's alright, he says. I feel that way too, all the time. And without knowing what he's saying he asks: Do you ever think about when we were together? She seems to swallow, wet sound, weight of her head against his chest. Do you? she says. Feel his face warm, his hands. I don't know, he answers. I find it difficult. With her fingers she's wiping at her eyes. Mm, she says. Here now he thinks and at the same time elsewhere ten years ago with their eyes closed, her head on his chest, half-sleeping. Later, to wake, wanting again. The closeness of that, as if visible behind a thin veil, through which even a hand could pass, touching, but not. The river never the same. And he is not the same man. You know, there are a lot of feelings there, he says. I feel guilty, for not being able to help you. And on some level, to be honest, I probably feel angry with you as well. For leaving me. Just to tell you the truth.

Quietly she answers: If we had stayed together, you would have ended up hating me, Peter. And if you had left me, I would have hated you.

Sometimes I think you do anyway, he says.

Her voice brittle. Why? she asks. Do you hate me?

No, he says. I just feel like I've failed you. You know, I feel like I let you down, and you're disgusted with me. I do feel that you hate me, sometimes. Yeah. This idea that it was all for my sake, that we broke up. As if I should be grateful to you. That's hurtful, it is very hurtful. It can feel, if I'm honest, it can feel like you're punishing me.

Still without lifting her head, hand at her face, her eyes. Maybe you should be grateful, she says. You've been living your life, haven't you? The last, whatever, six or seven years, you've had a life. I haven't.

You mean I've been out with other women, he says. That's what you call having a life. I can't imagine that you think I've been happy. How many times have I come pleading with you to take me back? The other week, when I was staying here. Trying to get you to talk to me. Or trying to touch you, or kiss you, whatever. You know, I think in a way you actually like it, watching me humiliate myself like that. And you get to reject me all over again. I think there's a part of you that enjoys it.

Quick and shallow her breath he can feel or is it his. Okay, she says. Maybe you're right. If you want to know the truth. Maybe I do enjoy it.

He falls still, halted, in silence. And then asks: Do you?

Well, it's flattering, obviously, she says. It is very flattering. And maybe it's nice to imagine, or to think about. That you still look at me in that way. I'm not made of stone. I have feelings. Maybe I do enjoy being pleaded with.

Warm he feels the weight of her body resting, her bare arm, and warm at his side, pressed against him. His eyes again closing just to feel or think of her wanting. Can I plead with you now? he asks. Without drawing away, without moving, she exhales quickly. You're just taking pity on me, she says. His hand stirring to touch her hair. Will you let me kiss you? he says. At last she lifts her head: and why, to retreat, or just to look in his eyes, or relent after all perhaps and permit him, he doesn't know, and without speaking again he kisses her mouth. Sense of her falling slowly still. Lying down on her side now with her head on the pillow and he lies facing. Softly her lips parting. Throb of desire he feels, his fingers in her fine soft hair. Held close to him, feeling, he thinks, yes. Hard, pressed against her. A faint indistinct sound like her breath catching he hears or thinks and idiotically he groans into her mouth, wanting. What, to hear that. Her breath, hot. And he also, rush of blood almost light-headed, touching. He shuts his eyes then. Like this, just to be with her like this, pressed close, to feel her breath at his lips. To make her feel, yes, to hear her cry out like that, it's nice. Warm her mouth and yes familiar. To think, as he has often thought, about her mouth, kissing her, and if she. Her fingers at the back of his neck. Can I touch your mouth? he asks. Feels or hears then somehow the flutter of her eyelids opening. Oh, she says. With your hand, you mean? He tries to swallow, throat tightening. Yeah, he says. Only if you don't mind. Looking at him now, she nods her head, tentative. He touches with the tip of his thumb her lips, soft, and damply parting. Wet of her tongue he can feel and closes again his eyes. Senses absurdly that if he moves at all, or tries to speak or look at her, he might come, just like this, exhausted, oversensitive, not even doing anything, his thumb only resting against her lower lip. And holding tightly closed his eyes he tries to breathe as normal. That's nice, he says. Thank you. Hears and feels her trembling. Her voice hardly at all suppressed she says quietly: Would you like— I don't know. Do you want me to touch you, maybe? Faint feeling, weakness in his limbs, and fumbling for words he answers: Jesus, yes, please. I want that, yes, thank you. At his waistband her fingertips and awkwardly he tries to help. Soft and cool her hand touching then, and she's shyly smiling, saying tentatively: Like this? Hot prickling feeling in his scalp, the back of his neck. Ah, it feels so good, he says. Tighter the pressure of her hand and he hears himself stupidly again groaning. Hem of her t-shirt lifted and the tip of his cock under the hollow of her navel. You're a little bit wet, she says. Tight throbbing sensation he feels inside himself, and closes his eyes again. Ah, sorry, he says. It's just nice, it feels so nice. Unseen she goes on touching him. Sound of her voice very low and sweet saying: I'd like to taste it. Groaning again he hears himself, loud hard stuttering sound. His eyes closed, feeling on her mouth the words as well as hearing, that she thinks, wants, pressed close against him, her small narrow body, tight her hand, and her wet mouth, tasting of salt, sweet, touching, and he's finished, saying nothing, only breathing hard. And then after all saying: Ah, I'm sorry. Opens his eyes to see her flushed, smiling, pulling back with her slim fingers the hem of her t-shirt, wet. Don't be, she says. Meeting her eye he feels his face still burning, his forehead, his throat. With a high sacred joyful feeling, he says aloud: Oh, well. Let me get you, ah— I'm sorry.

She's laughing, touching tenderly her face, shy. It's alright, she says. That was nice. If I had known it would be like that— I just always thought it would be so difficult. To make you feel— I don't know. I'm sorry.

He feels his eyes pricking, touched by her sweetness, by how easy it has been, friendly, fond, somehow even ordinary. Let's get married, he says. Again delightedly laughing she answers: Was it that good? They look at one another, pleased, foolish, and he touches her hair. Yes, he replies. How are you feeling, is the pain still very bad? Smiling with her cheeks and throat pink. No, it's okay, she says. The painkillers are working. And this was a nice distraction. Glancing at him quickly and away again she says: More than a distraction, thank you. Ease and lightness in his body he feels. I think it's one of those things where I should be thanking you, he says. She finds in her bedside drawer a packet of tissues. In companionable quiet for a time they lie there, tired he thinks, and happy, inexpressibly happy, saying nothing. He asks eventually if she feels up to eating and she says maybe a slice of toast or something plain like that. I'll go and put some on, he answers. Back in a minute. And leaning over he kisses her forehead. I love you, he says. Still smiling, still with the same shy look, she answers: I love you too.

In the kitchen, yawning, pleasantly dull of mind, he puts some bread in the toaster, finds the butter and jam in the fridge. Visits the bathroom, washes his hands. His reflection over the sink quite ordinary, his ordinary face, which he sees every day reflected in mirrors, darkened windows, the unlighted screens of devices. Appearing at times rather tired and rough, hollows under the eyes, and at others decent-looking and youthful still. Lines in his forehead though you notice now. With the overhead light especially. Hers also. To taste, she said: and a hard little after-rush of pleasure passes through him, involuntary, exhaling aloud, almost wanting again already. To feel again, to make her say more, yes. In the kitchen the toast isn't finished yet and he takes his phone from his pocket. Two work emails, missed call from his accountant, and a text from Naomi. Blankly he taps to open.

NAOMI: im cooking lol
NAOMI: if its bad we can order in
NAOMI: what time you home ?

She has attached a picture: his small green casserole dish on one of the hotplates. Disorientated feeling, as though his centre of gravity disturbed, walls shifting: like passing out, he thinks. As if he will pass out there and then, and at the thought, remembering, he sits down on a kitchen chair. The little green dish on the stovetop, what time you home. Christ, he thinks, what is he doing, what on earth. In the bath the other night, murmuring in her ear, I want you to be happy. Was he lying then: and why, for what, for what possible reason. Strong sudden impulse he feels to begin praying, already mouthing the silent words, and then frightened by himself he stops. To pray for what: forgiveness, guidance. From whom: God he barely believes in, sentimental Jesus commanding us to love one another. In over his head, fathoms over, and something has to be done. How capable he has been of holding in his mind with no apparent struggle such contradictory beliefs and feelings. The false true lover, the cynical idealist, the atheist at his prayers. Everything lethally intermixed, everything breaching its boundaries, nothing staying in its right place. She, the other, himself. Even Christine, Ivan, this married girlfriend of his. Their father: from beyond the grave. Conceptual collapse of one thing into another, all things into one. No. To answer first the simple question of where to sleep tonight. Marry me. I love you. What time you home.

# 12

The same night, a Thursday, Margaret is doing front-of-house for a performance of the *Goldberg Variations*. Young pianist from Belfast, some nice notices in the press, and a good audience in, she thinks, closing the outer foyer door. Plenty of the regulars, the music crowd, and elderly Mrs Harrington in her beautiful winter coat, and Eleanor Lawless with her husband, and students, some of them, young, with bad skin, and no coats at all, and at the last minute Anna, out of breath, laughing, wrestling with a half-broken umbrella. One by one Margaret has torn their tickets and directed them to their seats, and from the lighted foyer now she enters the hall herself, into the murmuring darkness, swinging the heavy door shut behind her, pulling the curtain clinking and stuttering along the rail. Fragrance of warm bodies, boots and overcoats damp with rain. Standing up on the stage-step she feels the light bright on her face, dust motes large and mobile before her eyes, while the murmur falls into hush. Danny upstairs in the control room tonight, his silhouette she thinks she can make out through the glass. Good evening and welcome to Clogherkeen Arts Centre, she says aloud. From backstage, while she without even listening to herself explains the location of the fire exits and asks the audience to switch off their mobile phones, she can hear underneath the so familiar noise of her own voice the sound of a footstep in the wings behind her, careful weight of tread. Thank you for your attention and please enjoy the show, she says. Scattering of applause. Making her way to her seat in the pleasant excitable quiet before the performance, she feels Anna's hand on her arm, voice saying in her ear: You're so glamorous. Absurdly, happily, Margaret laughs. Then the lights, dazzling, the young musician all in black, the sound of applause, wall of noise as she seats herself at the piano, tapering off into silence.

Into the still silent darkness, the first notes float high and even hesitant. Lighter higher tones followed slowly by lower, dragging a little, strange echo: an almost straggling effect. Pink fingers of the pianist on the glossy white keys, frowning in focus her youthful pink face. Margaret brought her a cup of coffee earlier, balanced on a tray with a plate of biscuits, and they talked about the tour, the musician soft-spoken and smiling uncertainly. Her bitten nails, reminding Margaret of Ivan. Reminded again now listening. On the phone with him last night, she mentioned the recital, and he told her that Bach was his favourite composer, that he would be sorry to miss the show. It gave her a tender feeling, this remark, suggestion of another reality. That he might, under different circumstances, be here with her in the darkness. After the performance, to hear his thoughts, and Anna's also. The three of them having a drink together, his gentle frowning manner, his thoughtfulness, ideas about mathematics and the baroque style. Pain in her heart to think. Abruptly now she hears the music changing: jaunty and rapid, clever, chattering back and forth. Quickly and easily the pianist's hands move over the keys, her head it seems nodding with the complex play of rhythms, faster and faster. Brighter now and glimmering the notes rise into the dark, chasing, light footsteps. The tense thrilled hush of listeners gathered together around the sound: sharing in silence this one brief consciousness. Hearing and listening together, following together the almost too quick bright brilliant passage of melody, dispersing and vanishing in the air. For an hour to share this without speaking. To sit here with other people in the dark. A small experience, small enough to hold in the hand, to touch and smooth later in a pocket. Last night on the phone, Ivan said he could come and see her during the week sometimes, if she wanted. Work at her house in the daytime, while she went into the office. Dinner together in the evening, maybe watch a film afterwards, his arm around her shoulders. All the unhappiness that life has visited on them both: dissolved however briefly in that feeling, shared image of that quiet contentment. Maybe, she said. Light and silvery high the music feathers through the air around her, sadly soft. And why not after all. Why not accept wholeheartedly life's offerings. This chess event he has coming up, the night she'll be in Dublin for the Music Ireland conference: they could meet in town, go for dinner. Or she could stop by the tournament, catch the end of one of his games. How they first met, after all: she the spectator, he the conquering hero. Introduce her to his friends afterwards perhaps. And she him, to her own friends, why not. Anna, this is Ivan, he's twenty-two. And extremely serious about chess. Is it impossible? Anna knows there's someone, each knowing that she knows. But Margaret can guess what she must imagine. Some nice man in his forties living above in Sligo, a paramedic or a librarian. Divorced or perhaps even widowed. Margaret bringing him hot meals and holding his hand in the cinema. It could never occur to her, how could it occur to anyone? A boy with braces on his teeth, mumbling in her ear: Ah, fuck. Anna cannot condemn what she does not know: and doesn't perhaps really want to know, not wanting to condemn. What the two of them have suffered together: grief, childbirth, sickness, misery. Full complement of the human body's excesses and inadequacies. Blood, excrement, vomit, yes, the accident and emergency, the late-night chemist, tears at the kitchen table. Anna tired now and happy, lines over her brow, arms strong with the weight of her firstborn. Margaret secretive and glamorous in her green velvet jacket doing front-of-house for a midweek piano concert. All their lives they have known each other. One loose handful of years left now before they are middle-aged together. Companionable silences of friendship. They will go on facing side by side the awful shocks of life, offering one another when needs be the old comfortable blanket of tacit understanding. Say no more. Better not to speak. I understand. Resounding now the music beats over them both, insisting, cresting, and then falling to silence. Margaret waits, watching, fluttering sensation, and finally, into the silence, the same quiet halting passage from the beginning, she thinks, uncertainly trilling itself into the dark, a tentative descent. Inexpressibly moved she feels by the strange stilted sound of the music, so strangely lilting, the final slow hesitant notes hanging suspended and trembling glittering in the empty air.

Into the silence at last spills the sound of applause. The audience rise to their feet, the noise grows louder, too loud, while the musician takes her bow, smiling with small white teeth. Bead of sweat trickling down her temple. Deafening the clamour of applause, Margaret's hands and arms growing sore with effort, and after returning for a second bow, the musician is gone. From upstairs in the box, Danny turns the house lights up, and Margaret goes to pull back the curtain from the door. Voices in the lobby, lights bright, dazzling, burbling laughter, rattle of car keys, while Margaret bids everyone goodnight. Eleanor Lawless stops to chat a minute, buttoning her coat up, good to see you Margaret, and you Anna, how's the little man, beautiful music wasn't it, take care now. Cold rush of rain from the street. Margaret and Anna walk across the car park together, linking arms. Great crowd in, Anna says. Pink halo of mist glowing around each streetlamp. I know, Margaret answers. Busy tonight the Cobweb with its old framed advertisements, sweetish stale odour of hops. Anna goes to order the drinks and Margaret settles into a little booth near the back of the bar, finding on her phone the photograph of her mother's dishwasher. When Anna returns with the lemonades, ice knocking softly against slices of lemon, Margaret shows her the picture, and Anna loyally takes the device from her hand for closer inspection. I hope you've sent this to your siblings, Anna says. Margaret laughing lifts her cold glass, condensation collecting wet at her fingertips. I'm not that bad, she says.

Handing the phone back, Anna answers: No, I'm being serious. You know your mother isn't going to tell them.

Margaret, after surveying briefly once more the resplendent white machine, puts her phone away. No, she agrees. But look, it doesn't matter. You start making a fuss over these things and you're just playing their game.

Anna looks pensive, turning her glass around on the branded yellow beer mat. Mm, she says. But you don't want to be the family martyr, either.

Margaret says the danger there lies not in buying dishwashers, but in growing emotionally invested in the buying of dishwashers. For a time, sipping their lemonades, they discuss, as they often have before, the personalities of their respective mothers. Margaret's mother Bridget, once the beleaguered matriarch of her household, assailed perpetually by the competing demands of her husband, her three young children, and her work as the principal of a local secondary school. Against this onslaught she developed in middle age a kind of permanently harassed disposition, almost a siege mentality; and at times, their family dynamic resembled nothing so much as an all-out tug-of-war for her attention, children imploring, mother withholding. This way of life, exasperating though it must have been for Bridget, did, however, come to an end a long time ago. She has long since retired, Margaret's father has passed away, and Margaret herself, though living close by, sees her mother in person perhaps once a month. And yet Bridget communicates, each time they do see each other, the same weary, overburdened attitude that is so familiar to Margaret from her early life, as if Bridget is still working full-time and parenting three children, while Margaret is still a teenager refusing to get out of bed on a school morning. Anna's mother Nuala, on the other hand, exerts influence over her husband and children primarily through a tendency to become irrationally anxious and 'upset'. Much of the family life has therefore always been arranged around their collective efforts to prevent Nuala from becoming 'upset', which involves concealing from her, by almost any means necessary, the existence of any problems or potential conflicts within the family circle. Nuala lives, to some degree, in a fictitious world acted out for her by a special dramatic troupe consisting of her own children and husband, a world in which none of her loved ones have ever been unhappy, sick, depressed, disappointed, hurt, anxious or frightened. But this, in Anna's view, has also had the perverse effect of making Nuala feel as if her own anxieties are in fact the only anxieties that anyone on earth has ever experienced, and that her suffering is something she alone, the only unhappy person in a world of thriving and self-confident individuals, can understand.

What kind of a life is that for her? Anna asks.

Well, I suppose it's the life she wants, Margaret says. There has to be some level on which she's actively working to make you all behave that way.

But we don't have to be so compliant.

No, of course. You just wonder whether at this stage she has the resources to cope with anything other than compliance.

Swallowing the last of her lemonade, replacing the glass softly on the beer mat, Anna says: I do wonder.

Can I get you another? Margaret asks.

Quickly Anna checks the time on her phone. Smiling up at Margaret then she says: Okay, why not.

At the bar, Margaret orders two more lemonades, and watches the barman turn away to fetch the glasses and bottles. She's thinking again about her family, her mother. Is Bridget really so cross and dismissive? Yes, often, but not only. A competent, dependable woman also, level-headed in a crisis, a rock of sense. On practical matters, insurance, car problems, treatment for sunburn, Margaret does, even now, sometimes solicit her mother's advice, which is invariably prompt and helpful.

The most distressing thing about Bridget's attitude to Margaret, and especially towards her marriage, is not the belief that Bridget is being cruel, so much as the suspicion, bred in the bone, a lifelong instinct, that after all she might be right. Can the deep childhood impulse to trust one's mother, to agree with her against oneself, ever be wrestled down by the comparatively thin force of reasoned argument? Are there even reasoned arguments to be made in matters of love, marriage, intimate life?

From behind her now, Margaret hears someone calling her name. Turning her head, she spots Ollie Lyons, the captain of the town chess club, waving from the other end of the bar. The sight of him, his outsized significance in her present life, makes her want to laugh; instead she smiles politely and says: Ah, Ollie, nice to see you again. He makes his way almost elbowing towards her, through a knot of others at the bar. Well, now, he says. How is life at the old town hall? His face has a bright beaming flushed quality, the lenses of his glasses glinting in the dim light. All well, she says. How are things in the world of chess?

Not bad, says Ollie. Not bad now. You know, on that subject, a funny thing.

The barman returns with two small lemonade bottles and two glasses with ice and lemon. Margaret roots in her handbag for her purse, saying distractedly to Ollie: What's that?

Just on the subject of chess, Ollie says. I was coming down Spencer Street in the car the other day, past the bus station there. Friday evening, it would have been. And who do you think I saw?

Margaret, turning her back to him, taps her card to pay for the drinks. Dry feeling in her mouth she swallows. Over her shoulder she says: Go on.

Ivan Koubek, says Ollie. I thought for a minute I must have been seeing things, but no, it was him alright. Distinctive-looking young chap.

She lifts while he speaks a small glass bottle of lemonade, yellow label moisture-wrinkled. Pours the hissing carbonated liquid into the glass. Is that so, she says.

You remember him.

She empties the first bottle and lifts the other. Yes, she says. I do.

We'd love to have him back again, Ollie says. If he is in town. His workshop went down a treat that morning.

Watching the liquid spill slowly over the ice, lemon slice slipping free now and bobbing to the surface, she answers tonelessly: Did it.

It did indeed, says Ollie. He was great with the kids. They're still talking about him.

Both glasses filled, she lifts them. Turning away from the bar to face Ollie, she tries, with what must be visible strain, to smile. That's nice, she says.

People say he could be our first grandmaster. Homegrown.

Cold and somehow heavy the glasses feel in her hands. Right, she says. I'm afraid I don't know much about that, Ollie. Have a nice evening now.

With a satisfied smiling look he answers: You too.

As if borne forward mechanically, a train along rails, she finds her way to the table where Anna is waiting, bent over her phone. I shouldn't stay long, Anna says without looking up, but I meant to ask you— She glances up and, seeing Margaret, her face changes, tenses. What? Anna says. Quickly she looks around, even rising slightly from her seat, half-crouching, surveying the bar. Then leaning over the table she adds in a low urgent tone: Is Ricky here? Margaret touching her earlobe gives a strange hollow laugh. No, she says. No one's here. Everything's fine. Anna reaches to touch her hand. What's wrong? she says.

No, nothing, says Margaret. They look at one another, and again Margaret laughs, horrible rasping sound. Oh, Anna, she says. I've been very foolish. I think I should go home. Is that alright?

Why don't you come back to our house? says Anna. We'll have a cup of tea. What do you think?

Drawn briefly to the image, Anna's house, baby clothes drying over the stove, Luke and his woodwork class. But it's not possible now, she thinks: she has made it impossible. No, she says, no, thanks. I should get home. I need to make a phone call. I'm sorry.

Anna watches her closely across the table, saying only: Don't worry, that's alright. Let's get going. I'll walk with you to the car.

They leave their drinks untasted, putting their coats on together under the pendant lights. If he didn't know before, Margaret thinks, he'll know now, seeing her leaving, white as a sheet probably, hanging on the arm of her friend. Raining again outside and she fumbles for her keys in her bag, Anna squeezing all the while her hand. Wide black car park deserted, the buildings of town looming dark all around, streaming, gutters dripping.

Are you okay to get home? Anna asks.

Sure, Margaret says. Of course.

Squeezing again her hand, Anna says in a whisper, although there's no one near: Is it to do with— someone you've been seeing?

With what feels like the last of her energy, Margaret lifts her head to look at her. Why, you've heard something? she asks.

Me? says Anna. God, no. After a moment's pause she says: Did someone say something to you at the bar just now?

Miserably she feels herself trying to shrug. I don't know, she says. It might have been nothing. Maybe I'm being paranoid. I should get home.

Anna puts her arms around her. Call me if you need me, she says.

For a moment Margaret rests in the pleasant bony discomfort of Anna's embrace, the scent of her house, apples, dish soap, all the fond unsuspecting loyalty of long friendship. Drawing away, she says bracingly: Thank you. See you soon. She gets into the car, turns on the engine. Lifts her fingers from the steering wheel in a final salute as Anna stands with her arms crossed in the rain, watching. Crunch of the wheels over gravel.

Driving home Margaret's thoughts are jumbled, almost as if she's been drinking. But no, she thinks: faster, not slower, tumbling forward over one another. Ollie's greasy little smile. Great with the kids, he said: about Ivan. As if that might be of particular interest to her. God in heaven. Talk of the chess club presumably. That man Hugh. And the chemist Tom O'Donnell, whose wife knows Margaret's mother. Her mother, yes. Hasn't she been longing for years to catch Margaret in the wrong? Running off on her poor husband to throw herself at some young lad hardly out of college. What has Ricky ever done to compare with that? And to think of Ricky. Anyone could tell him, could have told him already. What then? Turning up at the office again, drunk, asking to see her. Margaret, is that you upstairs? Come down, I want to ask you a question. I've heard something in town about you. Hand on heart she never when leaving had a thought of meeting anyone else. Only wanted to sleep alone in a safe clean room in the peace of her own company. Book on the nightstand, cup of tea, turning out the light at eleven o'clock. Cleanliness and quiet, that was all. No one could have imagined. Out of nowhere it came, unforeseen. And now she has to tell them. Can't now not, has to explain. Joanie. Linda at the office. Anna: better she hear it from Margaret surely than someone else. Lurid gossip in the supermarket. Old school friends sharing the latest. Margaret Kearns, can you imagine? I always had her down for a bit of a wild one. God forgive me she thinks.

Letting herself into the house with numb fingers, sightless, she forgoes the light switch. In the empty darkened kitchen she pulls a chair from the dining table and sits down, lights the screen of her phone. Selects his name from the contacts list. Ringing. Clicking sound and then Ivan says: Hello?

Muffled sort of thumping in the background she can hear: music, voices. Oh, you're busy, she says. I'm sorry.

No, no, he answers. I'm actually not at all. My roommates are having a party, kind of. If you can hear noises. But I'm just in my room, I'm doing nothing.

Calm familiar sound of his voice so soothing. In his room she has never seen, has only imagined from his descriptions. She closes her eyes. Ah, she says. Okay.

Was the music good?

Weakly, she smiles. Yes it was, she says. It was beautiful. You would have loved it.

I'm jealous, he replies. Bach is the best, isn't he? You listen to the later composers and it's actually sad how much lesser they were, in terms of talent.

She wipes at her nose with her fingers. In the oven door, a dark blue reflection of the window behind her, distended curvature in the glass. I went for a drink with Anna after the concert, she says. And I happened to run into Ollie.

Who?

Ollie Lyons. You remember, the captain of the chess club, here in town.

Oh, that guy, Ivan answers. I remember, you said he had a crush on me. Not that I think he did, I just remember you saying that.

Finds herself nodding her head, swallowing. He made quite a point of coming up to talk to me this evening, she says.

Yeah? That's funny. Maybe you're the one he has a crush on.

The sound of Ivan's voice with its inexplicably deep power to soothe her. Touching her forehead she says: He told me he saw you in town the other day. At the bus station. He was driving past.

For a moment Ivan says nothing. Then he says: Ah. After another pause, he adds: Hm. Finally he says: That's awkward, I'm sorry. I didn't see him, obviously.

It's not your fault, Margaret answers. Don't say sorry. From the way he was telling me about it, I got the impression— that maybe he thinks it has something to do with me. I don't know why he would think that, it's just the impression I got.

Over the confusion of noise in the background of the call, she can hear Ivan sighing. Then he says: Okay. Now that I'm thinking back on it, someone did say something to me at the workshop that time. About you. It was just a passing comment,

I didn't think it was necessarily hinting at anything. But I guess, if you think about it, maybe it's possible someone saw me in your car that morning, or something like that.

With her hand she massages her forehead. Of course: all along in that case they have known, or suspected. And Ollie, seeing Ivan at the bus stop, would merely have been gloating over the triumph of a rumour confirmed. Right, she says. That makes sense.

He falls silent for a time. Is this really bad? he asks.

Breathing in and then out again slowly. No, she says. It'll be okay. Nothing awful can happen.

Cool. I'm glad you're saying that. I think you're right.

In the cold dark emptiness of the kitchen she sits, hand moving over her forehead, back up over her hair. But if people are talking, she says, I suppose it's possible that someone might tell— my ex-husband.

Yeah, says Ivan.

I'm sorry about this. I don't want you to get dragged into it.

He answers in a sensible tone: It's not dragging me, Margaret. I'm actually the one who's causing the problem for you. Are you scared of what he'll do?

I don't know, she says. I mean, sorry, he's not violent or anything like that, obviously. Not at all. I'm just scared he'll be upset.

I get you. You don't want to hurt his feelings. But you haven't done anything wrong.

She closes her eyes. Well, I don't know if other people will see it that way, she says.

He pauses, as if to let her complete the thought, but she says nothing more. I know what you're saying, he says. People can be judgemental.

Opening her eyes again, swallowing, she answers weakly: Yes.

And you're judgemental on yourself, as well. So that doesn't help too much.

Feebly she feels herself trying to smile. I'm sorry, she repeats.

Yeah, I wish I was older, he says. It would make everything so easy. Like if I could be your age right now, I would take that in a second.

With painful fondness she replies: Ivan, that's your life. Don't wish it away.

It hasn't been that great of a life, believe me. To make you happy, I would wish it away, no problem. It's nothing, only a few years. Before I met you, the years were pretty bad anyway, I'm sorry.

She laughs. Her head uselessly shaking. Cold and dark the house around her, surfaces delineated dimly in the window light, blue and silver. Structure of her life she feels disintegrating: and yet the feeling is strangely calm. Her phone growing hot against the rim of her ear. His thoughtful silences. At last she says: We don't have to talk about it. How are you?

She hears him on the other end of the line clearing his throat. As it happens, he says, I have a small bit of news to tell you as well, although it's not important.

Swallowing, she tries again to smile. Oh? she says. Is it chess-related?

Actually not. It's no big deal. But remember my dog who I told you about?

Of course. Alexei. He's with your mother now, isn't he?

In response, Ivan makes a noise like: Hm. Then with what sounds like a nervous laugh, he says: Yeah. It's nothing to worry about, I'll figure it out. But basically, he's not staying with my mother anymore. He's actually staying with me. For the moment. Until I find somewhere else.

Bemused, Margaret says: He's there with you right now?

Literally, he's curled up beside me on my bed.

Image of Ivan on his bed: lying down, maybe, his head propped up on the pillows. The dog slim and soft beside him, small heartbeat. Oh, how nice, she says. I thought you weren't allowed to have pets in the flat.

We're not. It's just temporary.

She pauses a moment. Then, smiling, she says: Ah, I suppose you might not be able to visit this weekend, then.

Well, I was thinking about that.

It's okay, don't worry. We'll see each other another time.

After a moment, he asks: Your landlord is pretty strict about pets?

Mine? I have no idea. Why?

I was just thinking, I could bring the dog with me for the weekend. Theoretically I could, because I'm still insured on my dad's car. I would just need to get to Kildare somehow, to our old house, and then I could get the car from there and drive to Leitrim with the dog. He likes going on drives. And he's well behaved, he wouldn't be a big burden.

She's laughing again, puzzled, oddly touched. I'm not worried about that, she says. But how would you get to Kildare?

I know, it's so complicated. It's like the problem with the goats and the cabbages. Where you have to cross the river. But anyway, I could leave Alexei here for a few hours with Roland and get the train to Kildare myself. Because you can't bring pets on the intercity trains. And then I could drive back here to pick up the dog afterwards. It actually makes sense when you think about it, because once I have the car, I can just stay in Kildare for a while. Like however long I need to, really, while I'm figuring things out.

That sounds sensible, she says.

Cool, he replies. Then it's all arranged. I'll be there tomorrow evening like normal. Except you don't have to collect me, I'll drive straight to the house. Is that okay?

Perfect.

Neither of them speaking, they both stay on the phone. Margaret in the darkened kitchen with her elbow on the table, hand at her face, imagining Ivan on his bed, the dog asleep beside him. In shared silence the seconds pass.

Well, I'll let you go, she says. I'll see you tomorrow.

Yeah. Everything will be okay, you know. In my view. I don't really know what I'm talking about, obviously. But I just feel like it's going to be okay.

I think you're right. I hope so. See you soon.

They hang up. Margaret rises from the table, turns the lights on, fills the kettle. Rushing sound of the tap. Her reflection dim and bubbled in the dark window glass. Gradually these situations arise, she can see that now, just one step after another, and by the time a few weeks or months have passed, your life is no longer recognisable. You are lying to almost everyone you know. You have come to care too passionately, too fully and completely, for an unsuitable person. You can no longer visualise your own future: not only five years from now, but five months, even five weeks. Everything is in disarray. All this for one person, for the relation that exists between you. Your fidelity to the idea of that relation. In the light of that, you have come to hold too loosely many other important things: the respect of your family, the admiration of your colleagues and acquaintances, even the understanding of your closest friends. Life, after all, has not slipped free of its netting. There is no such life, slipping free: life is itself the netting, holding people in place, making sense of things. It is not possible to tear away the constraints and simply carry on a senseless existence. People, other people, make it impossible. But without other people, there would be no life at all. Judgement, reproval, disappointment, conflict: these are the means by which people remain connected to one another. Because of Margaret's friends, her former marriage, her family, colleagues, people in town, she is not entirely free to live the limitless spontaneous life that she has imagined for herself. But because of Ivan, because of whatever there is between them, she is, on the other hand, not entirely free to return to her previous existence either. The demands of other people do not dissolve; they only multiply. More and more complex, more difficult. Which is another way, she thinks, of saying: more life, more and more of life.

# 13

The same evening, still the same, Peter sits alone in Sylvia's kitchen looking down at the screen of his phone. Thoughtless feeling. Mind an emptied bowl almost echoing. Photograph of a casserole dish. When the screen begins to darken he taps to light it again: his only conscious action for a minute or two. No sound in the room except the faint occasional rumble of passing traffic at the front of the building. Toneless hum of the refrigerator. Finally with the same dull blankness of mind he texts Naomi that he won't be home for dinner. After many drafts and redrafts adds: Sylvia's not feeling great, so I'm going to hang around at hers for a bit in case she needs me. Is that ok? Naomi writes back promptly: oh ok, no worries. hope she feels better soon. Almost wants to tell her that he would do the same for her. For her, Naomi, if she were ill, which she was that time, and he did. Hang around, that is, in case she needed him. An ear infection, whenever it was, April, May. On the mattress in her old room, holding her small hot head in his lap, stroking her hair, saying nothing. For you I would do the same: and isn't that the basic problem, that he would do the same, wants to, and Christ in heaven, actually does. When civilisation is fundamentally premised on the exclusivity of such willingness. And why is it? Oh, who knows why, that doesn't matter now.

He rises to his feet and mechanically butters the toast he had put on before. Goes inside to help her sit up in bed when she's ready to eat. Her face tired, lined, smiling through the veil of her pain, and she thanks him. Takes some more painkillers and tries to eat what she can. After he clears the dishes, they watch a film on his laptop, something with Fred Astaire, but she falls asleep before it's finished. He sits for a time against the headboard watching her. His love for her poisoned he thinks. With guilt, with shame. Not as if she doesn't know of course: about the other. She does, always has. Not strictly monogamous he told her, which was true after all. Why then this feeling, claustrophobic, panic even, as if concealing on his person a murder weapon. Because he has given each woman reason to believe that he is actually in love with her. Worse: because he himself has believed it. Though he has been selfish, erratic, yes, bad-tempered, distant, he has not knowingly lied, not about that. And now, as if waking at last from a nonsensical dream, he surveys in terror the disorder of his life. Before, when they talked, and she touched him, everything was peaceful, simple, tender. Now, retreating from the small closed intimacy of that moment, taking into account the broader picture, the girlfriend he lives with, for instance, who is twenty-three, and sometimes gives him head in the morning before they get out of bed, he feels suddenly very frightened, and even shocked, as if this situation comes as news to him. Sweat breaking out under the collar of his sweatshirt he feels again, back of the neck, thinking about her, and the other. His own actions, which now seem so wrong as to be morally illegible. At least if you kill someone you have a motive. What on earth is he doing, what has he done. Beside him she turns over in her sleep, mouth half-open. He leaves her a note on the bedside table: Call any time you need me. Don't worry if it's late. I love you.

Outside on the street, the first mouthful of cold dark air, yes. No need to go home yet. Stay in town for a while, have a drink, settle his nerves. And on that point, he takes from his wallet a foil sheet and tosses back without tasting two pills. Slipping phone from pocket he walks back towards the Green, tapping out a few messages: You around? With what seems touching loyalty Gary replies: Few of us in Mulligan's. Seat here with your name on it. Phone locked, dropped dead into the pocket of his coat, heavy, and the misted air of the night wreathes itself in majesty around his body. Crowns of luminous streetlight hanging weightless and silent over the heads of passers-by. Talk to someone he would nearly like to. Quick opinion poll. Has to be one or the other, of course, that's a given. Nobody argues about that anymore, except those unnerving moon-faced people, the polyamorous, fetishists, and so forth. People who have cashed in their erotic stake in civil society and are doomed forever after to sexual irrelevance in the eyes of anyone normal, no offence. With all due respect he would rather drop dead. And yet, dreaded thought intruding, is he not, in some sense, already? Considering his feelings for, and not only wanting, but in fact, to some extent, having; in the sense of engaging in what might broadly be called sex acts, with more than one woman in the space of twenty-four hours. Might be alright if they were strangers, just girls he never intended to see again: bit over the top, but people in his experience tend not to judge. No, what makes it perverse is somehow confusingly the degree of his emotional involvement. The fact in other words that he actually likes them both. Is it so unthinkable? People can have affairs without exiting the sexual mainstream, surely, even if everyone agrees that affairs are wrong: wrong, of course, yes, but not suggestive of sexual deviance. That one might feel attached to both wife and mistress must be in limited circumstances, though not condoned, still basically accepted and understood. Certainly, when it comes to the question of his own self-esteem, he would rather be thought a cheater than some kind of freak. But then that would only be a case of borrowing someone else's self-esteem: because whatever he might gain would be the woman's loss. Or more than one woman's. God help him. No, he thinks, no, no: the only question is how to choose. Should he take the cash prize or the new car, what do you think. Pitting one philosophy against another. Maturity against youth. Yes, sobriety against decadence, intellect against appetite, he could go on. Better instead to specify. On the one hand, the love of his life, high principle of his conscience, his complicated feelings for whom have prevented him, let's be honest, from developing any kind of serious attachment to anyone else for the last, whatever, fourteen years. Certain difficulties, certain problems to be negotiated, but isn't that what it means to love someone? On the other hand, his captive, his tormentor, on whom he has lavished how much money, jewellery, gifts, who likes it a little rough, who has with mischievous pleasure outwitted him at every move, and with whom he is feebly and defeatedly in love. Each attempt to contend with her, to win back some little portion of his pride, has only sunk him deeper. Good against evil.

No. Never mind. No one to talk to in any case. Not his

friends: they know her a little, and the other, mutual acquaintances. Unfair to put them in that position. Whatever they might suspect, whatever they might already be saying amongst themselves. Discretion he thinks can render almost any eccentricity acceptable, at least for a limited time. As if it's not so much the tangled relations, but the desire for some transparency in one's personal life that is after all perverse. And maybe it is. Range of advice he can anyway imagine. Look, she's a lot of fun, but it's time to get serious. You're just playing with each other, it's some kind of power game, no one's going to win. You've only ever really loved one woman, just go and be with her. That young one knows how to look after herself. She'll find another fool with a nice big bank account, don't worry. The opposite line of course equally plausible. You have to move on, Peter. It's been over for a long time. What you're really clinging to, it's not her, it's your own youth, your hopes, dreams, trying impossibly to regain what you've lost. So you messed around for a few minutes, she gave you a handjob, so what. Jesus, it's pathetic, it doesn't change anything. She's gone: let go. You have a life to live. Nice little girlfriend at home to wreck your head for you, what else do you need. Feels sick thinking: and for who, for her, the other, for himself. Why anyway attachment, why always this attachment to particular people. Why never any sensual excitement at the idea of the unknown, the strangers as yet unmet. Make a break for it maybe. Get shot of the whole town, the whole country, go off somewhere new. Attachment, the cause of all suffering, so the Buddhists say. To cling to what you have, what you have had, the life you have known, the handful of people and places you have ever really loved, to cling and not let go. Never relenting, never accepting, becoming all the time more enmeshed, holding harder, loving and hating more.

At Mulligan's, the whole gang are in: Gary, Matt, Val Fitzgerald, Elaine Barrett, her friend Agnieszka. Chair to one side of the table piled high with coats and bags, which Gary starts rearranging when he sees him. Calls of greeting. Alright, big man, says Matt. Come here and see if you can settle an argument for us. Elaine laughing says: I think he's more of a man for starting arguments than settling them. Feels himself smiling now, fragrance of stale alcohol in the air, and aftershave, cocktail of scents signalling the inexorable approach of mild pleasurable drunkenness, half-heard conversation, laughter, yes, he takes off his coat and answers: Let me get a drink first. Anyone want anything? Back at the table with a glass in his hand, cold, the fresh wet taste faintly savoury in his mouth, he experiences a moment of peace in which nothing of significance seems to be wrong with his life after all. Around him his friends are arguing about the housing market, the extent to which the crisis is driven by a shortage in supply. Finishes the first drink, has another. It's nonsense, Elaine is saying. It's made up. Half the properties in the city are empty. And don't get me started on the office buildings. He drinks and in tranquillity listens to the stream of relevant vocabulary: high density, new build, compulsory purchase orders. What about Naomi's house? Gary asks. What ever happened to that? Peter puts down his drink, answering: I don't know. The guys they brought in for the eviction smashed the place up. Baseball bats and everything. Cries of horror from the others. Fucking hell, says Elaine.

I didn't know about that, says Val. She alright?

Naomi? says Peter. Yeah, she's good. She's fine.

But it must have been terrifying, says Agnieszka. Where is she living now?

Picking up his drink again Peter answers: Ah, she's staying at mine for a bit. Unofficially.

You know I still haven't met her, Elaine says. I've only seen a picture.

At this he notices in his peripheral vision Val and Matt glancing surreptitiously at one another, and then away again. Knowing, he realises. Didn't know they knew. Elaine doesn't mean that, obviously, or she wouldn't have said. How long he wonders have they known. Or seen for themselves perhaps. Jesus: fans of hers. Imagine. And answers offhandedly: Yeah, I must introduce you.

She's great, says Gary.

Wordlessly Peter contemplates the remark. Great, yes. Also very expensive and probably insane. No, she's a nice girl, it's not her fault. I just get off on messing with her head, I don't know why. I'm in love with someone else anyway. Once you meet your soulmate, there's no point pretending, is there? Feeling of solace you get when she's near you. To live the right life. Naomi can't complain, she's well looked after. It's all good, we have fun together. Too much fun if anything. Find myself fantasising sometimes about getting her pregnant. How pretty she would look and happy. Take her around town buying things for the nursery. Idea of running into people we know somehow erotic: look what I did to her, kind of thing. As sexual fantasies go, it's not the most unnatural, is it. Used to have the same one, once before. Differently. Long time ago. Yeah, when I think too hard about my life, I do start feeling suicidal, funny you should ask. Conversation has moved on, something about capital gains tax, and he finishes a third drink, gets up to order a fourth. Taste slightly sour in his mouth as usual. Need another to cleanse the palate. Had forgotten almost about her former career: ages he thinks since she's done any of that. And not as if she was really serious about it. He's seen the pictures himself, practically tasteful as these things go. Only one or two you could call truly pornographic, and she raked it in for those, special requests. Closed the account back in February or whenever it was. Subsisting since on his largesse, her desultory sale of prescription sedatives, and the occasional bar shifts she picks up from friends. Still, probably the talk of the Law Library by now. He too would be talking, if it were someone else. Half in scorn and half in jealousy. Involuntarily and for no reason he remembers the image of Sylvia this afternoon, clutching with her hand at the carpet in agony. Yes, too much against not enough. By the time the barman sees him he orders after all a shot of vodka as well. Drink it at the bar and no one will notice. Tastes of nothing, just settle his nerves. Cool damp cloth to the fever in his head. Asleep still he wonders: or waking has seen already the note he left. Call me. I love you. And the other: did she eat alone the dinner she had cooked for him. Or just give up and order Chinese food, lie on the sofa repainting her nails. A proliferation of inappropriate feeling he thinks. Disorder of sentiment. Remembering the way his father would write out on lined paper the doctor's instructions, spidery handwriting, names of medications. His meek deference, yes, even in the face of certain death, with no hope he would be spared, when his obedience could buy him nothing. Peter meanwhile in a blind rage at everything: the consultants, registrars, the hospital vending machines. Out at the house one day, in Kildare, on hold with the insurance people for twenty minutes, he kicked a hole in the garden fence. Said he'd get it fixed and never did. Sickened with shame. To find his father reduced in the end to a figure of pity. Couldn't even look at him, didn't want to. His timidity an embarrassment, or worse, an insult. As if he didn't mind what was being done to them, as if it was all okay. Cowed by the fury he would say nothing, do nothing, avert his eyes, pretending not to see. Peter like a child again, flare-ups of bad temper ignored. Unacknowledged. Look at me. Why do you have to leave. Why does everyone, why does everyone always have to leave me, why. Actually, I'm sorry, before I settle up, I'll have the same again. Vodka, yeah, thanks. Can I pay with card?

Back at the table Elaine is putting her coat on, Val checking the bus timetable. You were some time up there. Yeah, he says. I ran into someone. You're hardly heading off already? It's after eleven, Agnieszka replies. Don't want to miss the Dart. Turning to Gary he says: You're not going, are you? Hears too late the desperation in his own voice, which politely they all pretend not to notice, buttoning their coats, looking in handbags. Go on, I'll stay for one, Gary says. Stilted goodbyes they exchange. Gary only hanging on out of pity, everyone can see. Feeling sorry for him: they all are. Should have been obvious before. For weeks, months, his flat affect, strained conversation. Tired all the time and distracted. Poor man, it's really hit him hard. Never knew they were that close. What does it matter. Left alone with him at the table now Gary asks how he's getting on. He says something about Ivan blocking his number, and they talk vaguely about families, bereavement, affects people differently. He'll come around. Peter nods his head and then for no reason remarks: Well, to tell you the truth, we don't really like each other. Ever since he was a teenager, it's been like that. He hates me because he thinks I'm an arrogant prick, and I look down on him because I think he's a fucking loser. Smiling nervously Gary interjects: Ah, I don't think you think that, really.

Surface of Peter's drink catching the overhead light, bubbles winking at the brim. No, he says. I don't know. He has a girlfriend, did I tell you that? Some married woman over in Leitrim. Or she's divorced or whatever. Older than we are, a few years older.

Oh yeah? How long is that going on?

Another mouthful, lukewarm now and tasteless. I don't know, he says. A month or two. A few weeks after the funeral, he met her. That's why he's not speaking to me, I told him to stay away from her, more or less. I don't know, I said she was probably mental or something.

Ah, right, says Gary. That wasn't a great idea, maybe.

No, yeah, he says. I just thought, you know, how could anyone halfway normal want to hang around with him? Like, however you want to dress it up, that's what I really thought. I could tell you I was being protective. And I was, in a way, but only because I thought this woman must not be right in the head.

Slurring he can hear in some of his own consonants now, the pills, the alcohol. Sensibly, not unkindly, Gary offers: You probably hurt his feelings, saying that.

Watches the white froth sliding down the inside of his pint glass under the light. I'm sure I did, he says. And it's pure hypocrisy if you think about it, because he's the same age as Naomi. If I'm really honest with myself, I think that's probably the reason I reacted so badly. Part of the reason. When I look at how I've fucked things up for her, you know. She's twenty-three, she doesn't know any better. The sad thing is I actually like her, but what can I do? I don't know. I don't want my brother ending up in the situation she's in, that's the truth. If this woman he's seeing is as selfish as I am, he's fucked.

A few seconds pass in silence, and then Gary says: I'm not sure I'm following you there. Are things not going well between yourself and Naomi?

He picks up his glass and drains it, replaces it on the table. Checks for no reason his watch which in the light he can't anyway make out. No, he says. There's someone else. It's all kind of complicated. But look, I won't keep you.

Oh right, says Gary. Someone else—on your side, you mean?

Peter pulls his satchel up into his lap, starts fastening it shut, answering: Yeah.

In the same mild non-judgemental tone of voice Gary says: I see, okay. It wouldn't be your ex-girlfriend, would it? I think I met her at the funeral.

Peter looks up at him, exhausted, head beginning to ache. Sylvia, he says. Yeah. Gary gives a kind of understanding nod of his head and, unbelievably, says nothing, does not appear to feel the need to say anything. Peter in silence stares at him for a time, holding awkwardly his satchel in his lap, and finally saying: What do you think I should do?

In response, Gary raises his eyebrows, but with a mild look. Oh, he says. I suppose I wouldn't know, Peter. It's complicated, alright. It would depend on the situation.

Peter rises finally from his seat, starts putting his coat on, affecting disinterest now, as if all a joke, absently smiling. Bigamy, that's still illegal, isn't it? he says.

Gary gives a kind of bemused laugh, answering: Yeah, I think so. Come here, how are you getting home? You want me to call a taxi?

Prickling he feels in his eyes, his nose. No, I'll walk, he

says. Lays a hand on Gary's shoulder saying: The soul of decency, you are. And then he's outside, breathing the dirty air of Poolbeg Street, brackish odour of the quays. It's been raining: still is a little. Hanging in the air around him, freckles of cool water. Hands in his pockets up to College Green. Yes, it has to be done, has to be done. There is only one way out. She, or the other. Could of course just have done with the whole thing and walk in front of a bus but they've probably stopped running at this hour and it wouldn't be fair on them would it. Herself with nowhere to live. Ivan mortified no doubt after their little quarrel. And Sylvia: Christ in heaven, she might think it was because of her. Try to remember he thinks. This afternoon in bed, her fingers unbuttoning. That was good, wasn't it, and they were happy. Only a little rearrangement required now to make everything simple. Yes. To inflict pain knowingly on others he has always been too cowardly: though he has, for all that, inflicted probably more than his fair share of pain. The house in Kildare sitting empty, he thinks, at least there's that, if she needs it, and he won't be leaving her destitute on top of everything else. Drunk now finally and feeling sick at the thought. Try to recall instead the half-darkness in her room, the way she smiled, and it could be like that again, not only once but for the rest of their lives. Correcting undergraduate essays together in the evenings, reading aloud the worst sentences to make each other laugh. On her little stereo system, the Barenboim recording of the 40th Symphony. Walking over together to their tenants' union meetings arm in arm, heads bent, absorbed in conversation. With his fingers now he wipes his eyes. The image of that life: how beautiful, how painful, to believe it could after all be possible. For so long it has hurt too much even to think. And now everything hurts so much all the time that to think makes no difference, to think even lends a kind of sweetness to the terrible pain. The life they could have had together. The refuge of a shared home, their books, furniture, watercolours. Gatherings at the kitchen table, friends calling round for dinner, arguing, laughing. The love they could have given to their own children. Wanted to give. Impossible ever to feel again like a good person, even halfway good, when all the good he had wanted to do in life was closed off to him forever. Had no route left through which to travel. Remained inside him, trapped, festering, turning into something stranger and worse. Proliferation of inappropriate attachments. Holding hard, harder, clutching, not letting go. Well, if that's suffering, he thinks, let me suffer. Yes. To love whoever I have left. And if ever I lose someone, let me descend into a futile and prolonged rage, yes, despair, wanting to break things, furniture, appliances, wanting to get into fights, to scream, to walk in front of a bus, yes. Let me suffer, please. To love just these few people, to know myself capable of that, I would suffer every day of my life. Passing the Green he's badly drunk, not even walking straight anymore. She might be out when he gets in: probably for the best. Crawl like a coward into his empty bed. Wishes he had told his father. We've worked things out, Dad, we're getting back together. Don't worry about me, I'm happy. Everything's good. You know we all love you very much. That's the only important thing. Thought so wretched he feels his eyes getting blurry, yes, and has to wipe them, half-supporting himself against a lamp-post. If anyone he knows. Peter is that you. Oh yes, I'm sorry. I was just thinking about my father. He died, you see. Not knowing. That I still. That we both, he didn't know.

That I hated him for leaving me. That I loved him so much. Wiping with the heels of his hands his eyes he stands up, listing, stumbles on down Baggot Street and home.

Upstairs in the flat she's sitting in the dark watching snooker. Some old episode of *Crucible Classics* probably with her man O'Sullivan five frames in the lead. Armchair she has pulled over to rest her bare feet on. Hello stranger, she says. How's the other girlfriend feeling? Closing the door behind him he leans against the opposite wall, bracing, and answers: Yeah, she's okay. Glancing around at him she sits up, hard to see her expression. Are you drunk? she asks. Taking off his coat he answers yes. Fuck off, she says. I thought you told me you were looking after Sylvia. Feels as though if he bends even slightly to take his shoes off he will fall on the floor and for this reason enters the room with his shoes still on, feeling under his hand for various items of furniture. Jesus, Peter, she says. You're seriously out of it, are you alright? Yes he thinks he should have told. I love you. Her, the other. Finds himself holding the arm of the couch beside where she sits, saying aloud: I'm sorry. She has turned off the television, darker the room now, and she puts her hand on his, he can feel, and even kind of see, rotating strangely before his eyes. Has something happened? she asks. And with a kind of weakening dropping sensation he finds himself on the carpet, his head by her knee, and he's repeating: I'm sorry. Her hand he can feel on his head. You're freaking me out, she says. Is there something wrong, or you're just hammered? His forehead resting on her lap now, the soft ribbed cotton of her leggings: green he knows without looking. 'Forest green', from the website she likes. In a thick-sounding voice he says aloud: I have to talk to you about something. Her hand pauses in its motion over his hair but she doesn't lift it away. What? she asks.

His face still wet he thinks, and reaches vaguely to touch again his eyes. About Sylvia, he answers. I want to explain.

For no reason he stops speaking and she says with faintly anxious impatience: Yeah, go on.

Thick feeling in his mouth swallowing. Look, we were together before, he says. Like I told you. For a while, a long time, six years. And then when she was twenty-five, she was in an accident. It was serious. She was really badly injured, she was in terrible pain. And I couldn't do anything, I couldn't help her. She was the one who wanted to break up. I didn't want to. I wanted to help her, but I couldn't. Even now, she's still in pain, all the time, every day. I swear to God, we were so happy before, we really were. And I can't even think about it anymore. Even to remember it, I can't. Nothing has made any sense to me since then. Not one thing. My life, it's like it's this horrible dream that keeps going on and on, and I can't wake up. I mean never, no matter how long I wait, I'll never wake up again. You actually start thinking, Christ, at least I get to die at the end. Or even wishing it would happen. I'm sorry, I know I'm not supposed to say it, but I do wish that sometimes, just that it would be over. He lifts his face from her knee, wipes unseeing his streaming eyes, his nose running. The reason we don't sleep together, he says, it's because we can't. Because of what happened, she can't. But we're not just friends. And I'm still in love with her, Naomi. I always have been. I'm sorry.

For a time there's only silence, and he waits with his face in his hands, seeing nothing, hearing nothing. Finally she says: Okay. I knew there was something between you, obviously. But

I didn't understand the situation. It sounds really sad, what happened. Clearly. I don't know what to say. I feel for her.

Wiping once more his face he looks up. Darkness of the room lighted only by the streetlamp out the window. Young and beautiful in the dim bluish shadow she stares back at him. She knows about me? she says.

He answers quickly: Yeah, of course. She knows, of course she does. If anything she probably thinks I've been more honest with you, about the situation, than I actually have. And I'm sorry for that. Trembling with a rush of terrible feeling inside himself as if to get sick, he goes on: But I can't do this anymore. We have to stop. You and me. Whatever it is, I can't let it keep going on.

Slowly she nods her head while he's speaking. Then in a simple quiet voice she answers: Okay. You know I don't have anywhere else to live. But if you're saying you want me to go, I'll go.

He now also finds himself nodding his head. Room spinning in dim circles before his eyes. To catch and hold his gaze on a single spot: and then to feel it slide out, away, as if pulled from under him. I'll find you somewhere, he says. You know, my dad's house is there, if you need it. In Kildare, it's not convenient, but it's empty. There's a train. And I can help you out with money. I don't want to make life hard for you.

In the dark she makes some kind of gesture, like a shrug, her shoulders moving. Okay, she says. Touches her nose then with her fingers. Do you hate me? she asks. Then immediately she gives something like a strained laugh and adds: Actually, don't say, I don't want to know.

Feeling his jaw weakening again, sense in his throat that if he tries to answer he will only cry, so drunk he can hardly see, and he lays his head on her lap again. I don't hate you, he says. Tight and painful his throat. If I say what I really feel it's just worse, he says. But I don't hate you, not at all. Pathetic, he thinks. Hard to believe even real. What did he want her for if not to ruin his life.

Do you love me, she says.

And he answers: Yeah. I love you, of course I do.

Silence for a moment and then her tone thin and managed saying: But then why are you making me go away?

Without lifting his head he replies: I'm trying to explain. I don't know what else to do.

If you just want to keep on seeing Sylvia, you can, she says. I don't mind. I get that it's complicated, I'm not trying to interfere between you. We'll work something out.

Even closing his eyes now he still sees or senses the room spinning, sensation of orbit. That's not real life, he mutters. That kind of thing, what you're talking about, life doesn't work like that. A little sound he hears, quick release of her breath, as if frustrated. And how does it work? she says. You tell me you love me and then it's alright, goodbye, I never want to see you again. Just so you can delude yourself that you're normal, everything is normal. You're so fucking sick in the head you don't even see what you're doing to yourself. Trying to put everyone in their little box. And if we would all just stay there, then there wouldn't be any problems. Whatever. I'm sorry about what happened to your friend. I can see it's horrific, it's upsetting, I get that. You love each other, obviously. I didn't understand before. But I'm literally right here, like at this moment. I'm a real person, this is actually my life. I don't know. Fuck you, to be honest. I want to go to bed. She gets up, scrambling, knocking him away with her knee, and he also finds himself somehow upright, or halfway, holding to the arm of the couch again, swaying or the room is. Naomi, he says. Soft the feeling of her body in his arms again, soft, his hand touching her hip, her waist, and sensing her breath close, her mouth, wet, and they kiss. Deep, yes, the taste of her. Forget everything he thinks. Go and live together on the continent, somewhere no one knows them. See her tanned and laughing in some green garden, rich heavy fragrance of flowers in the air. Sitting in the shade while he's clearing the table, clinking of glasses. Infant at her breast. Real life, that would be, yes. Do you want to come to bed before you send me away? she murmurs. Opening his eyes vaguely into the rotating blackness around them, awake enough to be at least finally ashamed. Ah, that would be nice, he says. But I think I'm too out of it, I'm sorry. Her head she lets fall against his chest. Hurt, disappointed. Final move she had to play he thinks. Or perhaps just wanted to. Why always assign to her the ulterior motive: let himself off the hook as usual. At the back of her neck, warm, he traces his fingertips. Lifts her face to kiss once more her mouth. In the morning, he says. Before you go. Her lips dimly parted looking up at him. You won't want to in the morning, she answers. Again they kiss, wet depth of her mouth, familiar. No, he says, don't worry, I will. In a whisper she tells him to promise and he promises. Lower again and almost inaudible she says: And you'll tell me you love me. He closes his eyes. Because she wants that. To hear him say it to her when they. Happy woman: yes, to make her. What is he thinking. What on earth. Why, for what possible reason, why. To send her away. Aloud he hears himself say simply: Yeah. I'll tell you in the morning. Now let's get some sleep.

# PART THREE

# 14

On Sunday evening, Ivan is driving through Kildare town, with a large takeaway cheese pizza laid flat on the passenger seat, and the dog lying asleep in the back. Everything has gone according to plan, and in just a few minutes, he will arrive home, to his dad's house, with his things, with the dog's various accoutrements, ready to get settled in. The day before yesterday, he'd had to go out to the house to pick up the car, and while he was there he had a look around inside. That was sad, there's no point denying how sad it was, to see their home that way, abandoned and cold. The curtains hanging lank and grey at the windows, and a film of blue-grey dust on all the surfaces, the low hall table, the lips of the skirting boards. Every room had the sad cold feeling of death, a dead person's house, Ivan thought at the time, which was, after all, exactly what it was. To suppress or dispel this feeling, he went around purposefully turning the lights on and off in all the rooms, and then doing the same with the taps, the radiators, flushing the toilets, even trapping a spider in a piece of kitchen towel and releasing it into the back garden. Opening and closing the windows, things like that. When he got back, he thought, he would have time to do some cleaning, to make the house look more homely and normal. Afterwards, he got in the car, drove back to Dublin, picked up the dog from the flat, and then drove to Leitrim to see Margaret.

Arriving at the cottage on Friday night, Ivan got out of the car just as the front door came open, an oblong of yellow light, and Margaret was standing there, in silhouette at first, and then, as he reached her, plainly visible, smiling, in her red woollen jersey, and he took her in his arms, saying: Hello. Laughing, she looked up at him, they kissed, a warm contented kiss of simplicity and happiness. Where's the little Alexander? she asked. Oh, Ivan said, he's in the car. One second. Together they went out onto the gravel, Margaret in her slippers, and it was raining lightly, and Ivan opened the back door of the car to let the dog out. Alexei trotted right over to Margaret, tail wagging, and she crouched down over him, petting his ears and head, saying: Aren't you beautiful? Delightedly the dog licked at her hands, her wrists, while Ivan took his things from the car. Inside, in the hallway, Alexei ran circles around Margaret, getting under her feet, making her laugh. He's just overexcited, Ivan said. He'll calm down in a minute. Or I can tell him to stop. Flushed with pleasure, watching the dog frolic around the floorboards, Margaret answered: No, he's great. He's so handsome. A little aristocrat. Looking up at Ivan, she asked: Would you like to eat something? I have dinner on. They went into the kitchen and the dog followed after them, paws making a tick-tacking sound on the tiles. Margaret lifted a dish from the oven and left it on the cooktop, shutting the oven door, and asked Ivan how the drive had been. The kitchen was filled with the rich savoury smell of cooking, braised pork, onions, and her low voice was asking him thoughtful questions, and the dog was padding around the room cheerfully. I wish I lived here, Ivan wanted to say, but he didn't. Instead, he said the drive was fine, and they sat down to eat, soft shredded meat with rice and vegetables and salad, and Alexei lay stretched out under the table, his tail beating now and then against the floor. Margaret said she was sure that everyone was talking about her in town, but no one had said anything to her face yet. She tried to laugh, she said it would be the scandal of the month, and that people would move on eventually. She looked tired then, Ivan thought, but also very beautiful, and he loved her with a love that was powerful and even dangerous. If anyone ever said anything to hurt her, he knew that he would be capable of wreaking extreme violence on that person, although it was obvious she wouldn't want him to do that, but he knew the capability was there inside him, to protect her at all costs. Even the idea of an unkind word, an unkind glance, directed towards Margaret, it didn't matter by whom, the idea opened down into a deep well of vengeance, to the point that Ivan was practically picturing himself with some kind of sword in hand, ready to strike down the detractors, not that he had ever handled a sword or would want to in real life, being by conviction a pacifist, but there was something true in the feeling nonetheless.

When they were getting ready for bed that night, Margaret taking off her little necklace at the dressing table, she asked when his chess competition was coming up. He told her it was the week after next, running from Monday through until Friday. While she brushed her hair, he explained in more detail the format of the event, and she asked if there would be any spectators. Ivan said not really. Some people's parents or friends might be there, he said. But spectators, like random people, no, there wouldn't be any interest. Classical chess is very slow. And if you don't play, you wouldn't really understand what you were looking at anyway. Margaret nodded her head, rising from the dressing table, while Ivan was sitting on the end of the mattress watching her. Standing at the laundry basket, her back to him, she started to unbutton her blouse. But sorry, he said, why do you ask?

No real reason, she said. I'll be in Dublin one of those days, for a work thing. But no, I was just curious.

Quickly Ivan said: Oh, I didn't know. Which day? You know it's my birthday that week. Sorry, not that I even care, just to mention.

She looked back at him, smiling. You never said, she replied. I'm going to be there on the Friday. What day is your birthday?

Tuesday, he said.

Twenty-three. You're getting old.

He laughed, feeling light, bashful, happy. I know, he said. You want to see each other when you're in town? You don't have to come to the chess thing, obviously. Although it would make me look really cool if you did.

At that she gave a sheepish smile, folding her blouse into the laundry basket. Well, I doubt that, she said.

But she also seemed pleased, and he noticed that she didn't definitively say no. In his mind he couldn't help imagining the scenario, Margaret being there at the event, arriving perhaps just in time to see his opponent resign. Rising from the table then, victorious among defeated rivals, Ivan would see her, and what would she be wearing, another one of her light thin blouses perhaps, it felt good to imagine the details, her hair pinned back behind her head or thrown loosely over one shoulder, the little necklace at her throat. He would go to her, of course: and would she let him kiss her? The image was so intense it was kind of sexy, kissing her in front of all those people, allowing everyone to presume, and correctly, that they, which was true. To kiss her, yes, in front of everyone, to be seen with her in that way. Not standing alone as usual after his game had concluded, watching one of the other boards, chess notation passing at high almost hallucinatory speeds through his brain, some of it maybe nonsensical, moves that weren't even in the position, his head like an overheated computer with all the fans whirring. To see her there instead, yes, to go to her, and they would talk about where to have dinner, putting on their jackets: it was like a dream, beautiful. To exchange a simple kiss, heedless of the eyes of others, watched or not.

Now, parking up on the driveway outside his father's house, Ivan notices with a strange feeling that one of the upstairs lights is on: the light in what was once Peter's room. Ivan did check that bulb on Friday morning, along with all the others, but he was certain, almost certain, that he had turned everything off again before he left. Getting out of the car, he takes his backpack, balances the pizza box flat in one hand, and takes the dog's leash in the other, letting him scramble down from the back seat. Inside, in the hallway, after Ivan shuts the door, but before he can do anything else, before he can reach for the light switch, or put down the pizza, he realises, he knows, that something is different. And this realisation, this foreknowledge, prevents him somehow from feeling frightened when from upstairs he hears a voice calling out: Hello? It's a woman's voice. He stands in the hall not afraid but dumbfounded, a huge blank neutrality of shock breaking out over him, unable to speak, unable even to formulate coherent thought, as the light in the landing comes on overhead and someone appears at the top of the staircase: a young woman, a girl. She's holding her phone upright in her hand, like she's in the middle of a video call. Oh my God, she says. Wait one second, this is crazy. Let me call you back. This remark is addressed to the screen of her phone, which she taps, and then holds loose in her hand at her side. To Ivan, she says: I'm so sorry about this. I think I know who you are. She's wearing a tiny crop top with a big knitted cardigan. You're Ivan, aren't you? she asks.

Swallowing, Ivan answers: Right, but who are you?

She gives a wild little laugh. Oh my God, she repeats. I'm so sorry. I think your brother tried to tell you I was here, but you weren't answering your phone. I'm a friend of his.

Oh, Ivan says. Okay.

Yeah, I got evicted from the place where I was living. And Peter said I could stay here while I was looking for somewhere else. I'm sorry he didn't tell you. I think he did try, like I said.

Right, Ivan repeats.

For a moment they stand there facing one another down the staircase, under the pendant landing light. She looks, he thinks, like the kind of girl who would under normal circumstances never acknowledge his existence. Her nails, for instance, are painted a dark kind of shimmering purple colour, and she has a nose piercing, and her face has the fresh scrubbed look of someone who usually wears a lot of make-up but isn't wearing any right now. I'm Naomi, she says presently.

I'm Ivan, he answers. As you know.

Alexei, still on the leash, but obviously excited by the unexpected presence of a stranger in the house, now lets out a kind of playful howling bark, bowing his head down at the bottom step. Ivan looks at him and says distractedly: Oh, sorry. He's friendly, he's not aggressive.

No, he's super cute, the girl says. I thought he was living with your mother.

Disorientated by the level of information this person seems to possess about him and his life, Ivan answers: He was. But, uh, he's with me now.

Again they lapse into silence. The hand Ivan is using to hold the pizza box is growing sore and overly hot. The girl has her arms crossed over her chest. Do you want me to leave? she asks. I totally understand if you do, it's just awkward for tonight, because I don't have a car or anything.

Ivan is once again wrongfooted by her words, feeling that he has at no point succeeded in picking up the thread of this conversation. Oh, he says. No, you don't have to leave. It's just, from my point of view, I don't really have anywhere else I can go right now. With the dog.

But you shouldn't have to go anywhere. It's your house.

He swallows again, unable to produce in his brain a single meaningful thought, and says: Well, I might go and put down this pizza.

Oh right, she says. Totally.

Ivan lets Alexei off the lead and he instantly trots up the stairs to greet the girl. After repeating that he is going to put down the pizza, Ivan goes through the door at the back of the hall, to the kitchen. He rests the pizza box on the dining table and then stands, uncomprehending, staring down at the orange-and-red printed pattern on the top of the box, showing an image of a chef in a toque hat kissing his fingers. It's cleaner, he thinks: the house is cleaner, than it was on Friday morning. Someone has gone around with a vacuum, at the least, and probably a cloth and a basin of soapy water as well. Who, he wonders. The girl, it must have been. For some reason the idea makes him feel faint and dizzy. He can hear Alexei bolting back down the stairs now, and sees him entering the kitchen, his ears pricked, lively, with a sort of confused but happy look. The girl follows after him, apparently unfazed. Not knowing what to say, having absolutely no idea in his head whatsoever, Ivan hears himself saying aloud: You want some pizza? She gives a little smile at that and answers: Oh my God, that's so nice of you. I will take a slice, but only if you're sure you don't mind.

From the overhead cupboard Ivan takes two plates and lays them on the table. The girl sits down and they each take a slice of pizza and begin eating, while the dog wanders around the room cheerfully. What to tell Margaret, Ivan thinks. How to write a message explaining the situation. How to even describe the situation in his own mind.

So your brother tells me you're like, a chess genius, the girl says.

Ivan, chewing, gives no answer for a moment. Then, swallowing uncomfortably, he says: I'm not, at all. I play chess, but I'm very far from being a genius. I think Peter uses that word too lightly.

She's smiling, helping herself to some of the garlic dip. Well, I've never heard him call anyone else a genius, she says. He seems to think most people are idiots. Ivan tears a piece of crust into two smaller pieces, trying to think, trying to create in his brain one single phrase of thought. With her mouth full, the girl says innocuously: He never mentioned me to you?

Oh, says Ivan. Well, we don't talk a lot. Actually, we don't talk at all.

Recently, I know, yeah. But I mean before, when you were talking. He never mentioned anything about me then?

Inside his head a sensation like radio static. Recently, I know, she said. And what else does she know, he thinks, what else might Peter have chosen to tell her. Hm, Ivan says. I'm not sure. If he did, I might not remember.

Eating again, she says: It's cool. I didn't think he would have.

The dog goes out the open double doors into the living room and climbs up on his old spot on the sofa. Gradually a thought begins to form in Ivan's mind, which is that this girl is, now that he thinks about it, obviously, not just a friend of Peter's. But if she's more than a friend, Ivan thinks, why is she all the way out here in Kildare and not staying at Peter's flat in town? And, after all – the thought strikes him with sudden intensity – what age can this girl be? He finds himself looking at her closely now across the table, her pretty face, with the silver ring in her nose, her little crop top: and only when she looks back at him does he return his attention quickly to the pizza. If she and Peter are only friends, why would she ask Ivan whether he had ever mentioned her? Why would Peter be confiding in her about the fact that he and Ivan haven't been speaking recently? And yet if they're more than friends, what on earth is going on? What about the dinner, about Sylvia, I'm still in love with her, what to make of all that? In an unintentionally energetic tone of voice, Ivan says: How do the two of you know each other, if you don't mind me asking?

She's toying with the pizza slice in her fingers. Hm, she says. We met, I don't know. On a night out, at a New Year's thing.

Are you a lawyer as well? he asks.

God, no. I'm in college, kind of. In final year.

Nodding his head, Ivan feels the beat of his pulse growing harder and faster. Okay, he says. You're like my age, then.

She has folded the slice lengthwise to take a bite, and now with her mouth full again she answers: Yeah, why? Do I look older?

Ivan rises to his feet, not knowing why, and goes to the sink, on the pretext of pouring himself a glass of water. No, he says. That's why I was curious, how you and Peter became friends. From the age gap.

Behind him, she gives a little laugh. Well, I was just saying that to be polite, she says. We actually used to go out together. But we broke up. Like a few days ago, that's why I'm here.

Buzzing sort of feeling in his head and brain: like an empty glass jar with a bluebottle trapped inside. He pours the water and drinks it down, standing at the sink. After swallowing he says: Ah, okay. Then he thinks to add mechanically: Sorry about that.

That's Peter for you, she replies. I mean, we were together for nearly a year, and he never even told you that I exist.

Ivan turns back to face her, watching her dip a piece of crust into the pot of garlic sauce. Remembering again the night of the dinner. Do you think any normal woman. Standing at the countertop, his head strangely light and empty, Ivan replies: Yeah, he never tells me anything.

She's wiping her fingers now on one of the little paper napkins they give you. You ever hear of this person Sylvia? she asks.

Ivan is silent for a moment, the evident complexities of

the situation crowding around him in an oppressive way. But whose complexities, he thinks? Not his. Why should he have to be tactful and sensitive? On Peter's behalf? Why? Finally he answers: Right. He was together with her for a long time. She's like, basically part of our family.

Naomi nods her head, looking down at her plate. Is she pretty? she asks.

Ivan pauses. You haven't met her? he asks.

She shakes her head.

Oh, he says. Well, to me she's kind of like a sister, so it's hard to describe, if she's pretty or not.

She just nods and says nothing.

He waits a moment, watching her, and then he says: Obviously I don't know the situation. In my experience, Sylvia is a very genuine person. I wouldn't say the same for my brother, but for her, that's what I would say.

Naomi gives a kind of absent smile, touching her nose with her fingertips. Don't worry, she says. I have nothing against her. I'm just curious.

With an agitated feeling, which could be pity, or annoyance, revenge, or something else, even worse, Ivan hears himself saying: I can show you a picture, if you want.

She looks up at him, an intrigued smiling look. Yes please, she says.

And why not, Ivan thinks, making his way through the double doors into the living room, why not. The dog lifts his head mildly, blinking, awoken from sleep, as Ivan takes from the bottom shelf of the bookcase a glossy red photo album and goes back into the kitchen. With the buzzing growing louder in his head he sits down at the table and opens the half-empty book, leafing backwards through the unused plastic pockets to the most recent photographs, while Naomi watches on. He covers just slightly with his arm so that she can't see him flicking past some images of himself, at the age of sixteen, receiving the FIDE Master title, shaking hands with various chess people. He had terrible skin at the time and really long hair. Before that, pictures from a family wedding, and then Peter's college graduation ceremony. There, in front of the stone columns, black robes tossed back by the wind, the two of them, Peter and Sylvia, together. Ivan's head humming very loudly now, he turns the album for Naomi to see, pointing out with a finger the photograph in question. That's her, he says. Both of them, obviously.

Naomi is still holding the paper napkin crumpled in her fingers. Impassively she gazes down at the photograph for a time. Oh, she says. Then after another moment she adds: Jesus, he's the image of you.

Disconcerted, Ivan says nothing. He had expected her to be more interested in the picture of Sylvia. Also, his belief was, or at least it had always been said, that Peter was considered handsome, as far as these things went. Not knowing what to say, Ivan says weakly: Well, he didn't have braces.

With a laugh she looks up at him. You're funny, she says. When are you getting them off?

Soon. In the new year.

She's looking back down at the photograph again. So that's Sylvia, she remarks. Without saying anything else, she turns back another page of the album, and pauses a moment. Then, turning the book towards him, she asks: Is this your family?

In the background, the same stone columns, the cobblestones underfoot, and in the foreground, the whole group together. Peter and Sylvia in the centre, in their billowing robes, and Christine in a pale-blue skirt suit, standing at Sylvia's shoulder, and beside Peter, their father wearing suit and tie, which was something he always hated, getting dressed up like that. And there, in front of Peter and their dad, a little boy, only twelve years old, very pallid and timid-looking, which is Ivan himself. Yeah, he says aloud. That's us.

Turning the album back in her own direction, looking over the image again, she remarks: Your mother is elegant. I like the suit.

Mm, Ivan says.

Peter doesn't like her, does he?

Uncertainly, Ivan pauses again, and then says: Well, they both have strong personalities. Deep down I guess they do love each other, or whatever.

Naomi looks thoughtful again, nodding her head. Touching lightly the transparent plastic film over the photograph with a fingertip, she says: And this is your dad?

Right, he says.

I can see it, she replies. The resemblance, a little bit. Raising her eyes to look up at Ivan, she adds: I'm really sorry. I know you must miss him.

I do.

With her eyes once more drawn to the photograph she says: It sounds like he was a really good father.

Ivan feels touched, uncomfortably, by these words, and finds himself looking down at his fingernails. Peter said that? he asks.

Yeah, he thought the world of him.

Ivan swallows and says nothing.

Still looking at the photograph, Naomi says: She's different from what I pictured. What is she now, a professor or something?

Realising that she is once again talking about Sylvia, Ivan replies: Right.

I guess this is from before the accident.

With the recurring strange sensation of being unable to think clearly, to formulate clear thoughts, he answers disjointedly: It would have been. Like a few years before. Because they broke up after that.

She goes on gazing down at the image. But he's still in love with her, she says.

Once again, the complexities of the situation strike Ivan as pressing, and he begins to feel that they are not Peter's complexities alone, but also this person Naomi's, and Sylvia's, and perhaps he shouldn't have intervened to show her the photograph after all. His motivations in doing so were not, after all, entirely clear, and may not have been wholesome. She doesn't look upset, however, just pensive. After a moment Ivan says: It's not really my business. But it sounds like maybe Peter hasn't been that nice to you. And I'm sorry for that, if it is the case.

She shrugs her shoulders. Men are dogs, she says. No offence. Peter's not the worst.

He swallows. Well, I disagree, he says. But okay, it's your opinion.

Glancing up at him, she says: You disagree that men are dogs? Or you disagree that your brother isn't the worst?

Awkwardly he tries to give a little laugh. Hm, he says. Both.

Oh, there are worse guys around than Peter, believe me, she replies. I could tell you stories, Ivan. There are men out there who make your brother look like a prince. You mind if I have another slice of pizza?

He tells her to help herself, and she closes the photo album and moves it to another part of the table, away from the food, before taking a slice of pizza from the box. Sitting back in her chair, she chews contemplatively, and Ivan, beginning again to feel hungry, also takes another slice. After some time spent eating in silence, he ventures to say: Did you do a lot of cleaning? Around the house, I mean. I just notice it looks a lot better than when I was here before.

With her mouth full of food she grins at him. That was your brother, she says. Pretty much the whole day Friday he was cleaning, I just left him to it. You know him, he's a neat freak.

In some surprise, Ivan pauses. Friday, the same day he himself was here. They must have just missed each other. Then he answers: Yeah, I guess he's always been like that. Things annoy him easily. Like, if they're out of place.

Naomi makes a face then which is like a private smile to herself. So true, she says. People included. Why did you block his number, by the way?

He looks at her, sees her funny weird smile, and then looks back down at his pizza slice, glistening under the ceiling light. That's between us, he says. He knows why.

Something to do with your girlfriend?

As he suspected, he thinks, she knows everything, Peter has told her everything, he has betrayed Ivan's trust in order to confide in this person, this girl, whose existence he has been keeping secret for almost a year. And without looking up Ivan answers: With respect, it's private.

She's eating again, wiping her lips with her hand. You're

still seeing her? she asks. I don't know anything about it, except she's older. And she lives down the country somewhere.

Irritated now, not even at her, but as if through her at his brother, Ivan retorts: You're right, you don't know anything about it. And she's not even that much older, she's barely older than Peter.

Thirty-six, right?

Ivan blows out between his lips, getting up abruptly from the table, pacing to the patio door. It's private, he repeats. He shouldn't have told you that. And anyway, he's a hypocrite, because you're the same age I am.

From behind him, the girl says: What, he thinks she's too old for you?

It's nothing to do with him, Ivan says. He has no right to comment.

Ignoring this remark, she goes on: Yeah, he's weird about stuff like that. He thinks he's too old for me as well, he says it all the time. Or he used to anyway, before he got rid of me.

These words occasion in Ivan another strange feeling, unpleasant, and he shakes his head. Whatever, he says. That's his thing.

You know he's a mess at the moment, she says. Not that it's an excuse, but he's seriously not doing well. Ever since your dad died, I'm sorry. He hasn't been right in the head.

In a heavy pressured silence Ivan stands at the patio door, saying nothing, wanting not to have to speak at all. Finally he turns from the door, saying tersely: No, I didn't know that.

The girl is moving her head from side to side, looking down at the half-eaten slice of pizza on her plate. Yeah, she says. I'm kind of worried about him, to be honest. He has said some things, I don't know, that would make me concerned. But

I don't want to freak you out. I'm sure he's okay. He probably just drinks too much. Glancing up at Ivan she adds: And he's upset that you're not speaking to him, obviously. He brings it up a lot. When he's drunk, especially.

As Ivan listens to these words, the bad sensation intensifies, hard and compressing. Right, he says. Okay.

She goes on looking at him, a direct look, and her eyes are calm and deep. After a moment she says: You know he really loves you.

Ivan feels himself exhaling sharply, feels the breath exiting through his throat and mouth as if knocked out of him by force. Embarrassed by this, by everything, flushed, angry, he says: That's actually none of your business. Like, who even are you? I've never heard of you before in my life. This is our family you're talking about. And you're literally just some random girl.

She's still looking at him, the same deep look in her eyes. Fair enough, she says.

He forces his gaze down at the floorboards, inhaling slowly, willing himself to let the feeling cool away and dissolve before he speaks again. Finally in a thin detached voice he says: Look, I have some stuff I have to do. Work and all that. So I might go and do that now. You can stay, obviously. Needless to say. I'll be in my room.

For a moment she says nothing. Then she answers neutrally: Okay.

Okay, he repeats. Cool. And if you're speaking to Peter, I don't know if you are, but don't tell him that I'm here. Like, don't mention that you've seen me, or say anything about me at all. Alright?

Chancing a glance at her, he sees her shrugging. Whatever, she says. It's like you said, it has nothing to do with me.

Right, Ivan says. Well, goodnight then.

Looking away from him, she answers coolly: Yeah, goodnight.

Finally Ivan leaves the kitchen and makes his way upstairs, with a sense of dragging his drained and exhausted body behind him. From the living room, he can hear Alexei hopping down from his spot on the sofa and coming along the hall to follow him up the steps. And this sound, the familiar little footfall of the dog's paws, following, his innocent nature, his inability to understand anything, and yet always trusting, this sound fills Ivan with a terrible almost shameful pity. Upstairs he opens his bedroom door and lets Alexei in before him, lets Alexei jump up on the bed and stretch out playfully with his tail curled, as if the weekend has been wonderfully enjoyable for all concerned, making new friends, going on car journeys, and so forth. As if he doesn't know, which he probably doesn't, that Ivan's father is never coming home again, as if he is still cheerfully waiting to greet him whenever he returns. Getting onto the bed himself, Ivan puts his arms around the dog's little body and breathes in his mute animal warmth. Alexei, having no idea why Ivan might be upset, lies there politely, allowing himself to be enfolded in his arms, understanding nothing. He's a mess, the girl said, meaning Peter. He's not doing well at all. It's something Ivan doesn't want to think about: doesn't even feel he should have to think about, considering Peter's words, the disrespect, and, in particular, the flagrant hypocrisy that has just been uncovered. The fact that Peter himself, while pouring scorn on Margaret's good character, had and knew himself to have at that very moment a girlfriend of Ivan's own age. Ivan is supposed to be concerned for the mental well-being of someone who has shown him such rank contempt? No. But then why do these words exert this pressure on him, the girl's words, he's drinking too much, he's not right in the head. She was trying to make Ivan think about something that he does not want to think about, that he even intentionally blocks and pushes away from conscious thought. The presence, behind Peter's smooth careless facade, of a certain darkness, a certain suppressed despair or rage at the world. The sense that although he is always surrounded by supposed friends, Peter is in fact a very lonely person, disturbingly lonely, that he suffers from troubling and unhealthy thoughts. The unspeakable fear, yes, that he might be capable of acting on these thoughts in an irreparable way. Like when the girl said she was worried about him, that he sometimes said things, and Ivan automatically thought and at the same time refused to think about what she might mean. The possibility, the idea, of what Peter might do, what he might be capable of doing, planning to do, or even at this moment actually carrying out. This in itself is, of course, no reason for Ivan to reconcile with his brother: simply because of a groundless and irrational fear that something bad might happen if he doesn't. And yet, it lends to the conflict between them an unsavoury flavour somehow, an unresolved aspect that makes Ivan uncomfortable, sensing more and more the encroaching presence of thoughts and memories he would rather shut out. Like when he was a child, the way he looked up to his brother, idolised him. The way adults would listen when Peter was talking, practically hanging on his words, their father so shyly proud of him, and Christine pretending to be exasperated, calling him a little devil, saying he would be the death of her. He was the captain of his school chess club, he was the one who taught Ivan to play. It was Peter, who had never read any opening theory in his life, who could literally only play the Evans Gambit, who probably only joined the chess club for a girl or something, it was all because of him, everything, all the years of exultation and misery. And after Christine moved in with Frank and they had to spend every weekend in Skerries, the way Peter would stand up for Ivan, and remember what foods he didn't like to eat, and stay inside playing chess with him when the others were in the garden. At dinner, making little jokes only the two of them understood, so they would be cracking up together at the table while everyone else ate in silence. Myslím, že nepochopili vtip. But before long Peter had to go away to college. Alone with his step-siblings there was never anything for Ivan to laugh about. They only liked sports and outdoor activities, and Christine started saying it wasn't good for children to sit inside too much. Long periods of time would go by with no visits from Peter. Then one day he brought home a new visitor, which was a girl, his new girlfriend, and her name was Sylvia. They were in their dad's house then, this same house. Peter and Sylvia stood by the fireplace talking and smiling, and Ivan stared at them wordlessly, overawed. They looked very tall, the two of them, and beautiful, like film stars, and relaxed, happy. Ivan had never seen his brother looking so relaxed and happy. After that Peter came home more often, always with Sylvia, and the house would be noisy with conversation and laughter and footsteps racing up and down the stairs. Ivan used to confide in Peter then, telling him about problems at school, and Peter would always strongly take his side and even get annoyed on his behalf. Every year at Christmas, Peter and Sylvia would bring Ivan up to Dublin for a day to go shopping, and at lunchtime they would sit in the tea rooms on Grafton Street together, under the stained-glass windows, and Ivan would drink a hot chocolate with cream. The smell of coffee and hot butter he remembers, the crowded clamour of voices and crockery, and everyone's faces shiny and flushed from the cold outside. That was before. After the accident, it was different. Sylvia went into hospital, and then a different kind of hospital, and Peter came to live at home for a while. It's no good thinking about that now, going back over all that. Yes, in retrospect, Ivan can see, with the eyes of an adult, that Peter was not coping very well at the time. But in the real chronology of events, Ivan was only sixteen. He had his own problems, his chess, his school, and so on. His painful infatuation with that girl Kelly Heneghan who didn't seem to know he was alive. Frankly, if he had to admit the truth, Ivan found his brother's presence in the house uncomfortable. Peter barely spoke to anyone, barely made eye contact. For hours at a time he would just sit staring into space, doing nothing. And he cried, okay, not openly, but you could hear him crying in his room. It was awkward. Ivan had his own life to worry about. What was he supposed to do? In the evenings after school, he started avoiding Peter's company, excusing himself early from dinner, slipping out of the room whenever Peter entered. Obviously the situation was sad, with Sylvia being in hospital and everything, Ivan was sincerely sad for that, but the doctors said the recovery was going as well as could be expected, and it's not like Ivan could solve the problem. It was just something he didn't want to think about, honestly. What good would come from dwelling on it, worrying about it all the time? And the whole thing dragged on and on. Even after Peter moved back to Dublin, he would come home periodically and lie in his room for days on end, not talking, not even eating meals. For a year it was like this, on and off. The brother who had looked out for and defended Ivan was gone, and in his place was this unnerving kind of ghostly presence, practically haunting the house, making everyone feel bad. One of these nights, Ivan woke up thirsty and went downstairs to get himself a glass of water, yes, fine. And in the kitchen he found Peter sitting alone at the table. It was late, maybe three o'clock in the morning, and he tried to creep back out, but Peter had already seen him. You don't have to run away from me, he said. I'm not a monster. Ivan stood frozen in the doorway, saying nothing. Why even think about all this now? Peter was crying then, openly, with tears running down his face. I'm just really scared, Ivan, he said. I don't know what to do. I don't have anyone to talk to. That's what he said, I'm scared, I don't have anyone to talk to, that's how Ivan remembers it. And instead of acknowledging that he had heard these words spoken, Ivan just turned around silently and went back up to bed. It was a conversation he didn't want to have. Peter was like twenty-six, Ivan was only sixteen or seventeen, it wasn't any of his business. He was just a child. Wasn't it, in a way, actually wrong of Peter to put him in that position? Soon after, Peter went back to Dublin for good, and things returned to normal, more or less normal. In fact, not normal at all, because Peter and Sylvia, who had been practically married before, were broken up, and Peter stopped coming home, stopped sending Ivan funny messages and chess puzzles, started taking holidays with his new lawyer friends. He didn't like his family anymore, any of them, it was obvious. He avoided them, and in a way they avoided him too. You could tell their dad was relieved that Peter wasn't coming home so often, not that he didn't love him, but just that the situation had become so awkward. Ivan never told his parents about what happened that time, Peter crying and saying he was scared. He never even really thought about it again, in fact he deliberately avoided thinking about it, with a sense of embarrassment, and worse than embarrassment, something like shame, resentment, whenever it came into his head and he had to bat it away again. Peter was such a difficult person, always making life difficult. The two of them started getting into fights whenever they saw each other, about anything, nothing at all. Peter laughing, dismissive, rehearsing the most stale liberal talking points, calling Ivan a creep or an incel. I'm sorry, but you don't relate to people on a normal level. I'm trying to have a human conversation and you're talking like a robot. Ivan shouting at him, screaming, you're not even smart, you're actually fucking stupid, slamming doors in his face. Inside his own bedroom then, taking books from his bookshelves and throwing them at the wall, just to relieve the feeling, his brother's smirking superiority. Pictures on social media of Peter on holiday with his rich friends, drinking cocktails, always with some insanely perfect-looking girl beside him. And the pictures would have hundreds of likes, maybe thousands. While Ivan was at home alone with all the lights off, entering depressingly niche search terms into pornography websites. Okay, maybe he was a creep, maybe he was an incel. Maybe he didn't relate to people on a normal level. It was better than being an arrogant narcissist at least. Better than arranging his whole life around going to parties and getting blowjobs from brainless rich girls. Right, but was it actually better than that? No, of course not, of course it wasn't. At eighteen, nineteen years old, Ivan felt a crushing desire to arrange his own life in this exact way, going to parties, getting blowjobs, he would have given anything, he would have pretended to have almost any opinions he could think of, in order to make this happen to him. Which Peter knew very well, and thought was hilarious, because they hated each other. When he brought home that Italian girlfriend, who wore her blouse half-open at dinner and no bra. Throwing her head back laughing at Peter's jokes. Kill me now, actually just kill me. Their mutual hatred, yes. It goes back to that, Peter's behaviour, and Ivan's response, lack of response. From all of this, the disappointment, the contempt, fury, coruscating hostility. Desire to inflict pain on one another. Ivan has never again seen Peter crying, has never seen him showing any emotion at all, even when their father died, even afterwards, at the funeral, nothing, just the same polite distracted smile. Like their father was nothing to him, death was nothing, he was bored, he had no feelings. The eulogy he gave, so polished, full of clever observations and jokes, making everyone laugh indulgently, but expressing no sincere emotion at all. Underneath Peter's smooth demeanour, Ivan has always known there is something else, but he has not wanted to know that, to allow that knowledge into contact with his life. Like Peter's strange behaviour at the dinner, his words about Sylvia, I'm still in love with her, and now the fact of this college student, his ex-girlfriend, who knows all about Ivan, all about everything, and she's saying that Peter isn't doing well mentally, all of this suggests not only hypocrisy but something wrong, Ivan thinks, something actually not right. At this juncture, wriggling out of Ivan's grasp, Alexei gets up on his feet and shakes himself, his ears flapping back and forth. Gripping the quilt with his claws he stretches, yawns, and then hops down off the bed and curls up underneath Ivan's desk instead. He understands nothing, he's just a dog. Probably he was getting too hot with Ivan clasping onto him, that's all. For a few minutes Ivan lies on the bed not knowing what to think, what task to feed into his brain, to go on analysing past events, his own mistakes and regrets, the wrongs he has done to others, or the wrongs done by others to him, or the confusing events in his life that seem to involve both kinds of wrong, or to think about his father, or about the girl downstairs, or about Margaret, the tournament next week, the light thin blouse she might wear. But no: his mind is too sickened to think about anything. Finally, sliding his phone from his pocket in silence, he opens the app and begins without further consideration to play a game of chess.

# 15

Back at the flat Monday evening changing his clothes. Place seems empty without her somehow. Though she was only here a few weeks. Homely feeling produced by the proliferation of her things, brought with her from the station or collected later from Janine, her jacket on the hook, shoes, and the smell of hair conditioner, deodorant. Dishes piled in the sink. Now in her absence the flat is clean again and sterile and at the same time dingier, like a hospital waiting room. Reminds him how much he's always hated the place. The ugly furniture, glass dining table, Jesus Christ. Friday morning in bed he told her that he loved her and she cried. Naomi crying over him, yes. Final gruesome victory in a game he should never have played. What he wanted after all, to defeat her, ruin her life. In retaliation for what, making a fool of him. Making him like her so much. Whole thing in horribly poor taste, he thinks. Start to finish. She'll be alright at least. Survival instinct. Checking out the house in Kildare, nice bathtub, presume I can smoke in the garden. She'll be alright, she'll be fine. She's a carnivore.

Back home that night he took another two milligrams and went to sleep with the lights on. Dreamed of nothing. Up early Saturday morning he tidied, hoovered, washed the sheets, made from unthinking habit too much coffee, and sat at the dining table to call Sylvia. Took her some time to pick up, hello, and he asked if he could see her. Oh, she said. I'm at home for the weekend. Is everything okay? At home, in Waterford, of course. Everything's fine, he said. How are you feeling? She said she felt much better. Thank you for the other day, she added. I told my parents you took very good care of me. I mean— Sorry, obviously I didn't go into detail. They were both laughing then, awkwardly, and he said that was alright. They talked a little longer. Medicinal effect of her voice, her intelligence. She asked if he wanted to say hello to her mother and he said sure. Doors opening and closing then and Miriam's voice on the phone saying: Hello there, Peter. How are you keeping? Tired, still sitting at the dining table, he closed his eyes. Hi Miriam, he said. I'm alright, thank you. How are you and Joe getting on? Behind his closed eyes he could see their kitchen, with the low ceiling, the painted cabinet doors, and Miriam in her dressing-gown with her glasses pushed back into her hair. All well here, she said. We're thinking of you, of course. And your lovely dad, God rest him. Sore his eyes and hot he felt. Thank you, he said. You're very kind. They talked for a little longer, exchanging good wishes, and she passed the phone back to Sylvia. For a few seconds, neither of them spoke. Listen, he said then, I love you, alright? Let's see each other soon, if we can. Quietly and without hesitation she answered: How about Monday afternoon? I'll be home after four if you want to come over. They hung up and he made some breakfast, scrambled eggs, bacon, finding himself surprisingly hungry, a third and fourth slice of buttered toast.

Coming up on quarter past now. Puts his coat on and takes his umbrella from the stand by the door. Be at her building in ten minutes, eight if he walks quickly and doesn't get caught at the lights. The right life, yes, at last. Outside, the fresh damp winter air, clouds massed dark and heavy. He turns right towards the church and cars glide past through standing water, headlights dipped. Grand old terraces, coloured lights blinking on and off in the high handsome windows. His mistakes all behind him. Raw relief to contemplate. He has extricated himself, the wrongs are in the past, however many, however complicated, and his life is beginning again. And rounding the corner the way the wind comes bowling down Baggot Street, rattling through the trees. Everything rinsed fresh by cold air and water, everything clean and new, he thinks, yes. Because the past falls away behind you at every moment. And the lights are with him all the way and he's up the stairs by four twenty-three, letting himself inside. White daylight from the windows falling soft and silent on every surface. She's at the table, papers everywhere, rises to her feet to see him, looking wan he thinks, and happy, and he takes her in his arms and kisses her. Yes, because his life is starting again, the long terrible intermission at an end, the smoke is clearing, he is finally resuming his place. And drawing back she smiles at him.

You're in a good mood, she says. Did you have a nice weekend?

Uncertainly he hesitates, sensing how far he has proceeded past explanation. Trying to organise his thoughts, wanting not to have to, he says: Well, it was quiet.

Already she's going to the kitchen, asking if he wants tea or coffee. No, thanks, he replies.

I'm having tea, she says.

Unable to remember or visualise now how he thought

things would unfold once he arrived, he goes for no special reason to the mantelpiece, looks unseeing at a candlestick. You work away, he says.

Presently she comes out again, seats herself on the sofa, her feet pulled up under her. Sets the cup down on the side table to cool. You were saying about your weekend, she says.

No, I wasn't, he answers. I don't think I was. Listen, I want to tell you, I've ended things with Naomi. She's moved out. She's going to stay in my dad's house for a while, until she finds somewhere more permanent.

In shock with lips parted, bright and wide her eyes. Oh my God, Peter, she says. What happened?

Uncomprehending he stares at her, disorientated, and she stares back at him, the two of them silent. What do you mean what happened? he says. We— Breaking off, finding no available grammar with which to complete the sentence, he tries again: This was on Thursday, after we— She goes on staring at him, wordless, offering nothing, and finally he manages to say only: After I was here, with you.

She goes on looking at him, pink patches of colour forming on her face. What? she says. After you were here with me, what? You went home and broke up with Naomi?

Right, he says. Yes.

Why?

He says nothing. Astonishing he thinks that he even continues to breathe, standing there, the air moving mechanically in and out of his lungs, while he says nothing, holding with one hand the mantelpiece.

Peter, she goes on, I'm honestly trying to understand what you're saying. Why have you and Naomi broken up?

Somehow thoughtlessly the words produce themselves:

After what happened, I thought it was the only thing that made sense.

She lowers her eyes now, speaking quietly. You told me that she understood about that, she says. You said it wasn't monogamous.

He feels his head shaking, and the mantelpiece hard under his hand. Jesus, he says. It wasn't. I mean, she understood, she knew. But what's the point in dragging things out?

Dragging what out?

Desperation, to feel it all slipping somehow away, and almost angrily he says aloud: For fuck's sake, Sylvia, what are we talking about here?

She rubs her brow with her hands. You told me it was all okay, she says. There wasn't supposed to be any pressure. If something happened with us, it would be nice, and if it didn't, whatever. It was all relaxed, there was nothing to worry about. No one was going to get hurt. Now you're over here shouting at me, I broke up with my girlfriend for you, aren't you happy? Of course I'm not. I never wanted you to do that to her. If I had known that's what you were thinking of, nothing would have happened between us. You led me to believe it was something completely different. Frankly, I don't think you know what you're doing. And you're making all three of us miserable.

Shaking his head, his mouth moving, unspeaking. These words, all three of us, crowd into his brain horribly, all three, like an inappropriate joke. I don't understand, he says. We're in bed together, you're telling me you love me, and now you're saying it was all just a misunderstanding? You don't want to be together after all?

And she too is shaking her head, her eyes averted. But nothing has changed, she says. What happened between us the other day, it was nice, I'm not saying it wasn't, but my situation is the same as before. The kind of relationship you're talking about, where I'm the only woman in your life and you give up everything for me, I don't want that. Honestly, I don't. It's just too much pressure. I'm sorry.

Sick feeling, to have misunderstood so badly, and angrily he says: What did you think I was going to do, just keep stringing Naomi along to make you feel better? Jesus.

Who said anything about stringing her along? I thought you were fond of her.

Staring at the floor he hears his voice sullen now and inexpressive. She's twenty-three, he says. It wasn't going anywhere. We had fun, whatever. I liked her, but it was just a distraction.

After a moment's pause, Sylvia asks: Have you told her about me? I mean, about my situation. Have you talked about that with her?

Head throbbing he goes on staring down at his feet. Well, I felt like, I suppose, yeah, he says. I thought I should try and explain, to some extent. A little bit, I did talk to her about it.

Strangely, frighteningly, Sylvia gives a kind of laugh, and puts her hand in her hair. Looking at him, she's looking, and her face is different. That's alright, she says. I didn't understand before. But it makes sense to me now. You're in love with her, aren't you?

Fumbling with his hand at the mantelpiece, sweating, he says nothing, and neither does she. Finally he answers: No. I don't know. Yeah, maybe. But it doesn't matter now.

Because you think I'm going to come in and rescue you, she says. Well, I'm not.

Dry feeling in his mouth, his throat. I don't know what you're talking about, he replies.

Very controlled and intelligent her voice now, controlled and intent, and her eyes still glittering. Yes you do, she says. You've fallen in love with someone, and you're afraid. It's the usual thing, you don't like being vulnerable. And I suppose on top of that, she's not a very suitable person. She has no money, and she puts up these pictures online, maybe you think people are laughing at you. And you're looking back on how things were when you and I were together, how easy everything was, and everyone was jealous of us, and you just want that back again. For life to be easy. What happened between us the other day, I can see now, you did that because you wanted an exit strategy. Maybe not consciously, I don't know, but in the back of your mind. You were looking for a way out with Naomi. I thought we were just— whatever, in that moment, and for you it was something else. We should have talked then, or we should have, I don't know. I was in a lot of pain, I wasn't feeling well. But whatever it was, I was not trying to help you get out of your relationship. Okay? You can't use me like that. I'm a human being.

Sharp goring sensation, and he presses with his hand at his breastbone, feeling what, the bitterness of the accusation, and worse, that she is taking away from him the only right thing in his life. Eyes ranging around the room at random, helpless, and when he speaks he hears his voice cracking. That's not what it was at all, he says. Look, Sylvia, I understand the situation is fucked up. It's a mess. I get that, and I'm sorry. Obviously, you know, you and I haven't been together for a long time, which was what you said you wanted. To see other people. I never wanted that. And yeah, maybe, recently, there were feelings, I did develop certain feelings. That's my problem, I'm not asking you to do anything about it. I know it's awkward, but these things happen, you know, you meet people. You were the one who insisted I should be meeting people, and yeah, things got out of hand, I'm sorry. But I love you, I want to be with you, that's all that matters.

That look on her face, staring at him, as if from far away. What happened to me, she says. Let's be honest, Peter, it ruined my life. And I'm trying to tell you that I'm not going to let it ruin yours.

His eyes trained dully on the fringe of the rug at his feet, wavering, hot, blurred. It already has, he says.

For a moment he can only hear her breathing, hard. Then she says: I see. Okay. What do you want me to do, apologise? Well, I'm very sorry. I can see it's terribly hard for you, that I'm in pain all the time and I'm never going to get better. How cruel of me to ruin your life like that. And now I suppose I've ruined Naomi's life as well. I don't know how either of you can ever forgive me.

Blinking down at the floor he can hardly see. Okay, he says. You're jealous, you're jealous of her. And I'm sorry about that. But you're saying some stupid things.

Again she falls silent, for a longer time now, a long time. Then with a tremble in her voice she says slowly: I don't see what more I can do for you. I've tried to be your friend, and for some reason you've been determined to humiliate me and hurt me. I don't know why. Maybe deep down you really wish I was dead, and you're trying to punish me because I'm not.

His hand at the mantelpiece now he feels grabbing, seizing, and with a sudden downward gesture he slams something onto the floor, without even seeing what it is. Lands with a bang on the floorboards and rolls forward onto the rug, the brass candlestick, and something else also, a notecard, a piece of paper, floating down more slowly through the air.

How dare you, she says. Get out.

Wiping his wrist across his eyes he's already leaving. Half-blinded in the hallway he takes his coat from the hook, umbrella, bangs the door behind him. What happened, it changed her, she's right. Cold superior person now who takes pleasure in twisting the knife. Only pleasure she has left probably. Maybe deep down you really wish. And maybe he does, maybe he does. Darkening blue of the sky over the tops of buildings. Soft unsealing sound of the automatic doors at the Tesco Express. From the off-licence section he takes a shoulder bottle of vodka wrapped in a plastic security tag and brings it to the till. See the girl hitting the button that says Visibly Over 25 without even looking. Thank you, yes. I too was twenty-five once, and even younger, though I readily concede that for you at this moment it must be hard to imagine. Life, which is now the most painful ordeal conceivable, was happy then, the same life. A cruel kind of joke, you'll agree. Anyway, you're young, make the most of it. Enjoy every second. And on your twenty-fifth birthday, if you want my advice, jump off a fucking bridge. Thanks. The doors once again parting to extrude his body onto the street. Shoulder bottle in his pocket. What's the plan, there isn't one. Can't go back to the flat, doesn't trust himself. Down the bottle, finish a sheet of pills, and what else. Morbid fantasies about his own death and perhaps even more than fantasies. Walks along the Green towards Grafton Street instead and his nose is burning, his eyes. Maybe deep down you wish. Get to Heuston, he thinks. Catch a train, go and see her, the other. Come crying, morose, apologetic, fall asleep in his childhood bedroom. What harm. She already thinks he's a headcase. In the house, alone with her, even if they start fighting, at each other's throats, screaming, recriminating, at least it's a distraction, and nothing bad will happen. Across the bridge to Abbey Street. Bulky his coat pocket standing on the tram, obtrusive, and what is he thinking. To slip quietly away unnoticed. Yes. Only after months or years would someone say: What ever happened to that lad Koubek? Never see him around these days. No, I don't think he's living in town anymore. That's all. If it could be like that, painless. Emigrate, like so many others who have fallen out of social life, eventually unmentioned, but instead of moving away, just quietly ceasing to exist. Yes. And what about God. Well, what about him. Feels the old kick of his spirit to think. Nothing can force me to endure what I hate, compel me to suffer, to accept suffering, indignity, nothing, no one, not even God. Just try and you'll see. I won't take it. You can't make me. At the station with his head held high he alights from the carriage, yes, bowing to no one, alone with his conscience, yes, and he will not be forced.

Train in ten minutes and he gets a ticket from the machine, buys a bottle of lemonade and enters the toilets. Slides the lock shut on a cubicle and feeling overwarm pours out half the lemonade and then, with the lids in his coat pocket, attempts to decant carefully the vodka into the remainder. His hands are sweating again. Nothing can compel him, he bows to no one. Okay, he may at this moment be for some reason in a toilet cubicle in a train station pouring three hundred and fifty millilitres of vodka into a plastic bottle of supermarket lemonade, which feels a little unsanitary, but nonetheless, he prostrates himself before no authority, he will not be forced. At the sinks he washes his hands and then deposits in the waste bin the empty glass bottle and its serrated cap. Back out on the concourse, two lukewarm mouthfuls, stinging. And if she's in a good mood they could even go to bed. Hurt her, make her cry, why not.

Image of the candlestick suddenly re-enters the brain, heavy banging sound, and the back of his neck is prickling, because he did that. Shouting, throwing her things around. Another mouthful he swallows. Maybe deep down you wish. Sick with guilt thinking: then don't think. Watch instead the live display board ticking times and platforms overhead. Animated hands of the simulated analogue clock. Have another mouthful. And when the number appears, it's easy, insert the paper ticket right side up and walk along the platform with the bottle swinging in your pocket. What could be easier. To go and see her, say you're sorry, have it out. Distract yourself. She won't make things difficult, or if she does, it's only the minor pleasantly irritating kind of difficulty. Nothing serious. Come here, I love you. Forget about it.

Out the window of the train now the familiar scenery, the gable sides of buildings, blocks of flats, Park West and Cherry Orchard. Leaving the city in gathering darkness, the houses, the fields, all known to him. This singular ribbon cut through the countryside, endlessly repeating reel of film. Burned-out car that's been sitting there ten years, the old milking shed with its roof collapsing. Did he throw the candlestick or only drop it from the mantel, he wonders. Knock it over with the flat of his hand or seize and throw, he can't remember, and probably it doesn't matter. How dare you, she said. Get out. Living together five or six years they never once fought like that. Crushes they had on other people they would laugh about, tease each other. All their little running jokes drawn out over years, growing stupidly funnier and more incomprehensible. Before they retreated to the false formalities of their pretended friendship. Undressing her for bed he remembers, yes: though in his memories she's not so young. Looks much the same as she does now. At the time of course she was no older than Naomi. Strange to think of that, and somehow awful. I begin to like them at that age. Forty-seven minutes the journey and he finishes in the meantime the bottle of lemonade. Slow headache coming down from the top of his skull not even really painful. More like the idea of a headache. Pulling into the station and the window so dark it shows only his reflection. Empty bottle before him on the table. Pale luminescent feeling as if already dead, descending. Gets off the train half-drunk and it's raining again on the platform. Strikes him suddenly he has no umbrella: and when, where. On the tram he had it. Station toilet he thinks, yes, messing with the lemonade. For Jesus' sake, he's had that thing years. He actually liked it. Climbs into a taxi, cash in his pocket, out towards the old ring road please.

At the house the lights are on behind closed curtains. Finds with his fingers the front door key, and what will she be wearing he wonders. Or in the bath again perhaps, singing to herself. Look who's come crawling back. Inside, the hallway, lighted, and he pushes open the living room door, almost speaking to her already, syllable forming in his mouth, and then stops dead. At the table in the corner, the old homework table, sitting with a chessboard in front of him, thick paperback book held open with his phone, his brother. Ivan. As if, at the station, Peter boarded by some accident a train bound back into the past, as if he has arrived here not this evening but two years ago, four years ago, and Ivan is studying his chess quietly, or studying for his Leaving Cert, and in the kitchen their father is even now cooking dinner with the radio on. Their father: yes, alive and well. Across the room Ivan looks at him and Peter looks back.

From under the table, languorously, the dog unfolds itself, and comes padding up to Peter, comes to be petted and fussed over, the dog, with its long thin face almost smiling.

What are you doing here? Ivan asks.

I'm sorry, wait one minute, Peter says. What are you doing here?

I'm staying here, says Ivan. I needed somewhere to take the dog.

Before Peter can speak again, Ivan adds sombrely: She's gone out with her friends, if you're wondering. Someone collected her.

Feeling nothing at all, as if anaesthetised, or dead he thinks again, dead already, Peter sits down in his overcoat on the old sofa. The dog jumps up beside him and lies down with its head in his lap. Absently he tousles the creature's ears, silken, warm. Someone collected her, okay, he says. You've met, then.

Oh, we've met, Ivan replies. Very much so. We've had interesting discussions.

At these words, this idea, the interesting discussions that Ivan believes himself to have had with Naomi, Peter gives a sort of laugh. Okay, he says. I tried to call you, to let you know she was going to be here. You still have my number blocked, I believe.

The aspect of hypocrisy kind of jumps out, Ivan remarks.

Still playing idly with the ears of the dog, Peter answers: Does it, indeed. My hypocrisy, I suppose you mean.

With effort in his voice, Ivan answers: If you remember, when we discussed a certain other situation, you were not very understanding.

I remember, yes. Still seeing her, are you?

I don't answer questions from you about my personal life,

Ivan says. That's one thing I can tell you. I made that mistake before.

That's okay, he replies. Don't tell me if you'd rather not.

They lapse into silence. The dog closes its eyes serenely in Peter's lap. Soft elastic frill of its inner lip showing. Thin limbs tucked up on the cushions. Studying your chess? he asks.

Obviously, says Ivan.

Back competing again?

Ivan nods without speaking, his gaze directed at the board.

What's the book? Peter asks. *My 60 Memorable Games*.

After a pause, as if relenting slightly, Ivan answers: No, I wish. It's just this thing on the London System. Which I never play, but you have to know the lines.

How's the rating?

Still the same, Ivan says. But there's an event on in town next week, a norm event. So that could be good, if it goes well.

Fingers moving over the dog's small delicate ribs Peter answers: Ah, okay. Good luck with it. I'll keep my fingers crossed.

Ivan glances up at him now. Did you tell Naomi I'm a genius? he asks.

Feels himself almost fondly smiling. I don't know, he says. Probably. If she said I did, I'm sure I did.

Well, I hope you realise I'm not.

To me, you are.

Ivan looks back down at the chessboard, as if sheepishly pleased. I don't mind her being here, by the way, he says. I think she's worried I'm going to ask her to leave. But if you talk to her, you can tell her, I don't mind.

Quietly Peter answers: Okay. Thank you. If I do talk to her, I will tell her. I appreciate you're being very decent.

Nodding his head, moving his eyes over the pieces on the

board. And I won't ask you about the situation, he says, because it's not my business.

Carelessly Peter exhales. Oh, I doubt you'd be interested, Ivan, he says.

If I'm interested or not, it's irrelevant. I'm not going to pry.

Another little silence descends. Ivan it seems rather self-consciously moves a pawn and consults again the notation in the book. The dog shifts itself further up into Peter's lap, re-settles, heavy and warm. Back to sleep. Eye half-closed showing under the lid a thin grey sliver of membrane.

Perhaps I was a little harsh that time at dinner, Peter remarks.

Immediately Ivan answers: There's no perhaps. You were extremely harsh, not perhaps.

As I recall, I was trying to speak to you about something else. It doesn't matter now. We were talking at cross-purposes. I'm sorry if I hurt your feelings.

When Peter looks up, he can see Ivan is red in the face, no longer looking at the chess set, but breathing in and out between his lips. It's not an apology when it goes into 'if', Ivan says. 'I'm sorry if', that's not a sincere apology.

With an oddly cool feeling, getting on for drunk he remembers, Peter regards his brother. Well, alright then, he replies. I'm sorry I was harsh, is that better? I actually texted you to apologise, but you blocked my number.

Ivan rises to his feet now, and in Peter's lap the dog's eyes come open, watching. As far as the double doors to the kitchen Ivan paces and then turns back. There's more to it than that, he says. You don't show me respect.

I'm not sure that's entirely fair, Peter answers.

You look down on me. You treat me like a child.

Smoothing his hand slowly over the dog's coat, Peter replies: Well, you're my little brother. I'm a lot older than you are. Maybe I do find it difficult to accept that you're an adult now. But that's not to say I look down on you.

Flushed, raising his voice, Ivan retorts: Even right now. Even right now, you're doing it, using all these words. The explaining kind of voice. You think you're right about everything. That's how you act.

Obviously there are things we disagree on, Peter answers. And yes, when it comes to our disagreements, I think I'm right, of course. If I thought you were right, we wouldn't disagree.

Throwing his hands up, Ivan says: Right now, literally. The voice you're putting on, the way you're talking.

Peter watches him pacing over to the piano and chewing on one of his nails. Well, if you want to get into it, Ivan, he says, I do think you have some unpleasant opinions. There are things you've said about women, to be honest, I would describe as disturbing. What am I supposed to do, pretend I agree with you? While you sit there saying feminism is evil, or women make up lies about being raped, or whatever it is.

Ivan moving his hands around in front of his face, as if waving the words away. Okay, look, whatever, he says. You're getting off the topic now. That's not relevant.

Yes it is, says Peter. You're accusing me of acting like I'm right about everything. And I'm pointing out, yes, sometimes I'm right and you're wrong.

Well, I don't remember saying those things you're talking about. If I even did say them, it would be a long time ago, and I don't remember the context. But whatever, views can change. I'm not saying, you've never been right. I'm saying, not always.

Feels himself settling back on the sofa now, watching. Ah, I see, he says. You've changed your mind, then?

Rubbing at his face with his hands, pacing from the piano to the bookcase, Ivan replies: Oh my God, whatever. I don't want to get into this at all. What I said in the past, I don't remember what it was, but I'm sure I have developed different views since then. Which would be the normal, right, that beliefs can change over time. You know, you're making a big deal out of nothing now.

Lightly Peter shrugs his shoulders, scratching the dog's narrow pink belly with his fingers. Well, to me, it's not nothing, he says. It's a question of right and wrong. But if you've changed your mind, I'm glad to hear it.

Without looking around, Ivan retorts: Because you're so perfect towards women.

Pauses, without looking up. Cold feeling rather than hot. I was talking about your beliefs rather than your conduct, he answers.

Conduct is more important than beliefs.

Slowly lifts his hand away from the dog and brushes a stray hair off his lap. Well, I don't know what you're accusing me of, he says. I can only assume Naomi has been complaining about me. But of course I'm not perfect, I never said I was.

Ivan is silent a moment. Then he says: Actually she defended you, if you have to know. But I can draw my own conclusions. She's the same age as me, you realise.

Yes, I'm well aware, Peter answers. Although I don't see how you of all people can object to that.

Ivan does look around now, eyes flashing. I'm not the one who's messing around with two different women, he says.

With a jolting shock, Peter hears himself laughing out, a

hard unpleasant laugh, cruel-sounding. If I were you, he replies, I wouldn't talk about things I don't understand.

Ivan's face is red, flushed, angry. See, he says. Now you're being honest for once. You don't think I understand anything. For your information, I have my own life. And I understand things very well. You think you can just push me around and I won't stand up for myself. Always, you're always the same. With the eulogy, at the funeral. You pushed me into letting you do it, and I just had to sit there saying nothing. Because you always have to be in charge.

Calmly he answers: It had to be one or other of us. I believe it's usually the eldest. But I didn't realise you had strong feelings either way. You didn't express any.

I was closer with Dad, Ivan retorts.

Strange that feeling, and chilling. So familiar the room, their home, and Peter realises suddenly, remembers, how much he hates it, how hateful, the feeling of being again in this terrible house. I'm sure you're right about that, he says. I tried my best, but I suppose it's true, we weren't very close.

What does that mean, you tried your best?

For a moment he's silent. Flickering in his head, in his hands he feels, pulse of his blood. I didn't find him an easy person to be close with, he says. He wasn't always very open to talking about things.

Quietly, with a shaking voice, Ivan asks: You're criticising him?

You asked me why we weren't close. I'm just trying to explain.

It was his fault?

Peter shrugs his shoulders. We were as close as I imagine he wanted us to be, he replies. We had very different personalities.

Why don't you say the truth? Ivan asks. You didn't respect him. You never respected either of us. And your eulogy was horrible, by the way. It was embarrassing. You always think you're so good at everything, but you're not. People just flatter you because they're scared to give criticisms. Well, I'm not scared. All you do is tell lies and talk in clichés all the time. You never say anything true.

Strangely Peter is conscious of smiling now, yes, thin smile, and with an energy inside him, his hands, his arms, hot, towering sensation, he gets up, stands at the empty fireplace. Okay, he says. You want me to tell the truth. That's fine. The truth is that I've spent my life trying to protect you both. From the age of what, twelve, fifteen, I was the one who had to be the adult. That's the truth, if you want to know. Who was looking out for me, Ivan? When I was the one who needed help, where were the two of you? No, you didn't want to talk, you didn't want to know. Neither of you. And why, because it made you feel awkward, you didn't know what to say. You want to know why I treat you like a child? Because you are a fucking child. When things get difficult, you're gone. You're out of the room. And that's alright, I don't expect anything else. Maybe with Dad I did, but I learned my lesson. He didn't want me to be his son, he wanted me to be his protector. And yours. So that's what I was. All my life, I was looking out for the both of you. And neither of you ever even had the decency to say thanks.

Seems to feel before he sees. The sensation, sudden, jarring more than painful, shoved backwards against the hearth, and he has to step back, find his footing. Ivan has pushed him, Ivan has raised his hands and pushed him back tripping hard against the fireplace, Ivan, standing there before him, breathing heavily, yes, he did it, he shoved him, hands to his chest. Heat of rage flaring inside him now, hot light, Peter reaches out and slaps him hard across the face with the back of his hand. Behave yourself, he says. Clutching at his own jaw, Ivan retorts: Fuck you. And tries with his other hand to shove again, tries actually again to push him, attempts, yes, and with a blind sort of pounding behind his eyes Peter grasps him by his sweatshirt, both hands, holding hard, and throws him down on the floor, where his body lands heavily. Crying out, and the dog up on all fours now lets out a high sharp yelp. Out of breath, blood filling his head, standing over him, to lay a hand on me, he did that, Peter feels himself draw back to put the weight of his body into his foot, ready to slam it into his ribs, who's sorry now, you little worm, I'll fucking kill you. Before he can move however he catches in the eyes a glimpse, eyes looking at him. Ivan's. Turned up to him, widened in horror, pleading, whole face ashen sick, beyond white, grey. Terrified. Dropping sensation in the stomach. Frightened, he's really frightened, and Peter steps back now, steps away, clearing his throat. Sort of thudding in his chest still. What was that. He wouldn't really. It was just. I wasn't going to do anything, he says aloud. Hears Ivan scrambling up, retreating to the other end of the room. Dog trotting after him, ticking sound of its claws. Dizzy sort of spinning feeling, light-headed, vague tinny ringing in his ears. You shouldn't have started it, he goes on. Looks around to see Ivan holding his face, and yes, the lip is bleeding. Fear in his eyes still. I wasn't really going to hurt you, Peter says. Look, I'm going, alright? I'll leave you alone. Clearing his throat he adds once more: I wouldn't have actually done anything. Closes quietly the living room door, front door, out onto the driveway, and it's cold out, hands are cold, shaking, breath leaving his body.

Walks down in darkness as far as the road. Churning feeling, cold or is it hot, and his mouth filling with a thin sour fluid, yes, and turning back from the road now, towards the garden wall, he tries to inhale slowly, thoughts breaking up into rivulets, rapid, incoherent, a heaving sensation, and then he gets sick. Once, twice, and he's sweating again, back of his neck breaking out, underarms trickling. Taste of formic acid and the rancid sweetness of lemonade. Feels better after. Takes a handkerchief from an inside pocket of his coat, wipes his face, his lips, back of his neck. Shouldn't have pushed me if he didn't want to fight. Half an hour it'll take him walking back into town now he thinks and then what, the train, and then. Headlights silver the walkway, flash and vanish. His lip was bleeding. Must have caught him when he gave him that slap. An overreaction, that's all. Said he was sorry. Shouldn't have started on him like that. I didn't. His fault. Handkerchief from his pocket and he wipes again mechanically his face. Weak in his legs. He was going to kick him, he would have, he was about to, and he would. In truth, he wanted to and would have. Heat of rage in his body. Frightened himself. More frightened than Ivan he thinks when he realised what he was doing, what he was about to do, more scared than he was. Something wrong with his brain. What he said, did. Hitting him in the face like that. Talking that way about their father. Regrets that now, of course he regrets. It was different, it was more complicated. Difficult feelings, everyone was doing their best. He was a good person, he tried. No one is perfect. Sometimes you need people to be perfect and they can't be and you hate them forever for not being even though it isn't their fault and it's not yours either. You just needed something they didn't have in them to give you. And then in other people's lives you do the same thing, you're the person who lets everyone down, who fails to make anything better, and you hate yourself so much you wish you were dead. Takes his phone from his pocket, opens the contacts list and taps Ivan's name, see if he's okay, and the call disconnects. Blocked number he forgot or did he. Taps again for no reason. If he's hurt or something, just to tell him sorry. Shouldn't have pushed me. No, it wasn't your fault. Wave of weakness he feels as if to be sick again and finds himself touching, holding the slick wet side of wall beside him, passing cars, and he's leaning almost crouching, his back against the brickwork. Something wrong, he can't walk. Try Ivan again but of course there's no answer. Can't call Sylvia. She hates him now. Himself also he hates. Better off if he did it. Scrolling up unseeing and then finally tapping again, holding the phone to his ear. Breathing hard against the wall, picked out in the passing headlights, shielding with his hand his eyes, and the phone is ringing, three times, four, and then the voice.

Hello my darling, says his mother.

Steady voice he tries. Hey, he says.

Pause he detects and then lightly she says: Everything alright?

Yeah, he says. Yeah, I was just thinking. Are you at home?

Yes indeed.

Swallowing, sour in his mouth. I thought I might call round for dinner this evening, he says. Only if it suits you.

Of course it suits me, she replies. I'm killing the fatted calf as we speak. What time should I expect you?

Closes his eyes. Wet of the wall against his back. Well, I'm out in Naas just now, he lies. I had a meeting. But I'll hop on a train, I could be with you in an hour or two.

You take your time, she says. I'll rustle something up here. I think it'll be just the two of us, if that's alright.

Fine, he answers. Perfect, actually.

Okay, see you then.

He clears his throat. Christine, he says. Could you do me a favour, in the meantime? It's not a big thing. Could you maybe give Ivan a call, and see if he's alright? We've just had a bit of a row. I'm sure he's fine, but I'd feel better if you spoke to him. He's not picking up for me.

Dreading what she might ask, tightening in his jaw and throat. But all she says is: No problem, I'll call him now. Do you want me to say we've spoken?

Exhaling he answers: No, I think better not.

Understood, she says. I'll be back to you. See you soon.

Phone slipping down into his coat pocket. Stands up on his feet, reaches again for the handkerchief. Thirty-two years old and running to his mother. When only minutes ago he was the one calling Ivan a child. The aspect of hypocrisy kind of jumps out. On his feet again and trudging towards the train station. Minutes pass, and she texts. Spoke on the phone just now. All good I think. Bit monosyllabic but that's the usual. He didn't mention you. Nothing to worry about I suspect. xxx. Reads and reads again. He didn't mention you. Okay. Wonder why. Unlikely to be out of loyalty. Ashamed perhaps. Or still frightened. Jesus. Oh well, at least he picked up, at least he sounded alright. Alive and well. Ivan. I'm sorry. Closes for a moment his eyes. And then keeps walking.

You weren't long, she says when he arrives at the house. Come here to me. Do you feed yourself at all? I'll take your coat. No umbrella? Tells her he left it at the station. Ah, that's a shame, she says. You were fond of that thing. At least I'll know what to get you for Christmas. Perfumed interior of the kitchen. Relentless chatter of her conversation. Darren hardly ever home for dinner, you know these big firms, keep them in all hours, and Frank is playing tennis. He sits at the dining table while she's at the stovetop, stirring. Says she read something in *The Irish Times* about young people taking cocaine. It's everywhere these days. I suppose you probably take it yourself. Examining his fingernails. Now and then, he says. She looks up mildly from the saucepan. And tell us, where do you get the stuff? she asks. I buy it off the girl I've been seeing, he replies. That makes her laugh, she's shaking her head. Oh, very good, she says. I didn't know you were seeing anyone. He shrugs his shoulders. I was, he says. But I suppose we've broken up now. She lifts the lid off a smaller pot, releasing a cloud of steam. Well, you'll have to find a new drug dealer, she remarks. He too starts laughing, they both are, and he puts his face down on the table. I need to sort my life out, Christine, he says. Things are not good. Pouring the contents of one pan into another, she says: You're grieving, pet. It's to be expected. Do you want to tell me about this girl? Surface of the table cooling his face he closes his eyes. No, thanks, he says. But just so you know, she's staying in Dad's house for a bit. Your house, as it is now. Just until she finds somewhere more permanent. Is that alright? Christine says no problem.

After dinner in the living room, opposite ends of the sofa, with the television on. Opened tin of biscuits between them. I had a fight with Ivan, he remarks. She says he mentioned that on the phone. Yeah, he replies, but not an argument. I mean we actually had a fight. I hit him. Astonished now she looks around, the eyes goggling. God above, she says. Where was this? What happened? Feels himself again shrugging, his eyes on the television. He kind of shoved me, I don't know, he says. And I slapped him. I threw him on the ground, I think.

But he got up again. We were talking about Dad. I suppose he thought I was being harsh. Which I was being. She has taken up the remote control and hit the mute button. Reaches over now and puts a hand on his shoulder. Peter, sweetheart, she says. I know things were hard between you and your dad at times. But he loved you. And I know that you loved him. The hand on his shoulder so welcome, so painfully welcome that his eyes fill again with tears and he looks away. I'm sorry, he says. Ah, you're not yourself, she answers. You and your brother will patch things up. But you have to keep an eye on that temper of yours. Okay? He nods his head, wipes his nose with his fingers. Firm pressure of her hand. Why don't you stay here tonight? she asks. Finds himself trying to work out whether it would be alright. In his thirties, to be staying the night in his mother's house. But his dad died. Right, but they weren't together. Why does it even matter. Deluding himself that he's normal, isn't that what she said the other night. So sick in the head you don't even see what you're doing to yourself. You're making all three of us miserable. You little worm, I'll fucking kill you. No, I wouldn't, I wasn't going to. I wish I was dead. Yeah, he says aloud. I'll stay, I think I will stay. If that's alright, I will.

# 16

Once Peter has left, closing the door behind him, and a few minutes have passed, so that it seems unlikely he will come back, Ivan goes alone into the empty kitchen. His upper lip is still bleeding, trickle of wet blood through his fingers, and with his other hand he tears a piece of kitchen paper from the roll, folds it into a square and presses it to his mouth. His breath is so loud it seems to fill the whole house, swelling and receding. What is he feeling? Shaken, he thinks, okay, yes, with a sort of sick adrenaline sensation, like the time on school tour when they made him get on the mini-rollercoaster, and afterwards his knees were so weak he fell over. Also, and again similarly to that incident, he feels ashamed. What for, in this case? Mostly he thinks for provoking a physical confrontation with someone stronger and more violent than himself. For having in the end to rely on his adversary's conscience and self-control in order to escape more serious injury, for having implicitly to petition his opponent for mercy, which was granted, making him almost kind of queasily grateful to Peter, in a shameful way, for not murdering him.

Back in the living room, Ivan sits down on the sofa with the dog, holding the folded piece of kitchen paper to his lip. If their father had been here, he thinks, it wouldn't have happened. Raised voices, yes, but not violence. And why not? Their father's presence would have made it impossible. Not that he would have intervened, only that the fact of his presence, like a forcefield, would have prevented in itself the outbreak of violent acts. And not just that, Ivan thinks. Before then, what Peter said. Those words, he didn't want me to be his son. He wanted me to be his protector. In the past, Peter and Ivan might have called each other names, and worse: but to criticise their father in this way, no. That would not have been possible. Not because of any rules, but because of that feeling, the forcefield kind of feeling, which silently prevented certain words from being spoken, certain acts from taking place. What was that forcefield, what did it consist of? It's difficult for Ivan to say. Even to think about it is confusing: it seems to slip away from him as he tries to handle and examine it. He lifts now the kitchen paper from his lip, blots, finds it's no longer bleeding. In their mother's presence, he thinks, there is no similar force. You can shout and scream right at her, and far from cowering, she will shout and scream right back at you. How many times has Ivan witnessed Peter and Christine castigating each other, hurling insults, slamming doors. Fuck off, fuck you, get out of my house. With their father it wasn't like that. No: he was a gentle person, frightened and upset by the anger of others. He had to be protected, Ivan thinks. There was an element of protecting him, yes. Not telling him certain things, not complaining. Fighting only amongst themselves, never with him. By using such cold critical words, it was as if Peter was intent on proving the absence of their father, in whose presence the words could not have been spoken, and Ivan himself seemed to leap energetically into this absence, shoving Peter against the fireplace. New things are possible now, which were inconceivable before, things like violence and certain forms of cruelty. They have shown, they have demonstrated the possibility of these things, Ivan thinks, and therefore in a way proven to themselves and each other that their father is really gone, not only from the house, but from reality itself. This thought, the logic which has brought him so far as to have this thought, makes Ivan feel sick and hot in the head, as if he has lost, at some point in his reasoning, his grasp on reality, his confidence about what reality actually consists of. Rapidly and it seems illogically with strange disjointed connections, thoughts go on moving through Ivan's brain: memories of feelings, or feelings about memories. In other words, nothing real. How can it be real to think of these things, this forcefield sensation, this desire to hurt or protect? Things that are real belong to the material world. Feelings, memories, ideas, dreams: these things are outside the realm of objective reality, that perfect self-contained realm, like a snow globe, with everything real inside it. But where is their father now? Inside the realm, or outside? A fact, a reality, or just a memory, a feeling?

At this moment, his phone starts ringing, over on the table where he left it. Right away he thinks: it's him, it's Peter. Getting to his feet, he only belatedly remembers that the number is blocked, it couldn't be, and then he sees anyway that it's Christine. Picking up, he says cautiously: Hello?

Hello sweetheart, says his mother. How are you?

Promptly Ivan answers: I'm good. Then, feeling that this

response may err too far on the side of cheerfulness, he adds: I'm okay. How are you?

You know me, she says. Trucking along. How are you feeling about your event next week?

He sits down at the table, trying to produce a tone of voice that is normal and not in any way alarming. Fine, he says. Good. My online play is good. I'm out of practice with classical. But I think it should be okay.

How do you mean, you're out of practice? she says.

Remembering too late that he has been lying to his mother for weeks or months on end about his supposed attendance at various fictitious chess competitions, he says quickly: I mean, I've been doing a lot of rapid tournaments. You know, and blitz. But this is my first classical event.

After a pause, she says: I never remember there being so many competitions on the Irish circuit before.

There didn't used to be, he says. It's from the pandemic. The boost from that. There are a lot more events now.

In a light kind of twinkling tone of voice, she says: And how about the gender balance, has that improved at all?

A little bit, he replies. But it's pretty imbalanced, still.

I was just wondering if you might have met a nice female chess player lately.

Instantly he answers: Oh no. No, I haven't, no.

Or even a nice girl who isn't a chess player?

For a time he pauses, waiting, feeling inside himself a certain unexplained intuition. At last he says: Well, maybe. It's possible, but I'm not going to talk to you about it right now.

That's okay, says Christine smoothly. You don't have to tell your mother everything. Or in your case, maybe I should say, you don't have to tell your mother anything.

He feels himself awkwardly smiling. Hm, he says. Alright, thank you.

Any thoughts on Christmas? she asks.

With his free hand he picks up one of the captured bishops, turning it between his fingers. Nothing concrete, he says. I guess, what with not flying, I don't think it will be Scotland for me. But I don't want to hold you back from going.

But petal, she says, if I go over and you don't, what will you do?

I don't know.

I'm sure your girlfriend will be at home with her own family.

It gives him a sad tender feeling to hear his mother speak these words, your girlfriend, the nice sort of way she says it, how sad that is. Maybe, he says. I don't know her plans yet.

And you're hardly going to have Christmas dinner with your brother, she says.

He swallows, wanting to say nothing, and then saying only: Yeah. No.

She waits, as if for him to say more, but he doesn't. Finally she says: Well, keep in touch. I'm at your disposal, but I think I should let Pauline know sometime soon. Okay?

Sure. I understand. I'll get back to you.

Before I let you go, she says, how's the little hellhound keeping?

Ivan looks over at the dog, who looks back at him with deep dark attentive eyes. If you could see him right now, he replies. Literally, he's angelic. I can't believe you don't love him.

I'm a monster, she says. But I'm happy if you're happy. Take care now.

They hang up. Ivan puts down the captured bishop and looks again unseeing at the chessboard, remembering what took place just minutes ago, the open hand striking his head, and the hard sudden slam of the floorboards into the side of his body. Taste of blood in his mouth like chewing on a zip fastener, and he thought maybe he had bitten his tongue. Humiliating to think of himself cowering there on the ground, unspeaking, terrified. And Peter just turned away, walked away a few steps, and left the room. As if to say, I could kill you at any time, it would be like killing an insect, but the idea bores me. I hate him, Ivan thinks. It's cathartic even to formulate these special words, I hate him. And yet in the moment of catharsis, Ivan senses there is something else beneath, moving in the opposite direction. As in fluid dynamics when the undertow moves counter to the surface current. What is that contrary direction, away from hatred of his brother? Hatred of himself, maybe. To remember himself pushing Peter, petulantly, weakly, like a child. And then afterwards scrambling up awkwardly from the floor, tears in his eyes, clutching at his lip. The shame of that, the mortification, which is also bright and hot, like hatred. Rapid again and disjointed, his thoughts. Remembering their father in the ICU, in terrible pain then, and they had to give him morphine. Ivan sometimes wished it would happen. Yes, because he thought of death as an event, something that would happen and then be over. And indeed, when it came to be over, there was relief, there was a certain freedom with that, to be free of the anxiety of waiting. In the months since, Ivan has embraced this sense of freedom, he can see that now. He has made impulsive decisions, he has fallen in love, his life has been transformed, in an uncontrolled rush of energy and feeling. To live, he has needed to live, to overcome the terrible event, yes, it was needed. But now that the event has come and gone, the funeral, the various rituals, only the loss remains, which can never be recuperated. The event is over, the event has been overcome, and yet the loss is only beginning. Every day, it grows deeper, more and more is forgotten, less and less really known for certain. And nothing will ever bring his father back from the realm of memory into the reassuringly concrete world of material fact, tangible and specific fact: and how, how is it possible to accept this, or even to understand what it means?

Ivan looks down at the screen of his phone now and impulsively without further forethought picks it up again and calls Margaret's number. She answers on the third ring and says hello.

Hey, Ivan says. It's me.

With the beloved smile in her voice she says: I know. How are things?

He exhales, deeply, feeling that he has not exhaled once, or not completely, since Peter walked through the door earlier: and the feeling is soothing, the release of a confined breath. Okay, he says. How about you?

Oh, alright, she says. I've just been talking to my mother. She's heard the story. That we're seeing each other, I mean.

He gives a little silence to let Margaret continue, and when she doesn't, he asks: What did she say?

Well, she's not happy. But it's nothing unexpected. We can talk about it when I see you.

He has the sense of thoughts gathering inside his brain, too many, crowding. Are you okay? he asks.

Yeah, she says. I mean, I will be. The whole thing is so ridiculous, really. When you think about it. Or I hope it is, anyway. My sense is that it probably is ridiculous, but then I worry, maybe it isn't. I'll be alright, though.

Abruptly he says: Honest answer, Margaret. Am I ruining your life?

With something like a smiling frown in her voice now, she replies: No, of course not. Why would you ask that? Just because my mother has been giving out to me?

I don't know, he says.

She falls silent for a moment, as if listening to his breathing. Ivan, are you okay? she asks.

Yeah, he says. Or I don't know, actually. I had a fight with my brother.

Oh no, says Margaret. What happened?

All at once now, and seemingly from nowhere, Ivan starts to cry. The feeling comes down over him like a nosebleed, inescapable, and it's not only tears running out from his eyes, but his shoulders are heaving, and he holds the phone away from his face so Margaret can't hear his short constricted breaths. From the small earpiece speaker he hears her voice saying: Ivan? Are you there, are you alright? He tries to calm himself, feeling guilty and ashamed, and with his free hand he wipes at his face. In a feeble crying voice he answers: I'm here. I'm alright, I'm just a little bit upset. I shouldn't have called you, I'm sorry.

Don't worry about that, she says. What happened with your brother?

Tears go on running freely down his face, hot at first and then cooling as they stream down to his jaw. Trying again to slow his breathing, he says: Nothing really. It was stupid. We were just arguing at first and then it kind of escalated. I pushed him, and he hit me back. But it was nothing serious, no one got hurt.

Jesus, she says. Oh God, Ivan.

To hear his name in her voice, he closes his eyes. The name has become so precious to him, his own name, from the way it sounds in her mouth. He tries to swallow and a little sob rises and catches in his throat, painful. Yeah, he was being critical about our dad, he says. And I guess I lost my temper, and then so did he. I don't want to hear criticisms about our dad just now, to be honest.

Oh, Ivan, she repeats in a tender voice. Where are you, you're in Kildare?

With his hand he wipes at his nose, his eyes. At the house, yeah, he says.

And you're sure you're not hurt?

He hears his breath brittle and rasping in the receiver. My lip was bleeding before, he says, but it's not now. It was nothing that bad. I pushed him, and he kind of shoved me onto the ground, that's all. I don't know. For a second I was scared of what else he would do, but he didn't do anything else, he just left.

Ivan, I'm so sorry, she says. People aren't themselves when they're grieving. I'm just glad you didn't really hurt each other.

Another sob rises and he wipes his face with his sleeve. Yeah, he says. You're making me feel calmer. I'm upset, I guess I was upset, to be honest, but I'm feeling calmer now.

It's okay, she says. I'm getting upset listening to you, to tell the truth. But I'm trying to be calm.

Painfully he feels himself trying to smile. No, he says. Don't worry. Everything's alright. Shaking his head he seems to hear himself saying aloud: I feel like maybe I still don't accept it. The idea that my dad is gone. I don't really get how it could be the case, if you see what I mean.

I think I do, she says.

Like he just sort of exited from time, and we all have to keep going, within time. Do you know what I mean?

Quietly she says: In a way.

He wipes at his nose, his eyes, and tries to swallow. I just feel like there were certain things left unfinished, he says. You know, that we didn't talk about, or that I didn't understand. It is young actually, for your parent to die, if you're twenty-two. I didn't really think that before, but I do now. Because I didn't understand certain things. Another few years, honestly, would have been better. Is that a bad thing to say?

No, it's not bad, she says, of course not.

Just a few more years to think things over, it would have helped me. When I look back, I can't believe how much things I never discussed with him. And even when we did talk, nothing got written down. It's all just memory, and what if the memories fade?

You're never going to forget about him, Ivan.

He hears his voice in the phone now sounding uncontrolled, sounding manic. I practically am already, he says. I can tell you. Sometimes an hour will go by and he won't even come into my head. The honest truth. The hour is gone before I even think about him.

But that's normal, she says. When someone you love is still alive, you don't think about that person every hour of the day either.

Because a living person has their own reality, he says. The person who's gone has no reality anymore, except in thoughts. And once they're gone from thoughts, they actually are completely gone. If I don't think about him, literally, I'm ending his existence.

Low and insistent her voice answering: No, you're really not.

His head and hands feel terribly hot, his scalp is hot all over. I feel like, honestly, I might have done a lot of things wrong in my life, he says. Maybe a lot, a lot of things I've done wrong. In the past, which I can never go back on. Because I didn't understand anything. You know, I feel like my brother really hates me now. And maybe he should. Maybe we both should hate each other, I don't even know. We have actually been pretty bad to each other, both. When I think about it, neither has been that good. And I feel scared of him sometimes, because he's angry at me, or we're angry at each other. If our dad was here it would be different, but he's not here anymore. Do you get what I mean?

For a moment she says nothing, and in the silence Ivan becomes aware of how loudly he has been speaking, the echoing ring of his voice off the ceiling and walls. Into the phone her voice says: I think so. I'm trying to understand, I'm doing my best.

He can hear himself catching his breath now, low white noise repeating. Can I see you? he asks. I mean like, if I get in the car right now, can I come over? I think I could be there by nine, a little bit after nine. What do you think?

And in her low beautiful voice she answers: Yes, of course. Come over, of course you should.

Helplessly, frantically, he laughs, relieved. Okay, thank you, he says. I'm happy.

They exchange a few more words and then he hangs up the phone. Inside his body the sense of decision feels invigorating and exuberant. Once more he wipes his eyes with his sleeve, wipes his whole face, and then getting to his feet he lifts the dog off the sofa and kisses him repeatedly on the head and neck.

After putting him down again, he starts packing his things into his bag. With the invigorated feeling propelling him around the house he packs up in a fast but very inefficient way, going up and down the stairs too many times, and then he stands gazing at his chessboard absently, trying to remember what he was thinking before. Naomi: he should leave a note explaining, since he doesn't have her number. From his backpack he retrieves a notebook and tears out one of the perforated pages, smoothing it down on the table. Carefully he writes in clear large script: Hi Naomi. I'm going to stay with my girlfriend for a bit, not sure when I'll be back. Make yourself at home. Ivan. He looks down at the message for a time, and then lapses again into absentmindedness, when what he really wants is to be in the car already, driving out of town, on his way. Something is in his mind, he thinks, wriggling there under the soil, something forgotten. The open hand colliding with the side of his face, catching his lip against his braces, taste of blood. Yes. Bending over the table he adds to the end of the message: PS. Peter was here earlier. I think he was looking for you. This task completed, Ivan clips on Alexei's leash and goes out to the car, starts the engine. Glances with a feeling of calm certainty in the rear-view mirror while he reverses onto the road.

The next morning, Margaret unlocks the double doors of the town hall and lets herself inside. The building is always cold in the morning, with the tiled floors, and old single-glazed windows they can't have changed because the facade is listed. Downstairs in the lobby she disables the alarm, puts a copy of yesterday's paper in the recycling bin, moves a chair back against the wall. Ten to nine. She climbs the staircase, turns on the office lights, boots up the old computer, and then stands leaning against the radiator, getting warm. At ten o'clock, the coffee shop will open, she'll have her usual cup of tea, and then she'll unlock the community arts room to let Tina set up for the morning workshop. When her fingers and hands start throbbing with the heat of the radiator Margaret sits down finally at her desk. Answers some emails, does a little work on next month's programme layout, posts a reminder online about the Beckett next week, pulling quotes from the newspaper reviews. *A dazzlingly fresh take on a twentieth-century classic . . . This sly and intelligent drama still has the power to shock . . .* It's always a battle with David about these 'difficult' productions. Margaret will come to the meeting with sheaves of press clippings and audience statistics and pieties about bringing the arts to rural areas, reassuring, ingratiating, and David will frown and take his glasses on and off before finally, grimly, giving in. On your own head be it. *Beckett as you've never seen him before . . .*

Yesterday at her mother's house, Margaret said it was all true. She has been seeing someone, for a month or two now, and he is a little younger, a lot younger. The unpleasantness she expected. After you spent how many years giving out to that poor man. Getting on your high horse. Holier than thou. Yes, and that too was true. She did spend years giving out, acting the part of the long-suffering wife, the persecuted saint. Years of her life. Forced now to confess herself after all another humble sinner. Motivated not by conscience but by her own selfishness: and the worst, most vulgar form of selfishness at that, which is desire. A shameful thing, the sexual motive. In a woman, especially. I thought I could at least hold my head up and say I had raised decent children, her mother said. I could at least. Is that your way of saying, I may not like you very much, but even

I didn't think you would sink this low. You know, that pretty well sums it up. Afterwards alone at the cottage Margaret swept the floor, tidied the bathroom. Wiping down in a pair of yellow gloves the surfaces and fittings, she felt and allowed herself to feel the heat of fury she otherwise tried all the time to suppress. Yes, her elderly mother, tutting and wheedling on behalf of a son-in-law she never even liked. Blaming Margaret for everything. Her sister Louise, happy to borrow money when she needed it, happy to call Margaret up complaining about her office, her flatmates, even about Bridget. But when Ricky went into hospital, suddenly Louise stopped calling. In person, the blank politeness of impartiality. Don't try to get me involved. Even Anna, panicked, flustered, indecisive, trying to see the best in everyone. He doesn't mean any harm, Margaret. It's an illness. He can't help it. What about the time he fell down the staircase in Walsh's and the girl behind the bar had to call an ambulance. Half the town out on the street watching him carried away on a stretcher, all of them knowing full well that Margaret was just around the corner, in the town hall, checking tickets for the cinema club, while her husband was being carted off to the accident and emergency. Where was Anna then with her talk of common sense and good judgement? She was fretting and fawning over him like the rest. Poor man. Poor Ricky. Nothing was ever his fault, the blameless lamb. Not a word for the shame he brought on Margaret in the eyes of everyone they knew. No, Margaret didn't need anyone's sympathy, she could look after herself. It was weak people who needed compassion, weak men especially, like Ricky, the unfortunate soul. Margaret was strong, everyone always said so, a fine strong woman. For that alone, how many people hated her. And would relish her humiliation now at last it had come. Indecent, sordid, making a show of herself. No wonder that husband of hers took to the drink. Who would defend her now, speak up for her, take her side? Of all those who had relied on her, complained to her about their own sorrows and received her sympathy in return, her family, her friends, who among them now would come to her defence? What loyalty had she purchased with her lifetime of good behaviour and self-sacrifice? None, nothing. There would be no one to speak out, no one to take her part, nobody. Stripping off then finally her rubber gloves into the sink she pushed the heels of her hands into her closed eyes, remembering her mother's words, her blotched face, nobody, nobody to defend her, never anyone, and felt down inside her body a desire to scream out at the top of her lungs, to release from the depths of her body a cry of incandescent rage at the disloyalty of others, and no one would help, no one, not one. Deeply she breathed, pressing firmly with the heels of her hands, and watched behind her eyelids the irruption of strange visual forms, shapes of light blooming and disintegrating, blue-green, yellow.

That was when she got the call from Ivan. About his brother, his father, and he said he wanted to see her, he wanted to get in the car. What could she do or say. It was upsetting, to hear him so upset, and to feel that it was somehow all her fault. Ivan had seemed at first, she thought, like a way for her to leave the bad feelings behind, an open gate leading out into another kind of life, free of all the remorse and unhappiness she had accumulated before. Now she was beginning to see that he could also be a source of these same bad feelings, unhappiness, remorse, that he was not going to retain always the new fresh unencumbered quality he had presented to her when first they met. His life also was littered with difficulty, just as hers was, and these difficulties did not dissolve on contact, but rather seemed to coagulate and harden. Around nine o'clock he arrived, with the dog, with a suitcase, and he had a cut on his lip where his brother had hit him, a small dark groove on his lip almost black from which Margaret had to avert her eyes. In the kitchen he asked about her mother, and she was at the sink, distractedly washing up a few pieces of cutlery. Her head felt hot. She spoke a little about her mother, the conflict between them, and then she said she didn't feel like talking about it anymore. The dog was standing at the back door quietly whining and Ivan went to let him out. When the door was closed again Ivan said: I feel like you're angry with me.

Of course not, said Margaret. You haven't done anything wrong. I'm the one who should feel bad.

And what have you done wrong, he said, other than liking me?

She shrugged her shoulders, dropping onto the draining rack a clean teaspoon. Maybe I'm interfering too much in your life, she said. Preventing you from meeting someone your own age. I don't know. As much as we like seeing each other, it's not as if it's going to last forever.

Behind her, she could hear that he had been pacing the floor, and then he stopped. Why are you saying this? he asked. Telling me it's not going to last. Your mother put this in your head, or what? Because I thought you loved me.

Flushed, flustered, the tips of her ears painfully hot, she turned from the sink, saying: I do love you. Of course I do. That's why I'm trying to tell you it can't go on forever. Jesus, Ivan, by the time you're my age, I'll be in my fifties.

Throwing his hands up in frustration he cried: Again the

age thing. Oh my God. What do you think, if you bring it up one more time then I'll get to care about it?

She looked at him, feeling something flashing in her own eyes. You will get to care about it sooner or later, she said. Whether you want to or not. I'm just advising you not to leave it too late.

Angrily now he retorted: Don't talk to me like that. Don't condescend to me.

After speaking, Ivan turned away, as if ashamed, and rubbed at his face with his hands. What happens in the long run, if we keep seeing each other? Margaret asked him. We'll be girlfriend and boyfriend? You're going to introduce me to your family, is that the idea?

Outside the door, the dog gave another gentle whine and Ivan went over and let him in. The dog trotted back inside and shook himself briefly, paws clicking on the tiles, tiny droplets raining outward from his glossy coat. Finally, without looking back at Margaret, Ivan answered tersely: I don't get the relevance.

What do you think your mother would say? Margaret said.

I don't care, he replied. It's not her business, it's my life.

And what about your brother? How do you think he would feel about the fact that I'm older than he is?

For a few seconds Ivan did nothing. Then she watched in strange stillness as he sank down onto the floor, sank with his head in his hands until he was sitting on the floor by the radiator, hiding his face. The dog padded over and snuffled at him curiously, probing at his neck, his ear, tail loosely wagging.

Quietly Margaret said: You've told him already.

With an elbow Ivan tried in vain to push the dog away, saying nothing.

Many things began to make sense to her then. And without speaking, she walked away. Inside her bedroom she clicked the door closed, sat down on the bed, pressed the palms of her hands to her chest. This was how things went, this was what her mother had tried to warn her about. To know herself the object of disgust and vilification, not only imagined but real, and not only by her own family but Ivan's. To see herself as the brother must see her, a middle-aged woman taking advantage of a naive grieving boy, and for what, for her own gratification, her own pleasure. Distractedly with fluttering hands she prepared for bed, she lay down alone on her side. Listening to the sounds in the house around her, Ivan's footsteps, and the neat delicate sound of the dog's paws. Inside her a sick feeling, poisonous. Deep down, Ivan had probably come to hate her, she thought: and she could even sense in herself the potential to hate him, for the selfishness he had brought out in her, for the life of decency he had interrupted. In the darkness, the door of her bedroom came open, and she lay on her side silently watching. From the doorway Ivan asked: Is it okay if I come in? She said yes, and he entered, closing the door behind him. For a moment he stood there inside the closed door doing nothing. Do you mind if I sleep here? he asked. Or I can sleep in the other room if you prefer. She said she didn't mind. He waited, hoping perhaps that she would say something else, something affectionate, and then, with defeated gestures, he started to undress for bed. Her eyes having adjusted to the darkness she could watch him lifting off his dark sweater and t-shirt, revealing the soft bluish luminescence of his body beneath. Like pared fruit, she thought. His back to her, leaving his clothes on the chair. He undressed to his underwear and then plugged his phone into the wall. In his dejection, his unhappiness, of which she was the conscious cause, she found him more than ever beautiful and dignified. She wanted him, yes, with a terrible desire that threatened to destroy everything it touched. Their friendships, families, both their lives. He lifted the coverlet and climbed into bed beside her. The weight, closeness, radiant heat of his body. Just to be touched by him, she thought. For a time in stillness he lay there on his back. Are you looking at me? he asked. She answered yes. Hm, he said. In what way? At that she let out a little breath, nervous, and he turned over on his side to face her. His hand was cool and heavy at her hip, and she drew closer. He kissed her on the mouth. Nothing else needed to be said. He could feel her wanting to be kissed, she thought, could feel that she had been lying there only waiting for him to come to her, to erase from her mind the feverish bad thoughts, all this he must have felt and known at once. He turned her over on her back, gently, easily, and lying down on top of her he smoothed her hair from her face, and they kissed again. Feeling of his braces briefly hard against her mouth. And the taste of the cut on his lip, unseen. As if in a dream, she thought. Falling descending sort of feeling, slow, and yet not at all controlled. His hand between her legs, opening her. Okay? he asked. She was nodding her head. Pressed against her hip, through the cotton of his boxer shorts, she could feel his erection. Her body, in his hands, was differently capable, something different, she was not the same. To lose now this new capacity, this new body she inhabited in his arms, unthinkable. Slowly he touched her, his fingers inside her, saying: Is that alright? Her eyes closed, she made some garbled sound in her throat, wanting, and nothing mattered, her ideas, values, thin little scaffold of respectability she had called a life, no, not even the guilt, shame, only the feeling, wanting so much, wet, her nose running, eyes stinging at the force of it, the depth, deeper. With her hand she fumbled at his waistband, and he took off his underwear. Lay back down on top of her again, the tip of his cock just touching, pressing, opening her a little, and further. Please, she murmured, yes. He said nothing, only moved inside her more deeply, more completely, and she could feel his breath on her lips. Ah, he said quietly. Fuck. Her fingers in his hair, at the back of his neck, clutching at him. Still deeper until she was full, entirely. Just to lie there she thought and let him take her in that way. To let him fill her like that, however much he wanted to, again and again, and what else could matter. This, enclosed in ordinary existence, the desire from which all human life derived, the origin of everything. With an intense rich glowing feeling she lay in his arms and let him move inside her. In her ear, he said: I really love you. And she answered without thinking: Oh, I need that. Mint scent of his toothpaste, and he was looking down at her, his lips parted. You need that, he repeated. You need me to love you? Inside her an opening unfurling sensation, hot, tender, and she was nodding her head. Cool, he said. Well, I do, very much. Yeah. I like that feeling, actually, to give you what you need. Her eyes fluttered closed. Deep pressing almost hurting and she felt him throbbing, wanting to, and she wanted that also, wet inside, image of silver behind her closed eyelids, jetting, emptying inside her, slowly even somehow, as in her mouth last weekend, on the sofa, slow, the taste of it she liked, and afterwards he was so sweet, thanking her, laughing bashfully, yes, she wanted that again more deeply, to be held down by him like that and feel it, the way he wanted to give it to her, completely, she could tell, and even to think of it then she was coming, a hard gasping sound she heard in her throat, shuddering, trying to breathe. Inside her a hot wet sensation, and Ivan was saying: Jesus Christ, oh my God. Oh God. Damp, sweating, he rested against her, both breathing hard, saying nothing more for a moment. Gradually her heartbeat slowed again, sense of a haze lifting away, leaving her calm, tired. She understood what had happened, something stupid, but also ordinary, a simple mistake. Ivan's back wet and cooling under her arm. His face in the pillow beside her. Fuck, he murmured. I'm sorry. Is it okay? Again she was nodding her head. These things happen, she said. Don't worry. I'll go to the chemist in the morning. He sat up slightly, leaning on his arm, looking down at her. Deep and dark his eyes in the unlit room, knowing more than he said, knowing and understanding completely. Okay, he answered. I'm sorry. I really wanted that. She lowered her eyes. So did I, she said. At that Ivan let out a sudden hard exhalation, and for a moment he said nothing. Then he said in her ear: I love you. She felt herself flushed, her nose still running, and she tried to smile. I love you too, she said. I'd better go out of town to find a chemist, though. I've made enough of a scandal already without turning up in O'Donnell's tomorrow looking for the morning-after pill.

Ivan kissed her once more on the mouth and then drew away, lifted his weight from her body, rolled over on his back. The current of air over Margaret's skin felt cool, even cold, and she pulled the quilt up to her chin. You know, it was true what my mother was saying, she said aloud. That I was self-righteous. With my husband, I was. Because he had all these problems. And maybe that was the way I dealt with it, getting angry and self-righteous. I can't believe you're doing this to me, sort of thing. I don't know if I'm explaining myself very well. I suppose I got attached to being in the right all the time. Which in a way I was. But maybe it's not good to be too attached to that.

Ivan in stillness beside her breathing. His intelligence, his thoughtfulness. Yeah, he said, I get you.

I really hated being that person, she said. Scolding and giving out all the time. I felt very trapped, having to live that way. I don't know how to describe it, being trapped inside a feeling. Like crouching into an awkward pose, and you get trapped there. Being perfect, being in the right. But I find it's very hard to let go of that now. Even though I never wanted it. Still, I don't know why, but it's hard to let go.

For a time neither of them spoke, and with his hand behind his head Ivan lay beside her looking up at the ceiling. Finally he said aloud: Same for me, in a way. Although different. But say with my brother, I can get very focused on being in the right. And my brain sort of glosses over anything I've done wrong. Because I view him differently. I don't really think my actions affect him. I see myself very affected by his actions, but not the other way around.

I understand, she said.

He turned his head slightly to look at her. He doesn't hate you or anything, by the way, he said. Peter, my brother, he's not really against you, or anything like that. I just explained the whole thing kind of badly, and we had one little argument about it, barely even an argument. But he apologised later on. Tonight actually, he apologised, before we started fighting. Which was about different things, and nothing to do with you. Just for you to know that.

Tired then, she closed her eyes. Okay, she said.

Warm and heavy under the quilt, they were both quiet for

a time. Then into the silence Ivan said: You know when you told me just now, 'I need that.' Like, that you need me to love you. For me, that felt very good. Yeah. Honestly, one of the best feelings I've probably ever had in my life. I'm sorry to bring it up, because I know it was said in a certain context, and maybe it didn't mean anything beyond that. But to me, it was meaningful, very much. To give you what you need, it's so nice, you have no idea. I just want my whole life to go on like that. And I think it could, I don't see why not. I don't know, maybe you think I'm being weird. Since we've only been together a short time. I know a lot of things can change. Obviously we'll just see how it goes. The future is a mystery, and so on. But I don't think it's anything bad to imagine, or think about. That we could be very happy, like we are now, in the longer term. And all the different things that could go with that. I mean, we're both young, in reality, anything is possible. Life can change a lot.

She just watched him, understanding what he was saying, what he was carefully not saying, the anything that he meant was possible. He didn't understand, she thought, or didn't want to accept, what the passage of time would do to them both. She would soon grow older, too old, no longer beautiful, unable to give him children, while he was still a very young man. He didn't understand or want to know that now: and why should he have to, when they were lying there in bed together, languid, happy, in love, why think about the cruelty of time? Let him, she thought, have his fantasy, which was, after all, so touching, so gratifying to her vanity, and something more than that. Lying by his side, allowing her eyes once more to close, she said nothing, she articulated no contradiction, and his words remained spoken there between them, unrefuted. The future was a mystery, after all, that was true. Within its infinite folds it contained the possibility, however remote, that she might still be salvaged, her body, from the wreck of all her wasted years. In his arms, to be given life, yes, and to give life also. Something miraculous, inexpressible, perfect. Impossible of course to think: and yet it happened all the time. May have been happening even then, concealed inaccessibly inside her breathing body. Each generation that had gone before, hundreds, thousands. The only answer to death, she thought: to echo back its name in that way, with all the same intensity and senselessness, on the side of life. Why not allow him, why not allow herself, at least the idea, the image, the future, at once impossible and not, enveloping them both in its mystery in the dark stillness of her quiet bedroom, descending with them both into the depths of sleep.

Now, sitting in the office, with rain streaming down the window beside her, Margaret checks the desktop clock and sees it's ten, after ten, and the coffee shop will be open, she can go and have her cup of tea. Ask Doreen what she's planning for Christmas. She's heard, Margaret can be sure, they've all heard by now. You'll have the town scandalised. People sniggering, no doubt. And others saying: Well, hasn't she every right. Ricky too will have his day, his chance to crow and scold, and why not. Arm in a sling last time she saw him. Urinating on the street outside Flynn's. She didn't even stop the car. Her sense of rightness, dearer to her then than her life. And why remonstrate: with him, with herself. She had to survive. To get out, not to drown, to clutch and hold at something, anything. The danger long past now, she looks down and finds her hands still tightened, grasping. Her thankless and dutiful life. With a tremble of something like relief she thinks of him now, Ivan, remembers how she left him this morning, his chess book propped open on the kitchen table. The dog stretched out sleeping at his feet. She was leaving early, get to the chemist before work, drive out as far as Carrick. Half-rising from the chair, Ivan kissed her goodbye, have a good day, I love you. See you later, she said. Enjoy the chess. To be that person, yes, hands in the pockets of her long raincoat, walking out to the car, whistling to herself. Thinking about what film they might watch tonight, where they might take the dog for a walk. Introduce him some evening to Anna, to Luke, let them talk about polytunnels together, or genetically modified insects. And maybe it won't last: maybe, next month, or next year, Ivan will meet someone else, a girl, young and slender with long fair hair, and Margaret will have to let him go after all, to bear that, the pain, the embarrassment, caught out again, making a show of herself. Serves her right. Or in ten years' time, against the odds, they might look back and laugh together. Maybe. Sense of all the windows and doors of her life flung open. Everything exposed to the light and air. Nothing protected, nothing left to be protected anymore. A wild woman, her mother called her. A shocking piece of work. And so she is. Lord have mercy.

# 17

Wakes with a pounding headache. And where is he, window on the wrong side of the bed, fragrance of fabric softener, ceiling too low. Mouth full of some sour fluid, throbbing pain in the cavity between his brain and skull. Spare room he realises, Christine's house, and remembers. Closes his eyes again. The candlestick. And Ivan, his lip bleeding, terror in his eyes. Feels for his phone under the pillow, nothing, and then gropes on the nightstand, nearly knocking the lamp. Dead. Cold weight in his hand. Gets up, pulls on yesterday's clothes, to think, not to think. Downstairs, the fragrant glistening silence of an empty house. No one home. And what had he expected: Christine at the stovetop making him a bowl of porridge, cooing, chattering, scolding, distracting him a little longer from the disaster he has made of his life. Instead he's alone in an empty kitchen in Skerries and the time on the oven clock reads: 10.52. Christ, can he really have slept, what, eleven hours, twelve. Exhausted, disorientated, he tries to find a charger for his phone, looking around the outlets at random, checking the same one twice, nothing, uses the bathroom, no toothbrush, coffee machine he doesn't like, should he shower here or go home, try to eat something or don't bother, quarter past eleven now, still unshowered, unshaven, head pounding. Better perhaps that no one's home. Spared Frank's complaints, what's he doing here, how long is he staying. Darren with his obsequious devotion to his faceless corporate employers. And Christine, her divided loyalties, her false good cheer, trying to smooth things over, yes. She has her own family, her own role, with all its various demands. She cannot be always available. That lesson has to be learned sometime, and why not at sixteen, or at six. A mother is not an endless thing. She has done what she could. How long he tries to think since the last time he was alone with her. As last night, watching television, just the two of them. And when next, if ever. Leaves the house by half eleven with the nothing he arrived with, phone a dead weight in his pocket, and it's raining again, oh well.

Train rattling over the coast. Dark sea torn by brittle white breakers, gulls floating black against grey sky. Every option exhausted. Nowhere left to hide from himself. Back to the flat, trapped alone again in the incessant repetition of his own thoughts, sick, paranoid, drugging himself to sleep. Unwelcome, unwanted anywhere, unloved. No, no, he can't, he can't do it. Go looking online he thinks, easiest, painless, fastest most painless, easy foolproof. 12 simple pain-free methods that can't go wrong. Hasn't he apologised in advance to practically everyone, I'm sorry, I'm sorry, hasn't his life for the last year, last seven years, been a series of abject apologies, never good enough. You've been determined to humiliate me she said. And is that true after all, is that what he wanted. To destroy her. Force himself into her privacy, tear away all her careful pretences, expose her terrified and defenceless like everyone else. Or did he only mean to get close to her, in his lumbering way, knocking over and breaking everything in his path, to feel her nearer and nearer still. Flaring hot the memory of her saying: Maybe deep down you really wish I was dead. And against the thought he hears himself muttering involuntarily on the train the word: No. To deny what? The truth of what she said. Or the fact of her having said it. To deny that he was there at all, that it happened, that she, and he, the candlestick, that anything has ever changed between them, that any time has passed at all. That they are no longer identical with themselves. His partner, his helpmate. She offered him friendship, a kind of friendship, yes, but he needed more. Or perhaps she offered him more, screened behind a veil of friendship, and he tore at that veil, foolishly, frantically, believing he could get to her. What have they been doing all these years, what did they think would happen. How dare you. You're jealous. You're saying some stupid things.

Carriage pulling in at Malahide, hiss of opening doors. Few stragglers with umbrellas getting on. Salt smell of the air, fresh, and the doors slide shut. And if Naomi had been at the house last night, he thinks, if it had worked out the way he planned. Would she have been happy to see him? To have him come crawling after all, admitting defeat, pleading with her. Perhaps they too would have fought, you know what your problem is, you're a headcase, you need help. Or she may in the end have greeted him without surprise, offhandedly, rolling herself a cigarette on the arm of the couch. Oh hey, what's up. Can you pass me my filters? Watch TV together, talking about nothing. Feel the temperature of his blood return to normal. A human being again. And in bed, the warmth of her sleeping body in his arms.

Yes, she, his nemesis, his accomplice, his little plaything. That he has come to love her, such an absurdity: like a stage fight where it turns out the knives are real. Probably thought she could get the better of him, teach him a lesson, without getting her fingers burned. Have some fun, make a little bit of cash. Just a game. Too clever for her own good. Now she's worse off than when she started, no money, nowhere to live, rejected, cast aside. What she feels about the whole depressing experiment he can't imagine. If she had been there. To delay however briefly his next encounter with the meaninglessness of existence. Naomi, I love you. Her open mouth, wet, receptive, the taste of nicotine on her tongue. You can do whatever you want with me. And he has, that is exactly what he has done, whatever he wanted. As if attempting to reach the end of his desires, to find out what is there at the end. Discovering instead with horror that his desires even when instantly and gorgeously gratified only make him increasingly unhappy and insane. Wanting too much. To love, to be loved. By her, yes, but not only. And anyway by now she probably hates him.

Discarded coffee cup rolls with an empty sound between two unoccupied seats. Woman reading a folded-up newspaper, mottled damp at the edges. Everyone he loves has had to suffer, he thinks. She, the other. Christine, you'll be the death of me. And Ivan, of course, Ivan he has patronised, bullied, belittled. His brother, the watchful child, all-seeing, he has assaulted and wanted to kill. His father. Impressed by him, intimidated. I'll leave that to you, Peter, you know more about these things. If you say so, I'm sure you're right. Making himself small, and smaller, until no longer there. As if it was him, his own fault, taking up too much space. I'm sorry. Everybody I love has to suffer. There's something wrong with me. I don't know how, I don't know how to live. Out the streaming wet windows, the backs of houses, suburban gardens, chimneys loosing coils of black smoke. Thought rises with unutterable relief: if it were all over. Yes. Just to get to the end and be finished. The calm that comes over him, to think. Great deep all-enveloping calm that cannot be taken from him. Relish of allowing himself to contemplate, yes, he can feel it, pure and clean, to rest, only to rest at last. Almost believing now, and feeling consoled by his belief, all obligations dissolved, no more emails to send, no bills to pay, nothing left for which to apologise, he finds he can go on sitting politely on the train, unwashed, wearing yesterday's clothes, feeling a sort of empty wavering relief inside the hollow of his body. Taps out of Connolly Station and it's tipping down, of course it is, that doesn't matter now.

Walks home bareheaded, rain-drenched, half-delirious. Noisy and confusing the city, exotic alphabet of lights and faces. In his building at last unlocking the front door of his flat he seems in his confusion to hear someone speaking. Opening the door it grows clearer, yes, a voice, hers. Inside, he sees her standing there, in his living room, radiant among all his dreary sterile furniture. Sylvia. Long tweed coat fastened at the collar and she's looking at him. The expression in her eyes, looking, yes, at him, her intent meaningful gaze and for no reason it seems she says aloud: He's here, he's here, he's just come in. Having no idea what's going on, what she's saying, why, only the fact of her presence, real or hallucinated, he says: What? And still she looks intently at him, still searching, as if trying to convey to him some message, and at the same moment from the door of his room Naomi emerges, yes, she's holding something lighted he can see, his laptop maybe or hers, and is it real, is anything. Fine filigree before his eyes he thinks as if of light itself. Hears Naomi's voice saying: Where have you been? And Sylvia more quietly: Peter? Dim encircling halo around the outer edge of his vision moving inward enclosing and someone is mumbling something which may be himself saying, Oh no, I'm sorry, and then he can't see anything, only lights behind his eyes. Hot feeling inside his head if it is his head still because he is dead, dying, or it was all a dream, waking into darkness. Together he thought he saw them standing there and could hear them speaking, beloved voices, weakness in his limbs he felt, in his knees, and Peter someone was saying Peter are you okay oh good lord is he okay. Jesus Christ.

Afterwards Naomi says that was insane and thank God she was here. Because I would have lost my head completely at that. The way you went down, it was like a sack of potatoes, I'm sorry, no offence. But it was, wasn't it? And Sylvia in the kitchen boiling the kettle says yes he did go down pretty heavily and she was afraid he was going to hit his head which thankfully he didn't. He at this point Peter lying on the carpet and there are cushions under his legs. I never would have had you down for a fainter, Naomi says. Cross-legged on the floor beside him. Ankle socks with the stripe. Sylvia returns from the kitchen carrying a tray of tea. Pattern of marigolds. He always has been she remarks. I'm actually fine he says. Oh he says he's fine, says Naomi laughing. He looks fine, doesn't he? And clambers limber off the carpet out of sight. He was out for ten seconds, twenty seconds max, they explained that when he woke up. Because Ivan had left a note for Naomi saying Peter had been looking for her and she tried to call him last night but got no answer and then again in the morning no answer and she even came into town to see if he was at home but the buzzer rang and no one picked up. Then it was nearly eleven and she was starting to panic because he had been 'behaving erratically' and she thought Sylvia might know where he was so she went online and found her college email and then Sylvia who had also been trying to reach him said she had a spare key for the flat and they could go up and see if he was there which is what they did and were doing when he walked in and collapsed on the carpet. Probably dehydrated Naomi says. Like you literally never drink water. I'm surprised you don't collapse more. She's sitting at the table he can tell from the directionality of her voice though he can only from here see the ceiling and part of the far wall. Clink of teaspoon also he hears. I don't know, says Sylvia. I think it might have been the shock of seeing us in the same room together. Allowing his eyes to close he lets out something like a groan hearing them both laughing. Help, says Naomi. My girlfriends have unionised. Okay I'm getting up, he says, I'm getting up now, I'm fine. For the love of God, says Sylvia, stay where you are for a minute please. We don't want any more melodrama. And she asks him if he's eaten anything. No he says. Well that's not good either she replies. Naomi offers to bring him down a biscuit and crumble it into his mouth and then they're laughing again hilariously. I am literally fine, he says. I'm going to get up, this is silly. Sits up too quickly and his head hurts. See them now together at the table Sylvia in a silk blouse buttoned at the wrists and Naomi in a yellowish quarter-zip fleece. Yes and they look very beautiful there laughing, eating from a packet of chocolate digestives. Which looking he begins in his head to feel a certain warmth and to see colours faintly in or behind his eyes and without speaking he lies down again with his legs on the cushions. My girlfriends are unionising. I think I'm going to die. You're lying down again, are you alright? I'm good, very much so. I'm just enjoying the floor. We were about to ring your mother. What, when I fainted? No, before. That was going to be the next move. From the alliance. We thought you might be there. A completely innocent explanation. Simply having dinner in his mother's house and staying the night in the spare room, who could think of anything more innocuous. Phone ran out of battery because he hadn't brought a charger. Nothing sinister at all. Absolutely no reason to worry. And falling down on the carpet like a ton of bricks, that was no reason to worry? But that was from the shock remember. And he's dehydrated, hasn't eaten. Lying there on his back while they go on talking and eating biscuits he can hear them. The one voice rich low golden and the other with the clear high purity of a bell. Like a child he thinks himself. When sick and frightened to hear the reassuring sound of adult voices. Naomi again is saying thank God Sylvia was here because she knew exactly what to do. Well, I only knew from before. It hasn't happened lately. At the vaccine centre a few years ago, I suppose that's the last time. What, you're afraid of needles? says Naomi. Defensively he hears himself answering: It's not that I'm afraid, it's a neurological reaction. Both of them laughing again and even he reluctantly smiling. It is actually different, he says, but whatever. I'm going to sit up now. Gingerly this time and slow. Takes his coat off, leaves it folded over the arm of the sofa and sits reclining head throbbing and Sylvia brings over the cup of cooling tea. Thank you he says. I'm sorry about all this. That's alright. I'm glad you're okay. Everything that isn't said and can't be. Oh that's Janine, let me get this. Hey, no, it's cool, we found him. I wasn't really missing, he says as she closes the bedroom door. Well you can see how the mistake was made, says Sylvia. Sitting at the table again and she's opening her laptop. I hope you're not missing work because of me. No, I'm not in until this afternoon. If there's anything you feel like eating. Or if you want me to go. Please don't. Air filling his lungs and then recycling back out into the room. I suppose it would have been a lot less awkward if I'd introduced you before. You know, you'd be surprised. It really wasn't awkward at all. Sound of her fingertips tip-tapping on the laptop keyboard indescribably beautiful he thinks and closes his eyes. Door scraping along the bedroom carpet. Janine says she's glad you're alive. Great, thank you. Tell Janine I appreciate it. I'm sorry, I'm grateful, thank you for everything.

Later she asks him if he's having a nervous breakdown.

I don't know, he says. Maybe.

You should go off to one of those clinics in Switzerland, she says. Get them to reset your brain for you.

How rich do you think I am, he replies.

Sitting again on the sofa but he has showered by now, changed his clothes, and outside the window it's getting dark already. Raining. Way the water holds the light in falling. Her legs resting in his lap.

I was seriously worried about you, she says. I'm not even going to tell you where my mind went.

He says nothing.

You know if anything happened to you, that would be horrific for me, she goes on.

I don't really want that responsibility, he remarks.

He's looking out the window still but he can see her shaking her head. Yeah, well, tough, she says. How are you thirty-two and you're like, I don't want the responsibility. You think you can vanish into thin air and it won't affect me?

Yes I would like he thinks to live in such a way that I could vanish into thin air at any time without affecting anyone and in fact I feel that for me this would constitute the perfect and perhaps the only acceptable life. At the same time I want desperately to be loved. Aloud he says: Whatever, I don't know.

You think I don't have feelings?

For me? he says. I think it would be better if you didn't.

Why, you don't care about me? If something happened to me, it wouldn't affect you?

Feels himself flinching at the question and says: Don't talk like that. Of course it would. It's too upsetting, I don't want to think about it.

Her head she goes on shaking. Long and glossy blue her black hair. You know what you remind me of, she says. You remind me of a child. Did you ever try to play a game with a child, and they start laying all their toys out exactly where they want them. And they're making up all these rules, and they get annoyed if you don't follow along. That's you. That's actually how you treat people.

Automatically and too quickly as if not to hear he answers: No it's not.

Yes it is, she says. Look at how you acted with me. Every time we saw each other, you put me back in my little drawer afterwards and closed it shut. Be honest. We were together nearly a year, how is it your brother never heard of me? You didn't even tell me when your dad died because you didn't want me showing up at the funeral. You treated me like a doll. Literally, you even bought me outfits.

Hot feeling in his hands, in his scalp. As soon as we started seeing each other, you were asking me for money, to buy you things, he says. That didn't come from me.

Almost laughing, cheerful now, she says: Yeah, I'm not saying I'm the innocent. I was partner in crime number one. Maybe we both thought we could get away with it. Just messing with each other's heads without getting our feelings involved. What do you want me to say, I'm sorry? We were both playing games. And yeah, I wanted to win, and so did you.

He looks at her. Intelligence in her eyes flashing. Okay, he says.

Drops her head back reclining against the armrest. But I didn't know about your situation, she says. Like, I knew, but I didn't know. You get what I mean. That was kind of hard on me. Maybe I would have acted differently if I knew before.

You mean you would have played the game differently.

Shrugging movement of her shoulders. Maybe, she says.

Maybe that's why I didn't tell you.

Places a hand behind her head resting. I like her, she says. Your friend, Sylvia.

Again he thinks of saying nothing. Then exhausted says only: So do I.

I guess she's the love of your life, she says. And you were just using me.

Well, I thought we were just using each other. But my feelings got involved.

Funny look on her face smiling to herself. Same, she says.

I'm sorry.

Looks at him without lifting her head. Are we still broken up? she asks.

He too shrugs, knowing nothing.

I'm just wondering if I have to get the train, she adds.

Oh, he answers. Well, whatever. You can stay here, if you like.

For a time she falls silent. Then with her legs still resting in his lap she says quietly: I was really scared before. When you weren't picking up the phone, I was scared. But I don't think you would do anything really bad. Would you? I don't think you would in reality, even if it goes through your mind, I don't think you would do it.

Swallowing, hard, and he tries to clear his throat. No, of course not, he says. There's nothing to worry about.

Promise?

Yeah, I promise. Of course.

For a time they sit in stillness, saying nothing, and he closes his eyes again. I love you, she says finally. As stupid as that is, coming from me. Like it probably just makes everything worse. But anyway. Whatever. I love you too, he says. Sky outside darkening into night. She says if she's going to stay they should think about ordering dinner and he says sure. Watches her on her phone looking at online menus. Dark her lips slightly parted. Mouth he has how many times kissed. Nothing for it now he's promised. She knew of course what he had been thinking. Always knows. Maybe we both thought we could get away with it. To be loved, yes, for no reason, with no imaginable reward. Sudden proliferation of grace. It probably just makes everything worse. Which in a way it does, worse, more complicated. Tethering him down into the world, barring the emergency exits. Stay and suffer. I promise. Of course.

Cancels his meetings next day. Calls in sick to college. She goes out to her lectures and he makes himself eat breakfast, swallows down a glass of water. Alone in the apartment with the radiators clicking. Greyish-white walls. Are you having a nervous breakdown or what. Screen lights with a message from Sylvia: Do you feel up to going for a walk? Nothing strenuous. But no worries if not. Closes his eyes into the image, the idea, fresh air, yes, cold, wind sweeping, to walk, to breathe. Yes please, he replies. Stephen's Green? Out of the house then in his coat still damp from the day before and no umbrella. Mercifully no rain. Not to think, not to think, only to be near her, breathe each other's breath for a while, decide nothing. At the south gate he sees her, waiting. Faintly golden the colour of her hair like wheat, and she's holding two coffee cups, umbrella hooked over her arm. She sees him, starts to smile, waiting for him to cross. That feeling, he thinks: all he has wanted, all his life. To walk towards her, to reach her, to accept from her extended hand the warm paper cup of coffee. Thank you, he says. She says he's welcome, and they're smiling at one another, weakly, absurdly, or trying to smile. Shall we walk? she asks. He nods his head, please, and tentatively she lays her hand on his arm, and he repeats for some reason: Thank you. Bundled in their winter coats they pass together through the stone gate. Bare the trees and hanging low their slender leafless branches. Decanting now and then a handful of cool gathered rainwater onto the gravel. Along the avenues they make their way, saying nothing at first, only sipping coffee. To be there, just to be there at her side. She clears her throat, starts to tell him about a lecture she has to give on the historical context of literary modernism. As if to ask his advice. Only being kindly of course. Something about fascism he says and they go on walking, talking about fascist aesthetics and the modernist movement. Neoclassicism, obsessive fixation on ethnic difference, thematics of decadence, bodily strength and weakness. Purity or death. Pound, Eliot. And on the other hand, Woolf, Joyce. Usefulness and specificity of fascism as a political typology in the present day. Aesthetic nullity of contemporary political movements in general. Related to, or just coterminous with, the almost instantaneous corporate capture of emergent visual styles. Everything beautiful immediately recycled as advertising. Sense that nothing can mean anything anymore, aesthetically. The freedom of that, or not. The necessity of an ecological aesthetics, or not. We need an erotics of environmentalism. Stupidly making each other laugh. Turning here and there along the laneways at random, doubling back, retracing. Startling once a clutch of pigeons from the grass, heavy soft beating of wings as they lift themselves aloft. Her voice, which also is soft and heavy, talking about the last time she saw Ivan, the logic puzzle she asked him about, the green hats again. And Peter holding his empty coffee cup in his hand tells her about seeing Ivan the other night, the fight they had, the cut on his lip. Pained the look on her face. Oh God, she says. Where was all this, out in Kildare?

Yeah, he says. You knew he was staying out there?

With her eyes averted, she answers: Not before, but Naomi told me.

Embarrassed, he swallows, looks away again. Right, he says. Sorry.

Quickly, without looking, she says: Don't apologise, please. It's none of my business.

Neither of us believes that anymore, he doesn't say. No such hygienic partition exists: and you don't even think it exists, and neither do I, and neither does she. Conceptual collapse of one thing into another, all things into one. Instead he says meaninglessly: I don't know.

I liked her very much, she remarks. Naomi, I mean.

Pain in his chest to hear, to think. Mm, he says. She said the same about you.

That was kind of her.

Passing together through the central open space of the Green. The stilled fountain, empty benches, empty plots of soil. Maybe you don't want to go over all this, he says. But I just want to tell you, it wasn't what you said. An exit strategy, it wasn't. What happened between us the other day. I know I've hurt you, and you don't have to forgive me. But you should know I love you, and I loved being with you. I was very happy then. There was no other reason. And actually, I'm not sorry. I am sorry for a lot of things, but not that.

Quietly she only answers: No, I'm not sorry for that either.

Oh, he says. Well, I'm glad.

Reaching the little bridge, they stop and stand looking down at the black water. I don't think I've been very honest with you, Peter, she says. Or even with myself. You know, I don't think I really wanted you to go on with your life, without me. I always said that I wanted you to, but I didn't. And deep down I think you knew I didn't. It was impossible, the situation I put you in. Telling you to do one thing but wanting you to do something else. And now you feel you owe me all these apologies. For what? For meeting someone else, falling in love with someone else, which is exactly what I told you to do. I'm the one who should be sorry. I've been cruel. You said it yourself, I'm jealous. And it's true, I am.

Disorientated he stands listening, saying nothing. Blank impression at first as if difficult to understand. Jealous he called her, and she is. And he knew perhaps, must have known, and said it for that reason. Jealous, you're jealous, because she's healthy and happy and young, the way you were, when we. When life was. After a time with a strange empty light-headed feeling he says: No, you haven't been cruel. It's complicated. I don't think either of us knew what we were doing.

White and trembling she turns her face towards him. I'm sorry, she says.

So am I, he answers.

They look at one another a moment longer. Both of them believing themselves so clever, so capable. Always a step ahead, a move ahead, of each other, of everyone else. What a mess they have made, he thinks, yes, both of them. An impossible situation. Which they both have colluded to draw out and prolong over how many years. With what aim, with what end in mind, neither he supposes ever knew. Their love for one another, yes: which has survived its own death.

You were right about Naomi, he says. I mean, it was a stupid idea, trying to get rid of her like that. It was cowardly.

Turning her back to the water and resting against the stone balustrade of the bridge, she takes her gloves from her pocket. It wouldn't have lasted, she answers. Your heart wasn't in it. That's why you had her staying out at the house.

Feels himself as if disinterestedly shrugging. Maybe, he says. Not consciously.

You're in love with her.

I know that, he says. I admitted that already. Don't be accusatory about it.

Palely smiling she replies: I'm not.

They look at one another again, tired, and tender, affectionate again. Pitying themselves and one another. The old fond familiarity in her look, without which he thinks he could not live. Yes. When he saw her waiting for him at the gate: to encounter not only her, the beauty of her nearness renewed, but also himself, the self that is loved by her, and therefore worthy of his own respect.

You're grieving, she says. I know you're confused. And I haven't helped with that. But I think we both have to let each other go.

He goes on watching her. Fine lines around her eyes in the grey winter daylight. Pain inside his body he can feel or is it somehow outside. What does that mean? he asks. Naomi and I should get back together. Okay, and what then? I suppose I'll just try and delude myself that I don't have feelings for you anymore.

Averting her eyes she says quietly: Even if it's the case that we still have feelings for one another, surely it makes sense for you to be with someone who can make you happy.

He hears his voice growing less controlled. But what if there isn't one person? he asks. If I have to go back to pretending you and I are just good friends, I will go out of my mind. I can't live like that anymore, I can't. It isn't even fooling anyone. And yeah, maybe if I were with you and I couldn't see Naomi, maybe that would feel bad as well. You know, I'm too fond of her, it's probably true, I would miss her. I would want to see her. That's the way it is.

Finally she does look up. Dark and searching the look in her eyes. Then what do you think the solution is, Peter? she asks.

I'm telling you that I don't know, he answers. Maybe there is no solution. What do you want me to do? Pretend to have a different problem that's easier to solve? I'm just trying to be honest for once in my life. I have no idea what to do.

She goes on looking at him and says at last: Well, maybe we could come to some kind of arrangement. Between the three of us. It's not unheard of. What do you suppose Naomi would think?

He looks away, has to look away, in agony. His life, the widening black emptiness from which he has no escape. It's not realistic, he says. Things like that never work in real life.

Maybe not in a conventional sense, she says. But maybe we're not in a conventional situation.

He puts his face in his hands. Like a child with his toys Naomi said, yes, and so he is, terrified like a child, furious, uncomprehending, nothing in its right place. Jesus Christ, he says. I don't know. This is all my fault. Everything, the whole situation, everything is my fault. I honestly think you both would be better off. I'm sorry.

For some time she says nothing, allowing him to hide his face, hot in the palms of his hands, ashamed of what he has said, what he hasn't said. I understand you're feeling overwhelmed, she says. But you and Naomi will work it out. And I'm where I always was, I'm not going anywhere.

Rubbing hard with his fingertips at his forehead he answers without knowing what he's saying: I just want this year to be over.

It will be, she says. Very soon.

But that won't bring him back, will it?

No, it won't.

Descending down over him the feeling, horribly. To think of all his failures, catastrophe he has made of his life, litany of irretrievable losses. Everything that has gone from him, everything he can never have back again. His youth, his happiness. That man, who was himself, who was his father. Sick, the idea is sick, a frightening joke. Nothing can make sense of it. He wants to hurt himself, yes, he wants to die, and would have, maybe, if she hadn't been here to meet him, lecture on literary modernism, if the other hadn't come looking for him, I won't even tell you where my mind went. Trapping him, confining him inside, while the room goes on filling with smoke. Stay and suffer. You have to. She touches his arm now and he feels himself almost angrily seizing at her, desperate, forceful, and in a thin fluttering voice she's saying: Peter, I'm sorry. I know I haven't helped you, I've made everything worse. I didn't know what I was doing. Frightened she sounds: and he also is frightened. Clutching at her, her living body, he presses his face blindly into her hair. She has been cold, cruel, vain, yes, he thinks, she, Sylvia, she has lied to him, tried to manipulate him, she has made everything worse. And he too has been dishonest, cowardly, pretending to believe her lies, and his own. She has hated him all along for leaving her, he knows that, and he has hated her for telling him to go. I forgive you, he says. Do you forgive me? Hears the trembling little smile in her voice, answering: I forgive you, of course. Everything. I love you very much, and I forgive you, completely. The touch of her hand at his face, the same and not the same: both the same and not. To reunite him with himself he thinks she means to. To feel himself continuous with his own past, to accept for the rest of his life the permanent encircling shadow of everything he has lost. To stagger on, ashamed, vanquished, demanding nothing, forsaking all his pride and self-conceit. Grateful that his losses have as yet gone only so far and no further. That God in his unknowable wisdom and mercy has left him this much. The cool touch of her hand at his face. The flash of chewing gum, the black tights. His mother, his brother, safe and well. Cold wet windswept streets. Books he hasn't read yet. Opening theme of the Concerto No. 24. His friends, students, colleagues, their kindly and familiar voices. There he is. Hello stranger. What has not yet been lost, what still at least for this moment remains. To do what little good he can with his life. To ask for nothing more, to bow his head, pitifully grateful, God's humble and grateful servant. Can he imagine anything less like himself? And yet here he is, defeated, relieved, forgiving everything, praying only to be forgiven.

In a strange frail calm the days pass. As if recuperating slowly from some long illness. Tired, distracted, he misplaces things, forgets what he went to the shops for. Falls asleep on the sofa with the cup of tea still in his hand. Woke the other evening to find Naomi had done the washing-up. Touching actually, how proud of herself she was, although everything tasted of dish soap the next day. In the mornings he goes to work, reading, teaching. Nights she goes out with her friends he calls around to Sylvia's for dinner. Emily making the salad, complaining about the council, while Sylvia fills a carafe from the tap. Together they walked over from her apartment to the union meeting the other night, her hand on his arm. A philosophical problem. When they go out together, to be mistaken for what they aren't. Or rather: to be mistaken for what they are. And how is that possible. To see a man and a woman walking together: to name in the mind their relation to one another, as it were automatically. Which is to select from the assortment of existing names the one that seems appropriate to the particular case. To say to oneself that in relation to the man, this particular woman must be a friend, or else a girlfriend, or a wife, or sister. An act of naming which stands open to correction, but correction only in the form of replacement: that is, the replacement of one existing name for another. If you are mistaken in thinking this woman my friend, that means merely that you have chosen the wrong term from the assortment, and therefore that I can correct you by supplying the appropriate one in its place. *The decisive movement in the conjuring trick has been made*, says Wittgenstein, *and it was the very one that we thought quite innocent.* Because the name you give to a presumed relation between a man and woman may be both correct and incorrect at once. Each name including within itself a complex of assumptions. You say to yourself that a certain woman is my girlfriend: and intrinsic in this act of naming is the supposition of a number of independent facts. That this woman and I go to bed together, for instance; that neither of us goes to bed with anyone else; that while we are in bed certain particular acts take place, and so forth. And if you are corrected about the nature of the relation, you will therefore reasonably conclude that after all we don't go to bed together, certain acts don't take place between us, and so on. *Here saying 'There is no third possibility' or 'But there can't be a third possibility!' – expresses only our inability to turn our eyes away from this picture.* Is she or isn't she. Are they or not.

Social as well as philosophical of course: the problem. All very well if Emily knows or suspects, or if Janine, or Max, Leah, even Gary, maybe. But what about people in general, the public, the whole of Dublin talking. And with that idea in mind he almost wants to forget the idea, throw both of them over and find some nice normal girl instead, someone without any radical intellectual commitments or bizarre sexual proclivities, yes, someone normal. Get married, give Christine a few grandkids. Overhear the other legal wives saying pleasantly: She's *so* nice. To spend his life making conversation with such a person, working to finance the lifestyle of such a person, would, of course, represent a kind of spiritual death for him. But perhaps that would be preferable to the kind of social death that awaits him now. What will he tell people, what will he say. What does he think he's doing. Not to hold anything above anything else, to keep everything equal: a delusion, not even a fantasy, a burdensome quasi-administrative task at which he can only repeatedly fail. Encountering in everyday situations new irreducibly complex dilemmas, thickets of intersecting desires and preferences. Having to meet the needs of the moment, every moment, forever. But why. Why should it be so difficult. He likes her, likes the other, and they both like him. To hold a little space for that. Surely everyone knows and accepts privately that relationships are complicated. Forget anyway about what people think. If it were anyone else after all. He would be the first to say what harm, no one else's business, good for them. Why should you care, what are you so insecure about. No one is taking your beloved monogamy away, don't worry. Laughable the old-fashioned attitudes people have, think the sky is falling in because some girl has two boyfriends. Everyone rushing to pick her apart and make fun of her, something palpably anxious in all the jokes. Yes, he would be the first to take the empty seat beside her, of course, be friendly, he enjoys that kind of thing. Always on the side of the losers, the scorned, the unwelcome. Different however. Because he has never actually had to be one of them. There has never been anything about him, about his personhood, which could make the big men uncomfortable, the seniors, judges, cabinet ministers. He's not a woman, not gay. White, able-bodied, college-educated. Foreign surname, okay, but even that minimal tension is dispersed when they hear him talking, nice newsreader accent. Isn't that what he enjoys. Taking the side of the downtrodden, the marginalised, not out of self-interest, nothing to do with him, but from pure conviction. To be himself unaffected, to have no skin in the game. To need, for his own part, no defence, no justification. Noblesse oblige. Okay, he didn't grow up rich, didn't go to private school, didn't mix with their sons. But to be a little outside the circle, it's not the same as being an outcast, a laughing stock, is it. No, and he has never been that. In fact he has held himself superior, his manners, his taste, he has considered himself above it all, impeccable, supreme. To reveal himself now as one of the outsiders after all. Catch the looks exchanged when he enters the room. Seat left empty beside him. Castration anxiety, Sylvia suggested. Joking or was she. Well, it's true, I wouldn't want to be a woman, he said. Who would? No offence, but the level of disrespect, I couldn't take it. They were in her office then, she was sorting a batch of essays. Is that the sum total of your gender identity, she said, you're just desperate for everyone to respect you? He said he would have to think about it. Then added: I mean, maybe.

Impossible to interpret he thinks. You know you're seriously making a big deal out of nothing. My friend Megan is in a throuple basically. Please never say that word to me again. The complete cosmic joke which for her is life. Not one single serious line in it. Doesn't he, though: feel happy, that is, to contemplate his journey home in the evening, letting himself into the building with two pizza boxes balanced in the other hand, noise of the hairdryer when he comes in the door. Oh, hey babe. Pizza, amazing. Wait, I have something really funny I wanted to show you. Or the walk instead to Sylvia's apartment, to talk about work, read aloud entire paragraphs of legal argument, worst judge in Ireland, I'm sorry. Lying in bed later with his arm around her, the weight of her head resting. Her eyes half-open, her mouth. That's interesting, tell me more. How to live up to all this: which seems at times the only question. Feels he has at once too much power and too little, enough to make a mess of everything, not enough to sort it out. Is he humiliating them both, she, the other, inflicting on them some terrible exotic pain, for his own selfish satisfaction. Is it shame he feels, that hot blood pounding in his ears, or only embarrassment: the minor trifling embarrassment of an awkward situation or the true shame of a moral wrong. How is it possible to know. What can life be made to accommodate, what can one life hold inside itself without breaking. For him they will make the grand attempt in any case, he thinks, yes, and maybe for reasons of their own, curiosity, pleasure, pride, desire, and also the principle, the possibility, the ideal of another way of life. An experiment bound almost certainly for one kind of failure or another, and yet attaining for these few hours and days to a miraculous success, a perfection of beauty, inexchangeable, meant not to be interpreted, meant only to be lived and nothing more.

Friday evening Christine texts him. A link to the Chess Ireland website, talk about a throwback, and the headline is: FM Ivan Koubek on track for second IM norm. Clicks through and finds a photograph of Ivan and a few lines of text, posted the night before.

> 23-year-old FM Ivan Koubek will have a chance to earn his second of three IM norms at the Winter Tournament taking place this week in Clancy's Hotel, Dublin 1. After a phenomenal performance so far he will enter

> the tournament's final day at the top of the leaderboard. We at Chess Ireland wish him all the best and hope to see him secure a second norm. Good luck Ivan! For more details about the tournament so far, click here.

Taps for no reason the picture to enlarge. Ivan's serious face frowning over a chessboard as usual. Tried to call him on Tuesday, wish him a happy birthday. Number was still blocked. 23-year-old FM. From the gallery of the Law Library now he texts Christine back: Did he have a game this morning? She replies: Yes he won. Even if he loses his last game now he will still make norm! xxx. Getting on for six o'clock. Idly he opens the maps application, types in Clancy's. Just out of curiosity, never heard of the place. Off O'Connell Street it says, over by the pro-cathedral. No distance, walk it in fifteen. Closes out of the map, wakes his laptop screen. Cursor blinking in front of him. The Sectoral Employment Order again. Downstairs before him the main floor starting to empty out, people heading away. Friday evening in the run-up to Christmas. Lights twinkling. Homely festive feel to the place this time of year, collegial, friendly. Mulled wine and charity fundraisers. He would have been there of course he thinks. Dad, he would have been there tonight, at this place Clancy's, see Ivan getting his norm. There taking photographs the last time, the FM title out in Rathfarnham, while Ivan embarrassed tried to turn his face away. A long time ago. Yes, and never to be had back again. Just as one day this evening will seem also, long ago, never to return, tinged with the sweetness and melancholy of that feeling, bright warmth of the gallery against the darkened windows, people waving to one another out the door. And he too is heading away now, he too is waving, there's Elaine saying goodbye, and Val, take care.

First taste of the cold city air and he's crossing over to Chancery Park. Everything in shades of deep liquid darkness, the sky, the street, the grass enclosed behind its railings. December evenings, safe at last from the onslaught of raw daylight, the city reveals its hidden face of sublime velvet blue. Row of terraces he passes, Christmas trees in the windows glittering. Hands in his pockets against the cold. And for what. Just to congratulate him. Not to make a scene, not to draw attention, just to be there, say congratulations, go away again, that's all. First birthday without his father, come and gone. Tried to call him, he did try. And Sylvia texted of course, got back a nice response she said. Won't make a nuisance of himself but someone should be there, he shouldn't be on his own. Take a left up Jervis Street, rows of bicycles, black empty branches of trees. Headlights sweeping. And onto Mary Street, all the shops open, lights and music spilling out into the cold misted air. End of another year. Sound of voices, faces passing, laughter. Bad idea on the other hand perhaps to insert himself. In any case it might be over already, he hasn't even checked. Waiting at the lights to cross O'Connell Street he opens the link again, for more details click here. Live games starting 2 p.m., ten rooms listed with the names of participants. Glances up, pedestrian light still red, and back down again. Most of the games finished now with their scores displayed, 1–0, ½–½. Near the bottom of the list he finds it: IM Philip Fielding–FM Ivan Koubek. Link still open. Taps and the board appears on screen. Ivan with the black pieces. Move 52 and he's up, count them, two pawns. The light turns and with the other pedestrians now he's crossing under the constellation of hanging lights and passing the Spire crossing again. Clock over the jeweller's shows the time nearly half past six. Streetlights garlanded in glowing mist. Down one of the side streets and turn left, check the map again, and yes, there it is. Capital letters above the door spelling out: CLANCY'S HOTEL.

Through sliding glass doors he enters. Fan of warm air from overhead, bright interior of the lobby, high-gloss marble-effect tile. People sitting around with suitcases, staring at their phones. Printed paper sign he sees reading: Chess Winter Tournament: Conference Room 2. And underneath, the pawn emoji, and an arrow pointing over towards the lifts. Getting hot now already in his overcoat, face and ears still tingling from the cold outside, he follows the sign, finds the room. On the door, another printed page, with the details of the tournament and the words: Silence Please. Games in Progress. One corner peeling away from the blue tack. Past him a porter rolls a clicking trolley of luggage. Empty sofa opposite the door, black leather. From his pocket he takes his phone, taps, checks again the game. Move 55 and still two pawns up. Go in there now and Ivan will look up from the board and catch sight. Furious. Or worse, frightened. Last time they saw each other, cowering on the floorboards with his lip bleeding. Number still blocked. Wouldn't be right really, interrupt his game. Hello, me again. Don't worry, I'm not going to hit you this time. Instead he sits down half-perching on the sofa watching his phone waiting. Go in when it's finished. Move 56 now and the white king is in check, knight on c3. Position looks good but you need a computer to tell you really, little bar at the side that shows. Before him the door swings open and he glances: two young men filing out, backpacks slung over shoulders. Other players probably, games finished. On the bright yellowish walls of the corridor an incongruous assortment of framed pictures with strings of tinsel adorning the frames. Wonder whose job that was. Hotel work around Christmastime: a nightmare maybe, or half-decent, you don't know. Call centres he worked in himself, studying for the bar, and a bit of freelance tutoring, private-school debating coach. Like Ivan teaching chess to groups of bewildered and witless ten-year-olds. Yes, what the two of them have in common after all, impatient, ambitious, hard on other people, hard also on themselves. Finish this game he thinks, get the second norm, and then go and celebrate. He deserves that. Good end to a dreadful year. Just say congratulations. I won't stay. He would be so proud.

A woman in a long loose mackintosh passing he sees and pausing now at the conference room door, as if to read the printed sign. A woman, yes, white and pink her complexion like a flower, dark hair pinned loosely behind her head. Catches the eye, her beauty, among the luggage trolleys and strings of tinsel, the high-gloss tile flooring. Small practical leather bag she wears over her shoulder and rummages inside now, then looks up once more at the printed sign. Oh no, he thinks. Turning just as he turned, away from the door, not wanting yet to enter. As if seeing in a mirror, himself but not. And she looks at him. Both knowing somehow, each knowing the other knows. For a moment they wait in stillness, she standing there, he seated swallowing unspeaking. Then without thinking without knowing what he is doing he rises to his feet and extends his hand to her, and beautifully a smile breaks out over her face, coming to him, taking his hand in hers. And how like a flower he thinks her as if after rain that fresh cool quality. You must be Ivan's brother, she says. Her voice warm and bright, certain sweetness he hears like music. Coloratura soprano. Yes, he says, that's right, that's me. My name is Peter. Still with the same smile, gentle, embarrassed, she touches the strap of her bag where it rests on her shoulder. It's very nice to meet you, she says. I'm Margaret, I'm— a friend of Ivan's. How much depth he senses in the fraction of a pause she gives, a friend. I'm sorry if I'm intruding, she goes on. He didn't tell me you were going to be here. Swallows, tries to be bracing and cheerful, voice wavering in his throat. No, no, he says, I'm the one who's intruding. I didn't tell him I was coming, I just wanted to drop by and say congratulations. But I don't want to barge in while the game's still going on. Looking at him she gives another tentative smile. Oh, I see, she says. He's still playing, is he? Quickly, too quickly, he holds out his phone, tapping, live feed of the board, saying: Yes, this is his game here, I believe. She glances, self-deprecating face, and says: That's nice. To be able to follow along, I mean. Not that I can understand it myself. He smiles, pleased, nervous, saying: No, me neither, not really. I wish I could. After a pause he adds: You can go in, by the way. I'm sure there's an area inside for spectators. I just didn't want to distract him, while he's playing. Dark her eyes looking up at him. No, she says. I'm the same. It shouldn't be too long, should it? Or what do you think? Nervously he laughs. Hm, he says. Hard to know, I'm afraid. Clears his throat and goes on: You're more than welcome to wait here with me, if you'd like to. Needless to say. A moment longer she looks at him, her expression a kind of complex smile: tender, uncertain, searching, somehow even he thinks apologetic. As if to him, apologising. Then she says: Thank you.

Together they sit down side by side on the sofa and he holds his phone out to let her see. On screen, Ivan has moved the rook to attack another of the white pawns, the h-pawn. How much she knows, he wonders. If she knows anything. Weeks, months ago at dinner, I've always hated you. And the other night at the house. His lip bleeding. Could have told her. The intensity of her presence, the felt reality of that, her raincoat, her handbag, so close to him nearly touching. Powerful desire to speak to her without knowing what to say. And a sense somehow that she feels the same, that they are stirring towards one another painfully, unable to express anything at all. On screen Ivan's rook captures the pawn and it disappears from the interface, swallowed, gone. Reappears as a ghost off the side of the board. Think of something. I believe you're based in Leitrim, is that right? he asks. She's nodding her head. Mm, she says. In Clogherkeen, where I'm from. You're a Kildare man, of course. And he too is nodding, smiling. The painful pleasure of hearing her voice, way she handles the syllables, faintly rural her accent or does he only imagine. That's right, he says. Although I'm in Dublin, must be, fourteen or fifteen years now. Expressive her eyes even when not looking, he thinks, gentle, somehow amused. I like Dublin, she says. His eyes on the screen. White knight leaping. Yeah, it's a good spot, he says. Bit of a kip, obviously. Sweetly she's smiling, sees without looking the sweet white flash of her smile. True, but I like that about it, she says. I'm up and down for work now and then. That's why I'm around this evening, actually, I had to come up for a conference. He chances a look round at her. Ivan mentioned you work in the arts, I think, he says. She now avoids his eye shyly watching still the screen. Mm, she says. In the arts centre, at home. Putting our programme together. Being modest, he thinks. And what to say. As it happens I'm a pretty cultured man myself. Something of a connoisseur, to speak the truth. Instead he says meagrely: How interesting. Demure, she goes on smiling. And you practise law, she says. If I'm right. He says she is. They lapse again into a kind of closed pressured silence, not looking. Finally she says in a very low voice: I can imagine what you must think of me. And as if scalded, in shock, he answers too loudly: Oh, Jesus, don't start. I was just going to say the same thing to you. At that she laughs out aloud, and with relief he also is laughing, they both are, in relief, in horror, desperate, embarrassed. No, no, she says. I don't think anything. I mean, I only think families are complicated. Flushed he feels himself, and trembling, answering: Well, you're right about that.

She lifts one fine hand to indicate the screen, nails unvarnished, pink and pearl white. I suppose you know all about these norms he's after, she says.

He swallows, smiling foolishly, saying: The norms, yes. I know about them. They loom pretty large in our family life.

She gives another little kindly laugh. And he has this second one now, doesn't he? she says.

Right, he says. That's why I wanted to drop by, just to say congratulations. He's been years trying to get it.

Absently smiling she studies the screen and murmurs: He'll be so happy.

Her absent smile, her mouth delicate and flower-like, he thinks. So happy. Phone hot in his fingers and white moves the rook to g7. Our dad should be here, he says. And hearing himself, confused, goes on: I mean, I'm sorry, our dad would have been here. To congratulate Ivan. You know, he was very proud of him. We all are, very proud. But my dad, especially, he would be sad not to be here tonight.

Conscious that she's looking at him he goes on staring at the screen. I'm sorry, she says quietly. I know it must be very difficult.

Damp his fingers and trembling the phone almost slipping. Thank you, he says. It is hard. I miss him. You know, to be honest, we weren't always very close. But that's hard too, in a way. He was a really decent person. More so than I am, I'm afraid.

Glances and sees her smiling, how beautifully, and how sadly. Well, you're being very decent to me, she says.

From behind the door before them now the sound of applause, cheering, sudden and thunderous, feet stamping, and puzzled they look up, and in his fingers the screen at the same moment darkens, the board greyed out, white text reading: 0–1. Oh, she says. Does that mean it's over? And he answers: Yes, I think so, I believe so. Fumbling to pocket the phone, embarrassed, his eyes averted, he goes on: You should go on in. I'm sure Ivan will want to see you. Her little handbag clasped in her lap, her eyes dark and deep he thinks, and knowing. What about you? she says. Still with his eyes lowered he gives a kind of strained laugh. Ah, well, he says. I'm not sure he really wants to see me. If I'm honest, I suspect he'd rather not. But it's alright, don't worry. I just wanted to be here. And it's been very nice meeting you. So hard to look her in the eyes and when he does he can see yes she knows after all. Quietly she says: Will you wait? I'm going to go in and tell Ivan you're here. I feel he will want to see you. If you don't mind waiting. What do you think? Terribly childish wish he feels for once in his life to do as he's told. I don't know, he says. I don't want to intrude. Down the hall the artificial chime of the elevator. Different porter wheeling past an empty trolley. From inside the room a well of silence and then another burst of applause and she gets to her feet. I'll go in, she says. Please do wait. Look passing between them. Each a little uncertain, he thinks, a little humbled, to face the other, trying to make the best of it, each liking and wanting to be liked. She does, he realises, want him to like her. The long loose raincoat, strap of her handbag. Jesus Christ. Then lifting a hand to him she turns, pushes on the door, its opened edge revealing briefly a triangle of light, bright, sound of voices, and then swinging shut she disappears.

Waiting then in silence empty-handed. Suspended floating, overwarm, heavy overcoat he hasn't taken off. Before him the flat grey plane of the closed door. And was it real he wonders. She, the raincoat, flower-like her face, the live stream, captured pawn. You're being very decent she said. Half in love with her himself by the time she was walking away. How is it possible he could have been so wrong about everything. Sitting there beside him quietly she seemed to embody the inexpressible depth of his misunderstanding: of her, his brother, interpersonal relations, life itself. And yet she didn't remonstrate. I can imagine what you must think of me. To imagine, Ivan. To credit him that is with such taste. Like the Italian girlfriend he stared at over dinner. One thing to look of course. A woman like that: difficult actually to believe. Beautiful, yes, but not just that. Something more also. The way she held herself. From inside, another round of applause. Visualise the room, the layout, other players, Ivan's rivals and friends. The arbiter reading the final standings. Consoling to know she's there now. His happiness. Which makes no sense: or in making sense makes everything else not. A minute passing, three, five. Door opens to release other people, young men. Talking amongst themselves, laughing. Doesn't want to see him, he thinks. Will she reappear, pained smile, another time maybe. Let him enjoy his victory. Again the inward swing of the door and again a few faces emerge, two, three. Leave before he's told to go, surely better. And yet he doesn't leave, doesn't go, sits simply in his too-warm coat on the sofa facing. Six minutes, seven. Door opening once more, triangle of white light, and it's him this time. Ivan. The look on his face, staring. How to know what it means. Almost trusting or wanting to trust and at the same time wary. Rising to his feet Peter looks back at him, his brother, the watchful child, so young still, all of life ahead of him, and his eyes are filling with tears, hot, the corridor dimming and growing blurry. Embarrassing himself, and worse, embarrassing him, ruining everything, he tries horribly to laugh, dreadful noise, averting his eyes, and Ivan comes towards him, saying: Hey. Other people leaving and entering through the door behind them, heedless, talking, everything normal. And in desperation, as if not to be seen, to hide his face, he puts his arms around Ivan, embraces him. Congratulations, he says. I'm sorry, alright? Hand on his shoulder he feels, soothing, as you would soothe a child. I'm sorry as well, he says. Are you okay? Drawing away Peter tries again to laugh, or laughs without trying, wiping his eyes with his sleeve. Yeah, I'm okay, he says. I just want to tell you, Dad would be so proud of you. And I'm so proud of you.

You want to go out and get some air? Ivan says. Just outside, we could walk around.

Wiping again his face, rough coat sleeve. To go outside, avoid making a scene, yes. Sure, okay, he says. Margaret's alright in there on her own?

No problem, says Ivan. Don't worry.

Out through the foyer, lights dazzling on the blurred tiles, and a voice is calling: Fair play, Ivan, happy for you. Staring at the floor not to be spotted. Yeah, thanks, he hears Ivan answer. Sliding doors before them parting.

Outside, the stillness of dark night air, salt of the river. Weakly he asks: I'm not taking you away from anything important, am I? And Ivan answers: No, no. The others are doing a little speed chess thing, but I wasn't going to bother anyway. Cool on his face the air, his streaming eyes, and they walk in silence wreathed in mist of breath, undersea glow of the lighted lamps, Marlborough Street. Did you win the whole event? he asks.

Yeah, Ivan says. Eight out of nine.

Good Lord. What's that, eight wins and a loss?

No, seven wins and two draws. I didn't lose any games.

My brother, the genius.

Bashful Ivan's smile. Stop that, he says.

They go on walking. Finds in his pocket a tissue or perhaps just a used serviette and wipes anyway his face. Says for no reason aloud: She's great. Margaret.

I know, says Ivan.

Desperately he starts laughing, shaking his head, blurred street markings swimming before his eyes. I've been such an idiot, he says.

We both have, says Ivan.

I tried to call you, for your birthday. It doesn't matter. Just to say, I didn't forget.

Feels him looking, sees him nodding his head. I knew you didn't, he says. Sylvia texted me. And Naomi as well, sent me a message.

Did she really? he says.

Oh, she didn't mention? That's funny. She texted me, yeah, happy birthday. I like her, by the way. I don't think I was that nice to her, when we met at first. But if I see her again, I'll be nicer, because I do actually like her.

With the serviette Peter wipes his eyes again. She never said anything about you not being nice, he says.

Well, says Ivan, she was sort of telling me some things I didn't want to hear. If I could put it like that. And I wasn't too receptive, at the time.

Laughing again now, Peter says: Yeah, that sounds like her.

With a cautious half-smiling expression Ivan looks back at him, saying: And the two of you are back together, or?

Feels himself lifting his shoulders, his hands, helplessly. Austere fluted stone columns of the pro-cathedral in the dim darkness up ahead. She's there, he says vaguely. She's in my life, yeah. Naomi. And Sylvia, I suppose, also, she's in my life as well, if that makes sense.

Right, Ivan says. I kind of thought that. And I'm glad, because I feel like Sylvia is part of our family. You know, we love her. And actually, we kind of need her, I feel.

Tight his throat swallowing. Mm, he says. I agree.

Delicately Ivan pauses before saying: And they know? That they're both like, in your life, so to speak. They know that.

Oh God, says Peter. They know that, of course. I'm not that bad, am I? Maybe I am, but I'm trying not to be.

They look at each other and both start foolishly, sheepishly smiling. No, you're not that bad, Ivan says. Or if you are, I don't know if you are, but you have good points as well.

I don't know, he says. I think I could stand to be a lot more like you.

Ivan falls silent a moment, looks over at the wrought-iron railings across the street. Same, to be honest, he says. I think I could be more like you. I used to wish I was. And then I turned against you a little bit. But now I'm coming around to thinking, maybe I wouldn't mind being more like you after all. Not one hundred percent, but maybe just ten percent more.

Touched, pained, feels again his head shaking, staring down at his feet. No, no, he says. You're good the way you are.

Not always, says Ivan. I can get wrapped up in my own problems. And I don't remember that other people have problems. Or I don't want to remember that. You know what I'm talking about.

Without wanting to, Peter puts his face in his hands, his head shaking. No, he says.

Well, you do know, says Ivan. I haven't always been that caring towards you. And I just want to say, I regret that. I didn't think about your feelings. Or I felt like it was annoying for me that you would even have feelings. Because I wanted you to be above all that.

Fingers at his brow, touching, holding. It's okay, he says. Forget about it. You're going back a long time ago.

No, says Ivan. I'm not going back any time. Right up until the present, I'm talking about. With Dad, when he was sick. You did a lot for him. For both of us, and I never said thank you. I guess because I didn't think you would care to hear it, or I didn't think it would mean anything to you. But maybe for a lot of different reasons, to be honest.

Hot his damp breath returning against his face, fingers rubbing at his eyes. Don't start that, he says. I'm sorry for saying those things the other night. About you, and about Dad, I'm sorry. He was such a good person. And he would be so proud of you if he were here. That's why I wanted to be here, just to say that. And to say that he loved you, and I love you.

In a low voice Ivan answers: I love you too.

You don't have to, he says. I would forgive you if you didn't.

After a pause, Ivan replies: No, I do. Even though you annoy me a lot sometimes.

With a trembling laugh he looks up at the featureless sky. You annoy me too, Ivan, he says. It's mutual.

Outside the gates of the church they have come to a stop. Ivan with his hands in his pockets, toe of his shoe nosing the ironwork. She said you were really nice to her, he says. Margaret said.

Ah, well, he answers. She's easy to be nice to.

A little silence falls. Hands still buried in his pockets Ivan casts his eyes up at the church. You believe in God? he asks.

Oh, says Peter. I'm not sure, I don't know. I suppose I would say, I try to.

Ivan looks back at him calmly, somehow wisely. Same, he says. That I try to. Although it doesn't always work, but I do my best.

In his chest a sweet stirring pain like a hand catching holding tight. Mm, he says. Me too.

From between his lips Ivan exhales, cloud of mist forming, streetlight-coloured. You're going to Scotland for Christmas? he asks.

I don't know. I don't think so. I'll probably just hang on in town.

Head nodding, looking down the street, as if bracing. Cool, he says. Me and Margaret were thinking we might have Christmas together. Like in Kildare maybe, at the house. With the dog being there. But it's not a big thing, obviously.

Tight catching the feeling and idiotically he smiles. Ah, he says. That sounds very nice. That sounds lovely.

Something like a little cough Ivan gives, and then says: Yeah. Well, she was just saying to me, a minute ago, do you think you would want to join? Like for dinner, on the day of Christmas. Or whatever. No big deal if you don't.

His eyes again filling with tears, hot, and he goes on smiling. Ah, wow, he says. That's a nice idea, that's very kind. I would probably have to check, you know. See what the others are doing.

Well, bring anyone, says Ivan. Whoever would want to come, you should bring.

Streaming his eyes and laughing he touches with his fingers. Hm, he says. That could get a little bit unconventional. I'm not sure what Margaret would think.

Looking at him Ivan says: She's a really good person.

Yeah, that's what I'm afraid of.

Ivan gives at that a goofy sort of shy little laugh. No, he says. I mean she's very understanding. She understands everything, literally.

Nodding his head, half-smiling, palms of his hands wiping his face. I'll check in, he says, I'll see what the plans are. Okay? I'm very grateful to be invited.

It would mean a lot to me, Ivan says. The first Christmas without Dad, and everything like that. But whatever you want, whatever you prefer.

Unthinking unseeing he reaches, folds again in his arms, his brother, the watchful child, the man. I'll be there, he says.

Thank you. I'll let you get back to your friends now. Tell Margaret I'll look forward to seeing her again soon.

Cool, he says. I'll look forward as well.

His eyes closed. Tightening in his chest and finally he draws away. And tell her thank you, from me, he says. Okay?

Watching him now almost cautiously Ivan answers: Yeah, I'll tell her. Are you sure you're alright?

Tries to laugh, lifting a hand goodbye. I'm good, he says. I'm happy. I love you. See you soon. And he turns, hand still lifted, waving back as he walks away. Hears him saying again: I love you too. Down dark Marlborough Street along the tram tracks to the river. Dries his face on his sleeve half-smiling to himself. Looking like a lunatic. To care so much. Grief does that. Tell Naomi what he said, I'll be nicer. Make her laugh. And Sylvia, we love her, we need her, I feel. All of them loved and complicatedly needed, for better or worse. Inextricable. The tangled web. Have to eat something when he gets in. Call his mother tell her sorry. Everything forgiven. Thou know'st 'tis common; all that lives must die. Everyone in the end of course, even he, Ivan, strange to think. To make meaning of something so fleeting, life. Here and gone. Think of him there inside the closed room tonight with the sound of cheering, people calling his name, feet stamping. That is life as well as loss and pain. This married woman he's hanging around with, how did that start. Ask them maybe over Christmas dinner. Her horrified laughter. Crossing over now towards the Abbey, brown brickwork, handful of rain he thinks he feels and turns up his collar. Picture them all there together. To imagine also is life: the life that is only imagined. Clatter of saucepans, steam from the kettle. Even to think about it is to live. Hard cold wind blowing in from the sea, blowing his coat back, raising white hackles on the river. Nothing is fixed. She, the other. Ivan, the girlfriend. Christine, their father, from beyond the grave. It doesn't always work, but I do my best. See what happens. Go on in any case living.

# NOTES

This book incorporates many quotations from other texts. I have tried to list those sources here, both for the information of interested readers and to avoid the appearance of taking credit for work that is not my own. Some of the quoted texts are still in copyright; I am grateful to the rights holders for their permission to use these excerpts in the novel.

The epigraph to this book is taken from Part II (also known as the 'Philosophy of Psychology' fragment) of Ludwig Wittgenstein's *Philosophical Investigations*. The translation from the original German in that instance is my own.

In the text of the novel itself, I quote several times from G. E. M. Anscombe's translation of the same work. On page 64, I use the quote: 'If a lion could talk, we could not understand him.' On page 428, I quote: 'The decisive movement in the conjuring trick has been made, and it was the very one that we thought quite innocent.' Later in the same paragraph, I quote: 'Here saying "There is no third possibility" or "But there can't be a third possibility!" – expresses only our inability to turn our eyes away from this picture'. Each of these quotes is taken directly from the 1958 edition of Wittgenstein's *Philosophical Investigations*, translated by G. E. M. Anscombe.

The novel also includes several quotations from the text of Shakespeare's *Hamlet*. On page 70, I quote the words 'How weary, stale, flat and unprofitable', which are spoken by Hamlet in Act I, Scene ii of that play. On page 239, I use the words 'Very proud, revengeful, ambitious. With more offences at my beck than I have thoughts to put them in' – this is another quote from *Hamlet*, though with altered punctuation, originally spoken by Hamlet in Act III, Scene i. Finally, on page 447, the line 'Thou know'st 'tis common; all that lives must die' is again from *Hamlet*, spoken by Gertrude in Act I, Scene ii.

On page 4, the phrase 'In whose blent air all our compulsions meet' is a quotation from Philip Larkin's 'Church Going', published 1954.

On page 9, 'What lips my lips have' is a reference to Edna St Vincent Millay's 1920 poem 'What lips my lips have kissed, and where, and why'.

On page 10, the phrase 'Dublin in the rare, etc.' is a reference to the song 'The Rare Ould Times' or 'Dublin in the Rare Ould Times', composed by Pete St. John and first recorded by The Dublin City Ramblers in 1977.

On page 11, the phrase 'And few could know' is a quotation from William Wordsworth's 1798 poem 'She Dwelt Among the Untrodden Ways'.

On page 13, the phrase 'Mixing memory and desire' is taken from T. S. Eliot's 'The Waste Land', 1922.

On page 16, the words 'Love's austere and lonely offices' are taken from Robert Hayden's 1962 poem 'Those Winter Sundays'.

On page 17, the words 'In their autumn beauty' are quoted from W. B. Yeats's 1917 poem 'The Wild Swans at Coole'.

On page 28, the words 'Thank you, Bobby Fischer!' paraphrase the final words of Bobby Fischer's 1961 article 'A Bust to the King's Gambit': 'Thank you, Weaver Adams!' That article advocated 3 . . . d6 as a response to the King's Gambit in a variation now known as the Fischer Defense.

On page 68, Peter mentally quotes the phrases 'copper stepped saucer dome' and 'Portland stone balustraded parapet' from the technical description of the Fourt Courts on the Buildings of Ireland website (buildingsofireland.ie), a national architectural heritage service run by the Department of Housing.

On page 70, the phrase 'Woman much missed' is a reference to Thomas Hardy's 1914 poem 'The Voice'. Later in the same chapter, on page 80, the line 'Where you would wait for me: yes, as I knew you then' is another quotation from the same source.

On page 137, the phrase 'Forever warm and still to be enjoyed' is taken from John Keats's 1819 'Ode on a Grecian Urn', though with modernised spelling. Keats is quoted once more, on page 322, where the phrase 'bubbles winking at the brim' is taken from his 'Ode to a Nightingale'.

On page 222, the line 'These days, yesterday, last night, this morning, I've wanted everything' is a quotation from Henry James's 1904 novel *The Golden Bowl*.

In Chapter 10, Ivan's analysis of Sylvia's logic puzzle is influenced by the work of the mathematician and philosopher Bertrand Russell, particularly the theory of descriptions first proposed in Russell's 1905 paper 'On Denoting'. The concept of 'vacuous truth' is an artefact of the development and application of truth tables in philosophy and mathematics; the originator of the truth table was Ludwig Wittgenstein.

On page 369, the line 'I begin to like them at that age' is a quotation from the 'Nausicaa' episode of James Joyce's 1922 novel *Ulysses*.

On page 421, the line 'We need an erotics of environmentalism' is a paraphrase of the final line of Susan Sontag's 1964 essay 'Against Interpretation': 'In place of a hermeneutics we need an erotics of art.'

On page 430, the phrase 'Not one single serious line in it' is a quotation from James Joyce on the subject of his novel *Ulysses*, from an interview with Djuna Barnes in 1922.

# ACKNOWLEDGEMENTS

The writing of this novel required some research into both the practice of law and the game of chess. On that note, I would like to thank Sunniva McDonagh, David Kenny, Alan Brady and Katie Rooney for their invaluable advice and assistance on the subject of law and legal work in Ireland today.

Likewise, I want to express my gratitude to the Chess Society of Trinity College Dublin and to its members Seán Doyle, Conor Nolan and especially Peter Carroll. Their responses to my queries about contemporary competitive chess and tournament formats were truly generous and helpful.

Any factual errors remaining in the text – concerning law, chess, or any other matter – belong either to the novel's characters or to me.

I also want to thank my family and friends for supporting me and my work, including in some cases by reading early chapters or drafts of this manuscript. JP, Tom, Sheila, Mark, Aoife – thank you all so much for everything.

Thanks as ever to Tracy Bohan, whose kindness so often

sustained me through the writing of this book. To Mitzi Angel: working with you is one of the great honours of my career, and I'm grateful now and always. Warmest thanks also to Alex Bowler, Silvia Crompton and everyone at Faber.

Finally and most importantly, I would like to thank my husband John, for making all my work possible, in more ways than I can say. John, what a joy and a blessing it is for me to share my life with you.

## A NOTE ABOUT THE AUTHOR

Sally Rooney is an Irish novelist. She is the author of *Beautiful World, Where Are You*; *Conversations with Friends*; and *Normal People*. She also contributed to the writing and production of the Hulu/BBC television adaptation of *Normal People*.